I0766158

STORM PRINCESS

2

USA TODAY BESTSELLING AUTHORS
JAYMIN EVE & EVERLY FROST

Frost, Everly
Eve, Jaymin
Storm Princess: Book Two

Cover design by Covers by Aura.

Page edges by Painted Wings Publishing Services.

Chapter art and scene break illustrations from Samaiya Art.

For information on reproducing sections of this book or sales of this book, go to
www.jaymineve.com
www.everlyfrost.com

jaymineve@gmail.com
everlyfrost@gmail.com

To everyone who takes a difficult journey for someone you love.

May you conquer every mountain.

PROLOGUE

CASSIAN OF THE HIDEAWAY CLAN - 10 YEARS AGO

S unlight flickers through the quiet forest as I carry my prey along the well-worn path. The heavy sack hangs across one shoulder and bounces at my back in a worrying beat. I'm not sure what to make of the creature I found creeping through the forest behind the palace. I killed it when it attacked me, but I'm hoping the King's guard will have answers.

The path lets out to a still lake and continues along beside the water until it reaches Crimson Court—the meeting place where the King greets visiting leaders from the gargoyle clans.

Movement ahead makes me pause. A majestic cherry blossom grows at the water's edge and a woman kneels beneath it. She takes my breath away every time I'm lucky enough to see her.

Her hair cascades across her shoulder, the color of a crimson sunset, its strands dipping into the water as she leans out across the surface. Her translucent wings flutter in the breeze, catching the light and making the air around her sparkle. She stretches out, trying to reach a water lily that floats on the surface of the lake.

I hide a smile as she strains forward, only to nudge the flower… and bump it farther away. It spins slowly as it floats beyond her reach.

Her disappointed "Oh!" reaches my ears.

An empty basket rests beside her. The cherry blossom tree isn't in bloom and it looks like flowers are in short supply today.

As she rights herself, palms pressed against her thighs, I leave the sack and its gruesome contents beside the path to quietly cross the distance, careful to appear in her line of sight without startling her.

I stop at the water's edge a respectful distance away from where she sits. "May I help you, Elaina?"

She looks up, her bright eyes a pale cornflower blue that steals my breath away. Her lips curve into a smile that makes my heart skip multiple beats. "That's okay, Cassian. I don't think anyone can reach it now."

"Why don't I try anyway?" I press my lips together, suppressing my smile as I kneel beside her, still maintaining a respectful distance.

Very carefully, so I don't alarm her, I release my left wing, stretching it out across the water.

Her eyes grow wide as my wing continues to unfold, revealing its unusual size. Light grey patterns ripple through it, bright in the sunlight, even though my wings are impossibly dark.

I rarely have reason to unfold my wings in front of anyone, let alone Elaina. Unlike the King's soldiers, I seldom fly anywhere. I was born into the Hideaway Clan, the lowest of the low. The Royal Residence is my home, but I am no prince. My job is to sweep floors, dust furniture, and disappear into the background, unseen. It's only out here on the outskirts of the palace that I can stand tall.

I tip my wing and scoop the flower from the water, carefully retracting it with the flower inside. Close enough now, I scoop up the lily before it's crushed between the folds of my wing. I hold the flower out to Elaina in both my palms.

She doesn't take it, her eyes intently searching mine.

I don't mind. I could happily drown in them. She's from the Virtuous Clan, so far beyond my reach. Her parents are ambassadors for her clan and live permanently in the palace, but for some reason, she doesn't seem to mind my company. I've heard that elves are different, but in gargoyle culture, our women choose their mate and not the other way around. It's up to me to prove that I'm worthy of her choice.

We are both sixteen and she won't make a choice until she's eighteen. I hope that I have a chance when the time comes.

"Cassian," she breathes. "You have Hideaway's wings."

My ancestor—the gargoyle from whom my Clan derives its name—was said to have wings that were large enough to hide others inside them, reflecting the light so he was completely camouflaged against any rock face.

He was legendary, whereas I am… ordinary.

Her lips part as she inhales, her breathing soft. "Nobody has had wings like Hideaway in centuries."

I clear my throat, soaking up her gaze, not wanting it to end. "They come in handy sometimes. Such as for retrieving flowers."

She reaches for the lily, her right hand carefully lifting it while her left closes over mine, surprising me when she holds on to me. Her hand is much smaller than mine and I marvel at the way her fingers only reach halfway across my palm.

"Do you think…" A smile grows on her face, a hint of intensity entering her eyes as she leans forward. "Do you think you could fly me above the tree line?"

My heart jumps. She can fly herself above the trees. That she would ask me to fly her anywhere is a gesture of incredible trust.

I manage to speak. "Of course. I would be honored."

She swiftly deposits the flower into her basket and leaves it on the ground as she rises to her feet, the breeze wafting her sky-blue dress around her long legs. I'm amazed when she slips out of her shoes, steps onto my feet, tucks her wings tightly to her sides, and wraps her arms around my waist, pressing her head to my chest. All without a second's hesitation.

She is so delicate; she hardly weighs anything.

Flying a woman requires that I wrap one arm around her waist and the other across her hips. It's a very personal position to be in, which is why I'm stunned that she would ask me.

Very carefully, in case she changes her mind, I slide my arm around her waist first. I pause. Wait. Hold my breath as I slip my other arm across her hips, beneath her bottom.

She tilts her head back to meet my eyes. "Up?"

I spread my wings, extending them to their full width, sweep them, and then we rush upward. I sense her quick inhale, her cheek pressing to my chest again as we become weightless, soaring above the treetops within milliseconds. I can't help but grin. My wings make my flight faster than most gargoyles.

I steady us there, keeping my wing beats constant, maintaining our position without rising any higher. It's important that she remains in control of our movements. The moment she wants to return to the ground, I'll lower us down.

She gradually relaxes, her arms loosening a little, trusting me not to let her fall while her wings are closed. Erador stretches out beneath us—the sparkling lake that turns into a waterfall in the very far distance, cascading off the side of the mountain on which the palace is built, while Crimson Court rests farther to our left near the Royal Residence that is hewn out of the mountain itself.

After a long moment, Elaina tilts her head back. "What would you do if you hadn't been born into the Hideaway Clan?"

I consider the question carefully. Wishing for things that can never be is folly, but because she asked me, I want to answer truthfully. "I would join the King's guard."

She gives me a small nod. "You're already stronger than most of the soldiers. My father says that when you're of age, the King will offer you a place in his personal guard."

"What?" I can't help the exclamation.

Her smile grows wide. "Everyone knows about it, Cassian. Why don't you believe it?"

I shake my head. "Because I'm..."

"Hideaway Clan." She nods. "But think about it. The King allowed a gargoyle from the Grievous Clan into his personal guard. He recognizes skill when he sees it. Why shouldn't he recognize yours?"

I press my lips together, trying to conceal my disbelief. I'm nothing more than a servant to the King. It's very difficult to believe that I will ever be anything more.

Her gaze settles on my lips in a way that confuses me.

She speaks very softly. "You're always so helpful and polite to me, Cassian. But... I would appreciate it if sometimes... you were not so polite."

Her eyes rise to mine, a question in them, but I don't know what it means or what she wants from me. My forehead creases as I try to decipher the curve of her lips.

She reaches up and smooths her fingertips across my creased forehead. "There. That's better."

She rises up, and I sense her bare feet arch as she reaches up onto her tiptoes, her thighs pressed against mine, seeking to gain height. I freeze as she rises as far as she can, stops, and gives me a perplexed look, and I suddenly wonder if...

I lift the arm that supports her bottom, pulling her higher so we are eye height. Her fingertips that lingered across my forehead shift to rest against the back of my neck. She carefully presses her cheek to mine.

"Cassian," she whispers, her soft lips so close that her sweet breath whispers across my mouth. "I will choose you, no matter what."

My heart is suddenly... too happy, too full. I inhale her scent and my head fills with lilies and cherry blossoms and beneath it, the strong moral scent of her Clan. Virtuous gargoyles are the most compassionate and empathetic and Elaina is more than others. She is the first to help a child with a skinned knee, serve tea to the older women, and make sure others have what they need before she thinks about herself. In combat training, she never fails to help her opponent back up to their feet.

She brushes her lips across mine, the lightest touch that sends my senses into overdrive. I want more, want to tangle my hands in her hair and taste her mouth, but I control my emotions. Giving me a kiss is a precious gift and I don't want to break this moment.

"Cassian." She sighs, shaking her head slowly side to side, her lips brushing mine at the same time. "So polite."

I can't help the smile that breaks across my face. "Hmm," I say, running my hand up her back to her neck, my fingertips sliding into her hair as my palm supports her upper back and my wings beat gently. "Maybe not."

I press my lips to hers, fitting my mouth to the curve of her lips, inhaling her soft gasp as she opens her mouth to mine. She tastes like a sky full of freedom. The world disappears around us, the sunlight warm on my back as she arches into me and her eyes close. When I break the contact, my lips hovering above hers, she opens her eyes with a controlled sigh that doesn't quite match how rapid her breathing is or that one of her legs has curled around my calf. I turn slowly, the air moving around us as I fight the urge to kiss her again.

As the sky revolves around us, she suddenly freezes, her gaze fixed on a point in the distance. "Cassian! What is that?"

I spin in the direction of her gaze.

In the distance, a dark plume of smoke billows from the palace. Only a serious fire would cause that. I hesitate for only a second.

"We have to get back. Hold on!" I clasp her tightly as I swoop to the ground, spearing toward the sack I dropped. I can't leave the creature behind. I have to show it to the King, make him believe the danger that's approaching. I'm not one of his guards—yet—and I don't want elevation or accolades. All I want is to protect my country.

Holding Elaina tightly with one hand, I drop to the ground, bend to pick up the sack, and sling it over my shoulder before I reach for her again.

"We'll travel faster if I fly you," I say, reminding myself that I need her permission.

She steps onto my feet again. "Yes."

Wrapping one arm around her, I hold onto the sack with the other, confident that I won't drop either her or it. With a sweep of my wings, we soar upward, speeding high over the trees. It's awkward, but my wings are strong, quickly carrying us toward Crimson Court. The Court is open on all sides to allow gargoyles to fly in and out, giant golden pillars supporting a vast scarlet roof.

Fear grows thick and sharp inside me as the distant shapes, the flames, come into sharp focus.

Soldiers swarm around Crimson Court, their ranks spreading all the way to the palace, but they aren't the king's guards. These men are bare-chested, covered in blood, dragging bodies along the ground. Some of their victims are still alive, but others... I recognize some of the gargoyles being dragged as servants from the palace, visiting dignitaries…

In the distance, swords clash and the roar of battle assaults my ears. I pull up sharp. I can't believe what I'm seeing. "It's the Grievous Clan. They've attacked the palace."

The Grievous Clan is the most ferocious gargoyle clan. They're warrior gargoyles without any morals, the most distrusted clan of all.

I whisper, "The King has been betrayed." I clutch Elaina tightly. Grievous gargoyles have no respect for women. "I have to hide you."

Elaina begins to nod. Then she inhales sharply. "Wait! My parents!"

Below us, two men shove her mother and father inside Crimson Court. I catch sight of her parents' emerald robes, their frightened, bloody faces, before they disappear beneath the roof. There's a sickening pile of bodies growing beside the Court that tells me the Court is a slaughter ground. I fight the sick feeling spearing through me, fight the need to soar into battle and kill every Grievous gargoyle I can find.

I have to keep Elaina safe first. "It's too late for them. We have to go."

"No, Cassian!" She beats at my chest, struggling hard to be free. I don't want to let her go, every instinct in my body telling me to run. I have to protect her. No matter what happens to me, I have to make sure she's safe. "Let me hide you, Elaina!"

"I can't leave my parents." She grabs my face in her hands, forcing me to focus on her. "I know how to use a dagger, Cassian. I know how to fight. I won't leave them to be slaughtered."

I shake my head. My arms tighten around her, refusing to let her go, turning and sweeping my wings to carry us far away.

"Cassian! Let. Me. Go." She grits her teeth, shoving at me, writhing in my arms, her wings attempting to spread.

No! She is too little, too slender. Within moments, she's slipped my hold, her wings spreading as she soars to the ground.

I follow her, landing moments after she does.

The Grievous gargoyles around us jolt backward at our sudden appearance, clearing the space before my wings knock them over.

Elaina doesn't pause, running as soon as her feet touch the ground. She flits through the group of Grievous gargoyles moving between her and Crimson Court, her figure as lithe as a silver wraith. She steals their daggers as she goes, her fingers nimble as she spins and dances out of reach while the filthy men startle at her appearance and try to grab her.

She is little but she is strong. Flinging a dagger at a gargoyle who tries to get in her way, she hits him square in the heart. She spreads her wings, rises up, and kicks another in the teeth so hard that he falls in front of her and she uses his sinking body as leverage to run up and soar in the direction of her parents.

I follow her footsteps, protecting her back, knocking out a gargoyle who tries to grab her from behind. I snatch his dagger as he falls, spin, and drive the weapon into the chest of another who attempts to stab Elaina from the side. I wrench the blade out of him, knowing I'll need the weapon again.

The sack is hampering my movements, so I drop it, aware of a massive gargoyle—the largest I've ever seen—striding toward me from my left. He watches me with narrowed eyes but doesn't run after me. When I leave the sack behind, he stoops to pick it up, staring inside it.

Elaina plows ahead of me to her parents, screaming when she sees them.

At the center of the Court, a massive gargoyle with a sharp nose and dark gray wings holds her mother from behind, one thick arm around her chest, his foot stamping the back of her calves to force her into a kneeling position. His movements are fast and brutal, choking off her cry of fear and pain.

I spread my wings and soar toward them, but the gargoyle's blade is too quick. Far too efficient. As if he were cutting the throat of an animal.

Elaina's horrified shout washes over me as her mother's body hits the floor. *"Mother! No!"*

Her mother's killer pays no attention to us and I'm too far away to stop him moving onto her father, who is being held immobile by three men. Elaina shoves the next gargoyle who tries to grab her, ramming her last stolen dagger into his throat.

Her father shouts, struggles, roaring for his wife. The sharp-nosed gargoyle crunches his boot into the back of his calves, snapping bone, his thick arm tight around his neck.

Elaina races toward them, desperate to reach her father in time. My dagger is poised, only seconds away.

The sharp-nosed gargoyle glances up, but he doesn't stop. His knife hand cuts to the side in a brutal sweep.

Elaina catches her father as he closes his eyes, the deep cut across his neck stealing his life, covering her in blood. Her screams wash over me, triggering every protective instinct inside me.

With a roar, I crash into the man who held her father, driving my wing dagger into his shoulder. I was aiming for his heart, but he twitched just in time. Still impaling him, I force him downward. The moment he loses his footing, I retract my wing dagger, following his downward fall. I aim my fist and sweep my wings to give me extra force. His eyes widen. He tries to hit me, but my fist slams straight and true against his temple, knocking his head against the stone floor with a sickening crack.

Blood sprays, the gargoyle lies still, and I rear up over him, my wings spread wide. His shallow breathing fills the suddenly silent Court.

I spin to Elaina.

She struggles in the arms of three men, who are dragging her backward. Two of them hold her wings, preparing to rip them off.

The third clasps his hand over her mouth to silence her, his other fist gripping her hair, pulling her head back so that her eyes water.

Water or tears. Either makes my blood boil.

When I look around, I discover that the other gargoyles have cleared the space around us, all of them standing back from me, staying clear of my wings.

I ignore them, focusing on the men restraining Elaina.

"You will let her go, or you will die," I say.

The one gripping her hair snickers, but I'm already moving. My wings snap closed with a sweep that lifts me across the distance. The moment my wings close, my feet touch the ground and my wing daggers dart forward, impaling the men gripping her wings—this time right through their hearts. At the same time, my fist closes around the throat of the man holding her hair. He doesn't have time to shout, releasing her as I lift him off the ground. I expand my wings, flinging the other two dead men off my daggers. Their bodies hit the ground with a thud while my fist squeezes around the throat of the third, choking him to death within silent seconds. I throw him to the side and reach for Elaina.

Her gaze shoots to something behind me, fear reflected in her eyes. "Cassian!"

A thick arm snakes around my neck, a fist meets my lower back, and a boot hits my calves. The sharp-nosed gargoyle rams his face against mine, blood dripping from his forehead. I should have stabbed him in the eyes.

His blade jabs the air at the corner of my vision, a descending flash of silver, pressing to my throat, forcing me to freeze. If I try to free myself, I will cut my own throat.

At the same time, three more gargoyles dart forward to restrain Elaina, shoving her to her knees, holding her face so she has to look at me.

I don't want her to see me die. "Close your eyes, Elaina! *Close your eyes!*"

The blade shifts, pain pierces my skin—

A guttural roar sounds from the side of the Court. "Stop!"

The massive gargoyle who picked up the sack I dropped strides across the distance, holding my dead prey in his raised fist.

The creature's panther-like body dangles across the newcomer's arm as he holds it high. Like his brethren, he is naked to the waist and his bare chest bulges with corded muscles. His eyes are black ochre and his jaw is square with a cleft in his chin. He wears a metal chain around his neck with a single, silver claw attached to it. He is easily the largest gargoyle I have ever seen. Even more ferocious than the King.

The other gargoyles part for him, dangerous grins growing on their faces. The newcomer may have stopped my execution, but his arrival is bad news, not good.

He stops mere paces away from me. "I am Grievous Howl."

"The King will kill you," I snarl.

He laughs. "The King is dead. He lies in a pool of his own blood in his burning palace. I killed him myself."

Howl barely gives Elaina a glance as he leans down to me, his eyes filled with all sorts of crazy. "Who are you?"

Through gritted teeth, I say, "I am Cassian of the Hideaway Clan."

"I am your king now, Cassian." The animal's head lolls in Howl's arms, its teeth bared as he raises it high above his head again, shaking its dead body and shouting, "Brothers, behold! We have a new brother among us. Cassian is now Grievous."

The Grievous gargoyles inhale sharply before they roar, a deafening cry.

I stare at them in confusion. First they wanted to kill me and now I'm their brother? The blade pressing to my throat says I'm not out of danger.

Howl rips out one of the dead animal's claws, dropping the carcass to the floor before he compares it with the claw around his neck.

He gives me a satisfied smile. "Larger than the one I killed."

He turns in a circle to the increasing roars around us. "Here is Cassian… who killed a shadow panther—one of the most ferocious creatures in our land. Only Grievous are strong enough to kill shadow panthers!"

While the roars continue, Howl ducks down to me, the claw clutched in his fist. He whispers, "The warrior who holds you is Grievous Gerst. He is my second-in-command—stronger than any other in my Clan—and yet you bested him. Right now, the damage to his shoulder is a liability. If you wish, you will be able to escape his hold, fight him, and you will win. But then you will have to fight me."

His eyes gleam. "You have Hideaway's wings. The first in centuries. It would be a pity for me to kill you. So I'm going to give you a choice." He points at Elaina. "I will let you live if you kill the woman."

I stare beyond Howl to Elaina. She tugs fiercely, trying to free herself from the hold of the three gargoyles who leer at her.

All my hatred flows to the surface as I turn back to Howl. "No. Kill me instead and let her go."

He laughs. "*No?*"

He moves so fast that I don't have time to breathe. His arm snakes around my neck, yanking me out of Gerst's hold, lifting me so that I dangle beside him. He drags me like a helpless toy across the floor toward Elaina. I ram my elbow behind me as hard as I can, kick back, try to spread my wings, try to use my wing daggers, but he barely budges.

He's strong.

Too strong.

For the first time... I've met someone who is stronger than me. I'm not fully grown, not at the full peak of my power, but even if I were...

"You will never defeat me, Cassian." Howl continues whispering into my ear as he forces me to my knees right in front of Elaina. If we reach out, our fingertips would touch. "She's too beautiful to be a slave but too fertile for my harem. I can't let her live. You will kill her mercifully, whereas my clan..."

I raise my eyes to the other men. Elaina whimpers as one of

them smells her hair, sucking on the strands he holds, his lips drawing back into a snarl.

"She's going to die, Cassian. The only question is whether it will be quick."

"*No.*"

Elaina shifts opposite me, her arms pinned behind her back. Her dress is covered in blood, the pale blue turned crimson. Her eyes are wide, but suddenly… not frightened. All the fear drains out of her expression, her cornflower eyes becoming clear and focused.

The worry and pain on her face smooths away as she says, "Cassian?" Her voice compels me to focus only on her. "It's okay."

"No."

She tilts her head to Howl. Her gaze doesn't leave mine as she says, "Tell your soldiers to let me go, Grievous Howl. I won't run."

He takes a moment to consider her before he says, "Very well."

He nods to the men and they release her. She rises slowly to her feet. Her dress swishes around her legs, torn up one side. A patch of new blood grows on her thigh. Despite the wound, she doesn't limp, gliding the short distance between us, the most beautiful woman I have ever seen.

I can't lose her. I have to fight. I have to think of a way to win. I *will* think of a way. I just need a little more time to slip Howl's hold…

She kneels in front of me while Howl continues to squeeze my throat.

She ignores him, holding her arms close to her sides, one hand tangled in her dress. Her knees nudge mine. She smiles. Soft. Gentle. A smile only for me. "I'm sorry I didn't fly away with you, Cassian. I hope you will find me again one day. I'll be waiting for you."

I shake my head, a determined denial. "I won't let you die."

She leans forward, her hand untangling from her dress as the corner of her mouth hitches. "Remember not to be so polite."

Her arm rises.

Too late, I see the dagger she holds. She must have snatched it from one of the guards who held her. But she isn't pointing it at Howl. She places its tip over her own heart instead.

"No!" I surge forward. My hand stretches. My fingertips brush the handle—

Howl jolts me back.

She rams the dagger into her own chest, her eyes filling with tears, a cry rising from her lips as she collapses across my knees, her silver wings falling across us.

"No! Elaina!"

Howl finally releases me, freeing my arms so that I can wrap them around her, pulling her up to my chest.

I want to shout, roar, wrench her soul back to me.

"Why?" I grasp her shoulders, supporting her head as she inhales, dragging air into her lungs one last time. "Why did you do this?"

She presses her soft palm to my cheek, the brightness in her eyes fading. "One day… you will understand…"

Her final breath washes across my mouth, the scent of freedom fading as her hand drops away.

Howl grabs me, hauling me up so fast that Elaina's body crashes to the floor, her wings spread across it and her face turned away.

I want to kill him.

I *will* kill him.

Howl's cold smile greets me as he rises up beside me. "You belong to me now, Cassian," he says. "Heart and soul."

1

MARBELLA

For seven years, I lived my life according to a precise set of rules. At the top of the list: subdue the Storm every day, don't touch anyone, and follow the protocols. I obeyed all of them. Until the rules were swept out from under me like yesterday's dusty rug.

Now, there are no rules.

I set the Storm free. I touched Baelen. And the protocols? Actually, it wasn't me who burned those to the ground; it was the Elven Command when they tried to kill Baelen and take my power. That's when they made me their enemy.

The boundaries that once existed around my life are gone. Literally. Now there's open space and deep stretches of blue sky. And the determination that I will heal Baelen's wounds and bring him back to me. Whatever it takes.

The phoenix soars through the cloud cover floating over elven country. I lean forward in the moist air, tugging on the back of Jasper's armor to get his attention. We're riding on the phoenix's broad back while the Storm's spirit sails along behind us, connected to me just like she promised she'd be. At this moment, she's floating on her back, riding the slipstream created by the firebird's wings.

Baelen's head rests in my lap and his feet lie alongside Jasper, securely tethered between us by ropes made of lightning. It's not exactly the kind of thing I ever imagined, but the Storm bound him safely to the phoenix and promised me that he wouldn't fall during our journey. A journey I never thought I'd make. To gargoyle country. The home of our worst enemies.

Responding to my tug, Jasper maneuvers around so he's facing me. It's safe to talk now that we've ascended into cover and left the Elven Command far behind. "Princess?"

"I need to know what happened while Baelen and I were in the simulation."

Immediately, Jasper shakes his head and tries to turn away from me, but I grip his arm. His muscles tense under my sudden touch, his forearm big enough that my fingers don't make it all the way around. He's a warrior, trained all his life to be part of the elven military. He could shake me off in an instant. But for a long time, I wasn't allowed to touch anyone, let alone a man, so the fact that I won't let him go right now makes him pause.

"I need to know what really happened." As I speak, my other palm rests against Baelen's cheek. His eyes are closed. His skin is warm to the touch, but his chest doesn't rise and fall like it would if he were asleep.

To Jasper, I say, "I only know what I saw in the simulation, but that was all a trick."

"Are you sure?" Jasper's serious eyes drill into mine. Always serious. He never smiles. Except once during battle, and that was a scary grin I don't want to see again. He's completely loyal to Baelen and for some reason wants to protect me from things that will hurt me. What's more, he seems to know what those things are before I do.

I give him a single nod. I'm more certain about this than I am about anything else right now.

"Okay, then…" He clears his throat as I let his arm go. He keeps his tone even and unemotional, as if he's reporting facts that don't mean anything to either of us. It's so far from the truth. Everything he says cuts my heart into pieces.

"As soon as you and Baelen sat in the Chairs of Truth to enter the simulation, your faces went completely blank. We could tell you weren't with us anymore. We kept watch over both of you because we were worried the Elven Command might attack your bodies while you were vulnerable."

Baelen and I had gone into the arena to carry out the final trial in the fight for my hand—which was supposed to be a simulation where we each fought a gargoyle. The trials were part of the marriage protocols that were designed to end in the selection of the strongest man to be my husband.

Baelen and I had made it through all the other trials involving tests of strength, endurance, and intelligence, leaving us to face each other in the final fight to the death. Leaving me to face the prospect of killing him, the only man I've ever loved, or he would've been cursed by sorcery to kill me instead.

Jasper says, "At first it seemed like everything was going to be okay, but about an hour after you sat down, the crowd got restless. It was a long time to watch you sit still. One of the Elven Commanders—Elwyn Elder—told everyone to leave and come back later. That bothered me, but I didn't do anything until…"

Jasper pauses, breaking my gaze to contemplate his hands. His knuckles are bruised. Welts crisscross the exposed skin on his arms and legs where his armor didn't protect him. I had done that damage to him while I was in the simulation, but I didn't know what I was doing at the time. I thought I was defending myself.

I say, "Go on. Please."

"When the crowd left, two of the Elven Commanders—Pedr Bounty and Osian Valor—locked the arena doors. Teilo Splendor was the only Commander who didn't seem to know what was going on."

I murmur, "He was the only one who wasn't involved in the curse." Teilo Splendor's daughter is a talented healer, and his grandson, Sebastian, is one of Baelen's most trusted friends. The Elven Command is made up of elected members of the five highest Houses: the Houses of Elder, Splendor, Glory, Valor, and Bounty. Technically, Baelen's House—the House of Rath—is the highest

House of all, but the Elven Command did everything they could to keep him out of their business, appointing Baelen as the Commander of the Elven Army so he couldn't claim his place with them.

"Teilo demanded to know what the others were doing," Jasper says. "But Elwyn Elder knocked him out. Sebastian and I ran over to intervene and that was when Gideon Glory cast his sorcery over the Chairs of Truth."

Jasper shudders, rubbing his arms as if he's cold. I know him well enough to know that not much fazes him. He takes everything in stride with an immovable calm, but the spell that Gideon Glory cast wasn't anything ordinary... I can still feel its effect, crawling under my skin. The way it had immobilized me after I emerged from the simulation.

I shake it off as Jasper continues. "You and Baelen were wrenched out of your chairs. They cracked apart as soon as you fell to the floor. That's when you began to fight each other."

He swallows. "You and he... your faces were still blank. It was clear you didn't know what you were doing. Jordan tried to grab you. I tried to stop Baelen. You shook us off like we were nothing. You were going to kill each other..."

I stare at my own clenched fists. Inside the simulation, Baelen had appeared to me as a gargoyle—the kind that the elves had pedaled as our enemies for hundreds of years: vicious, unrelenting, horned, with salivating teeth. I met a gargoyle during one of the trials and discovered that they're nothing like that. Female gargoyles are particularly beautiful. While their male counterparts resemble stone, the women look like humans with gossamer wings. I'd fought Baelen with everything I had, believing him to be my enemy, not knowing I was fighting him in real life.

Jasper clears his throat. "It turned really bad when you got ahold of Baelen's dagger. You lit up like a lightning storm. That's when everyone got involved. Your Storm Command and Baelen's soldiers —all of them tried to stop you. Sebastian's mother saw what was coming and grabbed me and Sebastian, shouting at us to find shelter."

All it takes is a touch of metal and I can harness lightning as a weapon. I close my eyes, trying to banish the memory. The simulation had made my friends appear like a swarm of gargoyles. I was desperate to defend myself against them, so I'd struck the dagger's electrified hilt against the ground, sending a wave of deadly lightning through the very elves who were trying to protect me.

He sighs. "There wasn't any shelter. Everyone went down. Even your advisor, Elise. She was trying to counter the simulation with magic, but the electrical shock knocked her out cold. Then... something changed. You and Baelen stopped fighting. You talked to each other for the first time."

I nod. "We figured it out. Well, Baelen did. He recognized me because of what I did with the lightning. He realized we were actually fighting each other."

"You were looking around as if you couldn't see us. You couldn't see the Elven Commanders sneaking up on Baelen... I tried to run back to you, but they got to him first." Jasper swallows, and the unemotional tone of his voice fails, disappearing as the intensity of his feelings breaks through. "Gideon Glory strengthened their weapons with sorcery. It's the only way to pierce Rath armor. All four of them stabbed Baelen at the same time."

Like the corners of a square. I can see the four cuts in Baelen's chest plate as he rests in front of me now, each cut several inches long, the edges of the metal burned where the sorcery sliced through.

Jasper stops speaking and clears his throat, clearly struggling now. My heart wrenches, but I need him to go on. I need to know what I couldn't see.

"Their swords went right through and would have impaled you too, but Baelen... he pushed you away, so you were safe. You ran back to him. You tried to stop him from falling and then he wrapped you up in his arms like he was protecting you."

Inside the simulation, Baelen had cocooned me inside his gargoyle wings, telling me to stay where it was safe, holding me until the simulation ended.

Jasper takes a deep breath and lets it out again. "I think you know the rest."

My cheeks are cold where the wind beats at my tears. But I'm not sad. I'm angry. I'd surfaced from the simulation to discover that I'd been tricked into disabling all the elves who were there to protect us. I'd done exactly what the Elven Commanders wanted me to do and left Baelen vulnerable to attack. They knew they could never get to me as long as he was alive.

Jasper's back is straight and tense. The lightning welts across his arms are red and raw. I'd hurt him. I'd hurt all my friends. There aren't enough apologies to make up for it. "I'm sorry, Jasper. I'm sorry for what I did to you."

He nods, accepting my apology, but a question enters his voice. "You said you gave Baelen your storm power."

My power to control the Storm was the Elven Command's ultimate prize. I am the first Storm Princess who can use storm power as a weapon. They believed I could pass that power on to the first man I touched. They were right, but so wrong about the timing.

"I gave my power to Baelen Rath seven years ago on the night I became the Storm Princess," I say. "Nobody knew, including me. When the Storm chose me, it poured lightning into my body. Baelen was nearby, and I poured lightning into him, too. It was through that act that I passed him my power."

I shake my head with remembered horror. All the nightmares I'd had after that night. The helplessness I'd felt watching Baelen suffer. "I thought I killed him that night. I didn't know it meant he had my power."

The Storm said she didn't know how Baelen and I had stayed away from each other. Looking back, I know it was only because of guilt and pain. I blamed myself for what he went through. I blamed myself for the scar running the length of the side of his face. I had wanted to keep Baelen as far away from me as possible, so I didn't hurt him again.

And now...

Now I trace the line of the scar from his right temple down the side of his face. It splits at his jawline, one side curling behind his ear, the other under his chin. If I listen carefully I can hear his heartbeat inside my mind, beating out a slow rhythm. I close my eyes, clinging to the repetitive *thud-thud* while my fingers tingle where they rest against his cheek.

The sound of his heartbeat is the only thing keeping me sane right now. But it's not enough. It will never be enough. I can finally touch him without fear that I'll hurt him. I can touch him because I want to more than anything else in the world. Finally… but he's not here. Not really.

After the Elven Commanders attacked him, just a moment before he died, Baelen used the power of the thunder to pause everything, including himself, halting the progress of the deadly wounds. He paused his own death. He gave me the chance to save him. But it's tearing my heart out being so close to him and yet so far away. It's like having part of me ripped away and thrown into darkness.

I spiral downward inside my mind, tears dripping down my cheeks from beneath my closed eyelids. I search for the light, the warmth that I always felt when he was close to me, the dangerous response of my lightning to the nearness of his body. I understand it now. It was my storm power trying to connect with his.

My eyes are still closed, but I sense my fingers growing warmer against his skin and so do my thighs where his head rests. I drop my forehead to his, spiraling further and further while a glow appears inside my mind like a single, red flame––a single strike of lightning as red as blood.

I stop breathing because… I can hear him.

2

BAELEN

I stand in a darkened field. Tall blades of grass sweep my fingertips, swaying in a breeze that cools my skin. My feet are planted to the spot, as if they have become part of the soil where I stand. I hold a sword, both hands curled around its hilt while its blade points down, planted in the earth like my feet. Despite its weight, the sword feels insubstantial, as if it's still forming in this quiet place where my heart and mind exist, suspended until I can return to the world of the living.

All is quiet. Nothing moves except for the breeze and the grass. The light never changes.

I wear Rath armor, covered from my feet to my neck in finely sculpted metal plates that link together to protect my body, the red-and-black markings of my House proudly displayed across them, the armor my ancestors wore into battle.

It didn't save me.

Blood runs from the wounds in my chest, gaping slits burned at the edges from blades strengthened by sorcery, but the agony of the attack is a distant memory. Brighter is the memory of Marbella's shout as she stood over the younger version of me in the simulation, protecting my younger self.

Her determined shout keeps me calm in this deserted field, keeps me anchored and steady.

I will protect Baelen Rath to the death. Because I love him!

Words she'd never spoken to me before. Words I couldn't speak to her after she became the Storm Princess.

Now I wait until I can tell her again.

At the edge of the field, directly in front of me, the light suddenly changes. A brief spark glows and then fades fifty paces away. It brightens again. Dims. Brightens and this time, a silhouette appears within it. A woman, her auburn hair streaking across the dark like a flame, her golden armor a rising sun.

Marbella.

Her hand reaches out to me, her fingertips lifted as if she's searching for me in the dark. Her face is shadowed and her eyes are closed, dark lashes resting against her cheeks. She pushes through the long grass, pressing against the breeze that suddenly springs up around her.

My heart jumps and she veers directly toward me, as if she's seeking me by the heavy thumping of my heart alone. Her fingers twitch and a bright sapphire spark rises from her fingertip, dancing across the breeze toward me.

I can't move, can't shift my feet, frozen here, clutching an insubstantial sword. The spark reaches my chest, my heart, and sinks through my armor, warming me, finally releasing my voice.

She can't be here. This is the place between life and death. She can't cross this veil without consequences.

I open my mouth to speak, needing to warn her, protect her. *Marbella, you can't be here with me.*

She pauses thirty paces from me, her eyes still closed, her lips parting as she gasps. *Baelen?*

Her sharp inhale turns into a sob, her chest rising and falling as her hand strains farther forward. *I need you. You have to come back to me.*

I want to hold her more than anything, but if she opens her eyes in this place, she'll cross over and there's no telling what will happen if the Storm is released here.

Still, I take what I can from her presence, her voice. *I will come back to you. You have to trust me. You have to trust yourself.*

She speaks in a rush, her desperation nearing panic. *What if I can't get you to the springs in Mount Erador? What if the gargoyles stop me? What if the springs don't work—*

Marbella Mercy, I growl. *My stubborn, beautiful love. You stayed away from me for seven years because you were determined to keep me safe. You will find a way to the springs, because you're determined to do that too.*

Nothing will stop me, she whispers.

I want to stretch out this moment, keep her here, but already I sense the Storm growing beyond us in the place of the living. An unstoppable force presses against my back, seeping through me. At the same time, a droplet of liquid falls on my cheek and down my neck. Then another. Crimson clouds form in the air above me and my Storm power surges. I rein it in, barely keeping it under control.

I want to go to her, but if she stays with me any longer, our Storm powers will collide and whoever she is with will be hurt.

Far, far beyond her, I sense a flurry of movement. A voice I recognize—Jasper's?—shouts Marbella's name, calling to her with an urgency I can't ignore.

You have to go now, I say to her. *Before I lose my will to remain in this place. And before we hurt someone.*

Her hand drops to her side—the hand from which the blue spark flew—and the movement tugs my chest. I tilt my head to study the space between us. The light glints off her armor. For a split second, it looks like a sapphire thread stretches between her hand and my heart. Then it's gone.

I miss you, Baelen, she says.

She turns away and I let her go, willing her to return to the living, the breeze blowing at her back, even though it leaves my heart hurting.

The light around her silhouette fades.

That's when it starts to rain.

3

———

MARBELLA

The flame grows inside my mind as I reach for Baelen, gasping back a sob as his gravelly voice speaks, laced with concern. *Marbella, you can't be here with me.*

Baelen? I choke. Gasp. *I need you. You have to come back to me.*

His voice is warm like my whole body right now. *I will come back to you. You have to trust me. You have to trust yourself.*

All my worries bubble upward. *But what if I can't get you to the springs in Mount Erador? What if the gargoyles stop me? What if the springs don't work—*

Marbella Mercy, he growls. *My stubborn, beautiful love. You stayed away from me for seven years because you were determined to keep me safe. You will find a way to the springs, because you're determined to do that too.*

Nothing will stop me, I whisper.

You have to go now, he says. *Before I lose my will to remain in this place. And... before we hurt someone.*

Hurt someone?

Far, far away, I'm aware that someone is shouting my name. "Marbella! Princess!"

I miss you, Baelen.

I don't want to go. I don't want to swim upward, away from

27

Baelen's voice, away from this connection. He doesn't respond. Instead, a force pushes me upward, back through the lightning and the flames, back to myself. The sky is bright as I open my eyes, much brighter than it was before.

"Princess!" Jasper balances on his feet opposite me, half-crouched, fingers splayed out toward me, alarm etched in every line of his face.

Lightning streaks upward in front of my eyes, but it's not inside my mind now; it's rising between Baelen and me, glowing between us and forming droplets that shimmer upward like raindrops in reverse. Shock burns through me. It's not just my lightning. It's Baelen's, too.

It's warm and safe, but only to me. To everyone else… it's deadly.

I'm suddenly aware of a disturbance in the air on my right. The Storm soars up beside me, her chocolate eyes filled with urgent concern and a surprising amount of fury. "Marbella Mercy! Stop connecting to Baelen Rath. Right now!"

"I—"

"Now! Or you will kill your friend."

I jolt back to Jasper. The droplets quickly follow the lines of Baelen's body, rising like a cascade toward Jasper. I immediately unclasp my fingers from around Baelen's face, disconnecting and pulling backward.

The result is instant. The light fades between us. The burning raindrops fall back to Baelen's chest and neck, dispersing and vaporizing.

The rain is gone. Gone like Baelen's voice and his nearness. I want to cry with the pain of that loss, the pain of being wrenched back to the rest of the world.

Jasper sinks back into a sitting position, relief washing over him. "You had me worried there, Princess."

"I'm sorry." My hands remain in the air, frozen, afraid to touch Baelen again. "I don't know… what that was."

"Your heart's broken," Jasper says, far more simply than I expected.

The Storm isn't quite so forgiving. She observes me with a mix of concern and distrust. She was once a female gargoyle. All I know about her is what the phoenix told me—that she gave her life for revenge. She turned herself into a storm and raged through elven country hundreds of years ago, killing our last king and almost wiping out the entire elven race. When the Elven Command tried and failed to steal my power after the simulation, I called the Storm to me without knowing what I was doing.

Now, here she is: a silvery, wraith-like creature with delicate features, large, drown-inside-me-chocolate eyes, long legs like I've never seen before, and a broken wing that I don't want to ask her about.

The most difficult part about her presence is that Jasper doesn't know she's there. He can't see or hear her, which makes all my conversations with her one-sided. She gets to talk and I have to listen, even if I don't like what she's saying.

Her lips compress into a tight line. "You can't do that again."

I don't even know what *that* was.

"You combined your power with his," she says, as if she's reading my mind—not hard given my questioning stare. "But if you connect like that again, you'll not only hurt every living thing around you, you'll also draw Baelen out too soon and he'll die."

I jolt away from Baelen even further, using the bare minimum of contact to gently move his head off my lap and rest him against the phoenix's back instead. The phoenix's body is broad and long, but Baelen's large frame takes up most of it. I find myself sitting almost on the bird's tail. Once the Storm's finished chastising me, I'll have to apologize to the phoenix for this new discomfort.

The Storm's face softens. "Don't worry, you can't combine your power by accident."

I scowl at her, since that's exactly what I did.

She sighs. "Yes, I know you didn't mean to, but you deliberately sought him out just now, didn't you? Well, don't do that again and all will be fine."

I sigh. I don't think Jasper will think it's strange when I say, "I needed to hear his voice."

Jasper has already settled himself back onto the phoenix. He acts as if nothing happened and I'm grateful for his unshakable calm attitude and his ability to bounce back—despite the fact that I could have killed him. "It's okay, Princess."

He takes a moment before peering through the cloud cover beneath us. The Storm remains beside me, keeping pace with the phoenix as if she wants to keep an eye on me now. I guess I don't blame her. In fact, I'm reluctantly grateful. No Storm Princess has ever shared power with another elf before like I have with Baelen. I'm walking on new ground and the Storm is the only one who might be able to guide me.

I'm glad for the change of subject when Jasper says, "We should reach the border soon."

The phoenix's voice sounds in my mind then, reminding me of soft wind chimes. *We are approaching the Revenant Mountains behind Rath land. Beyond the mountains is the border between Erawind and Erador. Once we cross it, we will be in gargoyle country.*

A shiver races down my spine. The phoenix flies much faster than any other creature, so we reached the border within a few hours. The first time I flew with the giant bird was during the trial that brought me to these very mountains. Nobody had ever flown with a phoenix before. The firebird told me it had been waiting for me to summon it because I was the Storm. I'd thought that was because I could absorb storm power, but the phoenix insisted it was because I *was* the Storm. I'm still not completely sure what that means.

I say to Jasper, "The phoenix says we're almost at the Revenant Mountains."

"We need to be careful." Jasper half-twists back to me. "The gargoyles recently started patrolling the air space right up to their side of the border."

"But the border has always been a neutral zone. Why are they patrolling it now?" It would certainly explain why the Elven Command had become paranoid about a gargoyle attack. They'd tried multiple times to attack the gargoyles who had started nesting on our side of the border, but Baelen had cautioned against a pre-emptive strike, telling the Command they didn't have enough information to start a war.

"They're trying to stop other gargoyles from escaping."

"Escaping…" The gargoyle I'd encountered was sheltering his two newborn children, hiding them within elven borders. "The gargoyle on Scepter Peak told me that facing elves was safer than what was going on in his home country. What's driving them out?"

Jasper shakes his head. "We don't know. Baelen was trying to find out."

"Well, whatever the reason, if there are air patrols, then the phoenix won't get us as far as I hoped."

I worry at my lip, disappointment rushing through me. I'd hoped that the phoenix could fly us at least part of the way to the springs in the heart of Mount Erador. "I think this means we have to land in the mountains and travel on foot."

Jasper gives me an apologetic shrug. "If it's any consolation, Baelen hid supply packs in the mountain range in case he ever needed them. I know where to find them."

That raises my eyebrows. "Supply packs in the mountains?"

Jasper glances away and then at Baelen. "He planned for the possibility that you and he might need to disappear."

I contemplate Baelen's still features. There's so much I don't know about his life after I became the Storm Princess. After he finished military training, he'd disappeared for three whole years. I still have no idea where he went. Now there's no way for me to ask him. After the Storm's warning just now, I'm definitely not going to try speaking with him again.

Jasper draws my attention. "I don't know about you, but I could do with a change of clothes and some food."

"You're right." I scrub my eyes. The fact that Baelen planned ahead is a good thing. Jasper and I have very few supplies and even our armor isn't ideal for an overland trek. Jasper's is beat up, but mine is pristine. It's made from an inner suit spun from Elyria spider webs and lined on the outside with Shimmer Beetle husks. The Elyria web is unbreakable, and the husks are the hardest material in the land. It took my Storm Command seven years to gather enough webs and husks to sew the suit for me. It may be the safest thing I could wear but it won't guard against the freezing nighttime temperatures on the mountain. While sunny during the day, a layer of ice forms over the mountains at night.

"If only I could have a bath too." Baelen's blood still stains my hands and armor. I need the reminder gone.

Jasper keeps a straight face. "Sorry. Can't help you with that. But there are water sources where you can wash up."

"Thank you. Can you show me where we should land?"

He points. "We should head a little more south. There's a concealed pass through the mountains that way. We can use it to cross the border—" He cuts off and spins. "Wait…"

I hear it, too: the far-off beat of wings. Elves have very strong senses, but mine are especially honed to changes in air pressure because of my storm power. I kick myself for not paying closer attention. I should have heard it sooner.

The phoenix gives a warning cry inside my mind. *Princess! Gargoyles are flying in from the left. They'll reach our position within minutes.*

I keep my voice down. "The phoenix says it's gargoyles."

Jasper's surprise mirrors mine. "We haven't crossed the border. They're in our airspace."

I grit my teeth. "Has that ever happened before?"

"Not that I know of."

"Okay, well… we're higher up than they usually fly. We should stay inside the clouds. Let them fly right under us. And if they don't…"

The Storm sails along beside me. "Be careful using your storm power around Baelen. His heart is connected to yours and he will answer the call of the storm."

That's going to make things difficult, but I won't risk Baelen's safety. Or Jasper's, for that matter. This close to me, he could easily be hurt if I unleashed my lightning. I choose my words carefully, trying to answer her and speak to Jasper at the same time. "If they don't fly by, I'll be careful with my storm power. I don't want to hurt you or Baelen by accident. There's been enough danger of that kind already today."

He gives me a serious nod before bending to retrieve his weapons from the satchel draped beside Baelen. Multiple weapons disappear into belts and holders around his waist and chest, including two swords crisscrossing his back. I pull on my leather gloves since it's the only way to handle metal without igniting my storm power. Then I strap on my weapons belt, balancing beside Baelen's body while I give my weapons a final check.

"I'm ready."

The Storm points left and down. "That's good, because the female has found us."

So much for hiding in the clouds.

A female gargoyle shoots upward through the mist, her arms outstretched, her wings pinned close to her sides as if she's just swept them down in one massive beat to ascend into the clouds.

She shrieks in surprise and jolts to a stop, so she doesn't collide with Jasper.

"Whoa!" he exclaims, instinctively throwing his arms out in a protective gesture.

I brace for her to attack us, but after a quick assessment, I can tell that the young woman doesn't carry any weapons. In fact, her arms are scratched, her face is tear-stained, and her legs are dirty. She looks seriously frightened. At the same time, the phoenix lurches away from the newcomer, pausing long enough for her to take one look at Jasper and dive into his arms.

"Help me!" she cries.

He freezes, shock shooting across every plane of his chiseled face.

She clings to him like a cat that just jumped out of a lake. "I beg you. Help me, please!"

A female gargoyle asking a male elf for help?

I'm as shocked as Jasper. I have a fleeting vision of a perfect button nose, rosebud mouth, and fear-filled, emerald eyes before the young woman buries her head against his chest. She wraps her arms around his waist and hides herself beneath her wings, becoming a silvery bundle next to him. It's not much of a camouflage, especially because she's shaking like a slender piece of filigree in a gale-force wind.

Look to your left, Princess, the phoenix's normally calm lilt fills with warning as it beats its wings once more, picks up speed, and resumes its former pace. *They're here.*

At the same time, Jasper cries, "We have company!"

Large grey forms cut through the clouds around us—fifteen of them flying in from our left. They're approaching so fast that their flight patterns shred the mist, forming wind tunnels up from the clear blue below us.

At their head is a man with light grey patterns rippling through his dark wings, his warrior features cut from stone. His wingspan is massive, and he carries more weapons on his body than Jasper, even strapped across his bare chest and thick thighs. His jaw is square and eyes are a dazzling sapphire. He'd be gorgeous if it wasn't for the cruel sneer cutting across his face.

He and the other gargoyles surround the phoenix. Three of them speed directly in front of it, forcing it to pull up sharply. Their wings push backward to stop their own forward momentum, but their wing daggers are ready to be used as weapons. In response, the phoenix curves and lengthens its wings, forced to coast.

As the wash of air from all the flying creatures pulses at me, billowing my auburn braid in the wind, the lead man shouts to the others. "It's elves! And… a phoenix."

He backpedals away from my fiery friend, gesturing to his companions to back up also.

Yep, I have a phoenix. And right now, that phoenix looks angry enough about being penned in to start breathing fire at these heavily-armed morons. If I were the phoenix's only passenger, I have no doubt it would ignite its flames. My ability to absorb and wield the storm means the phoenix's fire doesn't hurt me. But it would definitely hurt Jasper and the female gargoyle.

Ignoring the danger, the intruders' wings beat slowly as they take up a holding formation around us, locking us in. Meanwhile, the lead man's gaze rakes over all of us and finally pauses on Baelen.

His eyes narrow. "I see you carry your dead."

Really? That's the first thing he's going to say to me?

Anger rises fast inside me, but I push it down as Jasper wraps both his arms around the cowering woman, sending a clear message to the newcomers that we don't intend to give her back to them.

The Storm floats behind me, quiet and observant. She promised me that if I ever need her to rage, she will, but again, with Jasper and the young woman in the firing line, the Storm's wrath has to be a last resort.

I may not be terribly tall or threatening in appearance, but I raise my voice to the sharpness of a whip. "You're in elven airspace. Explain yourselves."

The leader sucks in a breath, throwing a brief assessing glance at his surroundings—and then back to us dressed in our warrior's armor. It's clear from the quickly hidden concern flashing across his features that he didn't realize he'd crossed the border. And he certainly didn't expect to be caught by a couple of warrior elves in the process. No doubt he was so intent on capturing his prey that he wasn't watching where he was going. It doesn't look like he's about to admit his mistake though…

"I am General Cassian of the King's Army." He points at the woman curled up against Jasper like a caterpillar. "That woman is a fugitive from our law. We have a right to recover her."

I lift an eyebrow in a scathing gesture, but inside I'm worried. If he's telling the truth about who he is, then he's very high up in the gargoyle command. I don't know much about their military structure, but a general can't be many rungs below the top.

I bury my concern as I say, "There are many of you and one of her. She must be a fearsome creature to warrant this many pursuers."

Cassian's expression remains deadpan. "She stole from our King."

I study the young woman. From the brief glance before she hid herself against Jasper, I know she's not carrying anything at all—her clothing is too thin to conceal an object beneath it. "I see nothing of value. What do you claim she's stolen?"

The sneer returns to his lips. "Her body."

Her… what?

Oh, that's not good.

One glance at Jasper tells me he's grinning. The last time I saw that look on his face, he stared down a whole arena full of men who had ill intentions toward me and *my* body. I swallow my rage at the gargoyle's arrogance.

There's no way we're letting these gargoyles fly by.

4

MARBELLA

Jasper deftly repositions the clinging woman so she's attached to his side closest to me, freeing up his arms. He rests his fingers against his thighs, still grinning like a wild wolf. He hasn't reached for his swords yet and I know that's smart. There's still a chance we can convince the men to leave without a fight.

"Well now," he says. "She seems pretty attached to me. I'd say she's staying right where she is."

General Cassian leans in, snarling through his teeth. "I am not accustomed to being defied! You will hand her over to me, elf!"

"While you're in elven airspace? I'm pretty sure you want to move along and let this one go."

For a moment, I think that argument is going to work. Cassian takes stock of the terrain below us and the other gargoyles fan out a little, removing themselves just a tad, but then I realize… they're moving into position.

Cassian shoves his face right up into Jasper's. "She is the King's property, and you will give her to me. Now!"

Jasper's gaze flicks to mine for the briefest moment. He tried. There's no getting through to this man.

"Yeah…" The grin drops away from Jasper's chiseled features, turning his eyes cold and hard. "I don't think so."

He tilts his head to the right, moments before Cassian's wing dagger slices the air right next to him. The woman shrieks, but Jasper's left hand snaps up fast, seizes the wing dagger, and shoves it backward, throwing the gargoyle off balance.

"Insolent!" Cassian roars, regaining his flight, but it gave Jasper enough time to draw both his swords, deflecting attacks from two gargoyles launching at his back before spinning back to Cassian. The swiftness of Jasper's movements dislodges the woman. She falls backward with a cry, clutching the phoenix's feathers as she scoots away from the fighting men and their flashing swords. I have no fear about Jasper's ability to deflect the three men, but I won't let him fight this battle alone.

I close the short distance between me and the female gargoyle as I draw my weapons. "Stay beside me! But don't touch me!"

I don't want to hurt her if I need to harness my lightning.

Her eyes are as wide as mossy pools as she stares up at me, squinting as the sunlight glints across her terrified face. "Elyria!"

The spider web in my armor must be catching the light. I don't have time to explain it to her. Dagger in one hand, sword in the other, I spin back and forth, deflecting attacks from all sides.

Luckily, the gargoyles' wings are so wide that only three of them can attack me at once: one at my front, one at my back, and one at the phoenix's tail. Also by luck, they think Baelen's dead, so they don't bother with him. At least for now, he's safe. Unless one of them slips and impales him while fighting me…

I shudder, but stay focused, blocking the downward swing of a sword while kicking back into the stomach of the gargoyle behind me.

The fight is brutal, but fast. My armor repels their weapons, making me bolder than I would be otherwise, even though I'll suffer the impact bruises later. The phoenix maintains its steady soar to keep us balanced but descends from cloud cover so we have visibility in every direction.

The biggest problem we have is the gap between Jasper and me that leaves the woman vulnerable. We both see the danger at the same time and quickly work our way toward each other. Before we can close the gap, two gargoyles dart inward, each from opposite sides. One rips the woman's hands away from the phoenix's body in a flurry of burnished feathers. The other yanks her feet out from under her and pulls backward. Her face bounces against the bird as the gargoyle holding onto her ankles slings her out into the air and darts away with her.

The woman's scream fades as the gargoyle drops down and flies under the phoenix, obscuring my view for a moment. I locate him as he reappears on the other side except... he doesn't have the woman anymore.

He must have handed her off to another gargoyle. At the same time, the remaining gargoyles fall beneath us and scatter in all directions. Now that we're above them, all I can see is a jumble of grey wings. It's a clever ploy. One I'd appreciate if I wasn't on the receiving end of it.

Desperately, I search for any glimpse of the woman's silver dress that might tell me which gargoyle has her.

Cassian takes a final swipe at Jasper with a vehement snarl before taking off with the others. I swing back to the ones I was fighting only to find the air clear. They're all gone. And they're all flying in different directions to act as diversions.

Phoenix, do you see her?

I'm sorry, Princess. Their wings conceal much. Do you want to pursue the ones heading west?

West is the direction of the border. It would make sense for them to escape in that direction, but I wouldn't put it past them to fly further east into our airspace and then double back to confuse and evade us.

I spin. "Jasper—"

He shushes me, his eyes closed. One hand, palm out, tells me to wait.

The woman screams. *Clever.* We can locate her by the sound. We both spin left to a clump of three gargoyles flying westward. Turns out they're taking the quickest route to the border after all. The phoenix immediately turns and spears in that direction and both Jasper and I crouch to lower our centers of gravity, so we don't fall off. She screams again before the sound is muffled.

As the phoenix closes the gap, one of the gargoyles glances up at the shadow suddenly descending over him. His movement reveals a patch of the woman's shimmering dress. He's holding her close.

"That's her." That's all Jasper says before he takes a step back and leaps out from the phoenix's back, plunging into thin air.

His decision to leap off into space is so sudden that it leaves me stunned. "Jasper!" I shriek, dropping to my hands. "You can't fly!"

He presses his arms and legs together to streamline his body and gain speed as he dives. It's a testament to how strong gargoyle wings are that when Jasper lands right on top of one, he doesn't rip right through it. The gargoyle holding the woman shudders to and fro, dropping and spinning, with Jasper's sudden weight now on one side of him. The two others launch themselves at Jasper, ripping at him with their clawed feet. Funny, I never noticed gargoyle feet before, but it's suddenly clear that the bird-like claws they have instead of toes could be just as lethal as their wing daggers. Which is to say, they could rip apart Jasper's body in moments.

I need to get down there. Because if Jasper can't latch onto a gargoyle—or free the woman so she can carry him—he'll plummet to his death. I can harness the wind and thunder to stop my fall. At least… I think I can. It's not exactly something I've tried before.

Phoenix, stay close. Please try to catch Jasper if he falls. But also… protect Baelen.

I know I've just given the firebird two very contradictory tasks. Catching Jasper involves flying into the fight. Protecting Baelen requires flying as far away from it as possible.

I suddenly realize that the Storm is gone. She disappeared as soon as the fight began. I take one more glance around for her, giving up on calling her for help, only to step into her as I prepare to leap from the phoenix's back.

"I will catch Jasper," she says, her hair billowing around her as she floats at eye level with me. "Even if it frightens the life out of him to be caught by something he can't see. The phoenix should protect Baelen."

"Thank you!" I hesitate before I dive, but not because of the leap into space.

You have my word that Commander Rath will be safe, the phoenix says, sensing the fear that springs through me at the thought of leaving Baelen's side, of letting him out of my sight.

As soon as I leap off its back, I angle my body to the side so I can see the phoenix ascending high into the cloud cover, concealing itself far above us and Baelen with it. I trust the phoenix to keep its word, but even so, a deep-seated fear has found a place in my heart: I can't lose him.

The Storm flies beside me, a wind tunnel forming around her as she descends. The gargoyles are much lower and further west now and Jasper grapples with two of them, holding them off, but the third is free and flies onward with the young woman.

I have seconds to grill the Storm. "Where were you just now? We could have used your help back there."

Her expression shuts off, becoming remarkably blank for such an expressive woman. "I can't harm a gargoyle."

I'm stunned. "Not even these brutes?"

"I will catch Jasper if he falls, but I will not join the fight."

"But, how can you—"

Her gaze flashes over me with veiled menace. "They are my people, Marbella. Do not ask me to fight them."

I jolt away from the vehemence in her voice, reminding myself that I control her. Well, to a degree. But it's the edge of fear that enters her eyes as she maintains my gaze that softens any worry I have about her intentions. She's not trying to fight with me. She's afraid I'll make her do something she doesn't want to do. I don't know anything about her, nothing about her history or motivations. I need to change that, and soon. I need to understand what makes her tick and why she became the Storm. Just... not right now when Jasper's life is on the line and we're about to catapult into three angry gargoyles.

"I won't make you," I say, testing my theory that her anger is fueled by the fear that I'll coerce her into doing things she doesn't want to do.

The instant relief that washes over her face tells me I was right. "I'll stay nearby. If you drop from this height, you'll have a minute before you hit the ground. Don't worry about Jasper. I'll catch him."

With that, she shoots off to the right to watch and wait.

I draw my last dagger. My remaining weapons are with the phoenix. Holding the weapon with its blade down, I angle for the gargoyle on Jasper's right. I need to get those two off him so we can pursue the woman. To my shock, the dagger grates down the gargoyle's wings as if they're really made of rock. No wonder gargoyles use their wings as shields.

The gargoyle retaliates instantly, trying to dislodge me and I barely maintain hold of the dagger, let alone his wings. We're too close to Jasper for me to risk ungloving my hand and using lightning. It would be over in an instant if I could. As I grapple with the man, he splits off, picking up speed and hurtling toward the nearest mountain peak.

We've just reached the edges of the Revenant Mountains and the lower we fly, the more likely we are to crash into them. The only upside of splitting off from Jasper is that now I can use my storm power without fear of harming him. Except that I need both hands to remove my glove and I can't exactly do that and hold on to the gargoyle at the same time. Can I float? Can I fly? I've harnessed the lightning's power so many times that I'm familiar with it, but I've never tried to use a tornado to keep myself airborne. A growl of frustration rips through me as the gargoyle soars straight for the side of a cliff face, angles his body, and...

He's going to ram me into it.

As the rock approaches, I grip the gargoyle's wing where it meets his shoulder, bend my knees under me, and hoist myself upward in a vertical line away from him. He crashes into the cliff and without my body as a buffer, knocks himself into the rock. With a shake of his head, he recovers enough to locate me plummeting down and reaching for his wing—anything—to stop my fall.

As I sail past him, my clutching hand catches his wing and I hoist myself onto his back again.

The man shakes and roars, "Get off me, elf! You can't win this fight."

"Watch me try."

A shriek in the distance has us both snapping around to see what made it. It wasn't the woman's scream but something more guttural—a roar of pain. My heart sinks to think it might be Jasper, but it didn't sound like his voice and the Storm promised me she wouldn't let him fall.

Of course, she didn't promise he wouldn't be killed…

The gargoyle ignores me for a moment, shooting forward, darting through the mountain peaks and I have to admire the strength he shows to fly with my weight against his back and wings.

We soar between cliff faces to see the gargoyle carrying the woman ahead of us. That gargoyle's wing beats are ragged. It careens wildly from spot to spot, crashing against the rocks like a moth with a broken wing.

A broken wing!

A slender object is lodged in one of the male gargoyle's wings, but I can't make it out until we draw nearer. My eyes widen as I recognize the shape of an arrow. I'm astounded that such a thing is possible given that my dagger couldn't puncture their wings.

The gargoyle fighting Jasper soars overhead, closer to the wounded gargoyle than we are.

Another projectile flies through the air from a point beneath us in the mountains and Jasper's gargoyle shrieks as an arrow lodges in his arm. The gargoyle carrying me races toward the scene, aiming for the woman since it looks like the other gargoyle is going to drop her.

A moment later, a third arrow speeds toward my gargoyle and I jolt to the left just in time as it flies right through the man's wing, skimming past my right side. That was way too close. I can't be sure if the attacker with the arrows is aiming for the gargoyles or if we are targets too.

The gargoyle cries out and can't seem to control his flight now that his wing is pierced. Luckily, we had almost reached the young woman. Her terrified eyes meet mine as I whirl past. I tense, crouch, and leap for her, wrenching her from the first spinning gargoyle as the one I was riding spirals away from me.

A clearing made of jagged rocks rises up to meet us.

I scream, "Storm!"

She's already there, beneath us, a torrent of air rising upward from each of her hands. I turn to locate Jasper but can't see him. I scream out into the rushing wind and hope he will hear me, "Jasper! Jump into the wind tunnel!"

Further above us, General Cassian appears, his massive wings sweeping across the air, but two wind tunnels have already swallowed us up. I see Jasper now engulfed in one of them as the other encloses me and the young woman.

Out in the clear sky, another arrow narrowly misses Cassian, its path upset by the sudden torrent of air. He roars down at us, pausing for a brief moment before shrieking overhead. The last I see of him through the rushing white wind, he's plucking the two injured gargoyles out of the air, taking hold of them with his clawed feet before they can crash all the way to the jagged ground. The one who was lucky enough to only be struck in the arm races ahead of them.

They speed away and out of sight.

The wind tunnel sweeps around me and the young woman, drawing us downward in a controlled descent, finally allowing our feet to touch the ground on the mountain path. The Storm maintains the swirling wind around us while the gargoyles fly away.

The young woman shudders in my arms, clutching hold of me like a slender branch in what is literally now a gale-force wind. I stroke her hair, trying to keep her calm, until the phoenix's voice sounds inside my mind.

The gargoyles have gone. They are fleeing back behind the border with their injured. Jasper is safe and so is Baelen.

Relief floods me, but it's replaced by a new worry. *Do you know who shot the arrows?*

No, Princess. This new attacker is well concealed.

"Storm," I whisper. "The gargoyles have gone. You can release us now. But please remain alert. We don't know where the arrows came from."

The wind dies down around me, dropping away so suddenly that the quiet is unnerving. Jasper's running footsteps are a welcome relief against the sudden calm. The Storm draws away from all of us. The arrow that almost struck Cassian clatters down the cliff face and onto the rocks. It must have got caught up in the wind tunnel too.

The Storm follows it down with her eyes, crestfallen and shaken, moments before she hides her face behind her hair. I can't decipher her thoughts, but the fact that these arrows broke through gargoyle wings seems to have shocked her. It certainly surprised me. She finds a shadowed spot at the side of the clearing and stays there. I make a mental note to speak with her sooner rather than later.

"Are you okay?" Jasper looms over me, checking every part of me with his worried eyes before stopping on the female gargoyle.

"We're fine, Jasper. The woman is shaken and needs care, but we must take cover as soon as possible. Someone was shooting at us, and I don't know if they're friendly."

I'm startled as a piece of the landscape shifts on my left—the opposite side of the clearing to the Storm. I push the young woman behind me and reach for my dagger.

Curses. I lost it in the fight with the gargoyle. I have more weapons, but they're with the phoenix and it can't land in this narrow space.

A large, gray rock turns around on itself nearby, pieces of it sliding away from each other like petals of a flower opening. Except, this is no flower. The rock rises up and up, taking on a new form as Jasper and I usher the woman backward. I take stock of the growing form before us, making out clawed toes, muscled legs, a broad torso, and finally, an angular face. A quiver of arrows rests against his leg, supported by his wings, and a bow dangles from his enormous hands at a deceptively casual angle.

Nope. Definitely not a flower.

I lift my arms away from my body, showing that I don't hold a weapon, deliberately spreading my fingers in a gesture of peace. "You're the source of the helpful arrows. We should thank you."

The gargoyle drops to a knee, nocks an arrow, and points it directly at my chest. "Elf," he growls, menace dripping from every sound. His nostrils flare as he inhales. "Tell me why the next one shouldn't pierce your heart."

"Because… you didn't kill me before. I don't think you can now."

5

———

MARBELLA

The gargoyle inhales again and I sense the pull toward him. It's as magnetic now as it was all that time ago. Muscles ripple across his arms and bare torso as he keeps the bow taut. His lower half is covered in leather pants, well-worn and supple. I cast around for our location. We must be close to Scepter Peak, because this is the same gargoyle I met before—the one who allowed me to live.

"You are ice. And clouds," he says, the hint of a smile settling onto his curved lips, creating a startling contrast to the deadly weapon he keeps trained on me.

I take a hesitant step forward, my boots crunching much too loudly on the rocky pathway. I stop, not wanting to startle him. Although… I'm quite certain he's completely in control of his reflexes right now. "Do you remember me?"

"You are the Storm," he says. He rumples his nose at Jasper in distaste. "But the other one reeks of twisted metal."

Poor Jasper. His armor is well and truly banged up now.

The gargoyle adjusts his aim faster than I can blink; the arrow now pointed squarely at Jasper. "I will kill him if you want."

"No!" I step between the gargoyle and Jasper. My arms remain splayed to make myself wider. I'm close enough to Jasper that he

47

wraps his hands around my waist from behind. His grip tells me he's about to pick me up and pull me out of the firing line. I'm too small to be an effective shield anyway. The gargoyle has simply adjusted his aim again, this time pointing the arrow over my head. I'm guessing right at Jasper's face.

Jasper's fingers flex against my armor but he leaves me where I am. His growl is soft in my ear and very unhappy. "Princess, I want you to know I'm swallowing my pride right now. Something tells me this gargoyle will only listen to you, and I won't be any use to you dead."

Maintaining firm eye contact with the gargoyle, I raise my voice to the level of a stern order. "This elf is very important to me. I want him alive."

The gargoyle's lip curls at one corner as if he disapproves. "As you wish, Lady Storm."

But he still doesn't lower his bow. I glare at it, but my displeasure doesn't seem to have any impact on the man.

He asks, "What did Cassian want with you?"

I'm surprised the gargoyle knows our attackers. Before I can reply, the female gargoyle speaks, stepping to my side. "He wanted me."

I cast a quick assessing glance at her because her demeanor is different now that she's not terrified for her life. Her emerald eyes are hard and cold for the first time, surprisingly unafraid. It's a stark difference to how she appeared when she dived into Jasper's arms begging for help.

What's more… a tingle of air brushes against me as she passes. Goosebumps rise under my armor. It reminds me of the charge in the air when Elise is spellcasting, but it's not quite the same. Elise's spells are always contained and controlled. This woman gives off sparks in all directions. I don't know whether gargoyles have spellcasters—I assume they do. But if the woman is a spellcaster, then I'm not sure why she didn't use her power to save herself from Cassian before.

She snarls at the gargoyle, "These elves saved my life. You will not kill them, Grievous monster."

The man's eyebrows lift in surprise. "How do you know my Clan name?"

She spits like a hissing cat. "I see your mark."

He lowers his bow and arrow, but it's a kneejerk reaction rather than a calculated move—the first reflexive response he's given. One big hand shoots to his side. I peer at the spot he clutches, making out a fine silvery shape not much bigger than my thumb etched just above his right hip. It looks like some kind of ink mark, but the shape is indistinguishable because it appears to have been cut into, jagged scars crisscrossing it.

His expression turns from surprise to anger.

He drops his weapon on the ground with a clatter and advances on the woman, curling his hands into fists. She stands her ground in the face of his oncoming wrath. The only reason I don't go into full defense mode is that the man's wings are pinned tightly to his sides. Having fought this gargoyle before, I know he's only serious when he uses his wing daggers. Right now, they're held back.

Jasper isn't so restrained. "I'm not swallowing my pride anymore." His snarl reaches me moments before he sidesteps out from behind me, closes the gap to the young woman, and pulls her behind him, facing down the other man with a determination of his own.

"Careful, gargoyle," he warns. "We went to great lengths to protect this woman. We aren't about to stop now."

The gargoyle pulls up face-to-face with Jasper. Both men are equal in height and matched in strength. Where the gargoyle resembles an immovable stone force made of jagged edges, Jasper is like a sturdy oak, feet planted, taking on a defensive stance.

"Don't worry, Twisted Metal, I will not touch her." The gargoyle angles his head to the side and lowers it to mere inches from the woman as she peeks around Jasper.

Despite the threat in front of her, she doesn't flinch or back away. I brace, at war inside myself. I know this gargoyle to be capable of gentleness. He showed me his sleeping children and displayed only a desire to protect them. At the same time, there is danger in him—that same protectiveness turned into a need to attack first and ask questions later.

He leans down to the woman, eye-to-eye. "Grievous Howl is no friend of mine."

She snaps right back. "King Howl is your kin. Born of the Grievous Clan. Just like you."

The gargoyle inhales sharply as if she slapped him. "He killed my wife."

"I…" The fire leaves her eyes, and she falters. "I'm… sorry. I thought…"

He spins away from us, presenting us with his back, his wings tightly folded. His giant rib cage expands and contracts as he sighs a breath in and out.

"My name is Llion. Do not call me Grievous. I forsook my Clan long before Howl came to power." He half turns but doesn't meet my eyes. "We can't stay out here in the open. You will all come with me now. This way."

He gathers up his bow and arrows without a backward glance, striding away along the path. Despite the threat he poses, the woman follows him without hesitation. Her wings flutter at her sides, her head down, the fight gone out of her.

I catch Jasper's eye but before I can speak, he says, "That's the gargoyle you met on Scepter Peak."

When I'd encountered Llion the first time, I was determined to keep all the elves away from him, because they would attack his nest with his children in it. Jasper had been the only one to come close to the nest, and I'd immediately acted as a diversion and led Jasper away. Until now, he never gave me any indication that he had known the gargoyle was there.

I stare at him, incredulous. "You knew he was there that night?"

Jasper gives me an apologetic shrug. "Baelen warned me in advance. For what it's worth, I thought you were exceptionally brave." He runs his hand across his forehead. "I, uh, actually disagreed with Baelen's plan for you to act as a decoy to protect the gargoyle nest. I thought it was too dangerous. I told him I would do it, but he said you were the only one who could keep the other elves away."

For the first time ever, I consider thumping Jasper. He knows I can handle myself, although Llion *had* almost ripped me apart that night, only stopping when he scented my storm power.

"He was right," Jasper says, catching my eye. "And now I think this gargoyle has more to fear than us."

I keep my distance from Llion and the woman ahead of us as I follow in their direction. I sense the Storm floating behind me, staying close, but she remains silent. Worry settles in the base of my stomach. I glance up at the sky, seeking out the phoenix.

"Do we have time for this? Following these gargoyles, I mean." I search the distant clouds as I speak. I need to see the phoenix and Baelen. "The woman's safe now. We should keep moving…"

"Is she?" Jasper gives me a hard look. "We can't save her from one threat only to leave her with another."

I sag. My heart stretches thin. "I take your point, but we still haven't crossed the border…"

"Maybe that's a good thing," he insists. "These gargoyles can tell us exactly what we're heading into. If there are more gargoyles like Cassian waiting for us, we need to be prepared."

I swallow down the feeling of near panic that threatens to engulf me with every step I take further away from Baelen. "But… I…"

Jasper's expression softens. "I know you need to return to Baelen. I sense you pulling toward him even as you're walking away from him. Being separated is hard for you. But trust me, we need to be prepared and these gargoyles can help us."

I push hard at the feeling of being attached to a coil in the sky. It doesn't go away—I don't want it to—but it lessens enough that I can follow Jasper as he picks his way along the narrow path. I try to fill the silence with words to distract myself. "What do you know of this… what did they call it? Grievous Clan?"

"The gargoyles are born into Clans the same way we're born into Houses. I guess you could say the Grievous Clan is the equivalent of Baelen's House—the House of Rath. Except for all the wrong reasons. Where the House of Rath is sworn to protect, the Grievous Clan has a reputation for destruction."

"Do you know this Howl gargoyle they were talking about?"

He shakes his head. "She called him 'King'. I don't know much about their monarchy, but I know their rulers aren't supposed to be from the Grievous Clan." He clicks his tongue, scratching his chin in thought. "Baelen did tell me the Royal Clan name once… It's something powerful… And it's two words, not one like all the other clan names…"

The Storm leans toward me as if she's going to whisper in my ear. She must know more about what's going on. The breeze she creates tickles my ear. She hesitates, and I think she's going to draw away from me instead, but at the last moment, she whispers, "*Supreme Incorruptible…*"

Jasper snaps his fingers. "I remember now… it's Supreme Incorruptible." His focus shifts from me to our surroundings. Ahead of us, Llion stoops to retrieve one of his arrows, the weapon vanishing into the quiver slung between his wings.

Jasper says, "All I know is that their monarchy has remained in power since the elves and gargoyles first came here. Unlike ours."

Our last king—the last elf in the royal line—died without children so our monarchy died with him. He was feared, not loved. It was widely acknowledged that he dabbled in sorcery and abused his power relentlessly. It was his scheming that caused the war with the gargoyles and led to the gargoyles creating the Storm to wipe out our race.

Funny, now that I think about it, how the details of the story are never really clear. I don't doubt that the Elven King caused the war, but it's never been clear to me *how*. And, knowing there's more to the Storm than I previously believed makes me wonder what really happened to cause her to give her life for revenge. Was she asked to do it? Did her people nominate her? Or did she choose this path on her own?

We travel in silence for the next half hour until the pathway ends. I pull up, stare at the soaring rock face, glance at Jasper, and spin back to the rocks. "Llion was just here."

I jump back as the woman pops her head out of nowhere, right in front of me. "Sorry, I didn't mean to frighten you. Step to your right," she says. "I didn't see it at first either."

I do as she says, even though I don't quite believe her. *Is it a trick?* "Huh. An illusion."

Once I'm standing to the right, it's possible to see an opening: a walkway between two soaring cliff faces. When viewed head-on, the edges blur into each other and appear as if it's one unbroken rock. "Clever."

I follow the walkway along and to the right again. My boots crunch loudly on loose scattered pebbles, and I guess that's some sort of warning system. The walkway turns left and once I'm there the space opens, shafts of sunlight pouring through openings in a rocky overhang.

I gasp at the glittering space around me. In the dark corners, spider webs glisten like delicate lanterns. In the sunlit spaces, plants grow—tomato vines, squash, and even strawberries. Far on the opposite side, a mountain goat is tethered. A soft whooshing sound signals the flow of water to the right, which tells me there's a clean water source here. Further to the back, in the cave-like hollow, a large cradle made of piled rocks creates a bed for the two babies. One of them is awake, softly gurgling while its little arm waves in the air. Judging by its rock-like skin, it's the boy.

I pick up my jaw. "This is…" *Not what I expected.* "Not the same nest you had before," I say to Llion as he waits at the opening.

He doesn't reply but gives me a nod, as if my approval is somehow appreciated.

The woman hesitates for a single moment, her own eyes wide, before racing to the babies. "Precious ones," she coos over them. She reaches out to pick up the boy but Llion growls at her.

She freezes, her wings drooping in dismay. "I won't harm them."

He takes strides to the nest and pulls the alert boy into his arms, propping him up in the crook of his arm. The boy is old enough to hold up his own head but otherwise snuggles into his father's chest. Llion murmurs into the child's ear and that's all it takes to quiet him. "You will explain yourself before you touch my children."

She gulps and asks meekly, "Do you have some water?"

"You may drink from the fountain. Over there."

He points, and as my eyes adjust to the darkness, I identify the source of the water running along the rock face and out from a lip into a carved crevice beneath it. The woman retrieves a wooden bowl from the base of the water source, filling and drinking from it, and then filling it again. I'd like nothing more than to put my head under the water and cool the back of my neck, but I don't think the others would appreciate me sticking my head into the water source. I follow after the woman and drink my fill, handing the bowl to Jasper too.

The woman finds a flat stone as far from Llion as possible. Jasper leans against the wall near her and I find a seat next to him. The Storm remains close to my other side.

A tug pierces my chest, and I almost don't hear the young woman speak. The phoenix must have floated further away and the sensation is agony.

I need to take cover in the clouds, the phoenix apologizes, its voice more distant than before. The relief I feel at hearing it speak is dampened by the knowledge it's flying away.

I understand, I reply. But as it ascends, the air is sucked out of my lungs. I take deep, slow breaths and focus on the sparkling webs until my heart calms.

The woman clears her throat, addressing Llion. "For the sake of the elves, I will tell you what you already know, as well as what you don't." Her wings fold inward and across her shoulders, giving her the appearance of a fallen butterfly.

"My name is Talia. I once belonged to the Sunflight Clan, but now..." Her eyes flick to me and I'm not sure why. "I am a Priestess-in-training. I am the first trainee in three generations." She brightens a little as she speaks, pride filling her eyes.

She angles toward me, speaking to me now. "I believe elves have spellcasters, but none can control deep magic, yes? In Erador, our Priestesses wield deep magic."

The light in her eyes fades. "Except there are not many of us left. As we age, we lose our power. It is the natural order of things, that all power must pass. My power is new and Howl wants it."

Her hands suddenly shake, and she clasps them together in her lap. "The older Priestesses hid me from Howl for many years, but Cassian found out about me. I've been imprisoned in Howl's Palace on Mount Erador for the last month."

Something about what she said fills me with alarm. Mount Erador is the mountain at the heart of Erador and the location of the springs where I need to take Baelen. I try to keep my tone casual. "Did you say his palace is built *on* Mount Erador?"

Talia nods. "Right beside the entrance to our most sacred treasure—the deep springs. It's a sacrilege to build a palace there. But he thirsts for the power of deep magic more than anything else."

My heart plummets. Neither of the gargoyles knows where Jasper and I are headed. After all, we're still on our side of the border. From their point of view, we're just two elves who happened to be in the wrong place at the wrong time. Or, from Talia's point of view, the right place to save her.

Now, she's told us that Howl's Palace is built right on top of where we need to go. Jasper catches my eye. He knows how bad that is too.

Llion's growl breaks the silence. "Howl takes whatever he wants, whenever he wants. He killed the rightful heir to the throne ten years ago and now he seeks to find all sources of deep magic to make himself more powerful. He has… no limits." He turns to Talia and I sense a gentling of his attitude toward her for the first time. "How did you escape?"

Tears glisten in Talia's eyes. "The elves won't know this, so I'll explain: Priestesses can only use deep magic in defense of another. I cannot use it for personal gain or even to protect myself."

This stuns me. Then I remember how she'd come out of her shell when Llion revealed himself. She'd stared him down without fear. "So that explains why you suddenly found your courage when Llion appeared."

"If you need protecting, I can do it."

"But what use is a power when you can't use it to save yourself?"

"The right kind," she insists. "The kind that can't be used for my own, selfish purposes."

I chew on that for a moment. I find myself staring at the Storm. Talia said that Priestesses can only use deep magic in defense of another. I wonder if all deep magic has the same limitation. The Storm had used it to become the Storm—was she trying to protect someone? She doesn't meet my eyes and I stop staring in case the others think it's strange that I'm looking at the wall for so long.

Talia is openly crying now, tears falling down her cheeks. "When the High Priestess found out I was captured, she came to me in my prison cell. The others helped her get in and she used the very last of her deep magic to save me. She turned me into a bird, small enough to slip through the bars. But as I flew away, I realized she wasn't coming with me."

Talia hangs her head, tears flowing down her face. "She took on my appearance and took my place in the cell to give me time to escape."

Llion turns a very pale gray. "How long would her power last to sustain that façade?"

"Cassian came after me the very next day. I believe that was when her power ran out."

Llion leans against the cradle, clutching the edge of it with his free hand. "Then the High Priestess is captured."

"The others have no power left to save her."

"You have to go back." His order is so sudden that Talia jumps. "You know you have to get her out before it's too late."

Her response is quiet. "No. I must not go back."

Llion paces back and forth in front of the cradle, as if he's caged. His voice is low, but sharp and edgy. "There are no other rightful heirs to the throne. The High Priestess is the only one with the power to bestow the Supreme Incorruptible mark on a new king. You know that's what Howl wants. He wants that mark! He's been looking for her for years. He will force her to make him the lawful king. And once that happens… nothing will stop him."

"No." Talia's tears have stopped. She wipes her eyes, but unlike before, she isn't defiant. She looks tired, her eyes red-rimmed. "I will not go back."

Llion looks as if he's going to burst, and I realize the only reason he hasn't roared at Talia is because his son and daughter are close by. He won't want to scare them. I admire his restraint. His need to protect his children must be far greater than any fear or anger he feels toward this woman.

She stands, pulling herself as upright as she can despite her obvious exhaustion. "I can't go back, Llion, because the High Priestess did one more thing before she set me free."

He stares at her. We all do.

"She passed her title on to me. She made me the High Priestess."

6

———

MARBELLA

Talia lifts the bodice of her dress, separating the top from the bottom on the right side to reveal her hip. An intricate mark the size of my palm rests against her skin depicting a sea of green grass at the base of mountains with a golden sun above them. I'm floored by the simple beauty of the design and the way it appears as if the grass is moving in a gentle breeze, the rays of sunlight warming the slender stems while the mountains loom in the darkness behind them…

I jolt as I realize Talia is eyeing me again, as if she's assessing my reaction. I pull back and shutter my expression. Nobody else seems to notice. Least of all Llion, who looks like he's just been hit over the head with a dizzy stick.

"High Priestess." He sways on the spot. "This means Howl can't be made the lawful king."

"Not unless he captures me."

Llion chokes back a laugh, shaking his head in disbelief. "You really can't go back."

A smile breaks across Talia's face. "I really can't."

Jasper leans into me. "That explains why Cassian was willing to breach our airspace to chase after her."

58

"It certainly does."

Llion rubs his face with his free hand. "Twisted Metal," he says, breaking into our conversation with a cautious nod in Jasper's direction. "It seems the entire gargoyle race owes you a debt of gratitude."

Jasper eyes Llion with a look of distrust before acknowledging the thanks with a quick nod of his own.

Llion returns to the cradle as his daughter wakes, carefully drawing her into the crook of his other arm. Without a word, he passes her to Talia. She brightens, whispering to the baby, "Beautiful girl."

The little girl wraps her hand around Talia's golden hair, tugging and gurgling.

Talia asks, "How did you get your children out?"

"After my wife was killed, Cassian was supposed to kill me too, but he said I should live with my pain. He threw me in prison instead." Llion snarls. "He should have put more guards on my cell. I got out, rescued my children from the orphanage, and crawled through mud and tunnels with them strapped to my back. I stayed underground, crept through the trees, hid in rocky crevices. I stole goat's milk to feed them."

"I'm sorry I called you a monster. Please, tell me your wife's name so I can pray for her soul."

"Liliana." He whispers his wife's name like a remembered honey on his tongue. "Her name was Lightsworn Liliana."

Talia jolts. "The Lightsworn Clan is nobility. Second only to the Supreme Incorruptible. Yet you…"

A smile ghosts across Llion's face. "You don't believe me. Don't worry, it took me a long time to believe it myself. That she could love someone like me."

"You don't wear the Lightsworn mark next to your own mark like married couples customarily to do."

"We married in secret." His smile fades. "It led to her end."

Talia remains very still. The only change is the deep crease that appears between her eyes. "What did she look like?"

His face lights up. "She had chestnut hair and eyes the color of new leaves: pale, delicate. Her wings had golden spirals—"

"Like the branches of a tree?"

He casts a sharp glance at her. "You met my wife while she was alive?"

"Yes. I met her. At Howl's Palace." Her eyes are wide pools. "She was there when I escaped."

Llion is as lifeless as the rock he resembles. "No… that isn't possible…"

"I promise you I'm not lying—"

"Howl ran her through. He killed her because she defied him. I saw it with my own eyes."

"You were deceived. She's alive." Talia tries to take his hand, but he steps away from her. "I would never trick you, Llion. You have to believe me when I tell you I met her. Howl called her by her name: Lightsworn Liliana. She was there with him. He…" Her lips press together for a moment. "He…"

Llion advances on her, staring into her eyes. Across the room, I hold my breath. Instinctively, I reach for Jasper, anchoring my gloved hand on his forearm. All I see in Llion's face is the same desperation I felt when I found out Baelen wasn't dead.

The same shattering of my heart because hope feels the same as agony when you can't believe it's true, when you're so afraid it will slip through your fingers.

"He what, Priestess? What did he do?"

"He will force her to marry him."

Llion's expression doesn't change.

Talia rushes on, "She's the highest-ranking woman. He was gloating because he'd captured me and believed the High Priestess would be next. He said that once he was marked Supreme Incorruptible, he would take Liliana as his Queen."

Still, Llion hasn't moved. "What will he do now that you've escaped, and he doesn't have his mark?"

She doesn't answer. The silence stretches on for so long that I stare wide-eyed between the two of them.

Finally, Llion swings away from her. "Tell me one thing,

Sunflight Talia, High Priestess: when did you learn how to hold a child properly?"

Her voice is small. "The Priestesses have hidden themselves in orphanages across the country for many years, pretending to be matrons. I cared for the children at one of them."

"Then you know what I have to do."

Talia strokes the wisps of chestnut hair across the little girl's head, smiling down into the baby's eyes. "I do. And I thank you for allowing me to take refuge in your home. You never have to fear for your children's safety. I will protect them."

As she speaks, she runs her hand over the little girl's arms and back, creating a warm glow beneath her palm. The baby girl sighs, and Talia says, "Nothing will harm them."

Llion kisses the top of his son's head and hands him over to Talia who deftly juggles the boy onto her other hip.

I exchange glances with Jasper, not knowing what to expect next as Llion strides over to us.

"Lady Storm," he says. "I'm coming with you."

I stare back at him. "What are you talking about?"

"The phoenix was flying due west. You were about to cross the border. I'm coming with you."

My jaw drops. I meet Jasper's startled eyes. Even the Storm freezes in shock beside us.

"You can use my help. And my weapons," he says. "I have to collect some supplies, but I won't hold you up."

Jasper recovers faster than I do. "We need to collect supplies too. We'll meet you at the top of the next peak. But please don't be long."

He stands, gives Llion a nod, and ushers me away from the cave. I'm too stunned to object. I stare at Jasper as we exit into bright sunlight. "What just happened?"

Jasper scans the sky, and I'm glad he's looking for threats because right now, my head is buzzing from the fact that he agreed to take Llion along so quickly.

"We saved a Priestess, stopped an evil fake King from getting the mark of superiority, and made a gargoyle ally who has weapons that can take down his own kin."

"And we haven't even crossed the border."

Jasper cocks an eyebrow at me in a rare show of humor. "That pretty much sums it up."

7

———

MARBELLA

I call for the phoenix immediately, anxious to see that Baelen is okay. The bird can't land on this spot—the gargoyle deliberately chose a place that's hard to access—so Jasper and I have to leap off a nearby rocky outcrop onto its back.

Once we're safely seated, I slide up to cradle Baelen's head in my lap again, quietly checking him over to make sure he's okay. I don't dare rest my forehead against his after what happened earlier with our power joining, but I allow myself a moment to breathe normally.

He's unharmed, the phoenix chimes.

I speak aloud so Jasper can hear me. "Thank you, my friend. Can you carry us further through the mountains? Jasper knows a place we need to go."

Don't worry, Princess, the phoenix says. *The sun is high in the sky now and I'll keep it behind me until we land. If there are any gargoyles nearby, they won't see us.*

As much as I trust the phoenix to keep us safe, my heart remains in my throat until we touch down on a wide platform ten minutes later. A cliff forms a sheer drop on one side, with a deep cave on the other. A path stretches along the side of the cave, hewn between rock surfaces.

The platform is wide enough to accommodate the phoenix even with its wings fully spread, making it the perfect landing spot. I give Jasper a nod of appreciation as he slides from the bird's back.

Jasper promised there are supplies here, and I want nothing more than to wash my face and hands. But the problem of getting into gargoyle country plagues me—even with Llion on our side. There has to be a better way than trekking across a hundred miles of mountains…

The Storm alights behind us, her delicate feet a caramel shade against the dark slate. The mountain range stretches in every direction. We're so deep inside it now that Rath land is a distant memory.

Be careful, Princess, the phoenix warns. *We may as well be in gargoyle territory already. I will alert you, but stay on your guard.*

I will. I rest Baelen's head gently against the bird's back and slip to the ground, stretching out my legs, not realizing until now how sore I am from everything that's happened. My muscles scream at me for rest as Jasper disappears briefly inside the cave.

He reappears with a cloth in his hand. As he closes the gap between us, I eye him warily. It's taking me time to get used to the idea that someone can touch me and that I won't hurt them when they do.

He stops before he reaches me. "Princess, if I may? Your cheek is bleeding."

My hand shoots to the sting blooming across my cheek.

Jasper gently brushes the damp cloth across the wound, taking care to touch me only with the material and not skin on skin, handing over the cloth so I can press it to my cheek myself.

"Thank you, Jasper. And please, I don't think you should call me 'Princess' once we cross the border."

He doesn't miss a beat. He was one of the first elves to call me by my first name during the trials, and it's surprised me that he's started calling me Princess again now.

"Okay, Marbella." My name rolls off his tongue without hesitation as he assesses my wound and finally gives a satisfied nod.

"I'll head into the cave first and get changed. That way I can prepare our packs while you're washing up."

"Yes, thank you." I sigh as he walks away. I spend a lot of my time thanking this man for his care of me.

As he strides away, he pulls his armor off, dropping it at the cave's entrance with soft clangs, one piece at a time. His armor is standard military issue and so is the shirt under it, made of sturdy twill. Not the most comfortable of garments but Jasper is never one to complain.

Surprisingly uninhibited, he pulls his shirt off too, and drops it in the growing pile. His back is broad, muscled but lean, as he stretches out his neck and back. Without the heavy armor, he moves again with stealth, prowling into the cave without realizing his near-nakedness has caused a bit of a stir out here on the platform…

"He is not an ordinary elf." The Storm sidles up to me. Her eyes are bright with curiosity as she peers after Jasper, her wings cast forward in his direction.

I smile. "Jasper Grace is definitely one of a kind."

"He acts like your protective older brother even though he isn't."

I shrug. "He's loyal to Baelen, which means he's loyal to me too I guess."

"It's more than loyalty. He cares about you." Her forehead creases as she peers at the space he left behind. "But he doesn't lust after you."

I choke a little. It's true that Jasper has had at least one opportunity to see me naked and hasn't taken it. I swallow a laugh. "You know… It is possible to care for someone and not—*ahem*—lust after them."

Her expression is suddenly dark. Clouds fall over the space she occupies as she draws more and more of the dark substance to herself like a physical shield. "That is not what I know of elves."

She turns to leave before I can figure out how to interpret her comment, but I'm not about to let her get away. With Jasper out of earshot, there are things I need to know.

Baelen rests on the phoenix's back. He looks peaceful, and the giant bird doesn't seem anxious to have the burden of his body removed. In fact, it looks tranquil as it rests down on the ledge, keeping watch on the skies around us, the glacial white clouds floating through the crisp blue. It occurs to me that if Baelen has the Storm's power too, then the phoenix will have the same affinity with him as it does with me.

Finding comfort in that thought, I chase after the Storm to the edge of the cliff. She floats just beyond the sharp drop with her back to me as if she's trying to make herself unreachable. She's physically connected to me so I know she can't go far unless I let her, but the slump in her shoulders tells me she would rather be curled up in a dark place right now than face the midday sunlight pouring over the platform. I'm suddenly reminded that she's a gargoyle. Her favorite place would be a quiet nest lit only by silvery threads of Elyria spider webs.

"Storm, please come back. I need you to show me how to move Baelen and keep him safe."

She swings back to me. She looks like she's about to shoot a retort at me but then she switches gears, swiveling to Baelen. Whenever she looks at him her eyes fill with sadness, and it makes me wonder if she feels pain for him. She isn't tied to him the same way she's tied to me: if we were a chain, I would be the link in the middle. But he carries her power too and that must connect them on some level.

She sighs. "Yes, of course. Come with me."

By the time she reaches Baelen and the phoenix, the Storm has left her melancholy mood behind and taken on the role of bossy teacher. "You think you need metal to harness the lightning, but you don't—"

"I don't?"

She drops the bossy persona for a moment. "You really don't. You locked the power up inside yourself because you were afraid of it. Now you need to unlock it." She clamps her hand over my forearm. It feels strange when she touches me; my brain tells me she's there, that she's holding my arm right now, but it feels like a breeze, soft, gentle, and somehow transparent.

"Close your eyes," she orders.

I do as she asks, reluctant to let Baelen out of my sight even though I know he's right in front of me and the phoenix won't let anything happen to him.

"You are connected to Baelen body and soul," she says. "Listen for his heartbeat. It will help you. Don't follow it like you did before. Just listen."

His heartbeat. It's the easiest thing for me to hear. So easy I'm scared I'm mistaking it for my own. The rhythm sweeps me up, melding with the warmth of the sun on my shoulders, the light breeze across my hair, and the pressure of the Storm's fingers on my arm.

"Keep your eyes closed," she whispers. "But when you hear his heart thud… don't just hear the sound… *feel it* like a burst of light inside you…"

A spark lights the darkness behind my eyes. The rhythm of his heart takes on a visual aspect, echoing in my ears and igniting in front of me like water droplets splashing upward.

"Each beat is a burst of light," she says. "Now catch one of them and hold it… and imagine it stretching out thin. You want it to stretch beyond you… all the way over to Baelen where it can curl around him and lift him from the phoenix's back."

I keep my eyes closed and exhale slowly, feeling calmer than I thought I would practicing this new skill. A thin thread of blue lightning pulses inside my mind. Baelen's outline grows clear, a rainbow of colors forming his shape while the phoenix's silhouette glows beneath him.

The lightning thread I've sent out splits into many delicate ropes of light that seep under Baelen's body and curl up and over him, winding around his torso and legs. Then each thread splits again, as many times as it takes to form a webbed lattice supporting his head and back, arms and legs.

In my mind, the webbing lifts him from the phoenix's back and supports him all the way to the ground. It's wrapped securely enough around him to hold him upright. The image is so clear, so brilliant with light that he could be standing in front of me. He could be awake right now.

My eyes burn and a tear escapes down my cheek. He and I had stood together on a cliff like this one, all wrapped up in each other seven years ago. I would give anything for him to be awake right now. I swallow my sadness, still keeping my eyes closed.

I say, "I think I'm ready to try moving him now."

The Storm's laughter is soft, but further away than I thought she would be. "Open your eyes, Marbella."

Her hand is no longer on my arm. My line of sight travels from where I expected her to be, to where she actually is—several paces away—and then to what's in front of me.

Baelen hovers there, his feet an inch above the ground. He appears in the way he would want to be, the way I always picture him—tall, shoulders back, head up, but maybe just a little bit tilted toward me. He looks strong, but when I reach out to him, I worry about how vulnerable he is.

"He needs a shield," I say. "A defense. Anyone can attack him like this. An arrow, a sword… worse, a gargoyle's wing dagger could kill him while he can't fight back. It's lucky they didn't already."

The Storm floats over to me, grinning. "You already gave him a shield." She circles behind me, a crafty glow in her eyes. "Why don't we see whether it works?"

She points a finger at a loose pebble, causing it to rise off the ground on its own. Before I can stop her, she flicks her finger toward Baelen and the pebble shoots right at him.

I swallow a shout as the pebble collides with the space in front of his shoulder. It pops, sizzles, and disintegrates without touching him. A fine shower of dust wafts away in the breeze.

I round on her. "That was reckless!"

"Not at all. I knew he'd be fine. You would have known too if you used your Storm Eyes to see what's right in front of you."

"My Storm Eyes?"

She shakes her head at me. "Close your eyes and remember what you saw. Then open them and remember what you see."

I scowl at her. "I hate riddles."

"I don't know how else to describe it." She shrugs before she wafts away to the other side of the platform and presents me with her back, clearly deciding that her work is done.

I close my eyes and reach for Baelen's heartbeat again. His silhouette bursts into flame so fast that it takes my breath away. He glows in front of me, a powerful presence consuming every thought inside my mind. Now I can see that my lattice of blue lightning covers every part of him.

Well, what do you know? I did give him a shield.

I allow myself a moment of relief before I open my eyes as slowly as I can, trying to hold on to the image.

Remember what you see, Marbella.

I focus on his closed eyes, his dark eyelashes, adjusting my focus away from the surface of his face to a little beyond it. I catch the barest glint of lightning before the sunlight obscures it.

Determined not to be distracted, I shift slightly to the left, sighting along the surface of his high cheekbones and down to his lips, focusing on the curves at the top and bottom. The faintest glint of light glistens at the corner of his mouth, but it's not blue like my lightning. It's red like his.

It's the same red light flowing through his skin that I'd mistaken for his heartstone's light, but it was really his storm power. I follow the glow as it washes through his lips, turning them crimson. It flows down each side of his neck in an intricate series of threads to his collarbone then disappears beneath what remains of his armor.

Overlaid on top of his skin, beyond his own red light, my blue lattice suddenly burns so clear and intense that it's like looking into the sun. I blink away the bright spots it leaves behind. I'm not sure if I'll be able to see it again at will, but now I know it's there, protecting him.

Just then, Jasper emerges from the cave carrying a pack. Water runs from his wet hair and drips down his broad chest. He stops when he sees Baelen. He crosses the distance while the phoenix ruffles its feathers.

"You moved him into a standing position. That's great."

Jasper already thought I could move Baelen before now, so all I can say is, "It is."

It feels like a small victory, but I'll take any victory right now.

"I wasn't sure if I'd need to construct a frame to carry him down the mountain," Jasper continues. "To conserve your energy."

"Oh, no, I'll be fine, but thank you." I add quickly, "Just don't touch him. I've put a shield around him, and it could burn you."

"Noted. Thanks for the warning."

I'm glad to see that Jasper's armor must have protected his chest from the onslaught of my lightning because it isn't covered in welts like his arms and legs. He changed his pants but hasn't put on a new shirt yet. The sunlight highlights the breadth of his shoulders and his narrow waist as he gestures back at the cave. "It's not quite a bath, but there's enough water in there to wash off the battle."

He drops the pack of supplies next to the nearest rock and takes a seat, assessing its contents. "You'll find fresh clothing inside the cave. It's all yours, Marbella."

The Storm places herself on the opposite side of the cave's opening, choosing a rock where she can keep an eye on Jasper while I get changed. She leans against a rocky outcrop, her scrutiny unrelenting. Jasper seems to pose a puzzle for her that she's determined to figure out.

I check on Baelen one more time before I head inside. Similar to Llion's nest, this cave has its own small waterfall rushing off a jutting lip from above my head with a shallow pool below. I practically run over to it, stripping off my armor and underclothes and dropping them on a dry rock before immersing myself beneath the water. The water at my feet tinges red as the cuts on my face, neck, and hands wash clean. They're not from the gargoyle fight this morning. None of them came near my face. They're from the Elven Command grabbing and clawing at me, digging their fingernails into my skin as they tried to take my power from me. I allow myself to slump beneath the waterfall, letting it run across my shoulders and back, wishing it would soothe my nerves. I remind myself that I'm okay. Baelen's okay. Jasper is okay.

My friends are safe. Or… as safe as they can be hiding on Rath land. Baelen had signed all the paperwork before the final fight so that if anything happened to him, then the House of Mercy—my House—would become custodians of all Rath land. I trust my brother to look after everyone there. I have to believe they are safe for now.

When I emerge from the cave, my nerves are much calmer. I bring the pack I found inside the cave filled with female clothing and supplies with me. I'm now wearing a thermal suit, gray like the rocks around us to make it safe camouflage. The pack Baelen had ready for me even contains a hairbrush.

Off to the side, Baelen stands like a sentinel against the cliff face. At this angle, I can imagine he's merely standing guard. My heart is both full and breaking. I don't care if the Storm and Jasper see the tears filling my eyes. Baelen cared about our future together. He planned so carefully in case we needed to escape: leaving his land in the care of my family, whom he trusted, and making sure there were proper supplies hidden and ready in the mountains.

The only question I have is *where* he intended for us to escape *to*. It's just another question I'll have to ask him when he wakes up.

Jasper is studiously finishing cataloging the supplies. He clears his throat when he sees me. He peers at me for a moment as if he's waiting for me to say something. When I don't, he purses his lips, and peers at me some more. "Marbella, I think I've been patient enough."

I pause, eyeing him, my eyebrows lifting. "Um… huh?"

He gestures to the other side of the clearing as if I should understand what he's talking about.

I glance in that direction. The Storm shrugs back at me from the rock she's sitting on, checking around herself in case there's something she missed. "I don't know what he's talking about."

Jasper sighs. "When are you going to tell me who she is?"

I blink at him. "Who?"

"Her."

"Her…?"

"The female gargoyle sitting on that rock. The one who isn't like any other I've ever seen."

I scrape my jaw off the ground for the thousandth time today. Does he mean… the Storm?

Her eyes shoot so wide, so fast, that splashes of lightning pulse through her cheeks. She blurts, "You can see me?"

Jasper nods. "I can see you."

The Storm falls off her rock.

8

———

MARBELLA

"How is this possible?" the Storm demands. She picks herself up faster than I do and advances on Jasper like he's a new enemy. She progresses from extreme shock to attack mode in two seconds flat. "Who are you?"

Jasper's calm and slightly curious expression doesn't change but he draws to his feet, towering over her the same way that Baelen towers over me. It's not a dominance thing. In fact, it's almost protective, like some sort of shield he wants to wrap around her. The difference is that, unlike me, the Storm can float upward, drawing up to eye level with him. Dangerous clouds gather around her, and dark shadows cast over them both, pooling around my feet but not quite touching me.

"I am Jasper of the House of Grace."

Her eyes narrow to dark slits. "How is it that you can see what can't be seen, Jasper of the House of Grace?"

"Maybe because I recognize beauty when I'm in its presence."

"Beauty?" Her glare increases. Then she jolts a little as Jasper's cautious compliment echoes back to her, but she launches right back at him. "Who is your father? Do you have gargoyle blood?"

One eyebrow shoots up. The corner of his mouth tugs. If this wasn't Jasper, I'd say he almost smiled. "Do I look like a gargoyle?"

73

For some reason that enrages her even more. She roars, "Half-castes take the appearance of their mother. Your mother could have had an affair with a gargoyle, and nobody would ever know."

Her rage has brought her very close to him. She's practically chest-to-chest and she's throwing off lightning sparks every which way. Power crackles around her but it seems to be hurting her more than him.

"Storm…" I say sternly, a clear warning in my voice. "You need to calm down."

Jasper lifts a hand at me. He doesn't want me to get involved. She hasn't hurt him, and his expression tells me he doesn't think she will. No matter how upset she is.

"Calm down?" she shrieks, the wind lifting around her, plucking at her hair and dress. "Nobody is supposed to be able to see me. Not unless I choose it." She gasps for breath, and I don't think she's talking about Jasper anymore. "It was my choice!"

Jasper maintains his calm where anybody else would have retaliated. Or run for cover. "My grandmother used to sing songs to me when I was young."

He pauses, waiting to see if she'll let him continue, giving her the choice. She glares so hard at him, her chest heaving, fear and anger raging across her face, but she doesn't interrupt.

"She used to sing songs to me about the mountains. And about flying." He doesn't take his eyes off her, his gaze running across her delicate forehead, which is crinkled in wariness.

He shrugs. "I think perhaps you're right. I think she must have fallen in love with a gargoyle. Grace land is on the southern border between our two countries so it's within the realm of possibility. My father loved the dark. He'd come alive when the moon shone at its fullest."

She presses her lips together in a stern line. "That's a gargoyle trait. Our eyesight is far superior in the dark than an elf's."

Jasper rubs his neck where she zapped him but he doesn't look away. "I like the dark too. All the details come alive in the moonlight."

I smother a gasp, remembering the way Jasper had doused his

lamp on the night we climbed Scepter Peak; the way he'd stood taller, his voice stronger, under the light of the moon.

The Storm hesitates. "Then you are… part gargoyle?"

"I always wondered if I was. But I thought I'd look like one if that were the case."

She shakes her head, her voice lowering. "It's impossible to tell by sight. Only your grandmother can tell you."

"Well, I guess that means I'll never know. She passed away a few years back."

"Oh. I'm sorry." The wind dies down around us as the Storm's wrath vanishes.

"What's your name?" Jasper asks, paying no attention to the fading clouds.

"Elyria."

"Like the silver threads that light up the dark."

She tips her chin up. "Like the *unbreakable* silver threads."

She's speaking with him so freely that I don't want to interrupt. Her relationship with me is complicated and my conversations with her are filled with veiled riddles, but with Jasper, she's talking openly for the first time. A pang of sadness breaks across my heart as I realize that she never would have told me her real name.

Jasper says, "It's clear to me that nobody else can see you, so I understand if it's an unwelcome surprise that I can."

"Not unwelcome." Her response is quick and unguarded. Her eyes widen as she seems to realize what she said and how close she's standing to him. "Just… unexpected."

Her forehead crinkles again. She seems a little perplexed by the fact that he hasn't backed away from her. She keeps glancing at the space between them as if she expects him to be the one to break their stand-off. "Are you sure nobody else can see me? You definitely fooled me for a while there."

"Almost certain," he says.

"Only almost?"

The corner of his mouth twitches. Again, not quite a smile. "I'm certain."

"Okay then, Jasper… of the House of Grace." She blinks rapidly, finally drifting backward. She never uses her wings to fly, floating on air instead. There's no way he hasn't noticed her broken wing. Jasper is one of the most perceptive men I've ever met, but he doesn't say anything about it.

The Storm floats by me, suddenly smiling but without smugness. "I told you he is not an ordinary elf."

I already knew that. Jasper, like Baelen, is exceptional. I'm lucky to call him my friend. I roll my eyes, laughing. "Does this mean I can call you by your name now?"

A thoughtful furrow descends across her forehead but lifts just as quickly. "If you don't mind, Marbella, I think you should still call me 'Storm.' If you call me by my name it will be almost as if we're…"

I cock an eyebrow at her, half challenging. "Friends?"

"I was going to say 'sisters.' But gargoyle families only have one boy and one girl. Twins. Always. So that would be too strange for me."

I shrug. It feels like two steps forward, one step back in our relationship's progress but I'll have to accept it. "Okay, Storm."

The phoenix speaks: *The other gargoyle has returned.*

Within moments, Llion soars onto the ledge, landing smoothly. His body resembles a small armory; he carries more weapons than Cassian did strapped around his waist, chest, and across his back. Suddenly our own arsenal seems completely inadequate.

Jasper pulls on a shirt but carries his armor inside the cave to leave it there. It's too beat up to be of any use now and too unwieldy to carry with us.

"The High Priestess is safe," Llion announces. "And I'm ready to travel."

His weapons are made of steel except for one dagger that is coated in some sort of gold-tinted substance. It looks familiar to me. The corner of my armor peeks from the corner of my pack. Unlike Jasper's, mine is flexible enough to fold and take with me. A golden beetle husk protrudes over the edge of the bag, and it dawns on me why Llion's weapons look familiar.

"Shimmer Beetles," I say, pointing.

He gives me a grim smile. "Well spotted, Lady Storm. Their discarded shells are the only substance strong enough to pierce a gargoyle's wings. I use it only when absolutely necessary and only for those with the blackest hearts. To damage another gargoyle's wings is a terrible thing."

My gaze shoots to the Storm and her broken wing, but Llion continues without noticing. "I discovered the husks after I moved here—"

He freezes. It's so sudden that I immediately respond by spinning in the direction he's staring, ready for anything: gargoyles, Cassian, an attack…

There is only Baelen, waiting with his eyes closed. My quiet sentinel. I spin back to Llion. "Please don't be alarmed. He was injured."

To my surprise, Llion walks right up to him. "This is Baelen Rath."

My voice falters. "You know him?"

"He gave me permission to use the beetle husks from his land." He gestures but doesn't take his eyes off Baelen. "The northern mountains are Rath land where the beetles live."

I blink away my surprise. "You spoke to Baelen?"

"He warned me to move my nest." His hands clench into fists. In that formation they resemble large rocks. "Elven soldiers were on their way to kill my children."

The Elven Command had sent a battalion of soldiers into the mountains without Baelen's knowledge several days before our battle in the arena. As Commander of the Elven Army, only Baelen had the right to command the troops, but he'd refused to do what the Elven Command wanted and attack the gargoyles on our side of the border. My brother found out about their secret attack just in time, and he and Baelen intercepted the soldiers before there was bloodshed.

Llion continues, "I didn't believe him at first. I fought him until I sensed that he is like you, Lady Storm. He is not ice and clouds like you are, but scorched earth and acid rain."

Baelen had told me about the Elven Command's attempt to kill the gargoyles, but he hadn't told me that he fought Llion. I shudder at the thought of these two men in battle against each other. While Baelen's intent would have been to save Llion, Llion's need to protect his children from all possible threats would have driven him to fight Baelen with everything he had.

I say, "He's the first Storm Prince."

Llion grins suddenly. "I suspect he would have beaten me if we continued to fight."

I grin back. "I genuinely mean no offense when I say that is most likely true."

"What happened to him?"

"The Elven Command—they're our leaders—they used sorcery to try to kill him."

His smile fades. "Then you have your own leadership issues."

"That's one way to put it."

The Storm catches my eye and I try not to react when she creeps up from the side and menaces over Llion. "Can you see me?" she whispers, testing him.

When he doesn't respond, dark clouds form over our heads. Llion twists as the shadows deepen around us. He peers at the clouds, perplexed by their sudden appearance. "Lady Storm, are you doing that?"

A big smile breaks across the Storm's face, giving her the appearance of a grinning elven cat. "He doesn't see me." She skips across the clearing toward the phoenix, humming happily all the way. I have to resist the urge to chastise her but that would only confuse Llion. As the shadows clear and the darkness lifts, an idea occurs to me.

"Do you have storms in Erador?" I ask Llion.

He nods. "Bad ones."

I say, "Then I have a faster way to travel."

9

MARBELLA

Black clouds boil across the sky beneath us, creating a thick barrier between the phoenix and the ground. They spread half a mile in all directions, moving at the same speed as the bird flies. A lightning strike crackles further below, lighting up the space around us. I squint into the misty rain, holding onto Baelen's back, keeping him in a sitting position in front of me. Llion had at first insisted he would fly behind us, but as soon as the Storm got going, he discovered that was a really bad idea.

Now he and Jasper are huddled back-to-back, Jasper facing me while Llion is at the front, facing forward. It took them a little while to work out what they were comfortable with since neither of them can come near Baelen without risking death now that I've shielded him. And that meant there wasn't a lot of room left for them to share. I have to lean to the side to see Jasper around Baelen and when I do, I find Jasper, head tilted, lips parted slightly, watching the Storm with an expression of bemused awe.

She's in her element, reveling in the ability to let loose like she hasn't in hundreds of years.

"Freedom!" she whoops, laughing as she soars above us, creating a white slipstream and waving her hands around like some kind of magic wand. "Thunder! Lightning! Wind! Rain!"

Poor Llion thinks I'm making the storm. I don't dare use my power with Baelen so close, not with the danger of drawing him out. Especially now that I've unlocked the barrier inside my mind. I have to concentrate on *not* reacting to the pull of electricity, the charge in the air, the sharp patter of rain, and the thunder that rattles my rib cage in a way that makes me want to join the Storm in flight. Her rage is contagious. My body tingles where I press against Baelen's back, but I clamp down on that feeling before his body reacts to mine.

I need to wait.

The disadvantage of creating such good camouflage is that I can't see the ground or any of the landscape below us. What I know of Erador is that it is a spider web of mountains, all connected to each other like veins in a body that stretches on and on. Every single one of the mountain ranges connects and eventually leads to their heart: Mount Erador. I wish I could see the mountain formations as we fly over. I read once that the rocks are every color: deep mossy green, dark blood red, mulberry purple, and even indigo blue.

We've been flying all afternoon and it must be nighttime now. At this speed, we should reach Mount Erador by midnight. The perfect time for creeping around unseen.

Hours later, the Storm's enthusiasm hasn't let up. She soars down to my level but keeps her voice low, reminding me that Llion can't hear her. "We're a few minutes away from Mount Erador. Do you want me to cover us while we land?"

I give her a firm nod. Getting here is only half of the equation. I need her to keep hiding the phoenix until we get back from the springs and can leave again.

She grins. "My pleasure." She soars beneath the firebird, spreading a thick mist as she goes and the bird follows behind her, beginning its descent. The rain eases up as the mist takes over. I catch a glimpse of a dazzling city before the spray rolls over us again. The image of the city far below is tinged with blue, not the golden flame of lamplight like we have in Erawind, but an iridescent glow of spider webs.

I ask the phoenix, *Are there any guards around the mountain?*

I sense a wide opening at the side of the cliff but no life forms around it, the phoenix replies. *The palace is several hundred feet to the right and well-guarded, but your destination is clear.*

That worries me. If Howl built his palace close by because he covets deep magic, then I would have expected guards to be placed all around the mountain, especially around the springs. Maybe they've taken cover from the Storm?

We're here, the phoenix says as we touch down. *I'll keep a lookout for danger. Leave Baelen with me until you know it's safe.*

I can't see more than a few feet in any direction, barely making out the shape of a cliff face on our left side, let alone some sort of entrance into it.

Llion lifts off the phoenix's back, but keeps his wing beats to a minimum so he doesn't disrupt our foggy cover. Jasper and I slide to the ledge while the Storm hovers above us, maintaining the cloak of mist. I glance across the nearby edge again but still can't see far. For some reason, I thought there would be stairs up to this place; I have to remind myself that gargoyles simply fly to high places.

"This is where we part ways, Lady Storm," Llion murmurs, tapping his fist across his heart in the gesture of gratitude that an elf would give. "Thank you for transporting me here. I will get myself—and my wife—out on my own."

"You don't have to do that alone," I say, even though we already had this conversation before we crossed the border. "If you find her tonight, come back to this spot. We can take you with us when we leave."

"I don't think finding her will be that easy. And getting her out is going to be even harder." He shakes his head but lowers it in a gesture of friendship. "May we meet again, Lady Storm."

"I hope we do, Llion. In better days."

Jasper draws near as Llion flies away into the mist. "Worst case, he's discovered and creates a diversion for us," he says, stating the grim reality matter-of-factly. "But I hope that doesn't happen."

I spin away from the cliff's edge, my nerve endings firing. I'm so close to healing Baelen, so close to seeing him open his eyes again. "I don't like how quiet it is here. We need to move fast and leave quickly."

The Storm descends to my side, leaning forward and squinting. She grabs my arm, stopping me before I can move. "There's something over there…" She peers through the thick mist she's created, crossing ahead of me and disappearing into it. Silence follows her and then…

A sharp pain shoots across my chest. At the same time I hear her gasp, followed by a sob. I feel her pain as if it's mine, but it's not physical. It's an electric shock.

"Something's wrong…" I run through the thick fog with Jasper on my heels. The Storm's silver dress blends with the mist ahead of us, but there's a clear patch in front of her right up to the wide entrance in the side of the mountain. Her feet lower to the ground, her wings drooping low as if they're both broken.

A substance stretches over the entrance from side-to-side. It's thick and taut like some kind of elasticized fabric.

"What is that?" I whisper. *And more importantly: how do we get through it?*

The Storm's voice scratches against the silence. "Wings."

The breath catches in my throat as Jasper approaches the substance, stopping a safe distance from it. He doesn't look for long. He spins back to us, head held high, but he can't hide that he's closed his eyes. "It's made of gargoyle wings."

Horror races through me. The hairs on my arms stand on end. "What kind of monster would take gargoyle wings and do that to them?"

"It must be Howl." Jasper opens his eyes but keeps his back to the atrocity behind him. "The wings have been melded together and fused to the sides of the rock. There are no gaps. There's no way through."

I whisper, "No need for guards." We can't cut through gargoyle wings. Llion's dagger is the only weapon strong enough to break through and he's already flown away. My mind races as I consider whether I can somehow remove a shimmer beetle husk from my armor and use it as a knife. All the while, I push away the horror I feel about cutting through these wings. I'm not sure if I can… I remember what Llion said about hurting a gargoyle's wings, about it being a terrible thing. Just the thought of it feels wrong.

The Storm wobbles beside me before she drops to her knees. "If they're melded together… he must have a heartstone."

Worried by her shock, I kneel beside her, even more concerned when she leans into me for support. It's not like her to show any weakness. I'm not sure why she'd be so afraid of a heartstone, or what that has to do with the wings in front of us, but she's visibly shaking. "Talk to me, Storm."

She shudders, clutching my hand. Jasper moves to her other side, kneeling, but doesn't touch her.

The Storm says, "When elves and gargoyles first came to this place, the bravest among them gave their lives to create the world around us: the division of the earth, then the moon, sun, mountains, plants, and animals. But when they gave their lives, they left their hearts behind. Those are the heartstones."

This is news to me. Each elven House has a heartstone of a different color. Baelen's House has the most revered of the elven heartstones—a gorgeous, crimson rock the size of his fist. But the idea that they were actually once hearts of real-life elves… I glance at Jasper. He looks as confused as I am.

I shake my head, saying, "The heartstones are objects of magic created by the ancient spellcasters."

"No, Marbella. They are objects of deep magic that were literally the hearts of the ones whose sacrifice made our lives possible."

"I was never told this." I shoot a questioning glance at Jasper, needing to confirm: *did he know?* When he shakes his head, I say, "The Elven Command hid this knowledge from us."

"Or else it was lost over time," Jasper adds, willing to give them the benefit of the doubt, but I know the Elven Command better. They deliberately kept information from me in the past, including the fact that I was entitled to own land.

The Storm says, "The elves gave a heartstone to each of the

elven Houses, but the thirty gargoyle heartstones are buried beneath the mountains. This was for two reasons: the first was to fortify our foundations, to keep our land strong—which the heartstones have done for a thousand years. But the second reason…"

She points at the barrier over the entrance without looking at it. "We have no spellcasting here because gargoyles can't conjure spells like elves can. Only our Priestesses can use deep magic—and then only to defend someone. But our heartstones are fundamentally different than yours. *Your* heartstones contain deep magic that can be drawn out for particular tasks, such as revealing the truth of your heart, Marbella, during the trials for your hand."

"And the gargoyle heartstones?" I ask, not sure if I want to know the answer.

"Gargoyle heartstones can be used as weapons. To do whatever the holder desires."

My gaze shoots to Jasper. I exhale. Slowly. This is not good for so many reasons: Howl and the Elven Command being two of the biggest. Right now, I'm hoping that Jasper's right and the Elven Command doesn't know about this.

Tears track down the Storm's cheeks. "The location of each gargoyle heartstone was hidden because of the devastation the stones could cause. But those wings… The way they're fused together… That can't be done by fire or glue. Our wings are our shields. Until Llion used his arrows today, no known substance could cut them, let alone melt them."

Jasper's brow furrows in the darkness. "You're saying that Howl must have dug up a heartstone?"

"It's the only conclusion I can draw." The Storm meets my eyes. "If he has, I made a terrible mistake telling you to come here. You can't stay. You need to leave while you still can."

"No." I pull away from her. "You said this was the only way to heal Baelen. I can't walk away now. I need Llion's dagger. I will cut through, heal Baelen, and then we'll get out of here as fast as we can."

"No, you need to—"

"I'm not leaving until Baelen is healed!" My shout is too loud. Too reckless. There aren't any guards at this spot, but I can't see how close Howl's palace is and the phoenix warned me that there are hundreds of guards around it. I squeeze my mouth shut and my eyes close as anger and fear rage inside me. I'm surprised I'm not shooting electrical sparks everywhere right now.

The Storm's voice turns cold. "You cannot cut through the wings, Marbella. They don't belong to you. They were taken from living gargoyles. Don't you see?"

I open my eyes. She's pointing.

She demands again, "Please, can't you see?"

I follow her finger to the thick curtain of wings. It shivers a little in the breeze until I realize… there is no breeze. The Storm has kept everything still so the mist remains thick. I take a step closer and it dawns on me what Jasper saw that made him look away. The wings shiver again. They are… still alive.

A twisted sound cuts off inside my throat. I jolt backward. I can't touch them. I can't cut through them. Pain shoots through my heart. "There has to be another way inside."

"There's no other way," the Storm says, her shoulders and wings slumping. "That's what makes this so cruel. Nobody can access the springs. Nobody can be healed."

"What do I do now? How can I help Baelen?"

"What about the High Priestess?" Jasper asks, even though we all know he's clutching at straws. "Could she help him?"

The Storm shakes her head. "She could have stopped the Elven Command from hurting him, but she can't heal him after the fact."

"Then… how…?" I can't speak. I can't feel. I'm numb from the tips of my toes to the top of my head. I've come all this way, and now I have to turn around and take Baelen back, with no way to heal him. His state of suspension won't last forever. I can't watch him die a slow death.

I want to scream and shout but I can't because it's so quiet.

So very quiet.

Wait…

Phoenix?

I wait for an answer, my heart in my throat. A scratching sound reaches me through the mist, but there's no reply.

Phoenix!

I grab my weapon, spinning in the direction where we left the phoenix with Baelen. "Something's wrong."

Jasper draws his sword, waiting for me to make a move.

The Storm hovers. "I don't sense anything…" An alarmed crease puckers her forehead. "In fact, I sense nothing…"

"Storm, I need to see the phoenix. I want you to lift the fog."

In response to my request, the Storm lifts the white vapor around us. It floats upward like a soft blanket to clear the space between us and where the phoenix landed. The firebird is still there, but its body is twisted at a strange angle, its head turned away. Baelen floats upright beside it, appearing the same as when I left him.

I race toward the phoenix. Its neck and head are pressed down against the stone. Its talons scratching back and forth, pressing, trying to get up.

Phoenix, speak to me!

Silence greets me as I round it, balancing at the very edge of the cliff to see its face. Its eyes are wide and staring.

If it wasn't for its talons scrabbling at the stone beneath it, I would think it was dead. But that can't be true because it would have ignited. I don't know a lot about the phoenix—it's the only one of its kind—but I do know that when it dies, it ignites into flame and will rise again when it chooses.

A whisper reaches me, like a far-off wind chime. It's the phoenix's voice, strained and forced. It says: *Out… there.*

I can't see anything beyond the ledge and suddenly our cover feels like a cage. Without the phoenix to warn us about approaching threats, my inability to see is a dangerous weakness. Still, I should have been able to hear anything that could be out there. Jasper too.

"Storm," I whisper as she and Jasper draw level with me at the cliff's edge. "I need to see."

She rises from where she'd bent over the phoenix to examine it, worry creasing her forehead. She brushes her hand across the air in a slow circular motion. The fog lifts again, the thick white cloud rising away from the edge of the cliff.

Shapes move in the darkness beyond. Many… *many…*

A gasp catches in my throat. My stomach plummets.

Layers and layers of gargoyles wait for us beyond the edge, beating the air to maintain a holding formation from one side of the cliff to the other. They're close enough that if I leap from the edge, I will crash into the first line of them.

A second and third line holds formation behind the first. I estimate there are nearly a hundred gargoyles, all of them dressed in armor and bearing weapons made of glinting steel. They cover the air overhead, up and up, all the way over to the rock face behind us: a swarm creating a thick barrier preventing any thought of escape.

Just waiting for us to realize we're surrounded.

10

MARBELLA

A small army beats the air, but where I stand, it's completely silent. No sounds reach me. Not the clinking armor, not the vast whirling wind they must be creating with their wings. It's as if we're enclosed in a sound bubble.

"Marbella." Jasper keeps his voice low and soothing. It anchors me, stops me from spinning into panic. "Stay calm."

"I didn't hear them, Jasper. I didn't sense them. The phoenix can't talk to me."

"We'll be okay." It's such a simple statement. I meet his gentle eyes, knowing that within moments, he will turn to rage because he will fight every one of these gargoyles if he has to. And I will fight right beside him.

Jasper shifts his gaze, focusing on the panicking Storm. "Elyria."

She's frozen beside me, shaking her head as if she's gone into shock. "I didn't… I can't… hear… feel…"

Jasper says, "I'm right here. You're okay."

He has the same effect on her that he has on me, but if anything, for her it's more intense. Her focus swings from the army that's about to tear us apart to Jasper. She visibly relaxes and I'm grateful. The last thing we need is for the Storm to turn into a wobbly mess.

The wall of gargoyles parts to allow another gargoyle to fly through. He is much larger than the others. In fact, he's as tall as Baelen, his thick arms and legs bulging with corded muscles. His eyes are black ochre and his features are chiseled: square jaw, perfectly shaped lips, and a cleft in his chin. His wings are shot through with veins that run emerald green.

A rock rests against his bare chest, attached to molded metal straps that cross his shoulders. It's the same size as an elven heartstone, but a deep, mossy green color. He must be King Howl.

Cassian flies close behind him. He nods his head in my direction in a single downward beat as if to point me out. When Cassian speaks, I don't hear him. I don't hear anything.

The King flies right up to the cliff's edge, within touching distance, surveying us: the prone phoenix, Jasper gripping his sword, and last of all--me. The way he glosses over the space between us tells me he can't see the Storm. It's a small blessing.

A smile crosses King Howl's face as he runs his eyes from my head to my feet in a way that makes me shudder. His lips part. He speaks and it's impossible not to read his lips as he says: "Well, fuck me."

He continues talking but turns away so I can't read what he's saying. The gargoyles around him break into laughter. It doesn't take much to imagine what he said after he ran his eyes over me. The mockery in their expressions is obvious.

I whisper, "Jasper! Be ready!"

I rip off my glove and take hold of my dagger with my bare hands. Electricity shrieks through me. I need to move before it reaches Jasper. On top of that, I have seconds before I lose the advantage of surprise.

I don't hesitate. Quiet as a shadow panther, I launch myself across the gap with my weapon raised. My blade rips apart the invisible barrier between us, streaks of electricity raging outward. As the bubble breaks, sound rushes in.

Cassian is the only one who didn't join the joke, keeping watch on me instead. His lips part in astonishment. "My King!"

Howl twists, but the shouted warning comes too late.

My weapon slides neatly into the King's heart.

Lightning fires across his chest, sizzling up his neck and across his wings, shooting burning light through his limbs. The impact forces him backward, but I'm ready for that. I kick my legs into his stomach and use his body as leverage to propel myself back to the cliff's edge, somersaulting onto it, rolling, and returning to my feet. The momentum slides me right back into the phoenix.

Howl's wings snap forward and then back. He wobbles, regains his balance, stares at the weapon protruding from his chest. For a brief second, his eyes widen in shock. As the last remnants of the Storm's mist swirls around his torso, he inhales. The same way Llion does. He holds the breath inside his lungs, drawing in my scent. Then his eyes narrow.

The moment stretches out. He doesn't collapse… doesn't even seem to remember that I stabbed him…

Curses. The heartstone is protecting him.

He breaks the moment with a laugh, a gusty sound, but there's no humor in his eyes as he announces to his army: "She thinks she can kill me!"

He slips the blade from his chest, clutching it in his fist, his chest still rumbling with laughter. It looks like he's going to crush the weapon. I wouldn't be surprised if he could with those giant fists. With a quick flick of his wrist, he pitches the knife at Jasper who darts to the side, deftly avoiding it and sliding right up to me at the same time, holding his weapon in front of me like a shield.

The Storm gasps and backs away, gliding from the phoenix, all the way back to the rock face. She won't join the fight. She already made her feelings clear about fighting gargoyles and I can't force her to do it. As much as I'm going to need her help…

"Pretty little elf." Howl ignores Jasper as he flies closer to me while the heartstone casts a sickly green light up and across his face. "You will not succeed where others have failed."

My weapons satchel is right beside me on the phoenix's back. I resist the urge to look at it while I calculate how long it will take me to get ahold of it.

A grin lights up Howl's eyes, making them sparkle like gemstones. "You wish to fight me again?" He casts his arms wide and his wings wider. The veins in them stretch out like emerald rivers. "I have no objection, but you should know that every moment you fail to surrender, your phoenix suffers terrible agony."

My eyes snap to the twitching leg beside me. Howl is doing something to the phoenix. Hurting it. Pinning it down. *Phoenix...?*

Its voice grates inside my head. *Don't... give up...*

My hands form into fists. I could make a grab for my weapons but Howl will crush me before I reach them. I fought Baelen when he took on the appearance of a gargoyle and his greatest advantage was his weight. I can't let Howl pin me down. But I need a plan—and fast.

Nothing can kill Howl, not while he has the heartstone. The only way to defeat him is to take the stone from him. The Storm told me I don't need steel to harness my storm power. It's time to find out if that's true.

"Soldier," I say to Jasper. "Move away from me right now. I don't want to hurt you."

Jasper pauses for the briefest moment before he decides to play along. He lowers his sword, sheathing it in one fluid movement. He bows deeply to me. "Far be it from me to stand between you and your prey, Mistress."

Jasper shuffles backward and assumes a post ten paces away, placed neatly at the center of the ledge where he can defend himself against an attack from any direction. He folds his arms over his chest, appearing relaxed, but I know he's ready for anything.

I curl my lip at Howl. It's time to play a part. I gesture to the discarded dagger that Howl threw back at us. "That was just for fun."

Howl's forehead creases, the first sign that he doesn't know how to read the situation. "You have a particular scent," he says. "You are not an ordinary elf."

"Ice and clouds," I say, remembering the way Llion described me. "I'm told I smell like rain." I close my eyes for the smallest moment, listening for Baelen's heartbeat. I need it. I need his strength combined with mine, but I can't chance drawing him out.

Instead, I focus on the memory of his body close to mine, the power that ignited between us. I need that.

A slow smile breaks across Howl's face. "You smell like deep magic. The sweetest kind." His eyes turn hungry. The heartstone against his chest glows a deeper green, seeming to respond to his emotions. "But there's something else too… something missing…"

I saunter right up to him, tilting my head back to maintain eye contact. A glow begins at the corner of my eyes, and I know I'm lighting up. A soft crackle reaches my ears. It's lightning. Without steel.

I can't hide my smile as lightning dances across my back and chest, curling around my waist and neck, building inside my palms. The crackles of electricity grow louder and stronger much faster than I expected, almost to the point of breaking out of my control.

Howl stands his ground but narrows his eyes at me, growling, "That's an interesting trick. I will figure you out, Little Doll."

A deep calm takes over my mind. I've never harnessed lightning like this before. It's always been targeted through my weapon, never flowing freely through my entire body. It always felt like it was external to me, as if I was borrowing it. For the first time, it belongs to me. It's mine. If I were alone on this cliff with the gargoyles, I would let the power loose and watch every one of these monsters fall from the sky. But I can't hurt Jasper or Baelen.

I smile at Howl. "You can start with this."

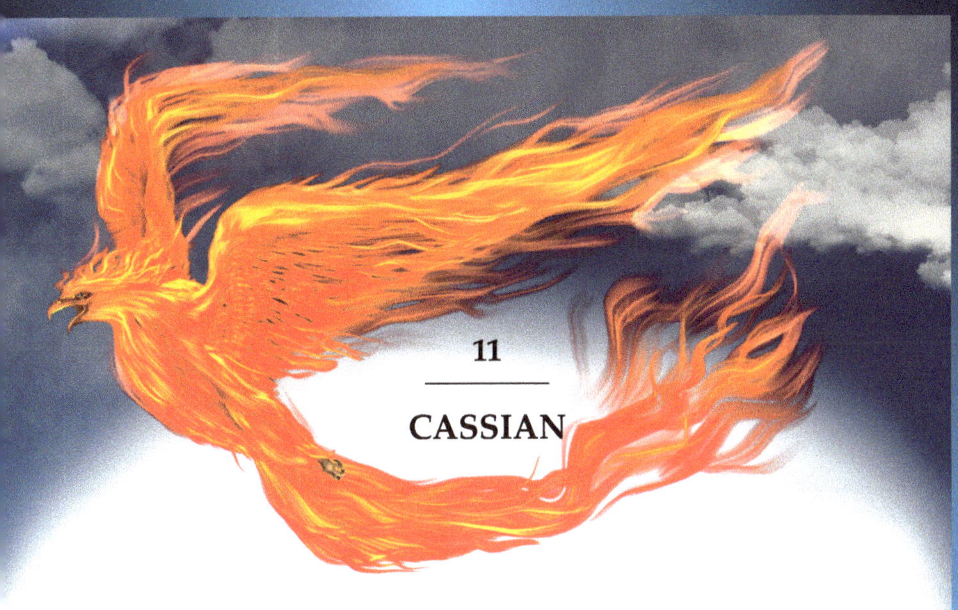

11

CASSIAN

Fog obscures the cliff as we fly in. Our wingbeats would normally clear the mist but Howl has already used his heartstone power to create a protective barrier around the deep springs—an invisible cage around the intruders that will prevent them from detecting our approach. His favorite trick. Luring his prey into a false sense of safety. It used to disturb me, but my heart has long since turned cold, the memories of the past banished from my mind.

Hope is nothing but an illusion.

Howl flicks his hand in my direction. Over time, I have learned to recognize all his moods, all his commands.

I call for the army of gargoyles to halt midair, directing them to swarm up and over the cliff. They fly carefully in the fog, avoiding the energy on this side of the invisible cage.

"It is as you reported," Howl says to me, his gaze distant and unfocused as he uses his power to see beyond the mist. "There are two elves and a phoenix. I have immobilized the phoenix and will take it as my prize. Let's see if the woman is as beautiful as you describe. She may be worth keeping as a plaything in my harem. Ah!" A cruel smile lights up his black eyes with anticipation of the kill ahead. "They have realized that something is amiss."

The fog clears, revealing the female elf and her male companion standing beside the prone phoenix. I hide my wince as the phoenix scrabbles against the ground, trying to escape the pain Howl is inflicting on it. I learned long ago that he's capable of incredible cruelty, learned to harden my heart against my rage and my inability to stop any of it.

The elves startle and brace, taking up defensive positions at the cliff's edge. The woman stands only five feet tall despite the way she carries herself with control and command. Her hair is pale auburn like the sun as it sinks below the horizon. For a second, I'm reminded of Elaina, the way loose strands of her sunset hair would curl against her soft cheeks.

I shake myself. I haven't thought of Elaina in a long time.

The male elf is like a giant next to the female, but even he is nothing compared to the warrior I saw strapped to the phoenix's back today. That elf would challenge most gargoyles—and most likely beat them. It makes me wonder what could have been strong enough to kill him.

The male elf says something to the woman but we can't hear it. It's clear he respects her—cares for her even. I press my lips into a line. Howl likes nothing more than to tear his victims apart in front of their loved ones.

Howl flies forward and I stay close beside him as the gargoyles part ahead of us. The veins in his wings glow brightly in the dim light, heartstone power pulsing through his chest and wings.

When he draws to a halt, close enough to the elves that I could leap forward and fight them, I incline my head toward the woman, keeping my movements sharp. "That is the woman who prevented our capture of the Priestess-in-training."

Howl glides within touching distance of her, his gaze running the length of her body. Consent is not in his vocabulary. The minute the barrier comes down, her body will be his toy.

He exhales, an appreciative smile growing on his face. "Well, fuck me."

The look on her face tells me she read his lips. She lifts her chin, shoulders squared, defiant, dagger gripped ready in her hand, her expression fierce in the face of the threat we pose. Just like this morning, she is ready to fight.

He turns to his soldiers with a grin. "I think I'll fuck her right here on the rocks. She'll need something hard against her back to take the pounding I'll give her."

The gargoyles around us break into laughter. Many of them are Grievous. Many of them follow Howl by choice, taking glory in every act of cruelty. Others don't. But they laugh anyway, because there isn't any other choice.

I don't take my eyes off the woman, frowning when the male elf steps away from her. If he was about to defend her, he wouldn't step back like that.

The woman moves fast. She rips off her glove, takes hold of the dagger in her bare hands and—

I jolt back with shock.

Electricity explodes from her hand and envelops her entire body in coils of light.

My breath stops as lightning bolts soar around her, lighting up her hair and face, making her more ferociously beautiful than anything I've ever seen.

She launches herself off the cliff's edge, her weapon raised. Her blade rips through the cage, her energy shrieking outward, destroying Howl's magic.

I can't tear my eyes away. Can't find my voice.

I have to find my voice. "My King!"

It wasn't what I'd meant to say. I swallow what I'd meant to say. *Kill him.* Dangerous words I will never speak aloud.

Howl twists back from the laughing gargoyles, shock registering on his face as she leaps toward him. His eyes fly wide and his lips part in a shout.

Her dagger thuds into his chest, a perfect, clean hit.

Electricity crackles from her dagger up his neck and through his wings, searing light burning my vision. He jolts under the impact, energy howling through him as he roars in the sudden quiet.

Concern shoots through me, but not for him. The woman has

nothing to hold on to except the dagger. She doesn't have wings. I prepare to fly forward and catch her, ignoring the fact that she could electrocute me, but in one swift move she kicks her feet into Howl's stomach and somersaults back onto the cliff's edge, sliding back into the phoenix.

Her face is flushed, fierce, a force washing out from her that I have never encountered before. A force that tore apart Howl's power, ripped through it like it was nothing more substantial than air. It gave her the power to stab him.

So much force flows from her that hope… *No, not hope. Never hope.*

Howl's wings snap back and forth as he wobbles before regaining his balance, his features frozen.

He inhales.

I smell it, too.

My stomach sinks, a dark cavern opening inside me that swallows my dangerous thoughts of hope.

Howl pulls the knife from his chest, pitching it at the male elf, who deftly avoids it. The male elf calmly steps out of the dagger's path to position himself close to the woman, his sword raised, ready to protect her.

Howl flies closer to them, dangerous laughter vibrating in his chest. "Pretty little elf. You will not succeed where others have failed."

She doesn't flinch, gesturing to the dagger embedded in the rock face with a curl of her lip. "That was just for fun."

Howl narrows his eyes at her. "You have a particular scent. You are not an ordinary elf."

"Ice and clouds," she says. "I'm told I smell like rain."

Howl gives her a hungry smile, nodding his head. "You smell like deep magic. The sweetest kind."

As electricity glows around her body, growing stronger, the cavern inside me closes, darkness and cold descending once more.

She's filled with deep magic, strong enough to fill my senses. The energy she controls is potent, as strong as Howl's, the kind he craves. He might have killed her quickly before, but now he will keep her, torment her, suck the life out of her moment by moment until she'll wish she were dead.

Now, she doesn't have a chance.

My fist snaps out. I bounce up at the same time, catching him right on the nose. It's not hard to miss his giant face. Streaks of electricity snake out from the spot where I hit him, coursing through his cheekbones and forehead. He roars and I know I hurt him.

He responds just as I expected—with brute force. His thick arms snap around the space where I was, attempting to wrap around me. Except that I'm already gone, bouncing backward, light on my feet, leaving him to grab at air.

I land several feet away and cock my eyebrow at him, baiting him. "Let's play, Howl."

"That's *King* Howl." He plows after me, fists swinging. I feint left and right, avoiding the swings, and duck under his arms, landing another electrified blow to his lower ribs. His bones light up behind his skin. This time lightning shoots upward toward his chest, traveling through his ribs as if his skeleton is a conduit. I land another blow square in his stomach before dancing away.

All I need to know is how close I have to get to the heartstone to shatter it. I don't think I'll be able to land a direct blow. He holds one arm in front of it at all times. He makes it look like he has his fists up for the fight, but his left arm is positioned close to the stone to protect it.

I focus on his exposed ribs and his legs, trying to upset his balance, as we exchange quick blows. He catches me on the shoulder when I don't expect it and pain explodes through my joint. Good thing I was moving—any harder and he would have dislocated my shoulder with a single punch. So far, he hasn't used his wing daggers, which tells me he doesn't want to kill me. Yet.

I leap, bouncing up from the balls of my feet. My fist glances off his jaw and he roars at me. This time electricity travels down his neck, stopping short at his collarbone.

I can't get close enough to the stone. My lightning doesn't travel far enough through his body to touch it.

Not unless I let him get close to me.

It's a dangerous move. It could end in disaster. But my options are getting slimmer. There's no way to warn Jasper. He'll react to defend me. So far, the other gargoyles have stayed out of the fight, but that could change in an instant.

I duck under Howl's next swing, keeping my arms close to my chest. Using my shorter height to my advantage, I step right into his chest, palms turned outward. His heartstone is at eye height. So close. My hands snap out.

Right before I reach the stone, he closes the circle of his arms and my hands smack against his pectoral muscles. The air whooshes out of my lungs. My left hand presses between his chest and shoulder, but my right hand is a mere inch away from the stone: right where I want it. As his arms close, forming a cage around my back and waist, I let the lightning loose.

It shrieks through his chest, lighting up his bones and sinew, his enormous beating heart, even the outline of his lungs. Brilliant cobalt light rushes all the way through his torso, beaming out his back and burning through his wings.

There's a flurry of sound behind Howl--shouts, falling screams, and gargoyles scattering outward. My assault has stretched far across the distance and burned anything in the way of it. I can't see how many I killed, and right now, my focus is only on the heartstone.

My lightning reaches it, slamming into it, flowing through it…

It doesn't break.

Howl shakes his head at me. "Little Doll, you have much to learn. You can't destroy a heartstone."

Cassian appears overhead, shouting orders, and suddenly a stream of gargoyles pours toward me. Jasper leaps up to meet them, scattering the mass before it can reach me.

But now he's made himself their target.

"Kill the man!" Cassian shouts.

I focus on Howl. "If I can't destroy it, then I'll take it from you."

He laughs. "You can try."

There's a *thump* against the air as his wings spread wide. With a single downward beat, he sweeps us into the air. I struggle against him, because this was definitely not part of the plan. Horror rushes through me at the possibility that he's going to fly away with me, and I won't know what's happening to Jasper or Baelen or the phoenix.

I don't know whether to be happy or terrified when he flies straight for the rock face behind me, knocking me against it and pinning me up high. His toe claws slide neatly into the rock, as do his wing daggers, leaving his hands free to push my shoulders against the smooth stone. He doesn't seal his wings against the rock, which means I can see past them. Down below, four gargoyles already lie dead at Jasper's feet, but he won't be able to defend himself against all of them.

Howl presses against me, forcing my hands hard up against his chest. The pressure makes it hard to move them, but I'm surprised he doesn't try to capture my hands since I just told him I was going to take his Heartstone.

"You won't succeed," he says. "Only a gargoyle can handle a gargoyle heartstone. One touch and it will kill you, elf. What I'm trying to decide is whether to let you kill yourself."

I don't know if I should believe him. It's bound to be a trick. I inch my hand across, trying to leverage my arm, my skin burning where it drags between us. I have one more trick up my sleeve.

Thunder.

The air thumps.

Thunder echoes out from me, freezing everything around us in a giant ripple. I can't see much beyond Howl's wings, but all sounds stop. For a moment.

And then the thump rushes back at me. My eyes widen as Howl blinks slowly, pausing and concentrating, inhaling at the same time as if he's sucking the effect of the thunder into himself, reversing it within seconds. Sound and movement strike up again and the fight resumes below us.

I didn't get any closer to the heartstone. "How…?"

"We are evenly matched," he says. "We could fight each other for days and neither one of us would win."

I grit my teeth and force my hand the final distance toward the heartstone. I'm a hairsbreadth away.

Howl peers down at my hand with amusement. "Do you really wish to die, Little Doll?"

At the last moment, when I'm about to curl my fingers around the heartstone, Howl lurches backward, releasing me from the pressure. At the same time, he gives himself leverage to wrench my hand away from the stone in a show of strength. He shoves both my arms back against the rock, pinning them bent upward beside me.

"It would be a shame to let you kill yourself… Storm Princess." He leans in, his mouth close to mine, inhaling against my cheek. "You are more beautiful than the stories say."

I shudder, repulsion racing through every nerve. "And you are more monstrous."

He laughs, his chest rumbling and hips pressing into mine. "I hear you are in need of a husband."

I grit my teeth. I seriously miss my armor right now. It's unbreakable—unlike the gray thermal suit I'm wearing. I would feel a lot safer if I was wearing it.

"Don't worry," he says, still chuckling. "I won't bed you. You are far too fertile, and I don't want an heir. Especially not a half-caste." His laughter dies and his mouth twists into a cruel line. "The only thing I'm uncertain about right now is whether or not to kill your friend."

My eyes snap to where I last saw Jasper. I find him further to the right, kneeling in a sea of dead gargoyles, maybe twenty, even thirty. He's ended them swiftly and cleanly, but now his wrists are shackled, chains pulling his arms out straight on both sides of his body by gargoyles. Cassian stands on the back of Jasper's calves, his claws pinning them against the rock. He pulls Jasper's head back and holds a knife against his throat.

I struggle against Howl but he doesn't budge. I'm pinned. The worst place I could be, and I let it happen willingly. I made the wrong choice.

Burning fear rushes through me as Cassian's blade glints. Jasper's weapon is thrown far to the right, resting at the Storm's feet. She huddles against the rock face, hands over her eyes, sobbing.

I scream, "Storm!"

She shakes her head. "I can't…"

"Storm! Please!"

Howl thinks I'm talking to myself. "You can scream for your power as much as you like, Little Doll. It won't do you any good."

The Storm lifts her head, her hair cascading around her pale face, but she doesn't speak to me. She cries to Jasper. "I… *can't*. I made a choice when I became the Storm. Please understand, I *can't* fight them."

Frustration replaces my fear. What on earth happened when she created herself? Whatever it was, it caged her somehow.

Jasper can't see either of us with his head tilted back. He calls, "It's okay. It's not your fault."

But it's definitely not okay. I'm pretty sure I've felt all the emotions because now it's rage that courses through me. Howl hasn't pinned my hand and I have no idea if it will work, but I flick my wrist and force as much lightning through my pointed finger as I can. A thin stream of it sizzles through the air, punching through the chest of the gargoyle holding Jasper's left arm and leaving a gaping hole behind. I quickly follow with a second, and the gargoyle holding the other chain drops dead on the spot.

Cassian is next. But he wrenches Jasper's head even further backward. "My blade is sharp, elf! If I fall, I will kill him."

I hesitate. The blade shines back at me. Am I so sure about my aim that I could dislodge the weapon and not hurt Jasper?

Howl smiles. "I see the male elf means something to you." He twists in Cassian's direction. "Keep him alive. I will use him as leverage."

Howl relaxes for the first time, seeming satisfied that he has the upper hand now. Hot anger boils through me. As two new gargoyles step forward and pick up the chains, dragging Jasper's arms upward again, I flick two quick warning bolts at their feet. I shout, "No chains! No weapons! He stands on his own."

Howl grins at me. "Do as she says," he calls, and to me, he says, "I'll give you this concession, but only because I've lost enough soldiers today." A curious crease appears on his forehead as he continues to press into me, seeming happy to stay right where he is. "Cassian told me you carried a dead man with you. Where is he?"

I search for Baelen beside the phoenix, amazed none of the gargoyles have collided with him. He's not where I left him and my heart stops for a moment. *Did they do something to him?*

I scan left, then right, finally locating Baelen in front of the gargoyle wings at the entrance to the cave. His expression hasn't changed. His eyes are still closed. The Storm gives me a bleak look, her shoulders slumped so far forward that her arms hang across her chest. "I moved him for you," she calls, staring at the ground. "That, at least, I *can* do."

A bemused expression flickers over Howl's face as he follows my line of sight to Baelen. "How does a dead elf stand up?"

He slides both arms around my back, pulling me away from the rock while keeping me imprisoned. He calls to his soldiers, "One of you, throw the dead elf over the cliff."

"No!" I shout, the breath squeezing out of my lungs as Howl crushes me tighter.

"He means something to you, too. Very interesting."

I gasp, trying to breathe. I have nothing to brace my feet against, scrabbling against his legs, and gravity is forcing my ribs against Howl's arms, making the circle around me even tighter. "They shouldn't touch him if they want to live. You said you've already lost enough—"

Howl isn't listening. He roars, "Throw him over the edge!"

The two gargoyles that I threw the warning shots of lightning at position themselves on either side of Baelen and prepare to take hold of his shoulders. I hold my breath, partly because I'm not sure what will happen, but mostly because I'm finding it very hard to breathe. Black spots appear across my vision and the ledge below me begins to slide sideways. I blink and try to focus, feeling like I'm going to throw up…

In the middle of my fuzzy vision, a bright spark of light suddenly glows, a small explosion that lights up the encroaching darkness. Shapes fall to the ground around Baelen's feet. An awful burning scent fills the air.

"Well, this night is full of surprises." Howl's crushing arms press closer and closer as my head swims. I need to focus on his face, but it blurs while the sounds around me swim and swirl.

I gasp. "Air… Need air…"

He shakes his head at me. "You bound your deep magic around that man. Even I won't be able to remove the shield you placed on him. But at least now I understand what is missing from you."

I make a last attempt to gain my freedom, releasing all the lightning I have into my hands pressed against his chest. The deadly blaze pours through Howl into the air beyond us, but the gargoyles in the background keep clear this time.

Howl doesn't react. I might as well be a butterfly beating at him. The last of my oxygen slips through my lips.

He leans over me, pressing his face close to mine. His lips caress my cheek and whisper into my ear, drawing out each word. "He holds your true power. If you hadn't given it to him... well... even my heartstone might not protect me from you."

He nuzzles my ear. "You would be truly formidable."

Darkness takes over.

"Sleep now, Little Doll."

13

CASSIAN

owl drops the female elf's unconscious body into my arms. He runs his fingers through her hair, pulling the strands to his nose and inhaling her scent deeply before he lets her go.

His pupils are dilated, his lungs filled with deep magic as he says, "Take her to the cells."

He crosses to the concealed mouth of the deep springs where the dead warrior elf stands, only ten paces away. Howl stops to study him while the gargoyles mobilize into ranks around us.

I expected the woman to be heavy because of her full-body armor, but she's light. Her hair cascades across my arms. One arm flops downward, but I gather her up, holding her safe. I try not to inhale, but it's impossible to ignore the scent of ice and clouds, just as she described herself.

The male elf stands only three paces away, released on Howl's orders. The other gargoyles are avoiding him now. I guess they're afraid that the Storm Princess will wake up and incinerate them if they appear anywhere near him.

The male elf takes a step toward me. He hides his fear for the woman, but there are hints of it in the crease of his forehead, the worry around his mouth. "I can carry her."

He doesn't realize that we have to fly him off this cliff. Without wings, he can't carry her through the air.

I check Howl's location. He's close by, but too intent on studying the warrior elf to listen to us. I shake my head, keeping my voice low. "She's safer with me."

The male elf's brow furrows. I don't expect him to trust me. I held a knife to his throat and threatened to end his life. Little does he know that I could have ended him well before that moment. He's a skilled and honorable fighter. The gargoyle bodies piled up around him, all clean, quick kills, without any torture or maiming. I held back the main army as long as I could before sending them in to fight him. But he's only one elf and I'm trained to recognize all the openings. I could have stabbed him in the back multiple times.

"What is your name?" I ask.

His shoulders square. He's clearly distrustful of me. As he should be. "I am Jasper of the House of Grace."

I incline my head toward the woman. "And hers?"

His eyes narrow, the furrow in his brow deepening. As he speaks, he glances to the side, fixating on a spot close by the dead warrior. It looks like Jasper is studying the warrior elf, but his line of sight is slightly off. It's odd the way he focuses on that bare spot as if he's watching something closely.

"Her name is Marbella," he says. "She belongs to the House of Mercy."

"Mercy?" I'm surprised. Over the years I've learned a little about elven culture and history. "Elves in the House of Mercy are slaves, aren't they?" *Like my clan used to be.*

"They serve the House of Rath," he says.

Rath. Now there's a name I know well. The House of Rath is both revered and hated by gargoyles. There were rumors several years ago about a wild elf who hunted in the wastelands of gargoyle territory. Some gargoyles whispered that it was Baelen Rath himself—rumors I could never verify.

I turn to the dead warrior that Howl is studying, suddenly suspicious. I don't know what Baelen Rath looks like. Neither does Howl. This could be him and we wouldn't know.

Howl stands in front of the dead warrior, studying him intently. Howl is shorter, which is a rare sight, but if the warrior were not floating, they would be eye to eye, both massive men, bodies honed for war.

I glance at Marbella, disconcerted by the way she seems to fit perfectly in my arms. Her motives for crossing the border are a mystery to me. Only someone desperate would travel into Erador. If she were bringing a warrior like Baelen Rath here to the deep springs, perhaps she thought she could revive him. There's no hope of that now. Not for him or for anyone.

A gargoyle appears with a sturdy basket gripped in his toe claws. I step back from Jasper, clearing my throat and raising my voice. The basket is big enough for him to crawl inside so we can fly him to the cells.

"Get inside," I order. "You will come quietly or your journey will not be pleasant."

To the waiting gargoyle army, I shout, "First and second legion, fly out!"

As the majority of the army flies away, Jasper refuses to budge. His hands twitch, seeking a weapon.

I growl a warning. "Do not resist, Jasper of the House of Grace. Not if you care about what happens to Marbella."

His jaw clenches before he finally clambers inside the cage.

Right before the hatch closes, emerald light sparks at the corner of my vision.

I spin to Howl, surprised to see him drawing on his heartstone power, his wings pulsing with rivers of emerald energy.

He reaches out toward the warrior elf. The determined set of his features tells me he wants to test his power against whatever magic is protecting the other man.

It's a reckless thing to do, even for him. The other gargoyles were incinerated the moment they made contact. Even if Howl isn't killed, everyone around him will be.

"Third legion, fly out!" I shout, relieved when the final band of soldiers immediately takes to the sky. That leaves a handful of gargoyles, as well as Jasper and the man whose job it is to carry him.

Howl's hand inches closer to the elf and the space between them sizzles. Electricity builds in the air around us, so thick that it steals the breath out of my lungs.

Behind me, Jasper shoves at the hatch to his cage so hard that it topples to the side. He scrambles out, his gaze on the same strange spot next to the warrior elf. His face turns pale, his reaction so intense that it's almost as if he's listening to a warning—

Howl's hand connects.

His heartstone power connects with a force so strong that a storm ignites around us.

Flames blast outward. Scorching heat roars past Howl and rips straight toward me in a giant plume.

I twist, drop, and my wings shoot out, curling around Marbella—

The flames hit my back. Not ordinary flames. These are like scorched rocks pelting against my back and wings. I squeeze my eyes closed, roaring out the heat and fear, a burning scent filling my lungs. I try to stop breathing it in, try to hold still when all I want to do is run, but if I do, I'll expose Marbella to the fire.

The roaring flames and fiery glow finally fade.

Dying screams wane into quiet.

I'm alive. I'm not sure how. My back should be burned to ashes, even if my wings would survive the blast.

I open my eyes.

Jasper crouches opposite me, his eyes wide, staring back at me. My wings stretch out on either side of him, forming a shield. I protected him from the blast.

I'm suddenly aware of a soft hand pressing against my heart. A cooling sensation radiates out from the point of contact against my chest. It's soothing like… *ice and clouds*. I stare down at Marbella's hand, deeply confused. Did she unconsciously protect me just now? Stop the heat of the flames? I can't believe she would do such a thing. But I can't deny that it's the only reason I'm alive.

Ignoring Jasper for the moment, I check Marbella first: her fingers, feet, hair—all the exposed parts of her body. She's unscathed, sleeping peacefully. In fact, her face has settled into an expression of such serenity, it's breathtaking, almost as if the power blasting around us was a comfort to her.

I snarl at Jasper, confusion making me angry. "Who is he? Who is the dead elf to her? Why does his power comfort her?"

Jasper's lips compress. Refusing to answer me, he glances side to side at my wings, which protected him. The basket he was in is now a smoldering mess and the gargoyle holding it lies dead on the cliff.

Marbella saved me, but I saved him.

With an unhappy sigh, I turn to Howl.

He stands in front of the warrior elf, unmoving. Soft growls meet my ears from his angry mouth.

"King Howl?"

He casts me a sudden glare, snarling at me. "Get the elves to the cells, Cassian."

As I turn away, his hand lowers to his side. Shock almost makes me freeze.

Howl's palm is burned.

Burned from where he touched the warrior elf.

He has never suffered an injury while wearing the heartstone. He is indestructible. But in one evening, Marbella broke through his power and stabbed him in the heart, and the warrior elf she brought with her burned Howl's hand.

A glance at Jasper tells me that he sees it too.

What is this feeling filling my chest? It can't be hope, because hope is dangerous.

I pull Marbella to my chest and rise into the air, my wings blowing ashes across the cliff where dead gargoyles lay. I catch Jasper's shoulders as I pass over his head, taking hold of his shoulders in my feet. I make sure my claws are retracted so I won't cut him. It won't be comfortable for him, but it's better than leaving him with Howl.

Behind us, Howl pounds across the cliff face toward its edge, his power dragging behind him, lifting the dead warrior without touching him. He releases his wings, a cloud of anger settling around his features.

I pick up speed, carrying my captives away, as far from Howl as I can get them.

14

MARBELLA

I awake pressed against cold stone.

"Marbella?" Jasper's worried face comes into focus, so close to mine that I can make out golden flecks in his brown eyes. I can't believe I never noticed them before.

I rub my pounding head, brushing off specks of dirt from the floor where I lay. "Jasper, what happened?" I shoot upright, squinting, ignoring the pain in my neck. "Where's Baelen?"

The first thing I see are the bars running from the floor to the ceiling opposite us. The second thing is the Storm floating next to them. Her shoulders shake as she glides back and forth as if she's pacing or maybe… crying?

I scan our cell from the moist stone walls to the dripping rivers of water running down on one side, back to the dirty floor. Beyond the bars, a long tunnel stretches into the distance. Light creeps in from a cluster of spider webs in one corner of the ceiling. A second cell rests next to ours, thick bars separating us. The phoenix slumps inside it, its head cast down. It doesn't twitch and fight like before. It looks unharmed, but its sad eyes blink at me from between the bars. I still can't hear its voice.

My blood runs cold. "Jasper, where's Baelen?"

"I'm sorry, Marbella. Howl moved him."

My world spins. I grip his shoulders, needing to anchor myself somehow. "That's not possible. Only I…" My pitch rises. I attempt to push away my growing panic, but it only gets worse. "Only I can move him. Nobody else can touch him. Only me…"

"Stop. Listen to me." Jasper's calm breaks through. "Howl moved Baelen using his heartstone power, but he couldn't touch him. Just like the other gargoyles, as soon as he went near Baelen, Howl got burned."

My eyes widen. I'd shot lightning through Howl without any effect on him. Now Jasper is telling me that Baelen hurt him? "He actually got hurt? Like… *hurt* hurt?"

Jasper's reply is grim. "His hand caught on fire. The skin on his palm burned away like he'd shoved it into acid. He definitely wasn't happy about it."

Llion had described Baelen as scorched earth and acid rain. I shake my head, remembering Howl's last words to me. "He told me that Baelen holds my true power. That I somehow weakened myself by giving it to him. You're seriously telling me that Baelen hurt him?"

The Storm speaks for the first time. "It's my fault." She falters toward me, but stops, worrying at her lip. "When you accidentally connected with Baelen yesterday, you merged your power for the first time, but you must have left some of it behind. Then when you were learning to move him, I told you to listen for his heartbeat. I should have realized… you love him so much that you gave him the most powerful shield you could. You layered your essence over him like a cloak."

"So, I accidentally gave him part of my power and then sealed it in with even more of my power?" I don't know how to receive this news. My greatest fear is that Baelen will be hurt while he's vulnerable. Knowing that he's safe and protected only goes halfway to calming my fears. I need to see that he's okay to truly believe it. At the same time, I've just found out that my power is diminished and that means I can't protect Jasper and the phoenix like I need to.

Jasper says, "Marbella, believe me when I say that right now, Baelen is a lot safer than we are."

I focus on Jasper, really focus for the first time. He's covered in blood. The welts I'd left on him are nothing compared to the new wounds across his body, the torn material at his chest, and the nick at the side of his neck where Cassian almost killed him. Yet, here he is, trying to comfort me.

I'm not ashamed when tears fill my eyes. "Jasper, I'm truly sorry. What I did was reckless. I thought I could beat Howl."

Jasper nods. "I thought you could too." He holds out his arms. "Come here."

I lean into him, and he slides his arms around me, gentle against my bruised ribs. I turn my face into his chest and let my tears fall, conscious not to press too hard against his wounds.

The Storm drops to the floor beside us. "I'm sorry I couldn't help you."

I turn my head to see her. "Storm, you have to explain what happened out there."

She swallows, twisting her hands in her lap. "When I became the Storm, I vowed that I would never harm a gargoyle. I wanted to protect my people... I never thought about the consequences of making that vow."

She lifts her eyes to mine. "Do you remember how I told you that a small part of me could escape the Vault when there was a natural storm outside?"

"I do."

"Well... ten years ago, I watched Howl kill the Gargoyle King." She shudders. "I never felt rage toward another gargoyle until that day. I tried to stop him. But every strike I aimed at him bounced right back at me, burned me, hurt me. I realized that if I tried to kill him, I would kill myself instead.

"Then the natural storm was over, and I was sucked back to the Vault. Mai Reverie was the Storm Princess then. I wept a river of rain that day and she was... so calm with me."

Fresh tears wash down my cheeks. The Elven Command had killed Mai, trying to make it look like the Storm's doing. They used her life to give them access to the deep magic they needed to create the curse that would have forced Baelen to kill me. Jasper strokes my hair, soothing motions across my head and down my back where my hair has come loose from its usual braid.

The Storm says, "My oath to never hurt a gargoyle is absolute. I can't touch Howl or his soldiers, no matter what they do."

Jasper says, "I guess that means you can never hurt me either."

Her eyes shoot wide. "I would never hurt you, Jasper Grace. Whether you are gargoyle or elf, or part of both... I only wish I could have helped you today."

"Jasper," I whisper, tilting my head back, something dawning on me. "If you're part gargoyle, you can handle a gargoyle heartstone."

He looks down at me, confused. He didn't hear my conversation with Howl, so he doesn't know what I'm talking about.

I explain, "Howl said that elves can't touch gargoyle heartstones. They kill us." I peer at the Storm. "Unless he was lying?"

"No, it's true but..."

"Then Jasper can try to take it—"

"No!" The Storm's shout echoes around us. "We aren't certain about Jasper's heritage. What if we're wrong? We can't risk his life like that." She shoots to her feet and resumes her pacing. "We've taken too many risks already. And Jasper has borne the brunt of them."

She stops in front of me. I stare up at her in surprise as swirls of lightning glint around her hands, suddenly clenched at her side. "I won't let you risk his life again, Princess."

Her emotion surprises me. I've only known her in her true form for a day, but until now she's been contained, almost aloof, definitely keeping a distance. For the first time, I see cracks of vulnerability. If the Storm is right about Jasper caring for me, then I'm pretty sure the Storm is beginning to care for him. No doubt a complication she doesn't want, but she isn't afraid to show it right now.

I give Jasper a final, gentle hug before I draw away from him. "The Storm is right. You've supported me all this way, Jasper. I acted out of fear and anger today and it led me down the wrong path. I won't take a risk like that again."

The Storm's show of emotion hasn't been lost on Jasper.

"Elyria," he says, drawing her attention from me. "I know you're worried," one corner of his mouth twitching upward, "but I'm not that easy to kill."

"I saw you take down twenty-eight gargoyles today. You are a great warrior." She's sincere. And deadly serious. "But all great warriors fall. There is always someone bigger, more brutish, more cruel… And I can't protect you from any of them in this place."

I understand her frustration. She and I share a power and we're still figuring out exactly what that means and how to use it. But what we do know is that it's useless against our enemies right now: I can't stop Howl and she can't stop the gargoyles that might attack Jasper. At the end of the day, she's as desperate to protect Jasper as I am.

Jasper brushes off his knees as he rises to his feet. "It's not your job to protect me, Elyria."

"But you're my friend. I'm new at this whole 'friend' thing, but isn't that what friends do?"

"I guess it is." He appraises her for a moment. His eyes crinkle at the corners. "Since we're friends, that means you have to let me protect you too."

"Protect me?" Her jaw drops. "I don't need protecting."

His gaze passes from the tiny crease between her eyebrows to the defiant tilt of her chin. "Protecting someone doesn't only mean making sure they don't die in battle. It means looking after them, making sure they aren't hurt in other ways."

"Nothing can hurt me."

"Are you sure?"

Her gaze drops to the ground. Once more I'm on the outside, an observer of their conversation, but I don't mind. The Storm definitely has trust issues and if Jasper can get her to open up, that can only make things easier for all of us.

The Storm chews her lip, clearly struggling with her emotions. She glares at the wall behind Jasper, not meeting his eyes. "It… would have hurt me… if you died today."

She immediately scowls, clearly not liking her own admission. Then her expression clears and her gaze shoots to his as if she's landed on a clever solution. "So you have to protect me... by not dying."

Jasper draws himself up to his full height before closing the gap between them. "I promise I'll protect you by not dying today. Or any other day."

Her chin shoots up. "Good."

"But you have to help me by telling me when you're scared or worried."

She gazes up at him, eyes wide, lips pressed together, suddenly vulnerable. "That will be hard for me." Her promise comes out as a whisper. "But, okay."

"Okay then." He gives her a gentle nod, an agreement reached. "Have you made any progress with the bars?"

The change of subject shifts her focus, and she seems relieved. It can't be easy for her to talk about her emotions after hundreds of years of continuous rage. "I've tried everything. Howl has used the heartstone to seal us in. I haven't been able to break through."

There are no windows to tell me what time it is. We'd reached the mountain at around midnight, and I can only assume we're now in Howl's Palace. "How long was I out?"

Jasper offers his hand to help me stand up. "Most of the night," he replies. "I was a little worried when you didn't wake up right away, but Elyria promised me you just needed time to recover. I was able to sleep while she kept watch over us."

The Storm shrugs. "I don't need sleep." Her brow furrows at my hand linked with Jasper's then she quickly looks away. "I can't sense what's going on outside this cell, but I estimate it's mid-morning by now. When he locked us in here, Howl said he would present you to his court today, but he didn't say when."

"Great. I'll be his trophy." And a fine trophy I'll be, looking like I've been dragged through mud. I run my hand through my hair and pull out a twig. "Seriously, what is on the floor of this place?"

The Storm wrinkles her nose. "I don't think we want to know."

Distant footsteps draw our attention to the tunnel beyond. Four figures appear in the distance—one silhouette is female and three are male, although one of the men looks different from the others.

The Storm moves to the side and Jasper draws level with me as the distant figures stride closer. It soon becomes apparent that two of the men are soldiers—that's if the wickedly sharp-tipped spears they carry are any indication. The woman and the different-looking man walk ahead of them. The soldiers don't exactly prod them, but the two in front hurry along the corridor as if they expect to be shoved at any moment.

They draw to a halt in front of the bars. The woman is scantily dressed in an aqua halter-neck top that barely conceals her breasts, her lower half swathed in a transparent skirt that wouldn't hide anything except for her barely-there underwear. The man wears a vest and long pants, both navy blue. The Storm gasps beside me and I know it's not the woman's attire that shocks her.

The man doesn't have wings.

I keep my expression deadpan as one of the soldiers leans forward and taps his spear against the bars. At the same time, the air inside my ears pops.

The Storm whispers, "The seal on this cage just broke."

That would explain the change of pressure in my ears.

The woman says, "My name is Carmen. King Howl says you won't cause any trouble. But he wants you to know that if you do, these soldiers are ordered to kill me."

She's completely expressionless. Blank eyes. Staring straight past me. She holds herself rigid, back straight, her spun-gold hair gathered upward in a loose bun. "Will you come with us, please?"

The soldier who broke the seal slides the bars to the side where they overlap with the cell the phoenix is still contained in.

The firebird's voice suddenly breaks into my mind. *Don't worry about me, Princess. Howl will keep me safe and well. He wants me as his prize. The same way he wants you.*

The seal on our cell must have been what was stopping us from communicating. My concern for her cannot be contained, and the phoenix rises up and gives me a stern look. *Focus on staying alive, Princess. I trust you to come for me when you can.*

I will, I say. *I promise.*

Now that our path is no longer barred, both soldiers quickly point their spears at the woman. She winces as one of them jabs her lower back.

"There's no need for that," I say, alarmed at the way he presses the blade against her side as if he *wants* me to make a move. "We won't cause you any trouble. Tell us where you want us to go, and we'll come quietly."

The woman swallows, her eyes watering. "You will come with me to Harem Hall." She gestures at the wingless man but doesn't look at him. "Your servant will go with Rhain to Slave Station."

I hesitate, sensing Jasper's gaze heavy on me. "We're to be separated?"

"Only while we prepare you both to be presented at Crimson Court. Please understand your male servant cannot enter Harem Hall. It is only for women."

I clear my throat. The name 'Harem Hall' combined with the woman's clothing doesn't leave much doubt about what goes on in the place where I'm headed.

"Please," I say. "Lead the way."

Carmen looks to the soldiers, waiting for them to raise their spears and allow her to pass by. They take their time and I have to grit my teeth against my rising anger as they finally permit her to turn and walk ahead of us. Blood trickles down her lower back where the soldier's spear punctured her skin.

The wingless man is next, taking his place beside her but keeping as far to the right as possible. He maintains firm eye contact with the ground. Jasper and I follow, and the soldiers bring up the rear. The Storm floats over our heads since there's plenty of space in the cavernous ceiling.

Halfway along the corridor, her urgent whisper breaks the silence. Thank goodness the gargoyles can't hear her. "If you're splitting up, who should I go with? You or Jasper?"

One glance at Jasper tells me he's going to say she should go with me, but I can tell by the deep furrow marring his forehead that he's still figuring out how to speak to Elyria without sounding odd.

I jump in first. "Jasper," I say. Then I turn my head as if I was addressing him instead of answering the Storm. "Don't forget to…

um… wash your feet." I cringe. *Seriously Marbella? That's the best you can come up with?*

He's not happy. And it has nothing to do with his feet. The muscle clenching in his jaw tells me he really doesn't like me going anywhere without the Storm, but I silently beg him not to argue.

"Good," says the Storm, "Because I don't like the sound of Slave Station. Even less than the sound of Harem Hall."

I feel better knowing that the Storm is going with Jasper when we reach the end of the tunnel and the wingless gargoyle, Rhain, gestures Jasper toward the staircase on the right side. Carmen proceeds up the stairs to the left and I don't want her to become a pincushion again. With a final worried exchange of looks with Jasper, I hurry after her, swiveling once as Jasper disappears up the other staircase with Rhain and one of the soldiers. The Storm floats behind him, worry radiating from her until she's out of sight.

For now, I'm on my own.

15

———

MARBELLA

The soldier following behind me is the one who jabbed Carmen. I consider the consequences if I were to accidentally-on-purpose trip and shoot a dose of lightning into him. But I promised the Storm I wouldn't take any more chances and I need to stick to my word.

We travel up several more flights of stairs. Each one is preceded by a landing and a tunnel stretching from it. Howl certainly didn't take any chances by throwing us in the deepest cell inside the mountain.

Finally, we emerge into an entryway and a courtyard. Sunlight streams around us and I have to blink for a full minute before I become accustomed to the light again. I try to focus on my surroundings as I follow Carmen, memorizing the route back to the phoenix.

At first I thought I was in the middle of a single large castle, but soon discover that Howl's Palace is made up of multiple disconnected buildings, each built into the natural rock structure. I'm surprised by the simple beauty of the rock gardens surrounding each building. We pass one covered with white vines bearing delicate ivory flowers. Another is constructed from rust-colored pebbles and flat amber stones interspersed with vibrant moss.

Several gargoyles dressed in navy blue vests tend the gardens as we walk through.

They glance up but quickly look away when they see Carmen. The wingless gargoyle had made a point of not looking at her either. I don't see dislike or distaste in their expressions, only fear.

She leads me to a single-level construction that backs onto a soaring rock face. It's surrounded by large, billowing saffron-yellow flags and a wooden verandah that stretches around the two sides that I can see. It's also surrounded by a wall of outward-facing soldiers.

They part for Carmen, giving her a wide berth and me with her. The soldier with the spear takes up position and closes the gap behind us. Then the soldiers turn to face outward, forming a barrier between us and the rest of the palace. Harem Hall is certainly well-guarded.

Carmen doesn't speak until we climb the stairs, cross the verandah, and reach the door. "The guards are not allowed inside. And Howl is not here." She waves her hand at the flags. "We fly the red flags when he's here."

I never thought I'd be grateful for the color yellow.

"Come with me, please."

We pass through a wide entryway into an opulent room scattered with plush cushions. A door at the other side takes us into another room, this one with a slate floor and a water feature. We pass through three more rooms until Carmen slides open a final door into a hallway with multiple rooms on either side.

"This is where we wash," she says. "There are towels inside. Leave your clothes in the dressing room. You won't need them anymore."

I'm not so sure about that. Judging by what she's wearing, there may not be a lot of suitable clothing options in this place.

"I'll be here when you're done," she says.

Inside the bathing room, about a thousand different scented soaps await me, as well as a lukewarm shower that leaves me shivering. I'd swap the soaps for a hot bath right now. The water runs dark with mud and whatever else was on the floor of the cell.

When I'm done, I squeeze as much water from my hair as I can and contemplate the discarded gray thermal. It's filthy. I'm going to have to take my chances with whatever clothing Carmen has to offer. I secure a large towel around myself before emerging into the hallway again.

She rises from a seat opposite the door and strides away. I think I'm meant to follow her. "Wait."

"Yes?"

"You haven't asked my name."

"I know who you are." She continues walking and I stalk her down the hall. Female voices project from the room beyond, but they stop talking when I enter. I count about twenty, all stunningly beautiful, some sitting, some standing. All dressed like Carmen. All staring at me.

We're in some sort of large dressing room with mirrors and tables around the edges laid out with hairpieces, hairbrushes, sashes, but not a lot of decent clothing in sight. I shudder, wishing I'd brought my ripped thermal suit with me after all.

"Sit, please. We don't have a lot of time."

I find a spare seat, ignoring the stares and whispers, while Carmen sets to work pulling a hairbrush through my tangled hair. Nobody has touched my hair in seven years. After I became the Storm Princess, I always did my own hair. In fact, even before that… except for Baelen. I close my eyes as I remember his hands sliding through my hair, releasing it from the braid I'd always tied it in, his fingers a light tingle across my shoulders as he followed the length of my hair down my arm.

I force myself to return to the present. Carmen is gentle and carries out the task without speaking. Silence seems to be her friend. I decide I'm willing to break it because I need information. "Why do the male gargoyles look away from you?"

"It's forbidden to look at a woman in the King's harem. Only the soldiers may see us. To the rest, we are ghosts."

Another woman approaches and I assess her in the mirror. Ebony hair cascades over one shoulder and reaches her waist. Intelligent olive-green eyes meet mine briefly. Where Carmen is silent and contained, this woman almost leaps out of her skin to speak with me.

"I am Gilda," she says. "Our King has sent you clothing to wear." A long silken dress drapes across both her arms and relief courses through me to see it. I don't hold my breath though. I can't see every detail of it from here and something tells me Howl won't be that kind to me.

Gilda hangs the dress over the nearest chair but doesn't walk away, commenting quietly on the way Carmen is twisting my hair. When she makes suggestions, Carmen considers them and makes changes. It's easy to see these two women are friends.

"Forgive me," I say, deciding to take advantage of Gilda's presence. "But the gargoyle back in the tunnel, the one called Rhain who took Jasper to Slave Station… Did Howl take his wings?"

Carmen freezes, her hands still entwined in my hair, turning into stone beside me. Gilda shoots concerned looks like fireworks at her friend. "You didn't tell me he made you walk with Rhain," she whispers to Carmen.

Carmen remains frozen. "I can't…"

It doesn't take a genius to see that I've stepped into something I shouldn't have. I try to gobble back the words as fast as I can. "I'm sorry, I've upset you. Please forgive my callous question."

"You are an elf," Carmen says, visibly swallowing as if there's a great lump stuck in her throat. "And a newcomer. So, of course, you wouldn't know…" She resumes twirling and pinning my hair, but her movements are overly focused, and her fingers are stiff. "Rhain's wings were taken as punishment for trying to free his wife from Harem Hall."

I study the room in the mirror. "Which one is his wife?"

Her movements slow down again, as if she's moving underwater. "I am."

I choke. "But… That's… You didn't look at him…"

"To acknowledge my husband is to kill him." Her movements become jerky and I'm impressed by the way she calms herself so she doesn't yank on my hair and hurt me. "To keep him alive, I must act as if I have no husband. No family. We all must. As I said, we are ghosts. That is how we keep breathing."

Gilda runs her arm across Carmen's back, giving her shoulder a quick squeeze. I remain silent for the remainder of the time it takes for Carmen to finish my hair. I've already put my foot in it. Royally. I'm lucky I haven't alienated her completely.

Once she finishes piling my hair on top of my head, she hands me two slips of material that I think are intended to be underwear. The bra has multiple clips and Carmen explains that's so they don't have to get the straps over their wings. I slip out of my towel and into the underwear and then the dress. The women in the room seem surprised when I drop the towel right in front of them, but I'm used to being surrounded at all times. Before everything went wrong back in Erawind, my Storm Command used to protect my every move. Admittedly, the bathroom was the one place I had privacy, but even so, I'd dressed in front of them too many times to be embarrassed now.

I take note of the bruises dotting my skin—from the fight with the gargoyles yesterday as well as with Howl last night—before sliding into the dress.

The sleeveless dress is jet black patterned with pale blue filigree that contrasts with my auburn hair and brings out the turquoise flecks in my eyes. I was right to be skeptical about Howl's intentions. The material plunges low at the front, and I'm grateful for the supportive bra because there's not much holding the dress together. Three ribbons circle my waist at intervals, holding the two wide straps that form the top of the dress together below my breasts. Luckily the skirt is fitted, flaring at my ankles, but it has a long slit up the back reaching my upper thighs between my legs. At least I can move in it, but the height of the slit makes me uncomfortable. The material itself is gorgeous, soft, and delicately embroidered. I just wish there was more of it.

I hold my head high as Gilda hands me a pair of heels.

I've never worn heels in my life. Give me boots or a pair of flats. Even to Jordan's wedding, I wore flat-heeled slippers. Gliding the heels onto my feet, I teeter on the spot, wobbling and trying to convince my ankles not to snap.

"You need to practice." Gilda takes my arm before I fall over. "Here, let me help you."

I wobble my way across the room, ignoring the stares of the women at the other end. Gilda asks, "When was the last time you ate something?"

I have to think hard about that. I ate at the cave on the border before we left Erawind, but I've been running on adrenaline ever since. "It's been a while."

"Well, there's the food table." She points with a twinkle in her eye at a table on the furthest side of the room laden with fruit, bread, and little cakes. "Go forth and eat."

Screw the heels. I have no idea when I'll get to eat again. I place all my energy into balancing and make it to the food table without falling flat on my face. Mission accomplished, I pick up the nearest red apple and crunch into it. It doesn't taste like I expected. I eye it warily. "What is this?"

"It's a giant cherry."

"Mmm. Not bad."

"Just watch out for the juice." She's about to take a step toward me when she freezes, pinned facing the direction behind me.

Whisper quiet, a shadow casts over me.

Gilda and every other woman in the room slides to their knees and bends flat to the floor, arms beside their heads as if they're praying. They tuck their faces down, foreheads pressed to the ground, becoming colorful mounds dotting the floor.

I'm the only one left standing. And, once I turn, the only one looking at *him*.

Howl towers over me. Unlike Jasper, the Howl version of towering is pure intimidation. I seek the sensation of my storm power deep inside: the electricity and thunder. I draw comfort from it and stand my ground. I will not cower to him.

The fruit remains clenched in my upturned hand. Some of the juice trickles down my wrist.

"I see the dress fits."

He remains at my side, and I discover the unwelcome secondary purpose of the slit in the back when he slides his large hand directly across my thigh. I grind my teeth together so hard that I might crack them. I'm glad Baelen's not around right now. Nothing would stop him from tearing Howl limb from limb.

Howl acts as if there's nobody else here—as if we're completely alone. Stopping the upward slide of his hand barely before he reaches my backside, he catches my upturned wrist in his other hand, trailing his thumb through the line of juice.

I narrow my eyes at him. For a second, the inside of his palm is exposed and I'm pretty sure I see burn marks. That must be the hand that Baelen burned. The knowledge that Howl isn't invincible gives me courage. "Let go of me. Right now."

He narrows his eyes right back at me, daring me to challenge him with my power. He lowers his mouth to my wrist, drawing his lips across the droplets left there. I remain as still as stone, suppressing the shudder rocking my spine as his eyes meet mine. His pupils dilate and I know it's not the taste of my skin that has that effect on him. It's my deep magic.

Well, he just ruined a perfectly good piece of fruit. There's no way I'm going to eat another giant-apple-cherry-thing after this.

"You are intoxicating," he whispers, and this time, I can't hide my shudder. My power is quickly becoming my curse.

I say, "I may not be able to hurt you, but I can definitely make a mess of your precious Harem Hall. Let me go or I'll start with the ceiling." That's the way my hand is pointed. May as well start with that.

He doesn't release my wrist, but removes his hand from my thigh, angling his body sideways, his wings kept close to his sides.

He scans the women. "Look up!"

Immediately, they obey. Their faces shoot up, but their bodies remain pressed against the floor. He inclines his head at Carmen and Gilda. "You and you."

I freeze. *Is he going to hurt them? Have I pushed him too far?*

I don't relax until he says, "You will come to Crimson Court today."

With the immediate threat to their safety gone, I scowl at him. "Do you even know their names?"

"I have no need for names."

Elves don't swear aloud, but I'm seriously tempted right now. We believe that curse words are curses that will return to the speaker. I don't chance it, but I have to bite my tongue to stop myself. Carmen's description of herself as a ghost is becoming more accurate with every passing second. Howl treats the women like they don't exist and even when he does acknowledge them, they are purely objects to be moved around or threatened.

As he waits for them to stand, I contemplate his features. Was he once handsome? I truly believe that every elf and gargoyle is born innocent. That our experiences mold and change us. But I find it very hard to believe that Howl was once a child without malice or hatred in his heart. A wave of pity rushes through me so strong it's like a physical force.

Howl's gaze snaps back to mine. His fist shudders around my wrist. The heartstone resting against his chest glows brighter than before, and he winces as if it suddenly hurts. He drops my hand, and the glow recedes.

My eyes widen in surprise. I have no idea what just happened, but it's very strange to me that my rage can't touch him, but my pity can. Unless… The Storm said that the heartstones are literally the hearts of brave gargoyles. I wonder if the stone will respond to particular emotions around it. It could all be connected to who the gargoyle was when it was alive.

I don't have time to test that theory because Howl jolts away from me as if he reads my thoughts. I'm quite certain pity isn't something he sees very often. More like fear, terror, agony, you name it… but not pity.

Carmen and Gilda wait obediently for further instructions, heads bowed again.

Howl snarls at them. "You will walk ahead of me."

They glide past me and I follow, deciding it's not worth jeopardizing their safety to resist Howl. I wobble in the heels but maintain pace behind them, tap-tapping through the rooms to the entrance. For such a large gargoyle, Howl is stealthy and light-footed. Half the time, it's possible to imagine he's not even there.

I wish he wasn't.

Cassian breaks off from the stiff line of guards ahead of us as we make our way down the stairs. From the way he waits until we reach them, it looks like he isn't allowed to step foot in Harem Hall either. The other guards peer past us, ignoring the women, no doubt awaiting orders from Howl.

He barks, "Ten of you. Break off. Either side."

Immediately they form two lines on both sides of us, keeping pace as we proceed along the wide walkways. Cassian falls in with Howl directly behind me and begins to converse with his leader.

Again, I catch my breath at the subtle beauty of the gardens around us. It's hard to imagine that Howl ordered any of this to be designed himself.

Carmen catches me gazing around. She whispers, "It's a replica of the Royal Palace. Howl destroyed the original palace when he seized power."

One of the guards gives her a sharp look and she stops speaking, keeping her eyes firmly forward and glazed over. In the absence of information from Carmen, I tune in to the conversation behind me.

Cassian says, "The Court is assembled as you ordered, King Howl."

"What about the Lightsworn Clan?"

"All there, including old Lightsworn Lance."

Howl says, "Good. What about the other Clans?"

"All represented. The Prime and Virtuous Clans were the most difficult, but they were open to… persuasion."

I wonder whether persuasion means bribes or, more likely, threats. Just like Carmen who won't look at her husband in case he's killed because of it.

Howl asks, "And what about the miners?"

"They were the easiest."

Howl sounds surprised. "Really?"

"We ordered them to stop digging for heartstones and offered them a proper meal, my King."

Howl grumbles, "A waste of good food."

Cassian clears his throat. "The stronger we keep them, the faster they dig. If you want to find more stones, you need to feed the miners more than gruel."

"Granted, that's true. They'll need more strength after today. Very well. One proper meal a day. But gruel for the other two meals."

With the number of times Howl makes me grind my teeth, I'm surprised I have any left. He starves his workers and rules through fear and subjugation. But what he says about the miners needing more strength after today worries me. If he's gathered all the Clans together, then he's clearly building up to some sort of announcement. It doesn't take much imagination to guess it has something to do with me.

We pass by a courtyard that looks directly west. I'm shocked to see that it faces the entrance to the springs. Sure, it's a thousand feet away, but I feel stupid that I ever thought I could get into this place undetected.

I stumble, the heels sliding out from under me, but a pair of wings slip around me, placing me firmly back on my feet. Howl's voice wraps around me. "Careful, Little Doll."

Stupid heels. I sigh with exasperation. Howl takes every opportunity to make contact. At least he doesn't allow the heartstone to touch me, which means he keeps himself just a little bit separate from the waist up. Even though his embrace this time is fleeting, it lasts too long.

As soon as he releases me, I continue walking, but I'm suddenly aware of a heavy silence behind me. Cassian has stopped talking. Howl clears his throat. I narrow my eyes as the silence stretches. *Has my skirt got stuck? Am I flashing my underwear at them? What on earth has shut them up?*

Cassian sounds hesitant. "My King, may I advise you—"

"No."

"But you—"

"I know. Don't worry. I have a solution."

Okay, that was cryptic. I decide I can't care about what they mean right now. An imposing building looms ahead of us—this must be the Crimson Court. Giant golden pillars support a scarlet roof. It's vast and wide, black flags fluttering from each high corner. A hum of voices emanates from it, and I guess it must be full of gargoyles.

I finally recognize the symbol on the flags—the same symbol that was scratched out of Llion's side: it's the silhouette of a shadow panther's head. It's etched in black with silver eyes and teeth and a claw next to its chin as if it's about to strike.

Howl's big paws slip around my waist again, pressing tightly. *What now? Surely he isn't going to starve me of oxygen again.*

There's a click. He leaves something cold around my waist. I jolt to a stop, staring at the metallic band he's locked around me. I twist for the first time, following the chain that links from the back of the waistband to his wrist. It's long enough to graze the ground, but won't let me move any further than a few steps away from him.

Anger flares. Lightning trickles across my palms. *He thinks he can chain me?* I can burn through this metal in seconds.

As soon as my power is visible, Howl leans into me, nuzzling my neck and inhaling. Tiny swirls of lightning leave my skin and dance across to him. My eyes widen as he literally inhales my power.

"Now you're ready to present to court," he says.

The moment he pulls back, I prepare to light up my shackles, but his big hand shoots out and grabs Carmen. She stifles a frightened shriek as he twists her arm, dragging her close and forcing her into an awkward half-crouched position. She tries to keep her balance while he squeezes her arm. He aims one of his deadly wing daggers right at her face.

Tears drip down her cheeks. Beside her, Gilda has frozen to the spot.

Howl barely looks at either of them. "Do as I say, Princess," he growls at me. "Or death will follow."

I squeeze my eyes shut. I swear I will end this man. I just… can't today. I fight my frustration as I open my eyes and nod. "That will be unnecessary."

"Good. Then keep your head down, eyes to the floor, and walk until I tell you to stop. No lightning. If you show your powers inside the Court, I will kill both women."

Unfortunately, I believe him. It's not an idle bluff. The sheer terror on Carmen's face tells me that. Howl doesn't want anyone to appear as powerful as him. If I show the gargoyles what I can do, Howl will punish the defenseless women.

Gilda grabs Carmen as Howl lets go, pulling her away from him and helping her back to her feet. Both of them give him a wide berth, practically brushing up against the guards who glare back at them. Of the two, I'd take my chances with the guards too.

I begin to walk as he ordered. Eyes cast down. One foot in front of the other. The chain pulls taut and only then does Howl walk with me, making it obvious that he controls me.

The guards fan out around us. Drums begin beating. In my head, the drums are Baelen's heartbeat. It's the only thing that keeps me moving.

16

MARBELLA

The drums don't stop until Howl takes his place on the throne. He tells me to stand on his left while he makes a show of resting his arm on the side of the enormous ornate chair, allowing the chain to dangle between us like a challenge.

As soon as we entered the Court, all talking stopped and silence descended. Which is why everyone hears him when he orders me to look up but to remain exactly where I stand.

Finally, I raise my eyes beyond the toes of my stupid heels. I find myself in an arena similar to the one I fought in during the marriage trials. Guards line each side and form a barrier at the back of the room. Their armor is decorated with the shadow panther crest, stylized black and silver.

There must be at least two hundred gargoyles crammed into the space, divided into segments, roughly identifiable by their different clothing and appearance. The front segments are clearly for the free gargoyles, given that they are clean and well-dressed in fine garments, while the back segments are filled with workers—slaves in navy vests and miners... Well, the miners are certainly interesting...

Yep, they're filthy. Even from this distance, I can see the dirt and dust coating their skin. But each one is large, imposing, and heavily muscled. They appear strong despite Howl's threats to starve them. In fact, a quick assessment of the miners compared to every other male gargoyle in this place tells me that Howl has chosen to send the strongest and biggest to the mines. They look more like they belong in an army than penned in together at the back of the room.

I appraise them and they stare right back at me, but I'm used to that. In Erawind, there were always elves peering at me and whispering as I passed by. The difference is that I was surrounded by my Storm Command. Jordan and Reisha, my Storm Commanders, always had my back, and my ladies were all taller than me, so more often than not, I couldn't see over their heads to notice the curious onlookers anyway.

What I'm more concerned about is what's behind me. The hairs on the back of my neck haven't stopped standing on end since I reached the stairs up to the dais I'm standing on.

I resist the urge to spin and see. Howl ordered me not to move and I don't want to risk triggering his rage by twisting to look around. He has deliberately placed Carmen and Gilda at the base of the dais, right where I can see the guards holding daggers to their backs. True to the rules, nobody else looks at them. I search the crowd in front of me for Jasper, clamping down on the worry rising inside me when I don't find him. I remind myself that the Storm is with him. Even if she can't do much to protect him, I have to believe that he's okay.

Howl leans back in his chair, taking his time to speak, exercising his control even in dragging out moments of silence at his whim.

"My people," he drawls, speaking to the crowd like he's a benevolent king and not a dictator. "I give you the elven Storm Princess." He doesn't bother looking my way as he gloats. "She is my prisoner."

If he expected applause, he must be disappointed. The crowd is completely silent as he rattles the chain between us. "Her power is no match for mine."

He stretches out a leg, making himself comfortable and seeming relaxed. "But her capture is not all we have to celebrate today."

He raises his free arm, signaling someone behind him. "Behold, my living statue."

There's a sliding sound, followed by the sound of flapping—is it cloth? Or maybe wings? I tense. I *need* to look around.

Howl grins at me, not budging from his seat. "And my phoenix."

He gloats up at me, daring me to disobey him. I fix my eyes firmly on his boots. Finally, he bounces out of his chair. "And the High Priestess."

He turns to survey his spoils, his wings half-spread, and I decide that's permission for me to shift so I can see.

My heart wrenches.

Set out in a row behind me, crimson sheets are swiftly pulled off three large cages. True to Howl's announcement, the first contains Baelen, the second cages the phoenix, and the third houses a petite woman I can only assume is the former High Priestess. Howl must know she isn't the High Priestess anymore, but if anyone else does, they aren't saying anything.

I hardly know where to look, especially when I see that Jasper stands beside the phoenix's cage, golden shackles like mine circling his wrists and ankles, connected by a chain that drops between his waist and feet. It's a clever design that will force him to walk at a shuffle.

"Oh, and another elf." Howl waves his hand dismissively at Jasper. Despite the way he ignores Jasper, Jasper's chains tell me Howl hasn't forgotten that he took down almost thirty warriors single-handedly. Howl isn't taking any chances with Jasper now.

To my relief, Jasper looks unharmed, dressed in clean clothing— a simple set of black pants and a shirt. Take away the chains and he might even look comfortable. If he's angry when his eyes land on me and quickly assess my own chains, he doesn't show it.

I'm also relieved to see the Storm, safe and well, gliding between the cages.

She gives me a nod as she considers Baelen. "He's okay," she whispers. Even though nobody can hear her, she must feel the weight of the heavy silence in the room the same way I do. "So is the phoenix. We're all okay."

"It's time to decide your fate, Princess."

My attention returns to Howl.

"The time has come for me to decide what to do with you." Howl resumes his seat and leans to one side, elbow on the arm of the throne, chin in his upturned hand, contemplating me. "I could hand you over to your people. I hear there is a country-wide search for you: a *storm*hunt so to speak."

When I left Erawind, all my friends and allies were forced into hiding. I'd sent them into the mountains behind Rath land hoping they would be safe there. I guess it was too much to hope that the Elven Command would just let me leave without searching for me.

Howl continues. "Your leaders are calling you a traitor. They say you murdered one of the Commanders."

Gideon Glory had used sorcery to create the curse that was intended to force Baelen to kill me. It was Gideon's sorcery that allowed the other Commanders to attack Baelen and nearly kill him. And yes, I'd killed Gideon, but in self-defense. However, the only elves who saw what really happened are now in hiding. I can only imagine the story the other Elven Commanders have come up with to brand me as a traitor and murderer.

"I also hear they are imprisoning elves who refuse to give up your whereabouts."

My stomach turns. I didn't think they'd go that far. Nobody knows where I am. I didn't tell anyone my plans. For my sake, that's a good thing, but not so much for anyone being imprisoned.

"But before I decide what to do with you, I want to know why you're really here."

Howl sounds almost reasonable but it's hard to breathe while I'm worried about my friends. I say, "I didn't come here to fight you, King Howl."

"Then why are you here, Little Doll?"

I consider my options. I could lie to him. Make something up. But that could land me in even hotter water. Baelen is safe right now. Safer than the rest of us. So, telling Howl the real reason we came to Erador doesn't feel like such a big risk.

I glance at the crowd, finding a woman in the first row whose gaze on me is so intense it's almost burning. Chestnut hair flows across her shoulders. Her eyes are green like new leaves—just like Llion described her. She must be his wife, Lightsworn Liliana. She looks desperate and I know how that feels. Her gaze keeps flicking between me and the former High Priestess. According to Talia, Howl intends to make Liliana his queen once the High Priestess gives him the mark of the lawful king. Liliana must believe that her freedom now is very limited.

The Priestess leans forward in her cage. She's slight and bony, but her wings are some of the most beautiful I've seen. A rainbow of colors shimmers through them as she moves close to the bars at the front of her cage. She has no power left—at least, not according to Talia—but her mouth moves and the hairs on the back of my neck shoot up again. Even without her power, her presence makes the air tingle. I read her lips. I'm sure she mouthed: *"Elyria."*

Strange. It was the first thing Talia said to me, too. "Elyria" is the Storm's name, but the High Priestess isn't looking anywhere near the Storm right now. She's looking right at me.

From the Priestess to Jasper, the phoenix, Baelen, Carmen, Gilda, and across to Liliana, I'm overwhelmed by how many lives hang in the balance around me at this very moment.

Which is why I can't try to spin a lie. Howl is like a spider waiting to trap me in the threads of my own making. If there's anything I can take away from the Priestess saying "Elyria," it's that I don't want to get caught in any web spun by Howl.

I say, "We came to heal our fallen warrior. The one you keep there." I point to Baelen. "If you allow us to access the deep springs, we will leave Erador as soon as he's healed. You need never see us again."

Howl appraises Baelen with new interest. "Why would you risk your life for this man? Who is he to you?"

"He is…" *My love. My heart. The other half of me.* "He is valuable to me and my race."

"Why?"

I clear my throat, taking a moment to think. "Are you familiar with the elven Houses, King Howl?"

"Of course." He waves his hand dismissively. "Glory, Valor, Elder." His lips twist as he peers at me. "And Mercy. I believe that is your House, Princess."

"Then you're also familiar with the House of Rath?"

Howl stiffens. His fists grip the armrest for a moment. "I thought that House was extinct."

"Almost," I acknowledge. "Baelen Rath is the last of his line. It would be a tragedy if his House perished with him."

"*This* is Baelen Rath?" Howl leaps to his feet, wings partially spread. He thuds over to Baelen, assessing his face and the open wounds in his armor. I'm forced to move with Howl since the chain isn't long enough for me to remain where I was.

I clatter across the dais in my heels. Being this close to Baelen is painful.

Being apart from him is painful.

No… Being close to Baelen is *more* painful than being apart. I feel like I'm being tossed around inside the Storm Vault again. The closer I am, the more the storm power within me reacts to his presence. There's a part of me that I have to shut off and shut down, and I have to do it fast. Otherwise my power is going to shine through whether I want it to or not, and that means bad things for Carmen and Gilda…

Luckily, Howl doesn't seem to notice. A deep crease settles on his forehead while he taps the heartstone at his chest. "Baelen Rath," he murmurs. "Here. Now. Right in front of me. And I can't kill him."

He curls one fist around a bar of the cage. It must be the hand that Baelen burned because it's blistered across the palm. Despite pawing at me earlier, Howl has kept that hand clenched in a fist. No doubt he wants to hide the damage.

I suck in a sharp breath as I realize he's staring at me now. His piercing eyes cut through me all of a sudden, his focus pinpointed, raking across me like blades. "I should have known. You would not wrap your power around anyone else."

He grabs my wrist and yanks me toward himself, hissing, "Careful, Princess, your storm is showing."

I may not be able to see myself, but I can sense it—a glow around my edges, a cool breeze that comes before a tornado. "I… need to… not be this close to Baelen…" Fear shoots through me, but so far Howl hasn't ordered Carmen or Gilda hurt, so I rush on. "I can't control it when I'm this close to him. I'm trying but I can't—"

"I see the thread," he says.

"What?"

"You've spun a thread from yourself to him. Like a little spider. You've wrapped it around him a hundred times. It connects you." Vehemence grows dark on his face, twisting his lips into a bitter line. "You think it's unbreakable, but I will sever it."

He lets go so abruptly that I stumble backward, but he very deliberately starts winding my chain around his burned hand, pulling me closer with every turn, until I'm forced to turn and stand with my back hard up against his side.

Jasper has clearly had enough and shuffles forward, pulling at his restraints, but Howl flings out his other hand, using his power to stop Jasper in his tracks. The Storm races to Jasper's side, alarmed, but there's nothing she can do.

Howl swivels to the crowd and raises his voice to an angry shout. "We have been digging for heartstones for the past five years! But only one has surfaced. Only one!"

At the back of the room, the miners remain silent, but a number of them shuffle where they stand.

"I have done everything to motivate you!" Howl roars, tugging the chain so tight that my midriff pulls upward. "I've taken your wives, put your children in orphanages, starved you, beaten you, cut off your wings. And yet you've only brought me one heartstone." He screams so loudly that he spits. "*One!*"

He wraps his free arm across my collarbone in a vise-like grip. "So now I'm going to do something new."

My heart thuds inside my chest. I tap into my power, trying to anticipate what Howl will do next in case I need to protect myself —or any one of the many vulnerable lives around me.

He roars at the silent onlookers. "Any gargoyle who finds a heartstone will win freedom for their loved one."

What? I didn't think the arena could get any quieter, but everything stops. Freezes. Then heads start turning. They're looking at each other, questioning. Like me, they must be wondering if they heard that right.

"There are twenty-seven more hearts!" Howl shouts, his mouth so close to my ear that the volume makes me wince. "That means there are twenty-seven chances to get back what you want."

His math is wrong. The Storm said there were thirty gargoyle heartstones and Howl only has one—that should leave twenty-nine.

I don't think about it any further, though, because he leans down to me, whispering into my ear. "You too, Princess. If you want your precious Baelen Rath back, you will find me a heartstone."

"Wh-what?"

I try to pull away, catching his grin before he yanks me close again. His smile reminds me of a jackal that just ripped out my heart and is about to swallow it down.

"You're going to the mines," he says.

17

MARBELLA

Everyone waits for Howl to descend from the dais—and me with him. He does everything except throw me over his shoulder, curling one large arm around my waist and dragging me along the pathway so I stumble down the center of the crowd, barely able to keep my feet on the ground.

As soon as we pass Carmen and Gilda and they aren't in his line of sight anymore, I elbow Howl as hard as I can in the ribs. "Stop dragging me! I won't fight you."

"But I'm having so much fun making you bump up against me."

Ugh. Seriously? "In front of your future bride?"

Howl pulls up short as we draw parallel with the Lightsworn Clan. It's easy to pick the patriarch, Lightsworn Lance, whom Cassian mentioned earlier. His skin is pale grey, fragile in appearance. He looks almost a hundred years old, but he displays the same bright-eyed depth of intelligence that Liliana does. The entire Clan is observing Howl's display with barely disguised disgust. I'm not sure if that's because they're offended or because they disapprove of the way he's treating me.

Howl seems thrown for the first time, which surprises me. He glances between me and the crowd, heaving me up against his side.

Rather than loosening his grip, he plasters me closer; one arm wedged against my back so the heartstone doesn't touch me, while his other arm presses inward across my collarbone in a painful opposing force. His left wing curls around me like a curtain hiding me from view.

I turn my head away from the green veins crisscrossing the inside of his wing as Cassian pulls up on Howl's other side. There's enough of a gap for me to see him. Jasper and two guards are close behind Cassian. Jasper glares at the way Howl's holding me, but as soon as he attempts to shuffle closer, one of the guards yanks him backward.

Cassian takes one look at Howl and immediately holds out his hand for my chain. Despite the urgency of his movement, his voice remains moderated and calm, even if it sounds forced. "If I may, King Howl? I can take the Princess from here."

Howl doesn't respond. If anything, he pulls me closer. I wince as his fist presses into my spine, forcing me to arch backward. It's as painful as a vise and I'm suddenly afraid my spine might snap. I try to take calming breaths as Cassian shoots alarmed looks at Howl.

"You have a solution, my King. Now you need to carry through with it." His jaw clenches. "Before anyone notices."

Their earlier cryptic conversation returns to me. A solution to what exactly? Dealing with me? Finding more heartstones?

Cassian makes a more forceful move toward my chain, and I hope Howl will release me because the pain shooting through my back is growing stronger.

In response, the King growls deep in his throat, a threatening sound. His right wing dagger descends toward Cassian, and his left wing extends the remainder of the way around me, like he's an animal that doesn't want to share its food. For a second, I think he's going to take Cassian's head off.

Cassian freezes, slowly lowering his hand and taking a careful step backward.

I crane my head back, trying to see Howl's face and figure out what's going on with him. His pupils are fully dilated. Light flickers across his neck. I can't see the heartstone, but the light is definitely shining upward from that. To my shock, Howl's face has descended in my direction far closer than I expected. I'm suddenly reminded of the way he absorbed the thunder last night, pulling it into himself, the way he inhaled my lightning and picked me up when I was about to trip, touching me at every opportunity, pulling me close to him at every chance he gets. He told me that my magic was intoxicating and now he's acting almost… possessive.

My eyes turn into saucers. The idea of Howl being possessive over me is terrifying. He told me he was sending me to the mines, but now it looks like he's changed his mind. Of the two options, I'd rather be as far away from him as possible. Especially because the pain in my back is only growing worse. Much worse. Too much.

I swallow a whimper. "Please… you're… hurting me."

The pressure on my chest eases so suddenly that I lurch forward into his now open palm. He catches me, the fingers of his right hand splayed across my stomach. The fist he held clenched against my spine opens at the same time, removing the painful force against my back. I'm suddenly resting on my two feet and not sure how I got there.

His wing doesn't open, but his hold has loosened enough that I can spin and face him. "You let go."

His eyes narrow, resembling slits of midnight. I sense a pull, but it's not his arms or hands. His lips part. At first, I think he's going to speak, but instead, he inhales. It's only then that I realize I'm glowing at the edges. I must have been accessing my power to deal with the pain.

Howl sucks in the glow around me, pulling it off my skin.

If my eyes were saucers before, then now they must be plates because the way he's reacting to my power… The way he let me go…

I can't see around the curtain of his wing, but I can see Cassian standing directly beside us where Howl's wing doesn't quite connect with his chest. He looks genuinely worried and the reason for his worry is slowly dawning on me.

"King Howl," I whisper, allowing the faintest glow of lightning to shimmer across my skin, watching him react to it. "Please remove my chain."

He lowers his hands. The metal band around my waist opens with a click at his touch. The chain slithers to the floor.

Now I know why Howl didn't want me showing my power here: he didn't want anyone to see how he reacts to it. Or that I might be able to use it against him.

I don't know how far I can go, but I'm going to try. I need to get away from here and take Baelen, Jasper, the Storm, and the phoenix with me. I reach up on tip-toes and plant both my hands on Howl's chest, either side of the heartstone. Allowing tiny pulses of lightning to travel through my hands, I feed magic straight into him and whisper, keeping my voice as low as I can so nobody else can hear me. "Release Jasper from his chains."

Howl's eyes meet mine, jet black. He looks completely gone as he lifts his head and orders the guards, "Release the male elf."

Through the slit between Howl's wing and chest, I catch glimpses of Cassian with Jasper's guards. They exchange glances as they bring Jasper forward and remove his chains, scooping up the metal loops. I can't see Jasper's face to know how he's reacting, but I'm sure he'll be suspicious. And probably worried, since he can't see me and I've been in here for a full minute.

I know I'm probably pushing it too far, but it's now or never. "Give me back Baelen. Let us go free."

Firelight flickers across Howl's eyes—lightning sparks that are evidence of an internal war. He doesn't want to let me go. I'm feeding him the magic he wants and now I'm asking him to part with me. I don't dare break the contact between us until he agrees to what I want. Even then, I'm not sure he won't retract his orders as soon as I leave his side.

I try again. "King Howl, let us go."

He growls. "I will…"

"Let me go."

He grins. "I will… never release you, Little Doll."

Disappointment burns through me. But I'm certain he wasn't

toying with me the whole time. The worry on Cassian's face tells me that.

Howl's wing opens, allowing me to step backward. He continues to grin at me, his expression turning lazy and confident. Despair fills me as he draws up to his full height, taking back his power over the situation.

I glance at the silent crowd. Howl's wing was around me the whole time. For all they know, he was torturing me for the last five minutes. I swallow down my bitter disappointment. Every time I think I can beat this man, he turns the situation around and gets the upper hand.

I stare past his right shoulder, waiting for his next order. Baelen is in my line of sight, and it horrifies me that I want to cry right now.

Then something moves in the distance above Baelen. I try not to react as a grey form unravels from one of the flags. It's a… flying thing. A streak of movement. A… male gargoyle. And it's suddenly speeding toward Howl.

It's Llion! I bury my reaction before I give him away as he soars directly toward Howl's exposed back, disappearing from sight as he flies right up behind the King's bulky form.

Howl continues grinning at me. "Well, Princess, to the mines you go. But don't think you won't see me again because I promise you—"

I lurch backward as two sword points shoot through Howl's chest, impaling him all the way through.

He roars and spins, the swords still embedded in his torso. His wings knock me to the side, his wing daggers sweeping around in an arc. Llion uses his powerful wings to push himself back and safely out of reach.

Howl curses. "Llion! You were supposed to be dead."

Without a word, Llion launches himself at Howl, his golden dagger flashing. It's the dagger that can cut through a gargoyle's wings.

I hit the ground at the same time that Cassian shouts for the guards. I roll backward and up to my feet, screaming, "Jasper! Storm!"

I shoot lightning into the nearest guard and wrench his sword right out of his hands before he hits the floor. Jasper deftly catches the sword when I throw it at him and spins to deflect the two attacking guards behind him.

Oddly enough, it's not the burst of lightning, but the thuds from when the guards hit the floor that sends the crowd into panic mode. They scramble backward, away from the fight. Women in the Lightsworn Clan grab Liliana, but she refuses to budge, curling down into a ball as gargoyles all around her take flight in a swarm.

"Llion!" Her scream is swallowed by the roar of the guards and Cassian's shout to let the crowd go.

"Get everyone out of here!" Cassian shouts as he spins back to the fight between Howl and Llion. I'm sure he's not worried about the crowd's safety—the grim determination on his face tells me he doesn't want anyone getting ideas about joining us in our fight against Howl.

Well, at least I can do something about Cassian. I shoot lightning at his feet before he can help Howl.

"Get back!" I scream at Cassian. I may not be able to stop Howl, but I can stop anyone trying to hurt Llion.

To the side, Liliana stays low, avoiding the final attempts of another woman to pull her out of here. "Liliana, you need to escape!"

"I'm staying with my husband!"

The woman flies away with a final worried glance. Within seconds, the entire congregation has taken flight and it suddenly makes sense why Crimson Court is open on three sides—fly in, fly out. I'm glad to see that Carmen and Gilda have also fled.

At the back of the room, the miners are the last to leave. The woman who tried to take Liliana with her shrieks over their heads. "Help Llion!"

For a moment, I think the miners are going to stay. For an even crazier second, I think they're going to start fighting the guards. One of them—a gargoyle with pale blue streaks in his wings, shouts to the others. But then the guards lining the back of the room turn and draw their bows and arrows. Suddenly all of the remaining guards are focused on the miners.

After a brief argument with the gargoyle beside him, the one with blue wings lowers his hands, head bowed. Even from this distance, I can see the clench of his jaw and the snarl on his lips. He inclines his head to the others, and, as one mass, they spread their wings and take flight, a formation soaring out and away.

Jasper, Liliana, and I are now the only ones remaining.

The guards form two wide circles around us: the outer circle faces outward against anyone who decides to come to our aid. The inner circle focuses on us.

Jasper and I take on the role of defense for Llion, stopping any guard who makes a move to tip the balance in Howl's favor. When one of them fires an arrow at Llion, I shoot the weapon out of the air, lightning crackling in the space above Howl's head.

Jasper takes up position on the opposite side and takes a less forgiving approach. He quickly dispatches two guards who try to enter the battle. Then another two, stabbing both and whirling to behead a third with such speed that the remaining guards back away, giving Jasper space.

I know that I could probably annihilate all of the guards if I need to, but Jasper's safety is at the forefront of my mind: I don't want him to get caught in the crossfire. I also don't know whether the guards have been coerced into serving Howl. I can't assume that they all want to be here.

In the center of the Court, Howl and Llion are—to my surprise—evenly matched. I'd thought Howl would crush Llion within moments, but Llion is deft and wields his weapons with an expertise I've rarely seen. I'm even more relieved now that I didn't see the fight between him and Baelen, or my heart would have been in my throat. It's more surprising to me than ever that I escaped this gargoyle's wrath.

Llion uses every part of his body as a weapon. From his clawed feet to his wing daggers, not to mention his gold-plated knife. Howl, on the other hand, relies on brute strength and bulk to try to overpower Llion, trying to turn Llion into a punching bag. But the more Llion evades him, the angrier he becomes.

Not to mention… Howl hasn't bothered to remove the swords from his chest and the constant energy he must be using to keep healing seems to be taking a toll. His movements are slowing. The next swipe he takes at Llion sails across Llion's head without touching him. He roars his frustration when Llion's dagger rips through his left wing, shredding it right down the middle.

"You think you can beat me," Howl roars, folding his wounded wing into his side. "You will burn, cousin."

Howl's right. Llion is an incredibly skilled fighter, but with the heartstone… Howl is indestructible. I sense the crackle in the air as Howl finally harnesses the stone's power. It doesn't matter how well Llion fights, Howl will always win.

As the two men circle each other, Llion takes a final plunge at Howl, aiming the knife at the heartstone itself. My heart leaps as I hope that the shimmer beetle casing—the most indestructible substance in our world—might actually damage the stone. A glimmer of worry crosses Howl's face, but the knife glances off the stone, tearing up and through Howl's shoulder instead. The knife lodges in his upper wing bone and sticks there. Llion skids to a halt several steps away from me and for the first time, dismay floods his features.

Howl's energy crackles around us as he turns. Streaks of electricity gather force around his torso and within his hands. He launches himself at Llion, palms out, ready to unleash a killing blow.

Llion reaches for his sword, still crouched, but Howl bats it out of his hand, gripping Llion's throat and squeezing. Electricity rockets through his arm, through his hand…

"No!" Liliana's scream echoes in my ears.

At the same time, Jasper runs at Howl, leaping toward his back. But it's a death plunge. As soon as he touches Howl, he'll be killed too.

Panic shoots through me, sharp and quick. Llion is choking,

Jasper is leaping to his death, and Howl still hasn't pulled the swords out of his chest, and suddenly…

He isn't Howl anymore.

His image morphs.

Suddenly all I see is Baelen in gargoyle form moments after the Elven Command stabbed him in the back.

Pain explodes in my heart. Blood rushes in my ears. A scream works its way out of my lungs, up into my mouth. "Baelen!"

A *boom* rocks the building.

Thunder crashes out from me, thudding through the entire space. The ceiling shudders and the supports tremble. Howl's head snaps up, focusing on me as everything slows and freezes.

Jasper stops, one foot already in the air, one still planted as he was about to launch off the ground. Cassian and the guards become statues in various stages of motion, some leering, others… to my surprise… turning their faces away as if they don't want to watch Llion die.

The Storm remains crouched next to the High Priestess's cage. She alone is moving while the older woman is frozen; the High Priestess points through the bars at me, or maybe at Howl, I can't tell which. Her mouth is open like she was shouting something, but I didn't hear her before she froze.

Howl's movements become labored, struggling, slowing. There's a moment of disbelief on his face before he slows to moving inches at a time.

I can't believe it. The thunder is working. I've actually slowed him down this time. But I haven't completely stopped him. I need to move fast—get Llion and Jasper out of here—before everything returns to normal speed. Which is happening faster than I want it to. Howl curls upward, regaining his feet, fighting the power, but instead of turning his fury on me, he pushes toward Baelen instead.

Suddenly, I'm the one who's frozen.

I realize why my power is working against Howl this time.

I see the thread Howl was talking about now—a thin, sapphire line of light connecting Baelen and me. A line of ruby light is entwined around the sapphire thread. Droplets of acid rain rise up from both of them, ascending into the air above the thread. It's just like when I was riding the phoenix.

I've connected with Baelen.

In the distance, Baelen twitches. One hand clenches at his side. It's a small movement but visible from where I stand.

He's waking up.

18

BAELEN

Rain drips down my hair and chest as I wait for Marbella to call my name. Blood-tainted water trickles down the sword I hold in my hands. The weapon remains partially formed, wild grass resting against its transparent blade.

I'm not tired. I never get hungry. I don't need to sleep.

I take one breath at a time, waiting to hear her voice.

Baelen!

My heart thuds to hear her scream. The connection between us tugs sharply, pulling me forward. For the first time since I entered this place, I take a step.

Power spears out from me. The sword's handle solidifies as I lift it from the ground, but it won't let me move beyond a single step.

A *boom* shudders through the field as I drive the sword's tip back into the earth. Thunder storms out from my location, rippling across the field. Lightning dances across the air, lighting up the sapphire thread between Marbella and me, the thin line that lets me hear her thoughts, know her fears.

She's terrified, her fear magnifying mine.

I reach out through the connection, seeking her voice.

Marbella, you're in trouble. What's wrong?

With a roar, I wrench the sword from the ground, the upper

portion of its blade turning into gleaming steel even though the tip remains translucent. I take another step, power thudding through me as I drive the sword back into the earth, one step closer to her. I will get to her, even if every step hurts.

Her scream makes me jolt. *Baelen, stop! You aren't healed. Don't come out or you'll die.*

I pause, confused. *But I feel stronger...*

That's because we're connected. Don't come back! Please, Baelen. Whatever you do. Don't come back until I ask you to.

I try to lift the sword again, but this time it's heavy, gripping the earth as if its tip has turned into a claw. It won't let me move.

Confused, I say, *You called me.*

She gasps. Sobs. The connection between us brightens, tugging at me, pulling at my chest, even though my legs can't move. I grip the sword tighter, pulling with all my strength, needing to go to her.

At the same time, a force I didn't anticipate washes across me, a powerful gale spinning around me, pinning me to the spot, forcing me to remain where I am.

I shudder as I realize she's pushing me away.

Her voice is broken and I don't know why. *Baelen, I love you.*

Marbella, let me help you.

She is bleak. *I won't let you die.*

I don't know what she's facing, what has hurt her, and she won't let me help. The wind—her power—grows stronger, dragging on my armor as it presses down on my shoulders, forcing my feet farther into the ground, forcing me to remain still.

Despite the ferocious force pinning me to the spot, the connection between us is so bright, I have to close my eyes.

How can I feel like she's right beside me, wanting me, and at the same time she's pushing me away with all her might?

All rational thought leaves my mind. I fight her as hard as I can. *Marbella! Let me help you!*

A golden light flashes.

She screams through our connection, her pain crashing over

me. It becomes my pain, ripping through my heart, shredding me into pieces.

The wind drops. There's a moment of silence and then—

The field explodes into thunder and lightning that tears through the grass, scorching the earth around my feet, the full fury of the Storm wailing around me.

I roar into the maelstrom. *Marbella!*

But this time, she doesn't answer.

19

———

MARBELLA

Baelen's voice sounds inside my mind, the connection so strong he could be standing beside me. *Marbella, you're in trouble. What's wrong?*

I shout so loudly inside my head that I slap my hands across my ears before I scream myself deaf. *Baelen, stop! You aren't healed. Don't come out or you'll die.*

There's a pause, confusion in his voice. *But I feel stronger...*

That's because we're connected. But that was a mistake. This is a mistake.

Somehow, I flashed back to the moment when Baelen died. The pain I felt was so strong, the memory of him was so strong, that I connected with him again without intending to.

Don't come back! Please, Baelen. Whatever you do. Don't come back until I ask you to.

But you did ask me. You called me.

Tears leak down my cheeks. I had called him. I'd shouted his name. I suddenly realize I've closed my eyes while Baelen and I were speaking, and I have to open them because I sense...

Howl.

Every laborious step he's taken has brought him within two

154

steps of me. His hands are outstretched and he's reaching, reaching for me and my power.

His lips move, the intense need in his eyes burning through me. "So. Much. Power."

I have to stop what's happening. I can't let Howl inhale our connected power like he did with mine earlier. I can't let him touch me. And not only because the thought of him touching the connection between Baelen and me fills me with horror and disgust and… just no.

There's a flicker of movement over Howl's shoulder. The Storm is shouting, but until this moment, I couldn't hear her. The connection with Baelen is so strong it blocked everything out except for what's right in front of me. She's pointing, finger jabbing in the same direction that the High Priestess is pointing.

Howl takes another step.

"Knife!" the Storm screams, pointing at his shoulder.

Llion's gold-plated knife is still embedded in the bone at the top of Howl's wing. Just like the swords in his chest, he hasn't taken the time to remove it.

It's a knife that can cut through anything.

My heart bleeds. *Baelen, I love you.*

Marbella, let me help you.

I know he could. Together, we could end Howl. Howl already told me that our power combined would be formidable. But it would only lead to Baelen's death. He wouldn't survive long enough to be healed. When he froze himself, he was literally seconds away from death.

I shake my head. *I won't let you die.*

Howl bends, crouching to my height, slowly, painstakingly pushing against the power that wants to pin him in place. I take two steps back for a run-up and then launch myself, feet first, into his chest. The blessed heels pierce his skin before I knock him backward. He has no control over his fall—all of his energy has been used to push toward me. He lands with a thud. I leave the heels embedded in his chest with the swords, race the two steps it takes me to run across his chest to his wing, bend, and wrench the knife out of him.

I keep running, plowing into Jasper to wake him up and knock him off course. He had been aiming for Howl's back when Howl was leaning over Llion. I don't want Jasper to end up plunging his sword into Llion instead.

"Marbella!"

"No time. I'm sorry."

I'm really sorry. I arc around, skirting around Howl who is regaining his feet, and head for a clear patch of floor where I can't be interrupted for a few precious seconds.

I stop, my heart pounding, banging in my chest so hard it's going to burst out of me. The thread between Baelen and I glows bright. Carefully, I take hold of it in my left hand, pulling it taut. It's attached to my heart, and what I'm about to do is going to cut my heart out.

Howl is already thudding up behind me, throwing the heels to the side and reaching back to wrench the swords out. He's speeding up. I don't have long.

With a scream, I run the knife through the thread.

The connection severs, pain screams through me, and droplets of acid rain splatter the floor. The knife shatters as it passes through the thread, spraying golden shells around me. A confetti of gold and ruby rains down around me--shattered pieces like my heart.

Everything snaps into motion before the shards hit the floor. I slump forward and Howl slams into me, wrapping one arm around my waist, keeping another over the heartstone—his standard approach for making sure I don't touch it. As he wrenches us both to a halt, his heartbeat drums so loudly that I can hear it from several inches away. He must have really been exerting himself to move toward me before.

My knees buckle. I push against his wings as they threaten to envelop me, forcing them apart long enough to see that Baelen is completely stationary again. The Storm rushes to him, sweeps her hand through the bars of his cage, and places her palm against his chest. She gives me a single, grim nod. He's going to be okay.

I stop fighting Howl, but to my relief, he doesn't close his wings around me like before.

"You severed your own connection." His condemning statement sounds far away and tinny. His voice becomes an angry growl in my ear. "You gave him all your power."

In the distance, the Storm suddenly lurches away from Baelen, causing my heart to go into panic mode. Was she mistaken? Is he dead? She spins in a tornado of movement and races toward me, panic-stricken, but halfway to me she jolts backward as if she has slammed into a wall. She rebounds toward Baelen like there's a rope attached to her spine and somebody just gave it a savage tug.

"Princess, I'm not bound to you anymore," she cries. "I'm bound to Baelen! I'm… stuck here."

I stare at her, stricken silent. I hardly know how to process what I've done. I wanted to stop Baelen waking up, but somehow, I've severed my connection with him and the Storm altogether. On top of that, if Howl is to be believed, I've given the last remnants of my power to Baelen. He holds it all now. And that means…

I don't even know what that means…

Howl wrenches me around so I'm facing him, both of his hands planted around my waist, squeezing. His nostrils flare and his mouth twists into a dangerous line. He shakes me so hard that my insides rattle. "You gave him all your power!"

There's a dark cavity inside my heart where my storm power used to be—where Baelen used to be. I think I must be numb or in shock. My body needs to sink, to connect with the floor. I wouldn't even be standing if it wasn't for Howl's steely grip.

I tip my head back, unable to connect with my limbs or my spine to keep myself straight. My hair has come loose and it cascades down my back, not quite as red as the Court, but bloody enough. I whisper, "I'm sorry to disappoint you."

He raises his open palm, a slap moments away from landing, when a female voice shouts, "Leave her be."

Howl spins to Liliana who has got ahold of a sword and clearly knows how to handle it, gripping it with two hands around the hilt, the tip pointed squarely between his sternum and his throat. "Your mistreatment of the Elven Princess has gone far enough, King Howl."

He cocks an eyebrow at her. "A gargoyle trying to help an elf. How unexpected." He rattles me again. "And you, *Princess*." He spits my title like it's something caught between his teeth. "You put yourself in harm's way for a gargoyle. One from the Grievous Clan, no less."

He spins me so I face Llion who stands in a clear patch of floor with Jasper beside him, the guards giving them both a wide berth for the moment.

"Grievous Llion, my cousin," Howl says, "I should cut off your wings and make you a slave. But that would mean keeping you around. On the other hand, killing you will be much too easy."

Liliana follows Howl's movements with her sword, but I sense her desperation when she looks at Llion. They haven't had a chance to reunite or reconnect. She won't know what happened to her children or where they are. She might not even know that Llion thought she was dead. She must be very practiced at keeping her emotions tucked away because, other than the first flicker of worry, she betrays nothing more than a determination to strike Howl if she has to.

Not that it would do much good.

"Let's see how long your loyalty lasts in the mines," Howl says, shoving me at Cassian. "Get them out of my sight!"

I swing inside a woven crate, the afternoon sunlight slanting through the gaps to warm my toes. I'm still wearing the dress with the ridiculous slit up the back, my knees held to my chest, curled up inside the container. When I grip the woven bars, my hands come away coated in flour. Apparently, they used these crates to transport food to the mines.

I'm a different kind of cargo.

In fact, I'm not entirely sure what I am anymore.

The Storm's panicked wail returns to me, her cry echoing in my ears. Storm clouds had gathered over Crimson Court as the guards dragged us away, but somehow Jasper had calmed her down. "We'll be okay," he'd shouted back to her.

"I'm scared, Jasper! You told me to tell you when I'm scared. Well, it's now."

"You'll be safe," he'd called, not even trying to pretend he was talking to me, although that's probably what the guards thought. "Watch over Baelen. That's your job now."

"Watch Baelen," she had whimpered, sinking to her knees beside his cage. "I'll stay and watch Baelen. Please be safe Jasper…"

Now, I peer through the gaps, trying to see the crate carrying Jasper and the one carrying Llion. Cassian's clawed feet are all I can see above me—he's the one transporting my crate—while flickers of color between sunlight tell me that there's a crate to my right and one further behind.

The trip takes less than an hour. Cassian said something about taking us to the western mine. The crate bumps to a stop and the lock at the side clicks open. I'm pretty sure they don't usually chain up their vegetables.

"Out." Cassian's brilliant sapphire eyes appear as the hatch opens and I scramble out on my hands and knees, preferring to go head-first than to shimmy out in this dress. "Watch your step," he says as he saunters away to the other crates.

Jasper and Llion both squeeze out of the baskets to my right.

A gust of wind hits me, whipping my hair around my face. We've landed on the uppermost peak of a mountain made primarily of rust-colored rock, bringing to mind an angry volcano.

A group of over twenty miners perches opposite us. They are all bare to the waist, their chests smudged with dust. I recognize the one with the blue streaks in his wings as well as the smaller, wiry one who had stood beside him back at the Court. If I thought they looked imposing from a distance, I have good reason to keep my distance now that they're up close. They're massive like Llion. Some of them give Llion a quick nod, acknowledging his presence, but none of them look happy to see Jasper or me.

The guards seem content to let us move around. They all carry long whips with black tips, curled up and attached to their belts. I eye this new weapon cautiously, but the guards don't try to stop Jasper or Llion when they position themselves on either side of me. I'm glad for their solidarity. As a bare-foot elf in a pretty dress and without any power, I know I'm in for a tough time.

"You okay, Marbella?" Jasper asks, to which I give him a quick nod.

"Thank you for saving my life, Lady Storm," Llion murmurs at my side. But when I raise my eyes to his, I catch a sudden confusion in the tilt of his head. As he leans down to me, I sense his short inhalation of breath and the deep thought in his eyes. Funny, I always thought his eyes were gray with gold flecks, but as he assesses me, I see that they're actually mostly golden.

"I know," I whisper when his confusion deepens. "I am not clouds and ice anymore."

"No, you are not." He leans in a little more, one hand reaching for my cheek. "You sacrificed much for my life."

His large hand is warm and surprisingly soft cupping my cheek. It's such a simple gesture, but it brings a burn of tears to the back of my eyes.

I say, "I'm sorry I broke your knife."

"That was for the best. I truly hoped it would be strong enough to shatter the heartstone, but it could only be used for evil if Howl got his hands on it."

He draws his palm across my cheek, the curious crease never leaving his forehead.

I ask, "What is it?"

He gives a small shake of his head. "Now that the storm is gone from you… I sense something else…"

Cassian's approach from across the clearing interrupts us. He and the guards have finished rounding up the miners into lines.

"Welcome to Mount Prime," he says, before turning his attention back to the miners. "Listen up, you no-clan filth!"

He paces across the space between us and them. "The rules have changed. From now on, you will dig in teams. Of which there will be five. That means…" He pauses and it seems to be for effect, although I'm not sure why. "There will be one team for each tunnel."

For some reason, that causes a big stir. The miners erupt, not quite into shouts, but definitely in unhappy disagreement with what Cassian just said. I eye them warily, trying to figure out why having one team for each tunnel would be a problem.

Cassian's sharp eye has them settling quickly. "Each week, you will fight to determine which team mines which tunnel. The winner will choose the tunnel they mine that week. But of course, as our generous King has decreed, any miner who finds a heartstone will get back what he… or she… wants."

He shouts five names, and five gargoyles step forward. They size each other up for a moment. One of them is the gargoyle with the blue wings.

Cassian addresses him first. "No-clan Roar, pick your first team member."

The gargoyle called Roar immediately claps his hand on the shoulder of the wiry gargoyle standing a step behind him. "I choose Iago."

Cassian moves on to the next team leader and it doesn't take a genius to figure out how this will go. Nobody will want me on their team. They will probably tolerate Jasper—even without wings, he's visibly strong, muscled, whereas I'm a tiny woman without wings. The fifth team leader glares at me with distaste. As the last to pick each time, he's going to be burdened with me.

The first picks are over and it's back to Roar for his second pick.

"I choose Llion," he says.

There's a stir among the others, but Roar growls at them. "What? Have you forgotten who this gargoyle is? I'm happy none of you picked him already."

A shadow of a smile passes across Llion's face as the others shuffle and murmur. Llion acknowledges Roar with a short nod, but his next statement causes an even bigger commotion. "With respect, Sunflight Roar, if you choose me, you must choose the Lady Storm next. Otherwise, I will be no help to you."

Roar is taken aback, glancing harshly between Llion and me. "You mean you wouldn't dig?"

"That is correct," Llion says. "No matter what punishment comes my way."

Cassian has stopped pacing and seems dangerously amused, rather than annoyed, at Llion's statement.

Roar asks, "Not even for the chance to free Lightsworn Liliana?"

"My fate is bound to the Storm Princess," Llion says, any hint of softness disappearing from his features. "My wife understands the debt I owe."

I consider his statement, remembering the way Liliana had attempted to defend me after I severed my connection with Baelen. It drives the fact home to me that the gargoyles have a whole culture that I know nothing about. Elven culture doesn't include the concept of a life debt, but maybe gargoyle society does. Even if it does, I'm not sure that Llion owes me such a debt. I stopped Howl from killing him, but it was as much about self-preservation as helping Llion. On top of that, Llion helped us at the border. Not to mention, he spared my life on Scepter Peak during the trials. On balance, I might owe him a debt and not the other way around.

Roar grits his teeth, the muscles in his jaw ticking. He sizes me up, looking me up and down. He must be trying to decide if I'm worth the risk. I've been underestimated enough times by enough men that I glare right back at him. If Baelen were here, he'd shake his head at the lot of them.

I catch Jasper's eye and have a very strong sense he's trying not to roll his eyes at the other men right now. There's a reason I made it to the final fight in my marriage trials and it has nothing to do with how tall I am.

"Very well," Roar says. "I'll choose the Princess next."

"Thank you, Sunflight Roar," Llion says. "You won't regret it."

"That's *no-clan* Roar," Cassian growls, finally deciding it's time to get in Llion's face. "Remember you have no clan here. I won't remind you again."

"Understood, General Cassian," Llion says, without giving any ground.

Cassian huffs and resumes his former position. The next team leader taps his fist against his thigh in thought, pausing before making a decision. He's an older man with a number of pale grey scars of varying lengths crossing his chest, and when he moves, his wings seem to follow the angles of his body. Right now, he leans forward a little, wing daggers slightly lowered, contemplating the waiting gargoyles as well as Jasper and me.

"I'll take the male elf," he says.

The team member he already chose startles beside him. "What are you doing, Badenoch?"

Badenoch inclines his head at Jasper. "That elf killed a legion of Howl's soldiers on Mount Erador. Everyone at Court was talking about it. If we're going to fight for tunnels, I want him on my team."

The team member glances around, his gaze becoming increasingly nervous as he checks out Roar and Llion who are now on the same team. "Yeah… okay."

Jasper takes his cue from Llion and even though he acknowledges Badenoch's choice, he remains at my side for now.

The choosing continues and when the choice returns to Roar, he's true to his word and picks me. I'm glad to be in a team with Llion, but worried about being separated from Jasper. There are many things Jasper knows that Llion doesn't, and I'm not sure how easy it will be to communicate with Jasper if the teams are pitted against each other. We're bound to be completely separated. I'm going to need Jasper's help if we're ever getting out of here.

In the end, there are four teams with five members and one team has six, but Cassian puts an end to any complaints about the uneven numbers with the command that the remaining gargoyle joins the fifth team instead of Roar's.

Jasper leans across me to draw Llion closer. "I don't know what Cassian has planned for these fights, but the other teams will target Marbella if they have the chance. They'll see her as a weak link and go after her. You'll need to watch your back and hers." His expression changes and his tone takes on a derisive edge. "Of course, they don't know how wrong they are."

I've never seen Jasper almost-smile as often as he has since we crossed the border, but there's another one when he looks at me right now. His mouth doesn't quite curve up, not quite a smile, but his eyes light up in a way that tells me that the day Jasper chooses to smile for real, it will be dazzling.

"You can use their misconception to your advantage. They'll underestimate you, Marbella," Jasper says before Cassian shouts for everyone to enter the mine. "I'll do what I can to make sure my team doesn't try any tricks."

As much as Jasper's faith in me bolsters my confidence, I can't deny that I'm worried. I don't have my power to fall back on, and Roar definitely doesn't want me on his team. As Jasper splits off, and Llion and I join Team Roar, I'm more than a little concerned that a threat might come from within my own team.

20

MARBELLA

We descend into the mine through a vertical shaft. It's wide enough that the gargoyles simply soar down. A metal ladder is attached to the side of it, which Cassian explains is for any gargoyle with a broken wing. Apparently, there are a lot of awful things that can happen in a mine: crushed limbs, toxic fume inhalation, collapsed tunnels that trap gargoyles until they starve––pretty much every gruesome death imaginable.

I'm still uncertain about why the miners seemed so unhappy about having a team for each tunnel, but I'm guessing I'll find out soon enough.

It's a long way down and by the time we reach the bottom of the shaft, my arms and legs are shaking from the effort. I'm grateful to find that we've entered an open area with two ramps: one heading down into the mine and the other heading up. One of the guards operates a pulley system and an empty minecart approaches along the tracks on the side heading up. The minecart halts in front of us and Cassian orders me to get in. The other miners have long since disappeared, so it's just Jasper, Llion, and me along with Cassian and the five remaining guards.

Once inside, the minecart speeds down the ramp far below the surface. I've spent enough time in the oppressive Storm Vault not to get freaked out by the weight of rock above us, but as glowing spider webs replace the last rays of natural light, my eyes take time to adjust to the new dark and the distance to the surface grows more oppressive.

I try to keep my mind clear by focusing on the seemingly endless rust-colored rock. It alternates between dark red and brown where the blue light from the webs mixes with the orange tones of the rocks around us.

Finally, Cassian applies the brakes, and the cart exits into a large, open area containing a number of structures that have been carved out of the mountain itself, jutting buildings transitioning seamlessly into the side of the enormous cave. It's hundreds of feet wide and deep. The ceiling soars far above us and is covered in webs attached to some sort of cloth, shedding gentle light through the whole area. I clamber out of the cart and count the structures as my eyes adjust: there are three.

Roar and Badenoch wait for us while a steady stream of gargoyles exit the building closest to our right. They're carrying pickaxes, shovels, hammers, and chisels, so I'm guessing that's some kind of tool room.

Cassian orders Roar to take us to the supply room. "Get them kitted up."

Roar pauses before he obeys. "Which tunnels are we mining today?"

"Today, we're taking a tour," Cassian replies. "So everyone knows what's at stake. Tomorrow, you'll fight for your tunnels."

Roar pauses beside Badenoch. It's easy to see that the two gargoyles respect each other.

Badenoch says, "I guess that means you're still our head foreman today, Roar. Tomorrow, well, sounds like we'll be enemies."

Roar shouts to the room. "Tools down. Wait where you are."

A chorus of clattering metal tools follows us into the supply structure where I'm relieved to find boots and work suits—none in my size as far as I can see at first. I'm not sure whether to be grateful or horrified when Roar shoves a pair of boots and clothing at me and says, "These are for kids. They should fit you. Get changed. We'll wait outside."

At least he has the decency to give me privacy. Still, I snag Jasper's arm before he leaves. "Stay. Please."

"I don't think I should. It won't look good."

"I don't care how it looks." I take a deep breath. "Okay, maybe I do. Just… please don't take your eyes off the door. And stay close to Llion for now. Being alone is as dangerous as being surrounded. For both of us."

"I understand, Marbella. Nobody's coming in here until you come out."

He closes the door behind him and it's strange how alone I feel as I strip off the dress and slide into the pants, shirt, and boots. I'm more accustomed to dressing in front of people. Not that I'd want to get changed in a room full of male gargoyles. Just that I'm used to being surrounded by women. Suddenly, there are none of those in sight. I shove aside the dilemma I'm going to be in when my cycle comes around. Luckily that's not due for another two weeks, so I have time to figure out how to manage it when the time comes.

I fold the dress and place it on the rack where Roar removed the work clothes for me. I quickly take the time to assess the other items in the supply room. It may as well be full of weapons—you can do as much damage with a pickaxe as with a dagger. I choose one and test it for weight and balance, sliding it into one of the sturdy pockets in the pants leg of my new clothing. There's a flap across the top of the pocket, but I leave it open and the tool visible. I want it to be obvious that I've got it.

Once again, I'm struck by the extent that Howl has oppressed his people. There's an army of miners outside this room and a hundred weapons inside it. Yet, they don't rebel.

When I push open the wooden door, Roar and Jasper stand right outside facing each other, eyebrows drawn down, the space between them charged with challenge. They seem to be having some sort of silent argument. Or a staring competition. Maybe both.

Roar waves his big hand at me without taking his eyes off Jasper. "She's here. She's safe. Now get back to your team."

Jasper ignores him. "You okay, Marbella?"

"Yes, thank you, Jasper."

"Okay." Jasper stalks away from whatever silent fight he was having with Roar, leaving me with the blue-winged gargoyle.

Roar spins to me. "Your friend seems to think I'm out to get you."

I decide to tackle this one head-on. "Are you?"

My directness seems to surprise him. Instead of invading my space, he takes a step back as if to emphasize his next words. "Listen, Princess. I don't want you on my team. Let's make that clear. But I'm not going to hurt you just because I don't like you. One more body on my team is better than one less." His assessing gaze rakes me again, sizing up my legs, arms, and torso, but not in any way that gives me the impression he's looking at anything other than to quantify it.

"Besides," he says, "You'll be able to squeeze into spaces we can't get through. That's got to be worth something the other teams don't have."

I shudder at the thought of whatever cramped spaces he imagines sending me into.

Across the way, Jasper has joined Badenoch. Llion waits with the rest of Roar's team. Llion may not have made his protection of me as obvious as staring Roar down like Jasper did, but his focus hasn't left me since I appeared. He reminds me of an eagle. Intent, focused, and very confident he can get to me fast if he needs to. It's not lost on Roar whose eyebrows have pretty much remained drawn down in a disgruntled expression.

"Let's go." Roar keeps his wings pinned to his sides, but they extend a little as he turns, revealing up close a glimpse of the intricate, blue-lit design etched across them.

"Lead the way," I say, the closest I can get to a statement of compliance. For now, at least, I'll trust his word that he isn't planning anything underhanded.

Seeing me emerge with Roar, Cassian takes charge of the

situation again. "Team leaders, choose a team member to bring with you. It's time to assess the status of the tunnels. No-clan Roar, you will bring both the Princess and No-clan Llion."

Cassian stalks away and ten guards round the team leaders into a group to follow him. The remaining guards order the other gargoyles to return to the food hall on the other side of the opening.

Roar and Llion take up positions on either side of me as we follow Cassian along an increasingly narrow pathway inside the mountain. "We call the place we just left the Cavity," Roar says. "It's home base. You'll see where we eat and sleep when we get back. The first tunnel is a hundred paces along. It's the easiest tunnel to mine, but it's least likely to contain a heartstone." He grins in the increasing dark. "We've focused mainly on that tunnel until now."

Mining the tunnel with the least likely chance of containing a heartstone makes sense if they don't want Howl to get another one. But I wonder how long that course of action will last now that Howl has promised to release a loved one to any gargoyle who finds a heartstone.

Up ahead, Cassian pauses at an opening in the rock. "Welcome to the first tunnel," he says as we crowd around the entrance.

Inside, the tunnel is lit at intervals with spider webs. So far, I haven't actually seen one of the spiders. In fact, I've never seen one. The chances of that happening are high here. To my knowledge, they don't bite, but there's a first time for everything.

The tunnel itself is clear of debris and well supported with solid-looking beams. Roar keeps his voice low. "Half the battle is keeping the tunnel from collapsing while we mine. Some days we spend all day working on the supports instead of digging. You'll see what happens if we don't when we get to the second tunnel."

Cassian catches Roar's last statement and passes me with a gleaming smile. He inclines his head at an upcoming shaft. "Down we go."

I sigh. Another ladder to descend. Jasper and I hurry down the wide shaft, our boots clanging on the metal rungs as the gargoyles wait impatiently at the bottom.

Unlike the others, Roar doesn't seem perturbed by the delay. When we reach him, he says, "Each tunnel is further down, and you have to climb multiple shafts to get to them. I'll get Iago to fix you both up with thick gloves to protect your hands and sliding plates on the inside of your boots. That way you can slide down the outer rungs instead of stepping."

Jasper inclines his head, his earlier distrust not entirely gone.

I say, "Thank you, Roar, that would be appreciated."

Cassian's shout comes from a little further along the tunnel. "Welcome to the second tunnel," he says. He gestures at a thick cascade of rubble. There's a small opening at the top, but otherwise, it's completely blocked.

"This one collapsed last year," Roar explains. "Whichever team gets this tunnel will spend most of their first week clearing the debris. It will take another week to start building the supports. Maybe by the third week, we can mine it again."

Tunnel number two is not such a great pick then. Not if you want to find a heartstone, but not so bad if you want to stall for time.

Cassian is already on the move and the guards press in behind us. When I hesitate, peering at the blockage for a moment too long, one of the guards reaches for the whip at his waist.

"Don't make me use this, Princess," he snarls. "Get a move on."

Roar grabs my arm and pulls me along. His palm is rough and calloused and big enough to encircle my forearm and cross his fingers past his thumb. My first instinct is to resist, but even Llion gives me a warning glance, picking up his pace beside me. Jasper is already ahead of us, and I'm glad he didn't hear the guard's threat, or we'd now be in the middle of a fight.

"What is that weapon they all carry?" I ask when we're a safe distance from the threatening guard.

Roar says, "It's called a Bone Lash."

"That doesn't sound good."

"The tip at the end is designed to shatter bone. If used to its full potential, it can tear a gargoyle's head right off their shoulders."

I can't suppress the shudder that runs the length of my spine. "Who would create such a thing?"

Roar doesn't say anything. His palm remains on my arm and he's in no hurry to remove it, urging me toward the next shaft down the mountain. Jasper disappears down it after a quick check in my direction confirms I'm safe.

This time, it's Llion who answers. "That would be me. I designed it."

My eyes shoot wide. Llion doesn't meet my gaze as he descends into the shaft, wings fully spread. Roar wraps his palm around my other arm and draws me close.

My focus snaps to him instead of Llion. "What are you doing?"

"Helping you. Trust me, you don't want the guards to target you. Place your feet on top of mine."

Both his arms slide around me, and I'm mortified to realize that I couldn't stop him even if I wanted to. As the threatening guard approaches, I decide it's worth sacrificing my pride for my safety. As I step onto Roar's feet and rest my head against his chest, he immediately spreads his wings. With one sweep, we ascend over the shaft and drop vertically into it. My stomach remains behind, but it's better than being left with the impatient guards.

Roar bends his head to the top of mine, and I'm a little alarmed and uncertain until he speaks in a low voice. "Grievous Llion was the King's armorer," he says. "The real King. Not Howl." His wings arch as he slows our descent a little, but not so much that the guards catch up with us. "He was the first Grievous gargoyle to prove himself loyal to the crown. I believe he even became one of the King's most trusted friends."

The flight down is too short. I want to ask so many questions, but we're already touching ground again. Roar wraps his wings around me for a second, sliding his hands back to my arms and lifting me off his feet.

To an onlooker, it must look as if he's simply setting me down, but he whispers one last thing. "Llion can make a weapon out of anything."

Roar steps away from me.

I seek Jasper and find him standing safely nearby with Badenoch. Llion has retreated to the background. He probably doesn't know how I'll react to his revelation.

Cassian is already speaking, and this time, he's the one giving us the run down on the tunnel. "The third tunnel is most likely to contain a heartstone," he says. "I expect this tunnel to be the tunnel of choice."

I glance at Roar. He shrugs as if to say that Cassian is right. From what I can see, this tunnel looks well supported by beams and its walls are more obviously made of rust-colored stone. I'm assuming that means we're looking for a similar colored Heartstone.

I let Llion have his space and don't try to avoid Roar when he offers me another lift down the next shaft. Roar has a quick word with Badenoch before Roar gathers me into his arms. Jasper quickly catches on to what they're saying.

As I step onto Roar's feet, Jasper backs away from Badenoch. "I'm not hugging you," he says with a growl.

The older gargoyle laughs. "I don't expect a warrior like you to do anything of the kind."

Without another word, Badenoch's wings sweep upward. He takes hold of Jasper's shoulders in his foot claws, and they both descend into the mining shaft.

Roar and I follow them down. Since Roar was open with me before about Llion, I decide to be forthright with him. "Why don't you fight back? You're all clearly strong enough."

He doesn't pretend to misunderstand me. "Howl has our wives and children." His muscles flex around me, sudden tension constricting the space around us as the air rushes past. I can't lean back far enough to see his face, but I sense the clench of his jaw, the growl in his chest. He speaks slowly, deliberately. "Howl's Harem is made up of the wives of the gargoyles who are most likely to rise up against him."

I swallow. "Your wife?"

"Yes."

I decide I've pushed the conversation far enough. I can't even begin to imagine his feelings. Baelen would tear apart any man who looked at me in a threatening way, let alone a man who used my body without my permission. In fact, he would have done exactly that during the battle in the arena when Rhydian Valor attacked me. Luckily for Rhydian, the fight ended when it did.

When I step away from Roar at the bottom of the shaft, I take a chance to check his expression.

Rage. Pure rage.

I acknowledge the emotion with a nod and decide to give him space. The fourth tunnel is a yawning gap in front of us. Not only are there few supports but patches of web across the floor reveal random jagged shafts along the way.

Roar clears his throat. His voice is still thick with emotion, but it disappears as he speaks. He's obviously working hard to set aside his anger. "The floor of this tunnel is unstable. There are pockets of air under it, sort of like gigantic bubbles. They're filled with poisonous fumes. It's not the fall that kills you, but the toxins. Believe it or not, this isn't the most dangerous tunnel."

I decide not to ask any more questions as we descend to the final tunnel. The air is warm now and the rock walls around us flicker with light that is more copper than blue. A sound I can't identify rushes to meet me as Roar lands. It crackles and pops. Hisses.

This time, when I step off his feet, Roar doesn't remove his hand from my arm. "Stay close."

Ahead of us, Cassian stands at the tunnel's entrance. Guards line up around us, herding us into a group, but they keep mostly to the back of the opening nearest to the exit.

A hand across my shoulder tells me Jasper's beside me.

Cassian says. "This tunnel is the closest to the heart of Mount Prime and its volcanic core." He swings aside, revealing the tunnel beyond. Patches of fire burn along it, small enough to avoid, but large enough to be a hazard. There are numerous collapses, rocks piled up along the sides and trailing across the center, and most of the supports are charred and blackened, barely holding the tunnel up.

Now I understand why the gargoyles were so unhappy to be put in five teams. Even setting up supports in this tunnel will be dangerous.

The same crackling and hissing sound I heard before grows louder. I peer at the various spot fires, trying to identify which one of them is producing the sound. It reminds me of logs falling on a fire, but as far as I can see, the spot fires burn without fuel. The sound hisses in the distance, whistling through the tunnel toward us. It's like a rushing fire, but nothing else happens and the sound disappears as quickly as it began.

I glance at Roar, but he doesn't seem to have noticed. Maybe it's just all the fires echoing in this enclosed space. I guess I'll get used to it.

"Hit the wrong rock and flames are the last thing you'll see." Cassian spreads his wings and beats down; the nearest fires respond to the extra oxygen by rushing higher, rising as high as the ceiling.

"We don't want this tunnel," I whisper to Roar, feeling like I'm stating the obvious. "I don't want Jasper's team mining it either."

Roar exhales. "I don't want *anyone* down here."

His comment brings home to me the fact that these gargoyles are his friends. All of them. I don't share allegiances with any of them other than Llion and Jasper. And maybe Roar now too. It's going to be easier for me to fight the others than it will be for Roar. Now I understand why Badenoch wanted Jasper on his team. Jasper and I are the outsiders. We won't worry about hurting our opponents. But it also makes us targets. The other team members will show us the same lack of mercy we will show them.

Jasper's fingers flex around my shoulder. The light from the spot fires flickers across his face, making his chocolate eyes glow molten. He doesn't have to speak for me to understand him. When we ascend from this place, we'll be enemies on different teams. But only on the outside. He'll do everything he can to protect me, and I will do the same for him.

21

MARBELLA

The rest of the day passes in a blur. Roar asks Iago to set Jasper and I up with gloves, and the wiry gargoyle attaches thick leather patches to the sides of our boots so we can slide down the mineshaft ladders. We test them out on the main shaft at the entrance to the Cavity while the guards watch closely. I'm not sure where they think we would escape to. There's nothing but desolate mountains out there.

As evening approaches, tensions grow. Dinner involves a rearrangement of seating so we can eat with our teams. That's when I meet the remaining member of Roar's team: a gargoyle called Welsian, who has the biggest biceps I've ever seen and stands a head taller than Roar when he draws himself up to his full height. Welsian mostly keeps to himself, shoulders down, hunkering over his bowl of gruel. Judging by what's on our plates, the "proper" meal that Howl promised once each day must be going to materialize for breakfast.

I try to tune out the nervous whispers and occasional outbursts at the surrounding tables. Snippets of conversation tell me the other teams are wondering the same things I am. Like how Cassian is going to decide who fights who, and what happens if someone's knocked out or injured—do they still get to mine with their team? All valid questions, but nobody has any answers.

When it's time for bed, Jasper leaves with his team, and I stay close to Llion. He hasn't spoken to me much since his revelation earlier.

He asks, "Do you still trust me, Lady Storm?"

"Of course. I know you didn't design those weapons for Howl."

He relaxes. "Then stay close to me. There are a lot of jumpy gargoyles here tonight and fear makes normally sensible men do stupid things."

"We sleep this way," Roar says, leading the way from the food hall. Outside, he points to the third structure. "That is the bathing area, but I don't expect you to go in there."

He's right about that. There was a small bathroom back in the food hall that I used, but I'll have to do without a proper shower for now. Right now that's not my biggest problem. I'd expected the final building to be some sort of barracks. "Where do we sleep?"

"Up there."

I don't particularly want to look up. I'm not going to like this. I give in and study the ceiling. The cloth that the Elyria web is attached to billows in at least a hundred places, sagging like lots of ribbons attached to the ceiling at their ends.

"Are those hammocks?"

Roar grins. "Don't worry, Elyria thread is unbreakable."

"You really sleep in them?"

"It keeps us close to the rock and Elyria light." Roar shrugs. "It's comforting for gargoyles."

Not so much for elves. The height of the hammocks isn't the only thing I have to worry about. As the evening draws on, I'm feeling the cold in a way that I haven't before. I remind myself that warm air rises, so sleeping close to the ceiling likely to be warmer than down here. Even so, I'm scared that the hollow inside me that I've been pushing away all day is about to rear its ugly head.

The Storm has been part of me for seven years. I absorbed her power every single day, *wielded* her power every single day. It made me strong physically and mentally. On top of that, my connection with Baelen was part of me the whole time—I just didn't know it. When he bound himself to me at the ceremony for choosing champions, he solidified what already existed between us. We made each other stronger.

Now a huge part of me is missing. I take a deep breath, close my eyes, and hope the emptiness doesn't get worse. "I guess you'll need to fly me up there."

Llion's deep voice breaks across Roar's. "I will fly Lady Storm up to her hammock."

"Okay. Let's head to the unoccupied area to the left. Over there." While Roar points it out, Welsian and Iago take flight in that direction, disappearing into their chosen hammocks.

Roar is next and finally Llion invites me to step on his feet.

"The last time we did this was the first night we met," Llion says.

"I remember. You let me live."

He sweeps one arm around my waist and the other across my shoulders, one hand curling against my neck to support my head. He pauses. "You are very cold, Lady Storm."

I shrug. "I don't feel like myself. I left a big part of myself behind today."

"With Baelen Rath."

"Yes." I rest my head against his chest, finding the warmth comforting.

"Lady Storm, you really are very cold."

We're the last to leave and the guards have started paying attention to us. We need to fly sooner rather than later. "I'll be okay, Llion. Thank you for your concern."

He sweeps us into the air, leaving the guards and their bone lashes behind. When I flew with Roar earlier, we'd plummeted downward. Flying upward is something else. It feels like floating, like rising from the bottom of a deep pool of water and taking the first breath of air as you break the surface. It reminds me of being the storm, not of containing the storm or controlling it, but *being* it. It reminds me of the way the phoenix called me the Storm, and the way Llion spared my life when we first battled because he said I was the Storm.

If only I could find it again. I have to believe that there's a tiny bit of it left because I can almost feel it, a connection, a spark. Almost…

It disappears as soon as Llion slides me inside the hammock he's chosen for me. The gap between it and the ceiling is large enough to sit up in. The material softly cushions my body but it's sturdy enough that I'm not afraid it will tear.

"Sleep well, Lady Storm." Llion releases the side of the hammock and takes hold of the next one. I can reach out my arm halfway to it. I pull my arm back in as the hammock rocks and I'm reminded of the distance to the ground. A glance left tells me that Roar has chosen the hammock on the other side of me. Iago is at my feet. Welsian is at my head, one big foot protruding from his hammock. They've surrounded me and I'm grateful.

I pull my boots off and curl my knees to my chest, wrapping my arms around them and hugging tight, trying to keep the hollow from expanding any further inside me.

My breath frosts in the air. So much for warmer air up here. I guess the gargoyles use their wings as blankets. I'll have to remember that and bring a blanket up here with me tomorrow. It's been a long day and I need to sleep. As the sounds around me quiet down, turning into the soft wash of deep breathing, I finally fall asleep.

I awake to a gentle touch on my shoulder. "Lady Storm, it's morning."

I crack open one eye. I'm not sure how Llion can tell. The Cavity isn't any lighter or darker than it was when we fell asleep. At some point in the night, I must have warmed up because my toes aren't freezing anymore.

I ask, "Are you sure?"

He grins. "The spider webs take on a greenish glow in the morning. Look."

True enough, the glow around me has changed to sea green. Not that I've ever seen the sea. But I've seen drawings in ancient elven books of what the surface of the Earth looks like. The color of the Elyria thread right now is exactly what I imagine a deep, calm ocean looks like. On top of that, the most delicious smells waft up from the kitchen below.

"Food. Real food." I slide out of the hammock into Llion's waiting arms, trusting him not to let me fall.

The rest of the team waits around me, wings spread to stay aloft. We descend together and it's not until we're halfway down that I realize how far I've come in regard to physical touch. A few days ago, I would have recoiled at the idea of anyone hugging me. Now, I stand on Llion's feet, my arms wrapped around his waist without thinking about it.

The food hall is a visual reminder of the upcoming fights. The other four teams have each chosen corners of the room as far away from each other as possible. We're left with the empty space in the middle. I sit wedged between Welsian and Llion, hunching over my plate, suddenly not so hungry anymore. We've barely finished eating when Cassian and the guards invade the room, placing themselves around the edges.

Cassian carries a copper cup with five, slender white sticks in it. As he enters the room, my ears ring, a high-pitched whine as if the air pressure in the room suddenly changed and my ears are adjusting. Rubbing the soft spot at the side of my face next to my ears, I try to shake off the distracting hum and focus on my teammates.

Iago nudges Roar. They both stare at the slender sticks. "Are those what I think they are?"

Roar ripples with visible anger, a dangerous air settling around him. "They'd better not be."

Cassian grips the cup, his expression unreadable. "Each team leader will choose a bone. The man who chooses the shortest bone gets to choose his team's opponent first. The fights will be one-on-one, hand-to-hand, no weapons."

Iago sighs, shaking his head. "It *is* the bones."

The fight goes out of Roar as he stands. "Nothing is sacred anymore."

For a second, the buzz inside my ears disappears. I grab Roar's arm before he leaves the table, keeping my voice down. "Choose the bone on the far left of the cup."

"What?"

That's a good question. I have no idea why I said that. I slump back to my seat, conscious of the eyes around me. "Um… I don't know… forget it."

He eyes me warily before he makes his way to Cassian and lines up with the other team leaders.

"The fifth team leader chooses first," Cassian announces. He stares at me as he speaks, but I still can't read his expression. I'm in the first team. If they're choosing from fifth to first, that means Roar gets whatever bone is left in the cup. What I told him about choosing a particular bone won't matter after all.

I don't yet know the name of the fifth team leader. I think the others call him Erit. He's the one who thought he'd be saddled with me when they were choosing teams yesterday. When Cassian presents him with the cup, he reaches for a bone and picks the one I wanted Roar to pick.

I watch carefully as he holds it up high to show everyone. It looks short, but we won't know for sure until everyone has chosen. One by one, the other team leaders pick bones of varying lengths, and as soon as Roar pulls the last bone from the cup, it's obvious that Erit chose the shortest. Badenoch has the next shortest and Roar has the third.

Roar gives me a questioning look. I'd told him which one to choose and it was the shortest—the one that would have given us the power to pick our fight. I have no answer for his silent question. I don't know how I knew that.

"What happens now?" Erit asks. He isn't quite smiling. It's hard to know yet whether picking the shortest bone will end up being a good thing or not.

"Pick a fighter from your team. Then pick his opponent from any opposing team. The winner of the first fight gets their tunnel of choice."

"And then?" Badenoch asks.

"If Erit's team loses, he picks another opponent until his team wins. After that, the holder of the next shortest bone in the remaining teams gets to choose their opponent. The fights continue until all tunnels are chosen," Cassian says. "The only rule is that you can't choose anyone who has already fought."

Erit spins to his team sitting in the far back corner of the room. He points. I follow his finger to a gargoyle who slowly rises from his seat. The standing gargoyle is not quite as bulky as Welsian, more like Roar in height and stature, but he moves in a way that tells me he considers each move. Whoever opposes him will have to strategize.

"I pick Arlo from my team," Erit says.

His finger swivels to Arlo's opponent.

Of course. I shouldn't be surprised. He's pointing at me.

"Arlo will fight her."

My jaw clenches. I narrow my eyes at Erit and rise to my feet in the same quietly confident way Arlo did, ignoring the stares around me. I'm silently wilting inside. None of these gargoyles has seen me fight. The miners all left before the fight at Crimson Court. If I still had my storm power, then picking me as an opponent would be suicide. But the simple fact is that I don't; they have nothing to be afraid of. I am a small, female elf and everyone knows it. I have no idea how I'm going to win this fight, let alone survive it.

I meet Jasper's eyes across the distance. His jaw ticks. I've seen that look on his face before—a mixture of concern and anger—and I've come to recognize it: he hates it when I get picked on by arrogant men. He knows that in a fair fight, I'm stronger than them, I can beat them, but he doesn't expect this to be a fair fight. He twitches like he's about to jump out of his seat, but before he can, Llion leans forward in his chair beside me, spreading his wings just enough that one of them extends across my back like a deadly backdrop. Or maybe a declaration of protection.

He appears relaxed and confident. "I don't think you thought this through, Erit. If Lady Storm wins, we get first pick of the tunnels."

Erit's brow furrows. "She isn't going to win."

Llion shrugs. "She fought King Howl on Mount Erador, stabbed him right in the heart, and dropped a legion of gargoyles from the sky. I heard they're still picking up the pieces. But sure... she probably won't win."

Standing beside Erit, Cassian suddenly grins, clearly entertained by Llion's attempt to psych out Erit and his fighter. He doesn't seem worried about Llion speaking about my fight with Howl. I guess that's because everyone knows that, in the end, I lost.

Cassian shouts, "Everyone outside."

Now I'm really regretting eating breakfast. A wave of nerves tells me that everything I consumed is going to very soon see the light of day again. Llion's palm between my shoulder blades is a comforting pressure, but it's Welsian who surprises me with advice.

He keeps his voice at a low murmur as he says, "Arlo favors his left leg. He hurt it last year when the second tunnel collapsed. His leg wasn't broken, but he was trapped under the fallen rocks for hours and since then he protects it. Focus your attacks on that leg and you'll beat him."

"Thank you, Welsian."

He taps his forehead. "You're little, but you're strong. You need to defeat him in here."

Iago also has pearls of wisdom to impart, wedging between me and Welsian as we exit the food hall to say, "Protect your head. Your face is level with his fists, so he'll try to knock you out fast. Also, he doesn't want to be injured or else he won't be able to mine. If you drag the fight out, he'll get nervous and make mistakes."

"Thanks, Iago." I pause outside, taking a deep breath and trying to focus on something other than the wide-open area in the center of the Cavity. Gargoyles are forming a large ring, inside which I'll have to fight. I remind myself that I fought Baelen in gargoyle form and he was a much more formidable opponent than any of these gargoyles. I try to ignore the fact that that was when I had my power. "What were those bones Roar chose from?"

Iago casts glances left and right before answering. "They're pin bones from a gargoyle's wings."

"Oh. That's..." *Very not okay.*

His expression hardens. "Those particular ones are the King's bones."

"But... why?"

Iago sighs. "Our wings are our protection, our strongest shield. To remove another gargoyle's wing bones after he dies is an act of aggression. You only do that if your anger against that gargoyle has not been satisfied by his death. It's a threat to the dead gargoyle's family. Except in this case, our young King had no family. He was the last of the royal line, so it was Howl's way of proclaiming that anyone loyal to the King is his enemy."

I watch from a distance as Cassian carries the cup with the bones away. The hum inside my ears eases. I don't try to shake off my emotions as my unease turns into a much stronger emotion: *determination.*

Iago and I are now alone at the entrance to the food hall. Everyone else has gathered to form the fighting ring. Llion, Roar, and Welsian wait for me at the closest edge. Jasper and Badenoch stand on the other side. Arlo has taken up position in the middle.

"I'm going to end Howl one day, Iago," I say. "I don't know how, but I will."

I hold on to the anger deep inside my chest as I stalk toward my opponent, ready now for the fight ahead.

22

———

MARBELLA

I focus on my game plan as I approach Arlo. *Attack his left leg. Protect my head. Wear him down.*

The wide circle of gargoyles around us quiets as I approach. My instinct is to leap into action, but I hold back, keeping at a distance, never taking my eyes off my opponent.

Cassian stands directly to my right, two guards on either side of him. They hold bone lashes in their hands, ready for any disruption, ensuring that the miners stand clear of them.

I shake out the tension in my shoulders, directing my question at Cassian. "How do we know who's won?"

Cassian folds his arms across his broad chest. "Whoever knocks the other one out first."

A single blow to the head can kill someone. Not to mention Arlo's head is quite a way above mine. I'd rather there was at least one other possibility.

"Is yielding an option?" I ask, drawing derisive laughter from Erit's team.

Erit calls, "Do you want to yield already, Lady Storm?"

I ignore him. My opponent, Arlo, doesn't laugh at me. Unlike Erit, this gargoyle appears to have smarts. He's calm, not edgy, already assessing the way I move, calculating how the fight will go

184

down. The way he studies me tells me he's not going to underestimate me like the others might. I'm actually sorry he's part of Erit's team. He seems like the kind of gargoyle Roar would have picked if Roar hadn't been forced to use up one of his choices on me.

"Sure," Cassian says, the corner of his mouth twitching upward, making his eyes smile in a way that doesn't quite match the fact that he's here to kill anyone who steps out of line. He seems oddly entertained by Erit's arrogance. Of course, unlike the other gargoyles here, he *has* seen me fight. "Either one of you may yield."

"Good." I stare hard at my opponent. "Because knocking Arlo out could mean he won't be able to mine today. I'd hate to do that to him."

Erit's team laughs and jeers, but I ignore them, circling Arlo to indicate that I'm done asking questions. I don't look back, but I sense Iago and Welsian's approval from where they stand behind me. The louder Erit's team shouts at me, the more I know my confidence is having an impact.

Arlo paces opposite me so we keep our distance from each other. I don't bother reaching for my storm power. I haven't felt its force since I cut the connection with Baelen yesterday. It's just me and my fists now. And perhaps my boots.

May as well get this thing started.

I dart forward.

Just like Iago predicted, Arlo goes for the quick knockout right away. A big fist cuts toward the side of my head, the size and color of a large rock. I have no doubt it will feel like one. I duck, and as his fist sails over my head, I follow through with a kick to his exposed side, connecting with his ribs. He's light on his feet and bounces sideways, reducing the impact my boot would have had. Nothing broken. This time.

As I dance around him, he keeps his fists up—just like I do. He speaks, keeping his voice neutral, matter-of-fact. "I figured I'd at least try for a quick end to this fight, Lady Storm."

"Fair enough, Arlo," I reply, acknowledging that he addressed me with respect. "I'm sorry this is how we get to meet each other."

He gives me a quick nod. He's done talking and so am I. He comes at me again, and this time, he hunches down to my level. Two quick jabs almost get through my defenses. I barely miss the blows. I'm going to have to truly dance around this man to avoid those rocks he calls fists.

As I spin around him, I kick out at his left leg. It's not a firm blow, but it lands. He reacts defensively, confirming Welsian's advice—he's vulnerable there. If not physically, then mentally.

We trade blows for another three minutes straight. It's clearly longer than the other gargoyles expected me to last because they fluctuate between shouting and silence. The silences tend to follow the hits I land. The shouting is when Arlo connects, which he does more often than I like. Mostly, it's when he uses his wings to give him speed, but in this closed in space, thankfully they aren't a massive advantage.

Another two minutes later, my boot connects with his left leg again, and this time panic flashes across his face, quickly hidden. I've lost count of the times I've got through his defenses—or how many times he's gotten through mine. Blood slides from a cut in my lip and another above my eye. I'm tired. But so is he. Iago told me to wear Arlo down, but I'm wearing down too.

It's time to admit that I don't know how to beat him. Our stamina is matched. He's worried about his leg, but so far he hasn't made any big mistakes in my favor.

He swings his giant fist once more, another knock-out blow, and I barely avoid contact with my temple. My vision blurs. Arlo has clipped my head one too many times. It will only take one more hit and I'm out.

If Cassian is true to his word, I won't have to fight again today, but I'm not sure when my team will have another chance to pick a tunnel. Erit only picked me because he believed Arlo could beat me. If Erit's team wins this round, then Badenoch gets to pick the next fight. He won't pick a battle against Roar or Llion or Welsian—or even Iago for that matter. It doesn't take a genius to know that my team has some of the most intimidating fighters in it. We could end up getting the fifth tunnel simply because nobody wants to fight us.

Desperation is a terrible emotion. I push at it, but it pushes back. It wants in. I can't let it, or *I'll* be the one making mistakes.

Whatever sounds the watching gargoyles make don't reach me anymore. At some point, I've blocked them out, focused only on my target. But as I feint right to miss another one of Arlo's knockout attempts, a voice reaches me across the distance.

It's Baelen's voice. Much younger. A memory I haven't thought about for years…

He says: *I've thought of a way for you to beat them.*

It's as clear as if he's standing beside me and we're fourteen years old again. I'm suddenly back in the Rath mansion, sweeping the hallway between the upper bedrooms, surrounded by carved wooden doorways and elegant tapestries…

The flashback is so vivid that it stuns me.

I almost don't move in time to avoid Arlo's swinging fist. At the last moment, I duck, glide, giving myself as much room as possible, because Baelen's voice is so insistent. I can't push it away. I have to let the memory in.

My body moves in the present, defending myself, moving without thought as the past consumes me, the memory takes over…

The broom hurt my hands. It was harder to sweep that day because of my bleeding palms. I'd hidden them from my mother and regretted it. Not bandaging my hands meant there was nothing between my raw skin and the wooden handle. I'd stopped sweeping, staring at my shaking hands, when I discovered that Baelen stood a little further down the hallway. A respectful distance. He never came close enough to invade my space.

He cast an acknowledging nod at my skinned knees and said, "I've thought of a way for you to beat them."

The visiting Valor boys had pushed me again. They spent every summer at the Rath House training with Baelen's father, as part of a group of boys chosen from the major Houses for the honor of being trained by the Commander of the Elven Army. They always managed to shove me when there was something sharp for me to fall against. And nobody to see them do it. This time it was the pebbled pathway at the side of the house and all its tiny, jagged rocks.

For now, it was shoves and trips, but I was worried about how much worse it could get, especially as we got older, and what else they might do. Entitled brutes.

Baelen waited for me to say something. Maybe he read my mind, my silent plea to him.

"I could beat them up for you." It was a statement of fact rather than conceit. He could turn them into pulp. "But that won't make them leave you alone. They'll get sneakier and I don't want that. You need to fight them yourself."

"I can't." The admission hurt more than the wounds. I tugged on my braid, a nervous gesture I was trying to conquer. "I'm too little."

I presented him with my back, snatching up the broom from where I'd laid it against the wall, wincing at the renewed pain. "There's no way for me to fight them."

He spoke at the same time I did, something I didn't hear. Funny how my misery had blanked out his softly spoken statement, my voice drowning out his. I'd said I was too little, and he'd whispered something in response. I hear it now in my memory... "You're perfect."

He paused, cleared his throat. "I've been thinking about what you could do. And I've figured out a way. A way that means being smaller is an advantage."

I propped the broom upright in the crook of my arm. "I appreciate what you're trying to do, Baelen, but I don't think..."

He took a step forward, the simple movement silencing me. He waited with one hand out, palm open. "It's a move I call 'the tangle.' But I'll have to touch you to show you." He waited, giving me time to consider, waiting for permission. "May I?"

Yes.

The tangle.

I haven't used that move since I left the biggest Valor boy screaming on the ground and told the others they'd get worse if they touched me again. It should work even better on a gargoyle with wings...

I snap back to the present and out of automatic defensive mode. Arlo jabs with his right hand, leaving his right side exposed. I bounce upward, left knee bent, connecting with the soft part of his stomach beneath his ribs. My left isn't my strongest leg, but it makes an impact.

With an *oomph*, he bends reactively at the waist and knees. I rebound to the ground, but I'm ready. I leap back to him and use his bent knee and then his slightly spread wings as platforms, one after the other, to stride up his body. Racing to the height of his shoulders, I kick my right leg out and swing both my legs around his neck. My calves close around his neck, and my body swings all the way around to his chest, where I drop my full weight to the ground, hands to the floor as if I'm doing a handstand. Except that my legs are locked around his neck.

The sudden weight jerks him forward. He drops head-first, rolls, and lands on his back with a cracking thud. Without releasing his neck, I use my stomach muscles to sit up, grab his right arm, and hook my own around it, locking my hands together around his arm. He kicks and thumps at my torso, but I tighten the tangle around his neck, squeezing his windpipes and lying against his arm to push it in the direction it doesn't want to go.

The whole move took seconds. Seconds to ground him and force him into compliance. The only difference between Arlo and the Valor boy is that I haven't broken Arlo's arm yet.

I'm leaning half on his arm and that means I'm propped up far enough to see his face. He's afraid. He can't mine with a broken arm. And if he can't mine… I don't know what will happen to him. I wish I'd asked Cassian what happened to the injured gargoyles he was telling me about yesterday.

"I don't want to break your arm," I whisper, trying not to let anyone else hear. "Yield!"

There's the barest flicker of his gaze to Erit. The rest of Erit's team is screaming at Arlo to get up, to beat me. The stark reality is that yielding isn't an option for him.

I slip my upper leg over his face, releasing his neck but not his arm yet, knowing that his instinct will be to get up, but because I still control his arm, he has to move in my direction. As soon as he leans toward me, I let go of his arm, freeing my left fist to strike his forehead. His own upward momentum adds to the force.

Lights out.

He slumps. His head falls back but my leg is there, ready to cushion his fall. *Ow.* I'll have a massive bruise across my calf later, but it's better than letting him crack the back of his head on the hard ground. He's already unconscious. I don't need him injured any more than that. He may be my opponent, but he's not my enemy.

I release him from the tangle, lower his head to the ground, and check his pulse. It's strong. He shouldn't be out for long.

I glide to my feet to the sound of silence, retying my hair and smoothing down my clothing. I scan the watching group from Erit to Roar, past Jasper's approving nod, and finally to Llion. Nobody says anything, not even Cassian, so I decide it's my turn to speak.

"You don't know me," I say, turning in a slow circle. "You don't know where I've come from or what I can do." I take a deep breath. I'm in the calm before the effects of the fight hit me—the bruises and the pain—but I'm determined to grip this moment with both hands and use it.

"My name is Marbella of the House of Mercy. In Erawind they call me the Storm Princess, but I wasn't born into privilege. I was raised as a servant in the House of Rath." I stop moving, finding myself facing Erit. "I didn't come here to fight you. I came here to help someone who is very important to me. I am not your enemy."

Cassian steps forward. I can't tell what he's thinking or whether I've taken up too much air space. He asks, "Which tunnel do you choose, Princess?"

I turn to Roar. As my leader, it has to be his choice. By deferring to him, I'll send a message to the other gargoyles that I'm part of Roar's team. I'm not fighting for myself. I'm a miner just like them.

Roar holds up three fingers in front of his chest. He wants me to choose the third tunnel—the safest one with the highest chance of containing a Heartstone. But as I open my mouth to speak, my ears buzz, drowning out my own voice in a high-pitched whine. I shake my head, trying to clear the sibilant whisper filling my ears: *The fifth one. Fifth one. Fifth. Fif-thththth.*

I've taken too many hits to the head and the pain is setting in. I ignore the suicidal urge to nominate the fifth tunnel. I have no idea where that idea's coming from, and I'm not about to give in to it. "The third tunnel," I say.

Most of the gargoyles visibly slump and many groan. Everyone wants the third tunnel. I'm only sorry about Badenoch's team. Because Erit lost, he gets to choose his next opponent and he won't choose to fight anyone from Badenoch's strong team. I just hope Erit wins the next round, because then Badenoch can choose after that. The first and second tunnels are still up for grabs, but very soon only the fourth and fifth will remain.

I lean down to Arlo, gesturing to the nearest gargoyles. "Help me move him, please. But be careful to support his head."

Erit sends two of his team members to take over. When I try to help them, Cassian gets in my way. "Get back to your team, Princess. And to your tunnel."

Already? "We don't stay for the next fight?"

"Why would you?" he asks. "You're wasting valuable digging time. You only get your tunnel for a week."

He's right, but I cast a worried glance at Jasper. I need to know where he ends up. Llion suddenly appears beside me, tugging me away before the guards can reach for their bone lashes.

He murmurs, "If Twisted Metal gets a tunnel below ours, we'll see his team pass by. You can worry about him then. For now, focus on your own recovery."

He's right. I need to conserve my energy. Allow my body to heal.

Unless Jasper gets hurt in a fight. Then he won't be going anywhere. I sense his chocolate eyes following me and when I glance back one last time, I find him standing tall beside Badenoch.

Jasper nods. Once. *Go on*, the gesture says. *I'll be okay.*

You'd better be.

23

MARBELLA

The third tunnel yawns before us. Five guards take up position at the mouth of the cave beside the entrance. Llion urges me inside the tunnel with the others, but it doesn't take him long to speak with Roar.

"Lady Storm fought hard," he says to the blue-winged gargoyle. "She needs to take it easy today."

Roar claps Llion on the shoulder. "I understand, friend. And I agree. Today she can learn about mining, but we won't push it."

Satisfied with that, Llion joins Welsian and Iago as they disappear further inside the tunnel. The faint clatter of buckets banging against their shovels as they walk tells me how far ahead they are.

"How do you know that a heartstone is buried under this mountain anyway?" I ask Roar as he hands me a pickaxe.

He ambles down the tunnel and says, "We don't know for sure. We only have legends to guide us. But the first heartstone was found in the heart of Mount Virtuous so there's some proof to support the stories."

"Virtuous is a clan name, isn't it? Are all of your mountains named after your clans?"

He laughs. "Actually, our clans are named after our mountains.

192

They are the names of the gargoyles who gave their lives for our new world: Prime, Virtuous, Lightsworn, Sunflight, Denrock, just to name a few. Even that son of a… er… even Grievous decided it was worth giving his life to save his people."

"What about the Supreme Incorruptible? Is there a mountain named after the royal line?"

Roar shakes his head. "The Gargoyle King Supreme gave his life to separate the layers of the Earth, which means that his body didn't form a mountain. His wife Queen Incorruptible became the moon, and the legend is that her heart remains in the moon above us. But as for the King's Heartstone, nobody knows. Some gargoyles say that Mount Erador hides it, but I don't think so. To answer your question: there isn't a Mount Supreme."

"Is that why Howl said there were twenty-seven more chances? He doesn't count the royal hearts?"

"That's right. And even if they are found, they're useless to him."

I slip the pickaxe into one of my pockets, wiping my mouth with my sleeve. Luckily, most of the bleeding has stopped. Before we leave the Cavity, Roar spreads a gummy sort of glue along the cut above my eye, telling me it would keep it closed so it can heal. "I would have thought the royal hearts would be the most powerful."

"Oh, they are. Incredibly dangerous. King Supreme's heart is the most dangerous of all. But only a gargoyle from the royal line can handle them and not be instantly killed. Even if he found one, Howl could never use it."

A heartstone that could kill Howl. The fact that there is *anything* in our world that could defeat that monster gives me hope. "You said the first heartstone was found in Mount Virtuous, so I'm guessing that's the heart of Virtuous then?"

"Virtuous was known for her kindness. Mercy. A bit like your elven House I guess." His expression turns dark in the light of the spider web. "It's ironic given the atrocities Howl has committed with her heart."

I remember that the Heartstone had caused Howl to react strongly to my pity while it was non-reactive to my anger. That would make sense if the gargoyle it belonged to was known for her kindness.

"So I guess we're looking for Prime's heart here?"

He exhales, gesturing at the end of the tunnel. The rust-colored rock wall rises up before me. "That's the idea." He gestures at the end of the tunnel ahead of us. "Here, I'll show you how to use your pickaxe."

I spend the rest of the morning learning my new trade, how to chip away at the stone, gather the debris, and tell if the rock wall is becoming unstable. Once he's satisfied that I'm not going to cut off my own fingers, Roar leaves me with strict instructions to go easy today.

He and the other men settle into a rhythm, pickaxes slamming into the rock one after the other, over and over. Their strength and resilience is breathtaking. They keep going even when sweat pours down their bodies and their chests heave. I marvel at the way they use their wing daggers to break the rock where their hands can't reach. At one stage, Iago flies up to the ceiling and hangs from the beams while he uses a combination of his chisel and wing daggers to even out the ceiling above us.

We stop twice to check the groups of gargoyles who travel past us to the fourth and fifth tunnels. Jasper isn't among them. Relief floods me, but it's quickly replaced with pity for the gargoyles headed down there. The first group has tied wet scarves across their mouths and noses to guard against the toxins in the air of the fourth tunnel. The second group carries buckets of water and have already doused their clothing in water, prepared for the fires in the fifth tunnel.

"They'll aim to survive," Welsian says at my shoulder. He's quiet for such a big gargoyle; I didn't hear him approach. "Digging will come second to staying alive."

"I'm glad that's not us. But I'm angry they're being made to go down there."

"Hold on to your anger, Princess. Use it for the next round of fights. Those teams will fight much harder next week to avoid this fate again. We don't want to be the ones mining those tunnels."

By the end of the day, I'm tired and sore all over. Only some of the pain is a consequence of the fight against Arlo. The rest of it is from repetitive digging and bending. I crave nothing more than an ice bath, but I'll be lucky to get a shower. As the only woman, I don't think they're going to clear the bathing room for me to use it in privacy.

As I enter the food hall, all talking stops. Every gargoyle turns to face me. I pull up sharp, my pain forgotten. Llion and Roar halt behind me with Welsian and Iago a few steps behind them.

The team in the back far right corner must have been the ones that ended up in the fifth tunnel. Their skin is dusty with ash, bearing smears across their cheeks and bare chests. The team at the table to my closest right have clean faces around their mouths and noses, but dust everywhere else—they were the ones in the fourth tunnel wearing face masks. Jasper and Badenoch are at my closest left. They're hunched, exhausted. At a guess, I'd say they spent the day clearing fallen rocks from the second tunnel. Only Erit's team looks like us: sweaty, dirty, but not in misery.

I can't read the gargoyles' intentions. Are they angry? Vengeful? Plain old tired? Nobody speaks. As I gaze over them, my fear of what their silence means turns to anger, but not at them. We shouldn't be divided like this. We're all here because Howl has imprisoned us and the ones we love. We all want freedom.

Cassian and his guards watch over the group in their usual spots around the edges, but as the silence extends, Cassian steps forward, reaching for his bone lash. He allows it to unravel, and the black tip hits the floor with a *snap*. To my surprise, he steps up beside me as if he's protecting me.

"Don't read anything into this, Princess," he hisses. "Howl wants to put you through hell, but he doesn't want you dead. I'm looking after myself, not you."

I'm not completely sure the silence means the miners are going to attack me, but that seems to be the way Cassian interprets it.

He growls at them. "You can get your revenge in the fights, scum. Now get back to your meals."

The team in the back corner is the first to obey, lowering their heads to their food, and resuming quiet conversation. I'm relieved when the other teams follow. The only one still looking at me is Jasper and I can't read his expression, oddly shuttered.

The only remaining free table is the one in the center of the room. That means no matter where I sit, my back will be exposed to someone. Not exactly a safe position. Llion takes my arm and guides me to a seat, sitting beside me, his wing partially extended across my back. Welsian and Roar bring us plates of mush, Roar takes the seat on my other side, and I dive into the food, knowing that whatever happens next, I have to eat while I can.

Between the fourth and fifth mouthfuls, Llion nudges me. I look up to see Roar shift from directly beside me so that someone else can slide into his seat.

My heartbeat returns to normal when I recognize Jasper. "Jasper, are you okay?"

His expression softens. "I'm fine. We got the second tunnel. It's hard work, but not as dangerous as other tunnels. Here, let me look at you."

I tilt my head so he can examine the cut above my eye. The glue that Roar applied has kept it closed. It hasn't bled all day.

"It looks as good as it can." He glances across the room, but the guards aren't paying attention to us anymore. "You made an impact today."

"I got that impression when I walked in." I shovel in another mouthful of food. As my dusty hand rises to my mouth, I wonder what I look like right now. Covered in dirt. Filthy. Sweaty. Tired. I probably should have made a trip to the small bathroom at the back of the food hall to wash my hands before I started eating, but there's no way I'm going anywhere alone this evening. Besides, the dirt hides the bruises so maybe it's better that I don't wash it off.

That way the gargoyles won't be able to see everywhere I'm hurt. "How many of them want to kill me?"

"None of them."

The spoon stops at my mouth.

Jasper reaches for it, pressing my hand back to the table, forcing my full attention. "You could have broken Arlo's arm this morning, but you chose not to. You told them that you aren't their enemy and they heard you. They heard Llion when he said you got closer to killing Howl than anyone ever has. Even the guards were talking about the fight in Crimson Court. I heard them myself. They said you could kill Howl."

I'm suddenly not hungry anymore. "Jasper... what are you saying?"

"I'm saying you started something. You lit a spark."

I stare at him. If he's talking about rebellion, then I want it to flare up and rage like wildfire. But sparks can be dangerous. Hope is dangerous. Uncontrolled fire can spread in directions you don't want it to, and it always results in death.

"That wasn't my intention, Jasper. I just wanted the others to stop targeting me." I shake my head vehemently. "I've lost my power. I won't get it back until I free Baelen. Even then, I don't know what will happen. I can't help the gargoyles. I can't even help myself."

I lean toward him. I'm the one grasping his hand this time, begging him to hear me. "I can't have their deaths on my conscience."

"Don't be afraid," he whispers back to me, dropping his forehead to mine. I close my eyes and try to absorb the calm he always carries with him. I want to go back to the moment when we were riding the phoenix together with the Storm sailing beside us—back when I had determination and hope, before I met Howl and discovered the destructive power of gargoyle heartstones or the cruelty of his actions.

Jasper whispers, "The gargoyles are smart. Careful. And..." He glances at the guards who are now looking our way. Jasper's comforting gesture hasn't gone unnoticed by anyone—none the least Cassian who wears a shuttered expression—but I don't care if it looks like weakness.

Jasper draws back, cupping his hand briefly against my cheek. To onlookers, it must appear as if he's saying something reassuring to me, but what he actually says is: "They want to talk to you."

He pushes back his chair, his touch slides away from me, and he returns to his team without looking back. The empty seat beside me leaves a hollow. I rub my face with my hands. I smear dirt everywhere but there's nothing I can do about it right now. Just like I can't help the gargoyles' hope of rebellion or my own desperation to get out of here and back to Baelen.

24

———

MARBELLA

The next day follows the same pattern of work in the third tunnel, except that we gain so much ground that we're going to need to put up new supports soon. Roar and Iago argue about whether our team should put up the supports before we finish for the week or leave it for the next team. In the end, Welsian steps in and asks, "What would be honorable?"

Roar promptly decides we'll put up the supports before the end of the week.

I keep my head down at breakfast and again at dinner, but it doesn't make much difference. Halfway through the meal, Roar vacates his seat again. I look up, expecting Jasper.

I freeze when I find myself looking at Badenoch. At the same time as he sits down, multiple gargoyles from different teams stand up, stretch, and move tables, making Badenoch's move to our table less conspicuous.

"Lady Storm," he says, addressing me the way Llion does. "I am Prime Badenoch. This Cavity was once the home of my clan, the Prime Clan."

He's speaking to me the same way that I spoke to all of the gargoyles after the fight with Arlo. I'd told them who I was and where I came from. Now, Badenoch is doing the same for me.

199

"You might be surprised to know that we gargoyles are not naturally warring folk," he says. "We are creators: farmers, carpenters, stone workers. We value beauty. Our women have always been sacred, protected, and valued." His expression hardens. "Howl took everything that was good about our culture and destroyed it."

He pauses for long enough that I whisper, "Why are you telling me this?"

"Because I sense my ancestor's heart in this mountain. The heart of Prime. Only the gargoyles from my clan feel it. But it *doesn't* call to us. It pushes us away. Prime's heart doesn't want to be found. Do you understand?"

He peers at me, his cautious eyes searching my own. "Sometimes I think I'm close to it and I deliberately dig in the wrong direction. I will not risk finding it. Not even to save my children. It doesn't matter what Howl has promised us. We won't find another heartstone for him."

"Who found the first one?"

"Virtuous Rhain."

I recognize that as the name of Carmen's husband. He was the gargoyle whose wings were taken.

Badenoch continues, "He thought he could use the heartstone against Howl. But its power was too immense. It knocked him unconscious. By the time he woke up, he was in chains."

My heart sinks. Ever since I heard about the heartstones, I'd secretly hoped that we might find one and somehow use it to defeat Howl. Howl had told me that only a gargoyle can handle a gargoyle heartstone and the Storm had confirmed that for me. She'd also warned me against asking Jasper to try using one. Now I understand why.

I swallow my disappointment. "Where are your children now?"

"Their mother is dead. She took her own life after Howl forced her into his harem." He doesn't stop speaking, but his voice scratches, becoming a hoarse whisper. "My children are in an orphanage, but I don't know which one."

After we rescued Talia on the border, she told us that she'd hidden as a worker in an orphanage—that all of the Priestesses had chosen to hide themselves in plain sight while helping the children there. I'm not sure if it will be any comfort to tell Badenoch this, but I say, "The Priestesses are taking care of them. They're scattered throughout the orphanages and are watching over the children."

Some of the tension releases from the set of his shoulders. "Thank you, Lady Storm. You've eased my mind with this news." He stands and as if on cue, random gargoyles at other tables stand at the same time, shuffling positions. Badenoch disappears among them.

Each night for the next four days, a new gargoyle sits beside me and tells me his story. They talk and I listen. I meet the leaders of the other teams and hear about their wives kept prisoner in Harem Hall or Slave Station and their children who had nowhere to go but orphanages.

On the sixth night, I look up to find Erit hovering beside me. I'm really not sure what to expect from this gargoyle. He was the most unwelcoming of them all when I first arrived, taunting me before and during the fight with Arlo. I really hope Jasper's right that Erit doesn't want to hurt me.

He stares at my hands instead of my face, clearly uncomfortable. The men shower at the end of each day and renew their cloak of work dust during the next. But me, I've washed my face and hands in the sink of the bathroom in the food hall and that's pretty much it. I'm quite certain I now stink. Possibly badly.

He slides into the vacant seat and says, "My name is… Grievous Erit."

My eyes snap to his, surprised that he's from Howl's Clan.

"Yeah," he says, finally meeting my eyes as if the admission about his clan is a relief. "I'm from *that* Clan. But I'm not with Howl. Some of us renounced our clan when Howl killed the King. I just wish I'd done it sooner. I… uh… didn't have the easiest upbringing."

"Please," I say, "Tell me about your clan."

"The simplest way to describe my clan is to tell you about

Grievous himself. You see, there's a legend that Grievous only gave his life when the new world was built because it gave him the chance to spawn the deadliest creatures: shadow panthers, slither snakes, and talon crows. To remind us that our lives remain in balance. That death is always around the corner."

I say, "I noticed that the shadow panther is the Grievous Clan's symbol."

Erit's expression becomes more hooded than before. "To be truly accepted into the Grievous Clan, teenagers must go alone into the darkest part of Mount Grievous to track and kill a shadow panther. If you return without one, you are beaten and cast out of your home. It took me three nights in the freezing cold, but I did it."

I remember my fight with the shadow panther during the marriage trials. It had smelled my blood and come after me. Jasper had tried to defend me, and I'd raced to save his life. It was the first time I held a knife and used lightning as a weapon. "They are certainly vicious creatures."

A curious expression settles over his gnarly features. "You've seen one?"

"Jasper and I fought a shadow panther on Scepter Peak back in Erawind."

His eyebrows lift. "You're still alive so you must have killed it. Or Jasper did?"

"I did."

His features remain in a state of surprise. "Have many elves have killed shadow panthers?"

I shrug. "I honestly don't know. I'd never seen one before that night. I was injured and it must have smelled my blood. We think that's why it came after me."

A thoughtful crease forms on his forehead. "Lady Storm, there must have been another reason. Shadow panthers don't crave elven blood—"

He stops speaking as Welsian makes a sharp warning gesture from across the table. A quick glance tells me that Cassian is approaching from the other side of the room. He must be concerned about Erit sitting beside me after all of Erit's threats and taunts during the fight.

Erit vacates his seat, keeping his head down, wings pinned close at his side, and his hands up. "Yeah, yeah," he says to Cassian. "I wasn't going to hurt her. I just wanted to tell her she won't beat us next week. You know, psych her out a little. No harm in that, is there?"

Cassian glares at him, letting the bone lash unravel and its tip drop to the ground.

I roll my eyes at the aggressive gesture. "It didn't work," I say, casting as much contempt as I can muster in Erit's direction. "My team could pulverize Erit in two seconds. Really, there's no need for lashing."

Cassian winds up the whip, but he does so slowly, leaving the threat to hang in the air. He glares at Erit as the other gargoyle backs away between the tables and chairs, putting as much distance between himself and Cassian as possible.

Cassian spins on his heel, his order clipped. "Princess, you will come with me."

My team shoots me varying looks of alarm. Cassian has left us alone all week other than being a malevolent presence in the background. Suddenly he wants me to come with him, and I'm not sure where he could want me to go. Or what's going to happen when I get there.

My hesitation is enough for him to twist back to me, the threatening bone lash now pointed at me. He winds the end of the whip around his hand and closes his fist around it. "Are you refusing?"

I shake my head, a rapid side-to-side. "No-o. Just not sure if I heard you right."

"This way."

I follow him out, but I'm worried. Nobody else has been called out with me. I have no idea what he could want with me. Maybe the conversations with the gargoyles haven't gone as unnoticed as I hoped. Maybe he's just been biding his time to confront me about them. A backward glance tells me that my entire team is on its feet at the center table, watching me go, fists clenched, wings arched. I can practically hear their growls from here. A row of guards closes around them, and I shoot my friends a rapid headshake that I hope they'll interpret correctly: *Don't make a move.*

The door closes behind me, sealing me off from my team, and I'm alone with Cassian inside the Cavity.

"Hurry up," he says, striding ahead of me as he tucks away his bone lash. My forehead puckers. Now that we're out of sight of the guards and miners he seems more impatient than threatening.

I keep my guard up, staying on his heels until he passes the bathing room and pulls up sharp on the other side of it. There's another door on this side that I never noticed before.

Cassian swings it open, and I crane my head to study the small room inside. It contains three chairs against one wall, a cupboard on the other, and nothing else other than another door beyond it.

"What is this?"

"My personal bathing chamber. There's a bath in the next room."

"Good for you." I fold my arms across my chest. "Can I go now?"

"You need a bath," he says, his nose wrinkling. "Badly."

I scowl at him. I've been dirty and stinky for days. "Why do you suddenly care if I'm filthy or not?"

"You need to be clean for tomorrow."

"To head back into the tunnel?" I scoff. "I'll be dirty again in seconds."

"You aren't going into the tunnel tomorrow."

All humor dies in my throat. I press my fist to my heart. "But tomorrow's the last day of the week. I have to help my team."

"Not tomorrow."

"Wait a minute—"

"Only you would argue against a day off."

I wrench my hand from my chest, glaring at him. "Because I'm worried about what I'll be doing instead!"

"You'll find out." He jerks his head in the direction of the bathing room. "Now get inside and bathe."

I storm across the room and grip the handle as he follows me inside. "You know what would help me more than a bath?"

He growls in exasperation. "What?"

"A blanket. It's freezing cold at night, and I don't have wings to keep me warm."

"Well, you're getting a bath instead."

There's no point arguing. In fact, I'm surprised he's let me argue this long. I shove open the door and enter the bathing room expecting to see some sort of water cascade forming a shower of sorts. I'm surprised to find an actual bath. What's more, it's full to the brim with water.

When I cross the distance and run my hand through it, it's warm. Not lukewarm, but toasty warm. A warm bath. A real bath. A small piece of heaven. I almost moan in anticipation of sliding into it. I clamp down on my excitement before Cassian catches my happiness.

Plastering myself with a cloak of disdain, I say, "Okay I'm here. You can go now."

Instead of vacating the room, he closes the door, takes a seat on the chair beside it, and kicks his boots out, crossing one foot over the other.

Denying what my eyes are telling me, I try again. "Are you leaving or…?"

"Or."

My eyes narrow so much that the edges of the room blur. A quick glance left and right tells me there's nothing in this room I can use to force him out. Other than the chair he's sitting on, the bathing room contains a bench with clean clothing and a towel folded on one end of it with a cake of soap resting on top. A bucket sits beside the bath. It's metal. Could be used to knock him out. Maybe.

He casually pulls out the bone lash again. I've never seen one in action, but the gargoyles are genuinely afraid of it. I guess if Llion designed it, then it's destined to be an efficient weapon.

"I'm not letting you out of my sight. Now bathe," Cassian orders.

I grind my teeth together and blow out an exasperated sigh.

"Fine." One thing at least, I'm not afraid he'll try anything. Purely because I'm an elf. Howl's mocking comments about my fertility and his contempt for half-breeds would cause Cassian to think twice before attempting anything his leader wouldn't like. At least… I don't think Cassian will try anything.

I slip off my boots, unbutton my shirt and pants, and rip them off. I hurl them at the empty end of the bench. They hit it with angry slaps. My underwear follows next. *Slap-slap.*

I plant my hands on my hips. He wanted me naked. Well, I'm naked.

He jumps to his feet, sapphire eyes wide, clearly taken back. I suppose he thought I'd at least attempt to cover up.

Show's not over yet, buddy. Because there's no way I'm getting into this beautiful bath without washing off some of the dirt first. Otherwise, the water will turn brown with grime, and I really don't want to soak in mud.

Hurling daggers at him with my eyes, I snatch up the bucket, drag it through the water, and pour it over myself. As the water rushes over me I fight the urge to close my eyes and soak it up. It's been far too long since I had a good wash. I keep a grip on the bucket in case he tries anything. I might even carry it into the bath with me just in case I need to use it as a weapon. I'm not sure how I'd feel about using the tangle on him while I'm naked—could be a bit awkward—but I'm prepared to break his arm if I have to.

Rivers of dirt run around my feet and disappear underneath the bath. Rushing water tells me there's a drain beneath it. Good thing, or I'd now be standing in a large puddle.

As I scoop up another bucketful, a soft click sounds behind me. I look up in time to see the door close and Cassian gone. The water sloshes in the bucket back and forth for five counts before I'm convinced he isn't coming back.

I sag against the side of the bath.

Now I can count the number of men who have seen me completely naked at… two. I scrub my eyes, pretending that the hot water trickling down my cheeks is from the bucket and not tears.

I want to hear Baelen's voice. I want him beside me. I crave his touch. His hands. His chest. His half-smile that makes my heart flip around in my chest. *Him.* I can defend myself and fight for myself, but I'm tired of doing it alone.

Badenoch said that he'll do anything to *not* find a heartstone, but I'm not sure I have any other choice. I need to free Baelen and heal him. To do that, I have to find a heartstone. And give it to Howl. Which will make him stronger than he already is. My shoulders slump. There's no way to win this.

Alone now, I take the time to scrub my body and hair thoroughly with soap before I slide into the bath. I leave the bucket outside of it but within arm's reach, just in case. I fully submerge myself, allowing the immersion to soothe my senses and halt my thoughts. I remain in the bath for another ten minutes, until the cooling water forces me to get out.

The world rushes back in as I slosh out of the bath. I dry myself as fast as I can and squeeze as much water from my hair, rubbing it with the towel. It might not have been a good idea to wash it given how cold it gets at night. The idea of trying to sleep while icicles form in my hair is not appealing.

When I exit the bathing room, Cassian waits on one of the seats, leaning forward, elbows on his knees, wings curved around his sides. I make enough noise to draw his attention, but he fixates on a point on the opposite wall, unusually subdued.

"I didn't expect you to do that," he says.

I assume he's referring to my earlier display of nakedness. I retort, "You thought I'd try to cover up or at least turn around? Maybe get into the bath fully clothed?"

"Something like that." He lifts himself from the seat, revealing a blanket in his arms. He turns to face me, his chiseled features appearing drawn and unsettled. "I didn't see it before, but now I do."

"See what?"

His eyes flash to mine. "Why Howl finds you intoxicating."

He passes me the blanket and I clutch it close to my chest. It's time for me to get out of here. He isn't blocking the doorway. I can walk straight past him. I head for the exit as fast as I can.

Outside, a flash of movement from above and to my right draws my attention to the bathing house roof. My eyes widen as I recognize Llion and Roar perched above me, foot claws gripping the edge, pickaxes in hand, ready to leap down if they must. Cassian is still inside and hasn't seen them. I shake my head, hoping they'll read it as: *I'm okay. He didn't touch me.*

The last thing I want is for a fight to break out. Especially when I'm okay.

They slink back into the shadows as Cassian follows me out. He didn't see them.

I focus on my feet and keep walking. According to Cassian, something is happening tomorrow that apparently requires me to be dirt-free and smell like vanilla-scented soap. I race back to the space below the hammocks where many of the men are taking flight to bed.

When Llion appears like normal and flies me up to my hammock, I tell him everything that happened, including my brazen behavior.

"I guess General Cassian didn't see that coming," Iago cackles. He was listening in from the hammock at my feet. Llion doesn't say anything as he reaches across from his hammock, one hand gripping the side of mine. I curl my hand inside his big palm and pull the blanket over myself, right up to my ears. It's thick and eases the chill seeping through my limbs.

"We'll miss you in the mine tomorrow," Welsian says from the hammock at my head. "We're putting up the supports. But we won't find anything while you're gone."

Was I scared that they might? That I wouldn't be there in case they unearth a heartstone? "What do you think will happen if we find a heartstone?" I ask. "Does our whole team get back what we want—or only one of us?"

My question hangs in the air. Nobody has an answer.

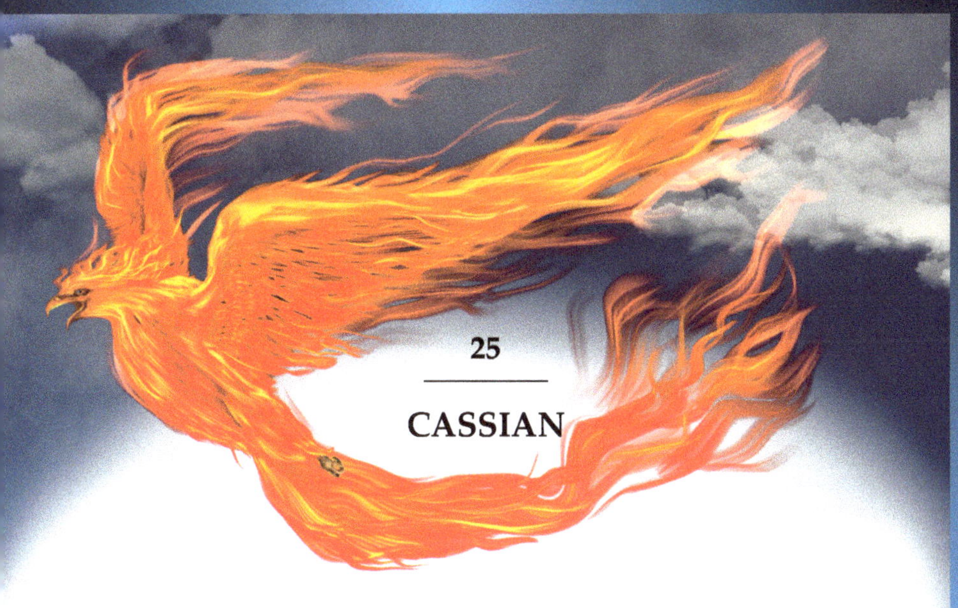

25

CASSIAN

Marbella is eating dinner inside the food hall and I shouldn't take my eyes off her, but she needs a bath before tomorrow. Layers of dust have caked onto her arms and neck, not to mention the ends of her hair—her pale tresses now a dull brown color. If Howl hears about her appearance, it will give him the excuse he wants to visit the mine and check up on her. That's the last thing I want.

Still, leaving her unattended is a risk. Tensions have been growing among the miners and I can't pinpoint the source. Every night, they rotate around while one of the men from another team sits with her. So far, none of them appears to have threatened her, but I have to treat their behavior with suspicion.

I hurry to the supply room to grab a new set of clothes for her, then I race to my bathing room, pausing in the entrance room to collect a towel and a cake of soap, depositing them onto the bench inside the bathroom.

A hidden faucet at the side of the room releases the water into the bucket I place beneath it. The water flows warm and soothing from a hot spring deep inside the mountain. So far, the tunnels haven't disturbed the spring, but I'm waiting for the day when the water runs cold or stops running altogether because the spring been destroyed.

I haul bucket after bucket to the bath, filling it to the brim. Normally, I don't bother using it, filling a bucket to wash myself, since my wings are too large for a bath to be much use to me. But at least if the bath is full, she can sink into it and undress behind its deep sides, get herself clean with some semblance of privacy since I won't be able to leave the room while she's here.

Finishing the task, I pause at the door, my hand pressing against the doorframe. I can't expect her to trust me, to follow me here if I ask politely.

I'll have to order her.

She won't like it, and neither will I, but I'll do what I have to.

Setting my features into a blank mask, I retrieve my bone lash from the entrance room and stride back to the food hall.

I freeze in the doorway. Grievous Erit is sitting beside her, leaning across her so I can't see her face. I can't see if she's threatened. Of all the gargoyles I could have left her with…

Dammit. I hurry across the distance, my wing daggers angled forward, my bone lash gripped in my fist.

Erit sees me coming and immediately rises from his seat, his eyes lowered, wings kept close to his sides in a subservient gesture. "I wasn't going to hurt her. I just wanted to psych her out a little. No harm in that, is there?"

I glare at him, allowing the bone lash to unravel. Its tip hits the ground with a snap while I check Marbella over. She looks relaxed enough.

She's dismissive, eyeing Erit with disdain. "My team could pulverize Erit in two seconds. Really, there's no need for lashing."

She's right. Llion could take Erit's head off. Roar is also an honorable man and even though he didn't want her on his team— an attitude that would have been his loss—he and his team have treated her with respect. It hasn't slipped my notice that they sleep around her in a protective square each night.

I wind up the lash, maintaining my aggressive attitude until Erit is a good distance away. He won't try anything now. I spin on my heel with a command thrown back at her. "Princess, you will come with me."

She hesitates, just like I knew she would, but I can't have her refusing. I slowly wind the lash around my hand. Dropping its tip is a more aggressive gesture, but she's seen me wallop a recalcitrant miner over the head with the lash wound around my fist. It packs a punch. "Are you refusing?"

She shakes her head, wide-eyed, her speech disjointed. "No-o. I wasn't sure if I heard you right."

Damn. She's not defiant—she's afraid. That's not what I wanted but it can't be helped. I incline my head in a sharp jab toward the door, waiting a beat for her to comply. "This way."

She finally follows me out and I exhale my relief as the door closes behind her. "Hurry up."

I listen for her footsteps, keeping her at the corner of my vision as I lead the way to the bathing room. She hasn't been in this area before, probably doesn't even know it's here. I swing open the door.

She digs in her heels, peering inside. "What is this?"

"My personal bathing chamber," I say. "There's a bath in the next room."

"Good for you."

I hide a grin. She's rebellious again. It's much better than afraid.

She folds her arms across her filthy chest. I'm surprised she can eat without getting dirt in her food.

She glares at me. "Can I go now?"

"You need a bath," I say, trying not to inhale. "Badly."

Of course, she asks me the difficult question: "Why do you suddenly care if I'm filthy or not?"

I attempt a partial truth. "You need to be clean for tomorrow."

"To head back into the tunnel?" She laughs. "I'll be dirty again in seconds."

"You aren't going into the tunnel tomorrow."

Her smile fades. So does her defiance. Worry settles across her face. Her fist presses against her heart as if it hurts. She's far too expressive, too vulnerable. Ever since she lost her storm power, there have been subtle changes in her expression, the way she carries herself, even the way her eyes reflect the light. I wonder whether the other gargoyles can see it or whether it's only me.

She takes a step toward me, imploring me with her eyes. They are pale blue in the light of the Elyria web high above us. "But tomorrow's the last day of the week. I have to help my team."

"Not tomorrow."

"Now, wait a minute—"

"Only you would argue against a holiday."

She glares at me. "Because I'm worried about what I'll be doing instead!"

I understand her concern, but I can't tell her. It would endanger not only her, but others who've already been harmed enough. All I can say is: "You'll find out." My voice turns to a snarl, my frustration getting the better of me. "Now get inside and bathe."

She storms across the anteroom. "You know what would help me more than a bath?"

Exasperation billows in my chest. She still hasn't entered the bathing room. "What?"

"A blanket. It's freezing cold at night and I don't have wings to keep me warm."

I grit my teeth. "Well, you're getting a bath instead."

She shoves the door open, but her anger evaporates instantly. I don't think she realizes she voiced her thoughts when she whispers, "An actual bath."

She crosses to it immediately, trailing her fingertips through the water, her eyes closing and a sigh leaving her lips. I guess she missed baths more than she let on. She quickly shakes herself, pressing her lips together and turning back to me, her chin up and her pleasure hidden. "Okay, I'm here. You can go now."

Not possible. There's too much tension among the miners to leave her alone. The only reason I sleep at all is because Llion is right beside her. He owes her a blood debt and won't let anyone touch her—even if remnants of her storm power light up the cavern ceiling at night, drawing the other men like moths to a flame.

The first night, they gathered in a swarm near her hammock while she slept, whispering about the strange crystalline Elyria web forming above her position. Llion threatened that if they dared come any closer, he'd break their arms. Roar and the other members of her team echoed his pledge. But it wasn't until I cracked my bone lash that the mob dispersed. Marbella slept through the whole thing and seemed oblivious in the morning.

If anything happens to her, Howl will come raging into the mountain. Nobody wins if that happens.

I close the door, take a seat, and stretch my legs, crossing one boot over the other, feigning nonchalance. She'll just have to get in the bath fully clothed, no matter how dirty it will make the water.

She frowns. "Are you leaving or…?"

"Or."

Her eyes narrow, and her glare is so fierce it could flay the skin off me. When her gaze shifts, I admire the way she's looking for a weapon, but there's not much she can use. I reach for my bone lash, casually resting it against my thigh. She needs to wash already.

"I'm not letting you out of my sight, Marbella. Now bathe."

"Fine." Her dagger-filled gaze doesn't ease up, but to my relief, she finally pulls off her boots. Except that she doesn't stop there, rapidly unbuttoning her shirt, ripping it off along with her pants and hurling them both onto the bench. Before I can stop her, she flings off her underpants and bra and pitches them against the wall, where they slap in the sudden silence.

Holy fuck.

I leap to my feet, my heart hammering an intense beat. I was not expecting her to do that. Nor was I expecting what the sight of her would do to me.

She plants her hands on her hips, completely naked and completely beautiful. All the way from her filthy hair to her perfect toes.

Rational thought scatters as my body's response takes control, freezing me to the spot. My head fills with the memory of her storm scent, her soft hair cascading across my arms, her hand pressed against my heart. I remember long ago, what it felt like to kiss someone who wanted to kiss me back.

Her expression dares me to touch her as she stoops to pick up the bucket, slipping it through the water to fill it. She tips her head back, arching her spine as she empties the entire bucket over her head. Water cascades down her face and neck, flowing across her breasts, hips, and thighs before trailing down her calves, tiny rivers that make me want to run my fingertips along their path. This time, she doesn't hide her moan of pleasure as the warm water sloshes over her body.

Her moan overwhelms my senses. I need her to make that sound because of me, because of my hands, not the water. *Need. Want. No...*

She reaches into the bath to fill the bucket again.

I can't watch the water cascade over her body again in places I suddenly want to touch. Not without crossing the distance between us, and I would never touch her like that unless she asked me to.

I have to leave.

I give myself a savage shake and force my feet to move, opening the door and closing it again. Quietly. Making sure I don't startle her. I stare at the closed door, press my hands against it, and try to breathe some sense into myself.

It's suddenly quiet inside the bathing room, only the faint trickle of water a reminder of her curves. I count the heartbeats until I sense her move again.

Her quiet sob reaches my ears.

Damn and fuck. What did I just do?

I drop into a seat in the anteroom, curving my wings around myself.

In the last ten years, I've done terrible things. I allowed my brethren to be maimed so they wouldn't be slaughtered. It's my fault Rhain lost his wings—the only punishment short of death that I could suggest that Howl would accept. I locked Llion up and told him his wife was dead so he wouldn't look back when he escaped, knowing that Howl would kill him otherwise.

But in the last ten years, I've never disrespected a woman. The first woman Howl sent to me was terrified. I gave her my bed and slept on the floor. But I kept her close, knowing that if she appeared to belong to me, she wouldn't be abused by the other men. Over time, I gathered my own small harem of women, those who had no other protection, making it clear that they were mine, even though they only warmed my bed when they chose to, not because I expected it. When a Grievous male slapped one of my women on her backside, I cut off his hand. *Don't touch what's mine.* It was a message that even the Grievous gargoyles understood.

Quietly, one by one, I found the women safe places to live far from the palace, some as matrons in orphanages, others picking fruit in the fields among other women. I keep an eye on all of them, making sure nobody threatens them.

I tell myself I'm trying to protect Marbella the same way I protected them, but I can't reconcile my physical response to her. More than physical. A deep need I haven't felt for a very long time. *Dammit, why did she have to remind me of Elaina?*

I jolt out of my chair, seeking safety in movement to calm my thoughts, hoping for redemption by retrieving a blanket from the cupboard at the side of the room. I grip it as I return to my chair and lean forward, my elbows on my knees. I stare at my hands—my enormous fists. I could crush her. That's what she sees when she looks at me. A captor with dangerous fists and a bone lash.

When she opens the door, I leave my wings where they are, curved around my shoulders in a gesture of remorse. I'm not sure if she'll recognize it, whether she understands that gargoyles communicate our emotions with our wings as much as we speak with our mouths.

It sounds like a useless apology when I say, "I didn't expect you to do that."

Her expression is blank. "You thought I'd try to cover up, at least turn around, get into the bath fully clothed maybe?"

"Yes." I lift myself from my seat, holding the blanket where she can see it. I don't want to shove it at her.

The truth is unsettling, but I speak it anyway. "I didn't see it before, but now I do."

"See what?"

I meet her eyes, trying and failing to forget the sound of her moan. "Why Howl finds you intoxicating."

I pass her the blanket. She accepts it, her face pale at my admission.

Moving to the side, I allow her to choose whether she stays or goes.

She chooses to leave, and I know it's for the best.

26

MARBELLA

The next morning, Cassian orders me to wait in the open area in the center of the Cavity while my team and the other gargoyles disappear into the tunnels. A group of guards remains around the opening to the shaft. Another group forms a crescent behind me. Security seems much more alert today.

Once the miners are well and truly out of sight, and the faint sounds of clanging metal indicate they've started work, Cassian signals a guard waiting at the entrance to the Cavity—the bottom of the ramp with the mine carts attached to it. The guard flies up and out of sight and I can only assume he's flying to the surface.

We wait another five minutes.

A breeze kicks up around me moments before a strong whooshing sound reaches me. It's different than the hum I heard when Cassian brought the King's bones to the food hall for choosing.

This is wings. Lots of wings.

A swarm of gargoyles shoots through the opening, pulling up high in the Cavity roof to slow down before settling to the ground. There are maybe fifteen of them, all carrying crates attached to their boots. Black robes cover their bodies from head to foot, complete with veils covering their faces, but their gossamer wings give them away. They're all female.

Sliding their feet out of the straps on top of the baskets before settling down, most of them head directly toward the tool room, ignoring me completely. Two hook their baskets over their arms and head in my direction.

"The miners don't know," Cassian says at my elbow. "Once each week, the women from Slave Station bring clean clothing and linens and take away the dirty ones. They also replenish our food supplies. The miners think that the cooking staff takes care of it all. You are not to tell your team, or any of the other gargoyles, what you've seen today."

The two women reach me, holding out their baskets. They don't remove their veils so I have no idea who they are underneath.

One of the women says, "We've brought provisions for the Princess."

Cassian clears his throat, shifting uncomfortably at the mention of "provisions." I roll my eyes at him but smile at the women. I'm happy to see them, whoever they are.

Cassian says to them, "You may use the food hall to show the Princess what you've brought. Once the door is closed, you may remove your veils. Nobody else will enter while you are there. I will knock when your time is up."

Provisions and the whole place to ourselves. It's practically a party. All my worry about what was going to happen today disappears. I lead the women to the food hall and wait for the cooking staff to vacate the room and close the door behind them.

Gilda and Carmen remove their veils, smiling at me. They both wear their gorgeous hair pulled back into tight buns, but they can't hide their beautiful wings. The patterns in them catch the light of the spider webs around us. "Hello, Princess."

I surprise them by embracing each of them. "I'm glad to see you, Gilda. Carmen." I shake my head in disbelief. "But Cassian said all of you were from Slave Station. How did you get permission to come here from Harem Hall?"

"Howl chose us personally. He probably thinks it will remind you of his threats at Crimson Court. To make sure you're still behaving yourself."

My happiness fades as I remember the way he'd hurt Carmen that day, telling me he'd kill her if I didn't obey him. "Well, you can assure him, I'm following the rules. I even had a bath when I was told to."

Gilda laughs, an infectious sound in the empty room. "I thought you were looking remarkably clean after spending a week in the mines." Her smile fades. "You should know that we're required to report back to Howl about your behavior, appearance, demeanor, basically everything about you that we witness today."

A wry answering laugh wrenches out of me. "I guess he misses me."

They exchange glances. Carmen tucks some stray hair behind her ear. "He's been in a particularly bad mood since he sent you away."

I study their faces and hands, wherever their skin is exposed. I'm looking for bruises. If he's taking out his bad mood on them… A sigh builds inside me. Knowing that I can't do a damn thing about it is killing me.

"What about my friends?" I ask. "The phoenix and Baelen Rath?"

"I'm sorry, we haven't seen either of them since that day at Court. But Howl did say something…" Carmen looks to Gilda. "Something about trophies? What was it?"

Gilda purses her lips, recalling, "He said he put his trophies in the Royal Residence. That's his home. It sounded like he meant your friends. As well as the High Priestess."

"Former High Priestess," I correct her.

She sighs. "Ah, yes, we all know the new High Priestess got away, but nobody dares call Howl out about it. As long as he claims to have the High Priestess, we all agree that's what she is." She changes the subject. "Here, let me show you what we've brought you."

Among the objects that spill out of the baskets are a hairbrush, toothbrush, two sets of Marbella-sized work clothing, and another blanket, much warmer looking than the one Cassian gave me. Not to mention the things I'll need when my cycle comes around. There's even a bag to keep everything in. I close my eyes with gratitude. "Thank you."

Gilda snatches up the hairbrush. "You may be clean, but you're in need of some grooming. May I?"

I'm glad she's gentle. My hair has become a bird's nest, made worse by its length, my tresses knotted from my scalp to my waist.

"We heard the tunnels here are some of the most dangerous," Carmen says.

"I haven't seen any of the other mountains, but the fourth and fifth tunnels are the worst. They've put us in teams, and nobody wants to mine those two tunnels." I skip the part about us fighting for tunnels. I'm sure Cassian will have reported back to Howl about my fight with Arlo. No need to worry Gilda or Carmen about it.

Carmen asks, "The teams can't help each other?"

Oh boy. How to explain that the teams are basically in competition with each other? "We aren't allowed to."

As she runs the brush through my hair, prying apart the worst knots with her fingers, Gilda asks, "Do you talk to many of the gargoyles here?"

It's a casual question, but Carmen immediately shoots warning daggers at her. I'm not sure why until I remember that Roar had said that Howl's harem is made up of the wives of the gargoyles most likely to oppose him. Gilda's husband could be any of the men here. I have no idea which one, and even in this empty room, I don't dare to ask outright.

I remain equally casual, saying, "My team has four men." I pause after I say each of their names, waiting in case Gilda gives me a signal. If I know which one she wants to hear more about, then I can tell her. "The men in my team are: Llion, who you saw at Crimson Court, Iago… Welsian… and Roar."

Gilda tugs my hair as soon as I say "Roar." I hope I've read the signal right because I continue speaking. "Roar is my team leader. He has these amazing wings with a blue pattern on them that reminds me of Elyria Web. Sometimes I think the pattern glows. He's very strong, never takes unnecessary risks, and always looks after his team. He didn't want to choose me at first. I guess he thought I'd be a liability." I smile, genuinely meaning it when I say, "I don't hold it against him."

I clasp my hands in front of me on the table. "He misses his wife. I'm pretty sure he would do anything to get her back. But he won't endanger her either. He stays alive for her."

Gilda is very quiet behind me. I can't see her face. She sniffles. Across the table, Carmen's eyes fill with tears for her friend, but it would be dangerous for either of them to break down.

Carmen gulps, takes a deep breath, and quickly changes the subject to distract Gilda. "Speaking of Elyria light, I'm surprised you haven't found it a problem, Princess. Most elves would struggle to see properly underground."

"I've adjusted, and now I love it, actually. It's warm and welcoming, and I can see the color changes, like in the morning when it turns green. I miss the sun though. I guess it's in my nature as an elf to miss the sun that the ancient Elven Queen gave her life to become."

"Just as we love the moon," Gilda says, her voice shaky but returning to normal. She leans down to my ear and whispers, "Thank you, Princess."

She finishes tying my hair just as there's a loud knock at the door. She and Carmen quickly flip their veils over their faces and retrieve their baskets. By the time I turn around, they look exactly like they did when they came in.

"Thank you for coming," I say. Words aren't enough for the gratitude I feel right now and not just because they brought me the basic necessities. For a few moments, I remembered what it was like to have female friends, to be surrounded by kind, caring women. I miss them the moment they take flight outside the food hall, joining the swarm of other women accompanied by guards.

I turn to Cassian, the bag of supplies filling my arms. Without thinking, I say, "I really want to put this in my hammock. Can you help me?"

He looks from me to the ceiling, eyebrows pulled down,

shoulders hunched. His response is clipped and dangerous. "How do you think I'm going to do that?"

I back away. I really didn't think my request through. A cold chill speeds down my spine. He allowed Gilda and Carmen to speak with me, but he's not my friend. Now he's either insulted because I talked to him like he's my errand boy--*bad move, Marbella*--or he's considering flying me up there himself, which would involve standing much closer to him than I'm prepared for. Considering he's seen me naked, very bad move.

"Sorry." I stumble as I step backward, righting myself just in time. "I forgot where I was for a moment."

With two more quick steps back, I spin and hurry away.

Not fast enough.

Two fully spread wings snap together in front of me, forcing me to halt.

27

———

CASSIAN

She's asking me to fly her up to her hammock—one of the purest gestures of trust a woman can show a male gargoyle. The kind of gesture she shouldn't make with me. Llion has flown her up and back many times, but his blood debt and the fact that he has a wife means that it's an act of assistance only. Likewise, when Roar flies her anywhere, it's out of pure necessity. But for her to ask me…

"Can you help me?" Her expression is trusting, relaxed, possibly even happy. Now that she's bathed and clean, her skin is luminescent, her cheeks glowing. I made sure she had complete privacy when she met with Carmen and Gilda. Even without observing her interactions with them, it's obvious that she took comfort from their presence.

My shoulders hunch over more than they already are. She doesn't know our customs. She doesn't know what she's asking me. She doesn't know that she shouldn't. I need her to take back her request immediately.

My response is a harsh rebuke. "How do you think I'm going to do that?"

She backpedals, all the happiness draining from her face, her emotions closing off completely. She's so anxious to get away from me that she stumbles as she turns away. She never stumbles. "I'm sorry. I forgot where I was for a moment."

My chest hurts. A sharp jab. I just stole her happiness. Like the thief that I am, my rebuke has destroyed any peace she felt—peace that, if I'm honest with myself, I wanted to give her. Regret storms through me, but I'm not sure how to make it right. I'm not sure if I can.

All I know is that I need her to stop walking away.

My wings shoot out, snapping together in front of her, their size giving me the ability to cocoon her where other gargoyles couldn't.

"Turn around," I order.

She shifts on the spot, avoiding touching my wings as I decrease the distance between us by striding forward. Even with my wings, she was almost out of range. She's wary and defensive now—as she should be.

I fixate on a spot on her shoulder, softening my voice, telling myself that she's an elf and flying her somewhere doesn't mean a damn thing. "Step on my feet. I'll fly you up."

I draw the line at saying 'please.' If anyone heard me, my reputation would be hit hard. I need to maintain control of this mine and the only way to do that is through the aggression I've honed for the last ten years.

She swallows. "I really don't need to take these up right now. I can wait until tonight—"

Frustration courses through me. She's so close to me now that I could wrap my arms around her waist and pull her to me. May the ancients forgive me, I want to. My voice is a growl as I meet her eyes, clear blue and cautious, and order her, "Step on my feet."

Her gaze fills with defiance. "Fine."

It's the same thing she said to me before she stripped in the bathroom. Heat fills my body, but this time I'm prepared for it, clamping down on my emotions.

Without missing a beat, she slips the bag over her shoulder, steps on my feet, and wraps her arms around my waist, pressing her head to my chest.

I fight the urge to close my wings even farther, to cocoon us like this. An emotion I haven't felt for a long time washes through me. It's so forgotten that I have trouble identifying it, no way to give it a name. Not peace, not happiness, not even lust. It eludes me so I push it away.

I spread my wings and we lift into the air.

28

MARBELLA

As Cassian's wings snap together in front of me, I pull up sharply, completely encircled.

I remember seeing his full wingspan when I first encountered him flying beside the phoenix. His wingspan is broader than any other gargoyle I've met, massive in fact, and that includes Howl.

"Turn around."

At least he draws the line at grabbing me. I pirouette on the spot, careful not to move closer to his wings in any direction. He focuses on a point at the edge of my shoulder. For a second, I sense regret in the line of his closely pressed lips and downward-cast eyes, but I'm not sure where that's coming from.

"Step on my feet. I'll fly you up."

Stepping on his feet requires leaning into his chest. I know that because Llion has flown me up to my hammock every night and that's the only way I don't topple backward. That, and Llion wraps his arms around me. It's perfectly fine with someone I trust. Not so much with Cassian.

My throat is dry. I try to find my voice. "I really don't need to take these up right now. I can wait until tonight—"

His scowl is back. Combined with a growl. He's not looking at my shoulder anymore, glaring directly into my eyes. "Step on my feet."

Somehow, it's easier to deal with him when he's mad than when he's bordering on helpful. "Fine."

He does a quick double take and I'm reminded that the last time I said "fine" to him was right before I threw off my clothes in disgust. Before he can get confused, I slip the bag over my shoulder, step on his feet, and slide my arms around his waist. I grit my teeth and close my eyes. He pauses for a moment. My nerves return.

Then he spread his wings and we lift effortlessly into the air. After a moment of silence, he says, "It might surprise you to know that I also started my life as a servant."

That does surprise me. I imagined him as evil General Cassian right from the moment of his birth. At the very least, I pictured him raised in some sort of military family like the children in many of the major elven Houses.

"I was a slave in the home of the Supreme Incorruptible, King Roman, himself."

He reaches my hammock but doesn't fly close enough for me to deposit my bag, choosing instead to wrap his hands around my waist and lever me backward so he can see my face. It's not a seriously dangerous angle, but it will be if he lets go. I keep my own grip firm on his waist. Otherwise, the only thing between me and the ground far below are his good intentions. I'm certainly not counting on those.

"I'm from the Hideaway Clan," he says. "The lowest of the low. You would be forgiven for thinking that all of Howl's Army is Grievous, but they aren't."

Since we left the ground, he's done all the talking. He seems to expect me to say something now while he maintains our position mid-air with light wing flaps. Not moving any closer to my hammock.

I ask the first question I can think of. "How did you become Howl's General?"

He answers my question with a question. "How did you become the Storm Princess?"

"The Storm chose me."

"Why? She was our storm. A *gargoyle* storm. Why would she choose any elf to calm her?"

I consider his question, searching for a reason. The truth is that she never told me. "I don't have an answer for that. I… she…" That awful memory returns to me, the full force of it so clear that Cassian blurs in front of me. I'd pushed Baelen out of the path of a lightning strike—a natural one—prepared to take the strike myself, but the Storm beat it to me. "I was trying to save someone's life, but I put my own in danger. When she chose me, she saved my life."

"Why would she do that?"

"I honestly don't know." I don't know what else to say. I need to ask the Storm these questions. I need to know why she became the Storm in the first place, as well as why she chose to save my life, and what triggered that choice for her. She could have let me fall. She could have allowed the last Storm Princess to die and never chosen another. She could have raged and killed us all.

Cassian pulls me back to him, leans in, and closes the gap. He inhales. His breath tickles my cheek. "You smell like…"

A deep furrow forms across his forehead, darkening his chiseled features. He peers into my eyes as if he's trying to draw something out of me. I have no idea what he wants. His eyes narrow and his voice lowers to a whisper. "But that's not possible."

He reminds me of Llion the day we came to the mines, telling me I smelled different now, and Erit the other day telling me about shadow panthers. I don't know how those things are connected, but both Llion and Erit wore identical expressions to Cassian right now, as if they're trying to discover the reason for something they sense but can't quite pinpoint. I have no idea what it is. I certainly have no idea why it's about me.

He contemplates me for another moment before he silently turns and allows me to place the bag into my hammock. His arms return to my waist. I only realize then that he hasn't brought his bone lash with him. He's completely bare of weapons. One arm wraps around my back and the other sweeps up into my hair, startling me until I realize he's supporting my head for the flight down.

He judges the distance to the ground before we drop. As the air rushes past us, he murmurs, "Definitely not possible."

A single beat of his wings slows the fall, and we glide to the ground. He releases me immediately, his wings snapping back into their usual position. "Be careful… Princess."

I step off his feet, not certain how to decipher his final comment. I back away and race to the entrance to the tunnels. I'm not staying up here any longer. I've never been so glad to enter the mine.

Welsian is the first to meet me in the third tunnel. He and Llion are in the middle of tapping planks of wood into place to create support beams.

"What happened?" Welsian asks. "Why did you have to stay back?"

I bite my tongue. I'm not supposed to mention the women. Not that I care about Cassian's rules, but I'm worried about the consequences. I don't know the identity of the other women, but if the miners knew that their wives and loved ones came here every week, they might attempt to see them. I meant what I said to Jasper: I don't want gargoyles getting killed because of me.

I clear my throat. I hate lying to my friends and I can feel my face flushing with guilt. Hopefully, they will interpret it as embarrassment. "A gargoyle brought me a basket of provisions." It's not a lie. Just not the full truth.

The mention of "provisions" does the trick. "Oh. Nothing nefarious then. Good." Llion changes the subject. "You're just in time to help finish the supports."

Anything to shift my focus off Cassian's cryptic remarks. I'm so busy trying not to think about what happened earlier in the day that I don't think about Gilda and Carmen's visit either. It's not until we finish work for the day that something Carmen said returns to me. We'd talked about how dangerous the tunnels are and she'd asked me whether the teams helped each other.

I stop at the entrance to the third tunnel on my way out.

Tomorrow the teams will fight each other again to determine which tunnel they'll work in next. The team from the fifth tunnel passes by, their clothing scorched. They look hopeful, but also afraid: can they survive another week in that place?

I swing back to Roar. "No team should have to mine the fourth or fifth tunnel twice in a row."

His pickaxe clatters into his bucket as he puts it down. The other members of our team pause behind him.

"True, it's cruel," he says. "But who would voluntarily take their place? And how would we even arrange it?"

"Well… we can't determine which bones get picked, but we can determine who wins the fights."

"You mean… throw the match?" Iago draws his chin back as if that's a horrifying thought. "Like Roar said, who would voluntarily do that?"

I sigh. "The teams who had the easiest tunnels this week."

"You mean us?" Welsian asks in his quiet voice. He rubs his arms and it's like watching tree trunks move.

I plow on. "What if we got all the teams to agree to a system? Random enough not to be obvious, but an order that gives everyone easy tunnels one week and harder ones the next. A week to recover before the next challenge."

I spin to the others. "Look, accidents happen, and people are more likely to get hurt when they're tired. The teams that go into those tunnels next week need to be fresh. That's us."

Llion has been quiet up until now. He lifts himself out of the shadows at the side of the tunnel. "And Erit's team. They mined the first tunnel this week. It's going to be hard to convince him to take the fourth or fifth next."

I say, "I can do it. I can convince him. But I need your help with the other teams. It only works if we all agree."

Iago asks, "I already hate the answer to this question, but which tunnel do you propose we mine next?"

I push away the suicidal urge to choose the fifth. I don't know enough about mining yet to attempt that, but I know the time will come when I have to. "The fourth."

Roar blows out a breath and drops himself against the side of the tunnel, shaking his head with a half-laugh. "What are you getting us into, Princess?"

"Control," I say. "We're taking back control."

ERIT WAITS FOR ME TO SPEAK. ALL WEEK, GARGOYLES HAVE BEEN coming to speak with me at dinnertime, but now I've asked for him specifically. He knows I have a question. But I don't intend to start with the one that really matters.

As the general hubbub of dinner washes over us, I ask, "Was General Cassian always stationed at this mine?"

He shakes his head. "I don't think he ever came here before."

I ask a question that I already know the answer to. "Why is he here now?"

"Because of you."

"Because of me." I prop my elbows on the table. "Why do you think that is? I have no power. I'm not a threat. What is Howl so afraid of that he sends his General to watch over me?"

A glimmer of a smile touches Erit's mouth. "He sees what we see."

"And what is that?"

"You're a leader." He shakes his head at me. He tries to hide his smile, but it doesn't work. "Wrapped up in a tiny package."

I hold his gaze. "I want to give Howl something to be afraid of, Erit. But I don't want him to know he should be afraid until it's too late."

"Well, I guess I'd like to know how you propose to do that."

"I want to start with the fights. I want us to take control of the outcome."

When I finish telling him my plan, he leans back in his chair, tapping the table, contemplating his hands. "You want my team to take the fifth tunnel next."

"Then you wouldn't get it for another four weeks."

"Assuming the other teams agree."

I lean forward. "They already have." It was easy to convince the teams who mined the fourth and fifth tunnels. Badenoch's team also agreed—I knew I could get him to see the plan's logic and Jasper backed me up.

"We cycle through the tunnels in the same order: three, four, two, one, five, and then three again. It means we get a break between the difficult tunnels and the burden never falls on one team more than the others."

"I don't know…"

"We have to take fear out of the equation. Howl rules by fear. If we start beating him in small ways, then the big ways will follow." I told Jasper I wasn't going to start a rebellion, but it's pouring out of me now, the need to fight back. "We're going to end him, Erit. I don't know how yet, but I know that this is where we start."

He rubs his face, scrubbing at his eyes. When I first met him, I thought he was an arrogant man. He'd underestimated me, but now I consider how much of that was fueled by fear. He pushes back his chair, and a number of random gargoyles stand up at the same time. They've been shifting around us at intervals for a while now and the guards have stopped paying attention.

"You're out of your mind." A grin breaks across his face. "But I'm in."

THE NEXT MORNING WHEN CASSIAN BRINGS IN THE BONES AND ROAR leans in for me to tell him which is the shortest, it's because he doesn't want to pick it.

"Third from the left," I whisper. At the same time, I hold my left hand behind my seat where the guards can't see it. I hold up three fingers. I'm sitting at one of the front tables and each of the passing team leaders glances my way. The leader of the team that mined the fifth tunnel is the one who will pick that bone.

The gargoyles don't question how I know which bone to pick. Even if they did, I couldn't tell them. All I know is that the hum that fills my body at night and makes me freezing cold, is the same hum that tells me which bone will give me the greatest power.

29

MARBELLA

We survive the fourth tunnel by wrapping wet cloths around our noses and mouths. The collapsed pockets in the floor are giant holes, at least six feet deep. While the rest of us spend time familiarizing ourselves with the safest pathway through, Iago comes up with something better. Identifying the solid sections of the floor, he shows Roar how we can run wooden planks across the holes—two spaced apart—then nail boards across them. He calls it a false floor. But we need flatter boards than the ones we have, which are all thick planks.

Roar asks to speak with Cassian who looms ominously in the entrance to the tunnel as Roar and Iago describe what we need. I wait in the background, but Cassian looks at me before he gives a curt nod. "You'll have them tomorrow."

As Iago passes me by, appearing pleased about the outcome, I understand why Roar had no hesitation about choosing Iago for his team. Whenever there's a difficult engineering issue, Iago always has a solution. When we need something enormous moved, on the other hand, Welsian is the gargoyle for the task. And Roar and Llion… I can't help but grin as I mentally label them as the workhorses. But me? I'm still not sure where I stand in all this. I just follow Roar's directions.

I catch his attention as he passes me. The wet cloth tied securely around my face muffles my voice. "Where does the wood come from?" All I have to do is turn around, and every week, there seems to be a new supply of it at the entrance to each tunnel, cut and ready to use.

"Groups of gargoyles work in the forests, chopping down trees, measuring out the planks. They're carpenters the same way we're miners. Then the couriers bring the supplies during the night."

"Why at night?"

He glances back to check that Cassian is gone. I can't see Roar's mouth because the cloth covers it, but I can't mistake his wry tone. "It's so we can't pass messages to them. We're stuck in our hammocks while they distribute the supplies without encountering us."

"How come I never noticed that?" A bunch of gargoyles lugging in wooden planks seems like a major disruption. Especially in the quiet of the night.

Roar scratches the back of his head and tightens his mask. I've gotten so used to seeing the gargoyles bare from the waist up that I hardly notice anymore. Sweat drips down the side of his face and down his chest. It's warm in the fourth tunnel.

"You… ah… you're a heavy sleeper," he says.

He seems oddly uncomfortable answering my question and I'm not sure why. I let it go even though I want to ask more. I was never a heavy sleeper in Erawind. In fact, light noises would wake me. I still remember the night Baelen woke me from my dreams when he sat outside my bedroom door, completely drunk, blaming the Storm for tearing us apart.

On top of that, the arrival of the female gargoyles the other day sounded like a tornado, so I don't understand how I could sleep through the arrival of a swarm of men.

That night, I'm determined to listen out for them. Cassian said there would be a delivery and I want to see it happen, even if I can't interact with the couriers. I fall asleep while my toes chill and my breath frosts, determined not to sleep so deeply, but I don't wake up until the next morning when my body temperature returns to normal. Curse these cold nights. It must be the night-time freeze that keeps me asleep.

We spend the following week finishing the work of the two teams before us to clear the collapsed second tunnel. The third week is the easiest when we get to mine the first tunnel, but our turn in the fifth tunnel approaches fast.

At the end of the third week, as he does at the end of each week now, Cassian calls me out of the food hall and shows me to the door of his bathing room. He closes the door behind him, and I don't see him again until the next morning. The night before we're due to mine the fifth tunnel, I emerge from the bath to find a silver handheld mirror resting on one of the chairs.

It's the first mirror I've seen since I left Harem Hall. The door is still closed, but Cassian is the only one who could have left it here for me.

I hesitate. I don't pick it up. I don't want to look at myself. I can see enough of my body to know that I've gained muscles I never had before, especially in my thighs and biceps—constant work will do that. I've spent a lot of time with my new hairbrush removing the bird nests from my head, so at least my hair won't look terrible, but as for my skin and eyes… I'm scared I'll look as bad as I feel. I can refuse to admit I'm exhausted if I don't see it written all over my face.

I turn the mirror face down and leave it on the chair. Half reach for it again, then take a step back before I do.

"Why don't you want to look at yourself?"

Cassian stays in the shadow of the door. I didn't hear him open it.

"I'm scared of what I'll see." There I go again, acting like he's my friend. I press my lips together, wondering what he'll do, but he doesn't move.

"You have nothing to be afraid of."

But I won't see the storm anymore. There it is. My greatest fear. For such a long time, I lived with lightning running across my skin, lighting up my eyes. Now it's gone and I don't want to see its absence. I don't want to see that little girl who used to tug on her braid when she was nervous.

He steps into the room, into the light, crossing the distance with quiet steps, and picks up the mirror, turning it to face me. Maybe it's fear or uncertainty or something else, but I don't look away.

He tilts the mirror so the first thing I see is my neck. My skin is paler than I remember, but that would be because I haven't been exposed to sunlight in four weeks.

The mirror reveals my chin and lips next, then my nose and eyes. *When did my face get so expressive? When did my eyes become so pale?*

Like my skin, my lips and eyes are glossy and translucent. Radiant in a way that I can't describe. *Who is this elf looking back at me?* She's definitely not what I expected. The storm is gone but a different glow has taken its place. Something I can't place. I press my finger to my lower lip, tracing the outline, tilting my head to examine my skin.

The mirror shivers. My attention snaps to Cassian, to the slight clench of his jaw, but he hasn't otherwise moved. He fixates on my finger, still pressed to my lips. I remove it slowly, but his focus remains on my lips. With minimal movements, he reaches for my other hand, running his palm across the back of my hand, curling my fingers around the mirror handle so I'm left holding it.

"It's yours," he says, his voice thicker than normal.

He tucks his wings closed, spins, and leaves me holding the gift.

Later, I crawl into my hammock after Llion flies me up. I'm colder than ever and desperate to bury myself in the blankets. My fingers are icy and my toes are popsicles. Llion didn't say anything when I stepped onto his feet, but he winced when I pressed my freezing hands against his back. For a few blessed moments, his body heat warmed me, but then we reached my bed, and I had to leave his warmth.

I double the blankets over, curl my knees to my chest, and pull the covers all the way over my head before I fall asleep.

For the first time in a long time, Baelen's voice echoes in my dreams. Memories flash through my sleeping mind.

He's holding out his hand to me in the hallway of his childhood home. *I've thought of a way for you to beat them.*

He's running his fingers through my braid on the cliff's edge, releasing my hair into the breeze before he kisses me. *May I have your permission?*

He's covered in flames. Acid rain drips upward into the sky. *Marbella, you're in trouble.*

You're running out of time.

Wake up.

A force as great as thunder blasts through me. The impact washes across me, right to left, lifting my body upward and casting it hard against the side of the hammock. Every bone shifts, weightless, released from gravity, and then snaps back into position as the blast passes.

I scream out in pain, my eyes squeezed closed as my cry shrieks through the Cavity.

The force wasn't me. I didn't do it. And it wasn't Baelen. I've combined my power with his enough times to know what his power feels like. The blast came from outside of me. From something far too powerful.

30

BAELEN

The rain no longer falls down my body. Instead, it drips upward into the sky. Tiny, blood-red drops lift from my shoulders as if the rain is peeling off me, taking me apart layer by layer, wearing me down.

The field of wild grass is scorched and flattened for a hundred paces all around me. Still, I hold this damn sword, its tip never solidifying, and as the days pass, my shoulders become heavy, my torso more bloody, the wounds in my chest opening up just a little more.

Ever since Marbella broke the thread that connected us, my view changed. Now, at the edge of the field, is a different sky, made up of moving pictures. Before, I sensed the world through her eyes, felt what she felt, heard what she heard. Now, I see it all as if it's far away.

Howl moves me around at his whim. One night, he puts me in a grand dining hall, where he eats dinner, gravy running down his chin as he orders a gargoyle to be imprisoned without food or water. The next, I'm placed in a dark room where the light doesn't reach. The next, of all the brutal places he could take me... his harem, where I clench my fists until I lose feeling in my hands, existing only for the day when I will cut his head from his

239

shoulders. I see Marbella in all their faces. I see her courage and determination. I see her pain.

No matter where I'm taken, the Storm remains at the corner of my vision, a silvery bundle. With every atrocity, she becomes more wilted, curling over herself, trying to hide beneath her wings. Sometimes she screams, but her power is anchored in me and she can't access it now. Like me, she doesn't sleep. She sees everything, all the things she shouldn't see. If I could break the chain that keeps her at my side, I would.

Now, I stand in Howl's personal quarters. It's the middle of the night but he paces opposite me, his wings slightly outstretched, veins pulsing green, his ochre eyes glinting as he prowls back and forth.

The door finally opens.

The gargoyle whose name is Gerst enters the room and takes a knee, offering up a wooden box to Howl. Gerst is ranked second after Cassian. Over time, I've pieced together that Cassian beat Gerst in a fight and replaced him as Howl's general, a fact about which Gerst is still sore.

Howl snatches the box from his fingers, flipping off the lid. It hits the floor next to the Storm, startling her, but she curves her body closer to me, hiding beneath her wings.

A smile grows on Howl's face as he studies the box's contents. I try to lean forward, not knowing what it contains. I catch sight of the edge of a glittering, sapphire object.

He snarls. "Now, I will make Marbella Mercy submit to me."

The fuck you will.

Rage flows through me so fast that I jolt forward, surprised by my own movement. I rally, pushing again, but the damn sword refuses to budge, holding me captive.

I roar into the upward rain, my voice turning to thunder. Raindrops splash against the edge of the field, cast in that direction by the force of the wind suddenly swirling around me.

I may not be able to move, but the rain can. I roar again, this time emptying my lungs, exhaling all my rage and all my fear for Marbella.

The raindrops ignite into flames.

Outside myself, I sense my body's real movement. My hands curl into fists and my head rises. I open my eyes, rage and heat filling them, flames licking across my vision.

Howl jolts so hard that he almost drops the box. He catches it before it falls, staring at me.

Suddenly, my sight changes and for a painful second, I can see Marbella, curled up asleep, her auburn hair peeking out from under her blanket, her eyes closed. She's peaceful. Serene. Crystalline Elyria web covers the space all around her.

Then, her image fades and so does my power.

Howl's quarters fill my vision once more. Gerst backs away from my location, taking paces toward the back of the room. "Is he waking up?"

Howl's lip curls. "No. He can't."

Gerst shakes his head. "You will need more than two heartstones to fight Baelen Rath when he wakes."

"You're right." Howl growls out his exasperation in a long, exhaled breath. "I will wait for a third."

My heart sinks. Howl has another heartstone.

Power from his first heartstone pulses through him, glowing emerald as he reaches into the box to take hold of the second stone. The minute his hand touches it, my senses explode. Power from both stones ripples through the field, shrieking toward me.

I hunch over my sword, bracing for impact. I need to warn Marbella, but I don't know how. I don't know if she'll hear me.

Marbella, you're in trouble.

You're running out of time.

Wake up.

31

———

MARBELLA

I cling to the swinging hammock as the aftershock rages through me, whimpering into my blanket. "A heartstone. Another heartstone."

Llion rears up from the hammock next to mine, launching himself across the distance. "Lady Storm!"

Tears leak down my face. I can barely open my eyes to look at him. "I felt it, Llion. I felt it."

Roar's voice is urgent from the other side. "What's wrong?"

"What happened?" Both Welsian and Iago are awake. In fact, it sounds like everyone is. *Lady Storm!* My name, the one the gargoyles have given me, echoes through the other hammocks as gargoyles wake up all around me.

I swallow and try to breathe. "Howl has another heartstone. I felt it like an explosion."

Murmurs of anger and despair filter through the listening gargoyles. Llion leans over me but directs his question to Roar. "Which heart could it be?"

"It's impossible to know, but at Crimson Court, the miners working in Mount Lightsworn said they were close to finding one. Howl's promise would have given them a reason to unearth it. I'm sorry, Llion. That's your wife's home."

Llion's shoulders slump. His wings form a protective curve around his torso. "Lightsworn's heart is the strongest one Howl could get his hands on. This is the worst thing that could happen."

Now that the initial shock and pain have faded, another sensation hits me.

I'm cold.

Burning and freezing at the same time. This is the first time I've woken up in the night since I got here and the deep freeze I find myself in is agony. Falling asleep was hard enough. Being awake is far worse. I shudder under the blankets, distracted by a light glowing beyond me.

I force my eyes all the way open. *What is that?*

My brow furrows as I look at the ceiling. Ice crystals cover it in a radiant white pattern glistening in the Elyria light. The nearest web has also turned white, its glowing strands resembling pure moonlight. The crystalline glow extends within several feet of my hammock, but not beyond. Further out, the ceiling is clear, and the spider web is silvery-blue like usual. The ice crystals have only formed around me.

It's too cold to lift my arm out of the blanket, but I raise a finger beside my chin, pointing at the ceiling. "What is that?"

"Ice," Llion says, before returning to his conversation with Roar.

"Yes-s-s." I interrupt him, my teeth suddenly chattering. "But how did it get there?"

He takes a closer look at me as all conversation dies down around me. For some reason, my question has dropped us into silence. He glances past me, maybe at Roar or Welsian. "We thought you knew."

I stare at him. "That I'm surrounded by ice?"

"It's been the same ever since you got here. Every night. We thought it was a storm thing. You always sleep through like it's normal."

A shiver rocks my body. Llion leans closer to me, concern washing away his puzzlement.

I say, "This is not a s-s-storm th-thing." I want to be asleep again. I don't want to be awake. Now that I am, the cold is eating me from the inside like acid. "Llion… I am… r-really c-c-cold…"

Icy shivers spear through my spine. My breath frosts. If what they're telling me is true, then *I'm* creating the cold. It's not the natural environment here. But I don't know how or why I'm doing it. I certainly can't make it stop.

"I-I'm so cold… it hurts… I d-don't think I'm okay…"

Llion touches his palm to my forehead. His eyes shoot wide. He lurches backward. "There's something wrong. We need to help her—"

The beat of a pair of strong wings interrupts him.

Llion rotates in the direction of the sound, blocking me from seeing who it is, but I recognize Cassian's growl. "What's going on?"

Nobody answers. The silence is thick.

Llion says, "Lady Storm needs help."

Cassian leans around him. I catch a brief glimpse of his sapphire eyes, narrowed and assessing, taking all of me in with that quick assessment, before Llion shifts sideways in a protective gesture, challenging Cassian. "Not your help."

Cassian snarls. "Get out of the way."

Llion pulls in closer to me, Roar closes in behind me, and Welsian and Iago draw up with them. It must be awkward maneuvering around the hammocks, but I'm surprised by how quickly my friends surround me in a protective circle. They spread their wings to cover the gaps between them, wingtip to wingtip forming a defensive wall. So far, none of the guards have approached us. Only Cassian.

Llion's response is swift. "You're not going anywhere near her."

Cassian's voice sounds like it's being grated through something sharp and unpleasant. Tense, but determined. Struggling to be patient. "I've ordered the guards to stay on the ground. I knew she was in trouble because I heard her scream. I'm not going to hurt her. She clearly needs warmth, and you don't have the wingspan to help her."

They don't budge. Their wings don't part.

Cassian's voice shifts closer. He must be right up in Llion's face by now. "Did you hear me? I'm the only one who can help her."

When Llion still doesn't move, Cassian exhales a sigh of exasperation. "Oh, fuck it… Llion, if she dies, Howl will remove my head from my shoulders. With my own bone lash. You know it's not an empty threat." He pauses. "Is that enough to convince you?"

I try to speak, but it's difficult. I force sound through my throat. "Llion… it's okay… Let him through."

Llion breaks the wall of wings, but only to check on me. He's so worried it hits me like a fist. Finally, he moves out of the way but doesn't take his eyes off the General. Cassian ducks under Llion's hammock and ascends directly next to mine.

He swiftly checks me over. "You need body heat. I need to get in there with you and then I'm going to wrap my wings around both of us to keep the warmth in. It means sealing you in with me." He pauses and I can't even begin to read his expression: desperately blank. "Will you give me your permission to do this?"

May I have your permission?

His voice blends with the memory of Baelen's. A sob tears out my chest and tears spring to my eyes, but as soon as they slide from my eyes, they freeze. Tiny, frozen pearls burn my cheeks. If Baelen were here, I would have sought his body heat already. Without hesitation, I would have closed the gap between us, knowing he would wrap me up in his arms and keep me warm for as long as I need him.

Cassian's eyes widen. He doesn't wait for my answer. I'm not sure I can even speak to give it.

He rips off his shirt, kicks off his boots, and slides into the hammock beside me, lifting the blankets so he's under them with me. His boots thud on the ground far below as he spreads his wings carefully in each direction, sliding one over the top of us and the other all the way under the hammock and around to the other side.

His wings overlap and settle against their own edges, gently forming a cocoon. Sealing us in just like he said. Under the blanket, he rapidly undoes the buttons on the front of my shirt, pushing the material apart. I'm naked underneath, but he doesn't pay any attention, supporting my torso and head with one arm as he leverages my shirt off with the other, sliding it down my arms and over my stiff fingers.

Hooking his upper leg over mine, he draws my hips up against his before pressing us chest to chest and gently fitting my head into the crook of his neck. His big arms close tight across my back, covering as much skin as he can.

I'm icy but he doesn't wince once.

"Focus on breathing," he says.

It's difficult and not only because of the cold. I haven't been this up close and personal with any man other than Baelen. For the next hour, my breath frosts against his skin, tiny crystals form before my eyes, and then… they melt. Like teardrops sliding against his chest, my breath freezes and warms, freezes and warms, over and over, one breath at a time, melting and evaporating. His skin changes color every time my breath touches it, and where my body presses against his, turning icy pale, returning to normal, then icy pale again, minute after minute, second after endless second until… finally…

I sense his breathing deepen. Relax. He didn't show any deliberate signs of being affected by the cold, but now I realize how furious his breathing had been as the freeze seeped from me into him. He was fighting the cold for both of us.

Closing my eyes, I greedily draw on his warmth. Everything around us has turned completely silent. I'm not sure if that's because the other gargoyles are sleeping or maybe listening to make sure I'm okay. Or maybe the seal formed by Cassian's wings blocks out all sound.

I find my voice for the first time in an hour. My vocal chords are stiff, but I manage to speak. "I'm sorry if I hurt you."

He stiffens. There's a long silence before he responds. "You're apologizing for hurting me."

"I know it hurt."

"It did hurt." In the same breath, he says, "You are very confusing."

"I guess I'm very confused right now. I don't know why this is happening. I don't deliberately do this every night. I didn't even know about it."

"It's only when the moon shines." His arms slide up and down against my back as he shrugs. "It's hard to miss the connection."

"But… why?"

He doesn't answer.

I tilt my head back a little. Funny thing, there used to be a permanent sneer on Cassian's face, but I haven't seen it for a while. When did that change? Over the last four weeks, I've heard the stories of almost all the gargoyles in this place, stories about their families, friends, loved ones, children. I haven't heard his.

I say, "Tell me about the Hideaway Clan."

"There's nothing to tell."

"There's always something to tell."

"Not this time," he says.

"Howl threatened you, but that's not the reason you're helping me. There's more to it than that."

His breath catches and he freezes up again, but he can't exactly run away. Not if he wants to keep me alive.

My turn to shrug. "Or you could tell me about your clan."

He's silent. I don't think I'm going to get an answer to either question. I return my head to his neck to show him that I won't ask again. Whatever part of me that was producing the cold has receded, but it's still there, deep somewhere. It will come back. I'm not safe until the sun rises again. I don't want to push him away given that he's my lifeline right now.

I'm not exactly sure what makes him change his mind about speaking, but he says, "Hideaway had the strongest wings. Even stronger than the King or Queen. They called him Hideaway because the color of his skin could change and camouflage against any rock and he could, well, hide someone in his wings and protect them. Humans walked straight past him, never knowing he was there. His wings could even block deep magic."

That doesn't sound like the kind of thing that would cause a whole clan to be treated as lower than the others. "Then… why?"

He seems to know what I'm asking: why did the Hideaway Clan become servants?

"Something went wrong. Maybe he hid the wrong person. Maybe he didn't protect someone he should have. We don't know why, but the King became very angry with him. To make up for it, Hideaway offered up his clan to serve the King for the rest of our days."

"So that is how you came to be a servant in the King's home."

He turns my statement back on me. "Why did you serve in the House of Rath?"

"All of the minor elven houses serve the major ones. We don't own homes or land. The House of Mercy has always served the House of Rath."

"But *you* became the Storm Princess. Not them. They wouldn't have been very happy about that."

Is he grinning? I tilt my head back to see, startled at the way Cassian's smile changes his face. It's lazy and confident, with a hint of challenge.

I say, "Well… I guess… I was the first Princess from a minor house."

"What about your former master?"

"Rordan Rath? Baelen's father avoided me while I was Princess." Even though he was the only man allowed near me. "I thought it was because I nearly killed his son. But now I think it was for my protection. He tried to keep me separated from elven politics for as long as he could."

I shift a little, feeling like I have to defend Baelen's house. "The House of Rath isn't like the other major houses. They are warriors. *Were* warriors, devoted to protecting others. I guess it's a different kind of servitude. Not cleaning floors but preventing death. Most of them died when the Storm first struck. Rath land sits on the border between our countries. It was hit first and the devastation was… So many elves died…"

I clear my throat, wondering why I told him all of that. And whether I should have.

Of all the things I said, Cassian hones in on the one thing I don't want him to. "You almost killed Baelen Rath?"

"I… uh…" My thoughts whirl. What was I thinking talking about my past? It's dangerous to tell Cassian any of this. I keep my answer to the minimum. "The Storm chose me, but he was standing close to me at the time and it struck him too. He was badly hurt."

"That's why he shares the Storm's power."

Because I poured lightning into Baelen while the Storm poured lightning into me. "Yes."

Cassian is quiet for another moment. "There's something I want to tell you. Then you're going to stop asking questions, and I'm going to stop answering them, and we're going to sleep."

"Okay?"

"Growing up in King Roman's home, I had access to a lot of information. Most of it, I gave myself access to, if you know what I mean."

"You mean you sneaked into places you shouldn't have?"

"I found out something I wasn't supposed to know. When the King died, he took the secret with him. Nobody else knows. Not even Howl."

If I was worried about telling him things I shouldn't, then what he's about to tell me might make us scarily even. I glance around, wide-eyed. If the other gargoyles weren't listening before, they are now.

"They can't hear us," Cassian says, another rare smile gracing his face. It changes him, relaxes his mouth, and lights up his eyes in mesmerizing ways. "We're sealed in here. I have the same wings as Hideaway. I'm the only gargoyle in my generation whose wings block everything—magic, sound. The only reason we've had this conversation is because nobody else can hear us."

I whisper, "What do you know?"

His smile remains. "The gargoyle who became the Storm, who gave her life to become the destructive force that killed your Elven King… She was Supreme Incorruptible. The heir to the throne. She was royalty."

The Storm was a Princess? *But... how... what...?* I can't even identify which question screams at me first.

Cassian's arms tighten again, one hand rubbing my back between my shoulder blades, easing out the sudden tension in my torso. "Now sleep."

True to my promise, I don't ask any more questions, even though I burn with them. The Storm, *my* Storm, my Elyria with the broken wing, was royalty.

Despite the tornado of questions churning at the back of my mind, the soothing motion of his hand on my back is impossible to ignore.

My eyes drift closed. My breathing slows. And I fall asleep in the arms of this ferocious gargoyle.

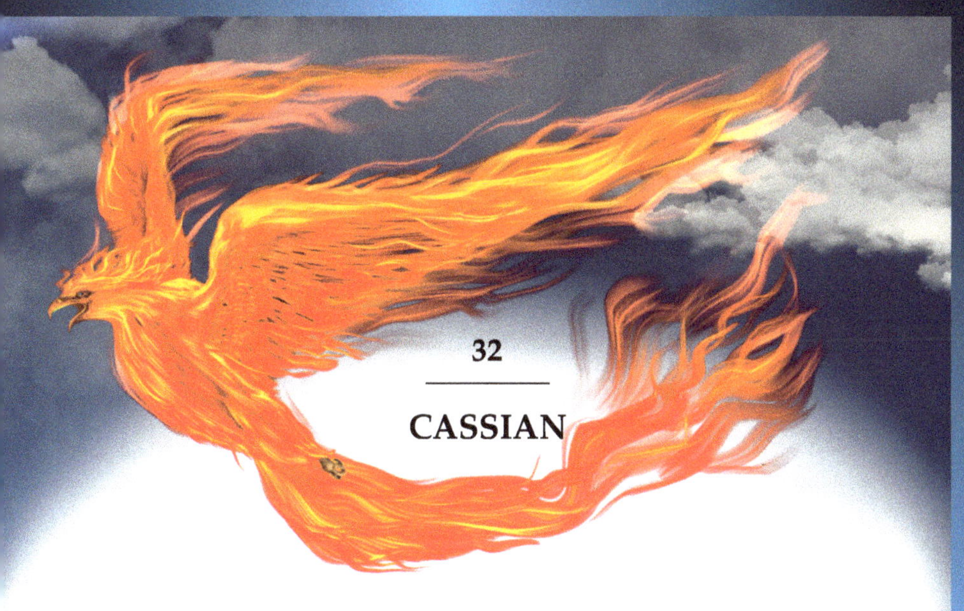

32

———

CASSIAN

Marbella sleeps, but I can't.

Up close, her scent is too strong, too dangerous. Her storm power used to mask it. Then the stench of the mine covered her skin. But now, the deep, familiar scent is unmistakable—a scent she shouldn't have. I inhaled it when I flew her up to her hammock, but I put it down to a confused memory. Lying with her now in this enclosed space, her naked chest pressed against mine, it's undeniable.

There are mysteries about her that I can't solve and lying awake won't do me any good. She's warm now, safe.

I exhale against her hair, my palm pressed against her back, my leg hooked over hers. My fingers rest against the nape of her neck, curled into her hair. As I shift, her head tilts back, but she doesn't wake, her breathing deep and trusting. She let me help her when the others tried to protect her from me.

Contentment.

I finally have a description for the feeling inside me. Odd, that that's the way I feel despite my burning need to kiss her, explore her body, and stroke the fire she keeps tightly controlled, to give her a different reason to sigh.

251

I wonder what would happen if I woke her and asked her for permission to do more than stroke her back.

Remember not to be so polite.

Elaina's final admonition is a painful challenge. She's gone. I lost her, but every time I look at Marbella, I see Elaina's red hair, her determination. But not her love.

I nearly stroke Marbella's cheek, almost nuzzle her awake, nearly ask for what I want, but then I remember the look on her face when she spoke about Baelen Rath, the way she looked at Crimson Court when she severed the connection between them. She traveled into the heart of Erador to heal him. Only the truest, most unbreakable love could cause her to do that.

Her heart is missing. It stays with him and I can't fill that wound.

I have no choice but to be polite.

33

MARBELLA

I wake to Cassian pulling my shirt back over my arms. His wings still seal us in, and I'm glad for that because otherwise, I'd be putting on quite a show right now. He buttons up the front even though my fingers have thawed, and I could do it myself.

When I'm fully clothed, he says, "The sun is up."

The seal breaks and the morning air rushes in. He slips over the hammock's edge, spreads his wings to stay afloat, and shakes them out, rolling his shoulders and turning his neck side-to-side. Then, he drops out of sight.

I lean over the edge, watching him go. Just as he reaches the ground, another gargoyle swoops in from the Cavity's entrance, someone I haven't seen before. Cassian stiffens as the newcomer speaks. The conversation finishes when Cassian gives the stranger a curt nod, and then the other gargoyle flies away.

I look up to find my whole team waiting for me to speak. They look like they barely slept.

"I'm okay," I say, guilt spreading through me as I wonder how long they stayed awake and on guard during the night. There was no way I could have given them a signal though. I was completely sealed in.

Llion looks relieved. "I'm very glad to see it, Lady Storm."

"What's going on down there?"

Far below, Cassian has called a number of guards into a group.

Llion shakes his head. "I guess we'll find out. Are you ready?"

The flight down is too short for my liking. The other team leaders are already there, herded into a group by the guards. The closer I get to the ground, the more agitated Cassian seems to become.

As soon as we touch down, Cassian speaks to everyone. "There will be no mining for three days." He waits a moment for the news to sink in. "The King has declared a celebration in honor of finding the Lightsworn Heartstone. He will be sending extra food. You may all rest and eat."

He spins to me, the stern lines back on his face. Any hint of the protective personality I saw the night before has disappeared. He is General Cassian again. "Except you, Princess."

Instinctively, I recoil, bumping into Llion. My friend steadies me, his reassuring hands remaining on my arms. Jasper edges toward me through the group. I haven't had a chance to speak with him in days.

Cassian's delivery of the next news is flat and unemotional. "You have been called to the Palace." He glares at Jasper as he reaches my side. "Alone."

"When?"

"Now."

Instinctively, I catch Jasper's hand. Howl is calling me back. No doubt to gloat about his new toy. If my face is as expressive as it looked the other day, then there's no disguising the contempt I feel right now. Despite my lost storm power, I feel stronger than when I left Crimson Court.

I ask, "Will you be coming with me, General Cassian?"

"Yes."

Of course. He goes where I go. I probably shouldn't feel this way, but it's a comfort that he's coming with me. Especially if I wake up in the night and need help again. Hopefully, that won't happen since it took a heartstone to wake me from my icy sleep the first time. "When you're ready then."

A smile ghosts around his mouth, quickly hidden. He signals the waiting guards and they bring the large crate I arrived in. I squeeze Jasper's hand before I clamber inside. "Use the time wisely," I whisper to him and Llion.

"We will."

My team's concerned faces are my final view before a guard closes the hatch and the crate rises into the air.

I TUMBLE OUT OF THE BASKET ONTO THE GRASS RIGHT OUTSIDE Harem Hall. The only advantage to being transported in the basket is that it was dark inside and allowed my eyes to adjust to the brighter sunlight. Steely-eyed guards watch my every move as I straighten my clothes. At least I'm not in a dress this time, although something tells me that's not going to last.

Cassian looms over me, grabbing my arm, making me wince. His jaw clenches. If there was a hint of a smile before, it's long gone. He growls, keeping it low, "Don't forget where you are."

It's a warning. I paste a suitably terrified expression on my face, although my wince is real. But the fact is… I'm not afraid of Cassian anymore. He had plenty of chances to hurt me and didn't. I'm not afraid and… I don't think he wants me to be.

I stumble across the grass as he pushes me through the line of guards. He isn't allowed beyond that line, so he shoves me toward the steps where two women I don't recognize wait to take me inside. I follow them without speaking, passing through the opulent rooms at the front of the building.

Like last time, they direct me to the bathroom first. After I've washed, I opt for putting my underwear back on before I pull a clean robe over the top. Then the women lead me to the room at the back where the women dress.

I stop short. The room is empty. "Where are the others?"

One of the women directs me to a chair and the other starts brushing my hair. "Where are Carmen and Gilda?"

The one brushing my hair places a finger against her lips. Okay, so they can't talk to me, but now I'm worried about the two women who brought me provisions. I sit surrounded by anxiety while they put my hair up into an intricate design that allows long strands to fall across one shoulder. So far they haven't presented me with a dress. My gaze darts around the room. I don't see one anywhere. But they're clearly getting me ready for something.

I take a moment to check myself in the mirror and I'm startled by what I see. My skin is pale, translucent from top to bottom, even my hair is a lighter shade of auburn. My eyes are washed-out green, glinting with an edge they didn't have before. My shoulders and upper arms are defined with visible muscles, but my lips are brighter red, flushing darker when I press them together. Could all this be a consequence of being underground and working hard for the last month? Or more to do with the way I turn into ice when the moon is out?

The women finish their work and leave without a word. I remain in my seat, not sure what to expect or do. So much time passes that I eventually slouch forward, leaning on the mirrored bench in front of me.

A sixth sense warns me, and I glance up into the mirror.

"I've missed you, Little Doll."

I glide from the chair, ready to face Howl as he prowls into the room, making it seem small and cramped. He rolls his broad shoulders back, displaying his wings and the now multi-colored veins running through them, some green, some blue. A second heartstone—this one the color of an icy blue pond—rests next to the first. It's their colors that intertwine through his wings.

A garment is draped over his arm, but I can't see the detail of it yet.

I draw myself up to my full height. Not very tall or intimidating but, hey, I can try.

He pulls up short, mid-stride inside the room. His harsh gaze moves from my head to my bare feet.

"How curious," he says. "Cassian was right."

"About what?"

"You've changed."

I circle around him as he approaches so he remains at the same distance. This seems to amuse him. "I heard you had a difficult night last night."

Cassian must have told him everything. I'm guessing that was the deal: watch over me and report back. "It wasn't the first."

"I suspected the heartstone's awakening might cause you some pain. You may not have your power anymore, but deep magic will always recognize itself."

My forehead creases. He seems to think my bad night was purely because of the heartstone. It had started that way, but the rest of it wasn't. Maybe Cassian didn't tell him everything after all. Maybe Cassian is smart enough not to tell him everything. Howl interprets my scowl as an unwillingness to admit weakness.

"Don't fret, Little Doll. It hurt me too. Holding a heartstone for the first time is like… well… connecting with lightning. You would know what that feels like."

Painful. Terrifying. I hope it hurt him a lot.

"Why am I here?" I haven't been able to maintain the distance between us and before I know it, I'm pinned in the corner. I smother a sigh. At least I tried.

"Your old friends want to see you." He runs the fingers of his free hand through my hair, brushing my shoulders and making my skin crawl. "But first you need to get dressed."

He holds up the garment draped over his arm. "This is for you."

It resembles the kind of dress that women in the major elven Houses wear to big events. And I mean *big* events. Like major House weddings or the appointment of a new Elven Commander. The last Elven Commander appointed was Pedr Bounty. His appointment happened soon after I became the Storm Princess and I still remember the stir I caused when I refused to wear the dress that the most senior Elven Commander, Elwyn Elder, presented to me—somehow, I knew even then that I couldn't accept their gifts or be seen to owe them anything.

In typical Howl style, the dress plunges low at the front but its structured shape tells me there's a corset under the bodice. The material is fine silver, satin, long, with silver filigree and pale gemstones in a floral pattern to the waist where the material streams outward.

"This too." Hanging around his wrist, dangling like a bracelet, is a tiara that sparkles with white diamonds. It was concealed under the dress until now.

I eye both the dress and tiara with increasing concern. He said I was meeting old friends. I thought he meant Baelen and the phoenix. Now I'm not so sure.

He looks very pleased with himself when he says, "You can't get into this dress on your own. You'll need help."

It doesn't take a genius to see where he's going with this. It seems this is make-Marbella-strip month. Howl has mauled me enough that I'm not surprised. What does surprise me is that I'm not afraid of him. It's an unexpected realization. I've spent the last month deep underground surrounded by fierce gargoyles who have proven that they are loyal to each other and willing to help each other, despite what Howl has done to them. Despite the threats the guards pose on a daily basis, they've never used their bone lashes. Of course, the gargoyles haven't given the guards any reason to take violent action, but even so, I find myself holding onto a shred of hope and faith for the first time.

I take a moment to consider my options—fight Howl, which will inevitably lead to him using his new Heartstone and all sorts of other unpleasantness or swallow my pride and save my fight for later. Just when I decide that a fight is worth it, Howl clicks his fingers, and the two women race back into the room.

I guess he didn't fancy himself a handmaid after all. He hands the dress to them and draws up a chair on the other side of the room to watch.

The first woman immediately instructs me to put my arms down at my sides. I'm not sure how that's going to work—I still have a robe and underwear on. But I do it anyway. She and the other woman hold the dress high above my head and slip it over me, robe and all. As I suspected, it contains a corset. But the pleasant surprise is that with the back fully unlaced, the dress itself turns into a screen around me.

The two women hold the dress in place as I wriggle around inside it removing my shirt and bra and then my long pants.

Huh. Take that Howl. No peep show for you. He seems amused, rather than disgruntled, stretching his legs out in front of him, lips curled into a half-grin as he watches me struggle not to reveal anything. Something has made him extra happy today. I should probably worry about what that is.

I decide to distract him with talk just in case his mood changes. "No chains this time?"

"No," he says. "You already know what's at stake."

The two women stiffen slightly before returning to the task of tying me into the dress. Howl's threat hangs in the air. The last time I was here, Howl threatened to kill Carmen and Gilda if I stepped out of line. I don't know these new women very well, but they could be the wives of any of the gargoyles I met in the mine.

"I do," I say, more for their sake than his.

They pin the tiara to the top of my head and last of all, hand me a pair of flats. Thank goodness, no heels this time. The corset makes up as a torture device, pushing my breasts up so they're in danger of popping out.

When I'm fully dressed, Howl lurches upward and flicks his head to the door. I thank the women before following him out. As we walk, Howl drops beside me and then slightly behind, resting his hand on my lower back in a possessive gesture.

When we exit the building, Cassian paces at the guard line. His wings are angled forward and his boots stamp the turf. On the surface, he appears impatient, but as I pause on the balcony, I sense… *fear?*

For himself or me?

His eyes meet mine across the distance. Agonized. Desperate. Flicking to Howl and back to me.

Fear for me.

Surprise shoots through me as his gaze assesses me, checking my status, searching for signs of abuse. I hold myself high and aloof to disguise my shock at his concern. I glide down the stairs after Howl. The other guards are well trained and don't spare me a second look as they walk in a line on each side of us, but Cassian takes up a close position behind me.

The sun is well up in the sky now, but a breeze helps keep me cool. It looks like we're headed to Crimson Court, but then Howl changes direction, leading me along a wide pathway that ascends through a thick forest of trees.

A palace looms in the distance, built partially into the side of the mountain, eerily camouflaged against the dark gray rock. As the pathway winds through the thinning trees, the palace catches the light in different ways, making it look like it conforms into the mountain itself.

Rows of guards stand watch outside it, peering at us as we pass through the wide-open door but none of them follow us inside. Even the guards who came with us file off before we reach the door. As Howl leads me through hallway after hallway, it's difficult to gauge the sheer size of the structure. It must have taken all of Howl's ten-year rule to build it.

Finally, we stop inside a small room facing a large wooden door elaborately decorated with the silhouette of a golden panther. Howl squeezes my waist and tells me to wait with Cassian before he disappears inside. Voices—mostly male—float out before the door closes again.

Cassian catches my arm, his question sharp and urgent. "Did he scent you?"

Scent me? That thing the gargoyles do when they inhale? Before I lost my power, Howl literally inhaled the storm into himself whenever he had the chance, but he has no reason to do that now. "I don't think so."

"Don't let him."

"Why?" I tilt my head back, trying to figure out why he's so unsettled. The night before, he'd told me a secret about the Storm. Something only he knew. Now I wonder what new secret he's keeping. "What aren't you telling me?"

"Your storm power hid it before. But if Howl catches your true scent…" He releases my arm, resuming his former position at my elbow as footsteps sound on the other side of the door. "He'll kill you."

The wide doors swing apart and Howl fills the opening, spreading his wings in an elaborate gesture. I can't see them yet, but I sense people in the room behind him—a large room—along with an expectant silence.

The half-grin that Howl has been wearing for the last half hour widens into pure delight. Shudders shoot down my spine at the sight. In the space of one breath, Cassian has told me Howl will kill me and Howl has appeared wearing a grin that drips with malice and anticipation.

"Little Doll," Howl says, "Come and see your old friends."

He sweeps his wings aside, revealing two men standing at a distance behind him. They are regal in robes that meet the floor, their lips stretched into smiles while their cold eyes are daggers. The last time I saw them, they'd killed Baelen and were trying to take my storm power.

Howl leans into me. "I think you know Elwyn Elder and Pedr Bounty. They came to see if you're dead yet."

34

———

MARBELLA

I never *ever* thought I would see elves in Howl's palace. Maybe in my worst nightmare, they would be here as prisoners. But that they're here as guests to see firsthand Howl's imprisonment of me is beyond my greatest horror.

The world spins, the contents of my stomach shift, and I suddenly lose the ability to breathe. The room is lined with an equal number of Howl's guards to elven soldiers, all dressed in armor. Each Elven Commander is joined by a small entourage of elves—advisors and personal staff—casually clustered behind them, sipping from glasses of wine.

Further inside the room, an enormous table filled with food takes center stage. Serving staff wearing the Slave Station uniform wait patiently at the other end of the room, and near them are the women from Harem Hall, dressed more demurely than the last time I saw them. Now they wear long dresses, not transparent this time.

The two Elven Commanders move only to speak, while for me, everything is spinning.

"We thought she would be in chains," Elwyn Elder says, clearly unhappy about my unbound state. I wonder if Howl has told them I

262

lost my powers—if not, it would explain why they are uneasy about me being free.

"And not quite so well dressed." Pedr Bounty's eyes narrow. He was always the bulkiest of the Commanders—broad-shouldered and imposing.

"I like to dress her up," Howl says, pushing me into the room. "You don't need to fear anything from my Little Doll. She's learned to be compliant."

Howl's condescending attitude slams my spinning world to a complete stop. The one thing this bastard is good at, is making me focus. I fight the urge to smash his nose in and show everyone just how compliant I am. Strategically it's better if the elves believe him. The less they fear me, the more complacent they will become.

I recognize some of the elves in the entourage. One in particular, I don't count as an enemy.

As the Elven Commanders move aside for Howl, Eli Elder steps directly into Howl's path. Maybe he doesn't realize he's in Howl's way. Or… maybe he does.

He bows his head to me. "Storm Princess," he says, reverting to the customary way to greet me. "Are you well?"

"I am well, thank you Eli of the House of Elder."

"I'm glad to see it." His eyes are crystal blue, not quite as brilliant as Cassian's but just as intelligent. He's lean and tall, an elegant fighter. I saved his life once—and he saved mine. He steps aside before Howl has a chance to get really annoyed, bowing to the King, although he hides a quick glance in my direction. I have to find a way to speak with him. He could have information about what happened to my family, my advisor Elise, and the women in my Storm Command.

I definitely don't think it was Howl's intention to give me hope, but for the first time I can see a lifeline back to Erawind, even if it's only in the form of information.

One other person waits at the far end of the table. The former High Priestess isn't dressed anywhere near as elaborately as I am. A simple but elegant robe covers her frame, and she waits quietly for Howl's order to sit.

He takes the seat at the head of the table with the High Priestess opposite me on his left. Elwyn Elder sits beside me and Pedr Bounty is next to the High Priestess. It forces them to lean across us to speak to Howl and I suspect he takes perverse delight in making them uncomfortable. The advisors are next, followed by their entourage. Eli ends up much further down the table, and Cassian takes up position standing guard in the space behind Howl and me.

As lunch progresses, the steady stream of food and alcohol is nauseating. I don't touch my drink and I pick through the food. After a month of eating gruel, most of it is too rich for my stomach and will only make me sick.

After what seems like the third dessert, Howl waves Cassian forward. "Take the Priestess and make sure our guests enjoy dancing in the next room. I have business to discuss with the Elven Commanders."

I scoot my chair backward, ready to follow Cassian and the others, but Howl's palm slams onto my arm. "Not you, Little Doll."

He curls his fingers around my forearm, and I flinch and try to hide the pain as he squeezes until I drag my chair awkwardly back into place.

"I apologize, King Howl. You gave me a party dress. I was confused."

The door closes and I'm suddenly alone with Howl and the Elven Commanders.

"You see," Howl says to Elwyn and Pedr. "She just needed to be tamed."

Pedr leans back in his chair, appearing relaxed. "We thought we would be celebrating your wedding by now, Howl."

A growl replaces Howl's smirk. "It turned out that my chosen bride wasn't a widow after all."

He's still gripping my arm and the topic of conversation hasn't relaxed him. My skin burns and my eyes water.

"You're hurting her," Pedr says, but it's a statement of fact. There's nothing in his tone that suggests Howl should stop.

"The Princess has learned that I can hurt her whenever I want."

He continues gripping my arm as he angles toward a door on the opposite side of the room. It's not the one the guests left through and is smaller and narrower. The heartstones resting on Howl's chest flicker for a moment as he uses his power to open the door without moving.

A large, golden object floats out through it, at first appearing flat, but as the full object emerges, it becomes a golden cage, tipped on its side like a coffin.

It's Baelen's cage. As it comes to a stop where I have a full view of it, Baelen floats inside the cage, suspended and completely still.

But there's something wrong with this picture: where is the Storm? The last time I saw her, she couldn't move beyond a hundred paces of him. I search for her in the shadows of the door Baelen came from. It's close enough that she could be hiding there. A puddle of silver is all I can see. It could be her or it might be a trick of the light.

The Elven Commanders jump to their feet, but not in fear. Eagerness to see Howl's prisoner is written all over their greedy faces.

"Yes, yes," Howl says. "But don't get too close to him. The bars are there for your protection."

When they're done peering at Baelen, Howl calls them back. "We need to talk about our deal."

More somber, Elwyn and Pedr settle back into their seats.

Howl finally lets go of my arm and feeling returns to my fingertips, the sudden rush of blood a different painful sensation. He's left a conspicuous red mark all around my skin.

He rubs his chin. "Our deal," he says. "As you well know, I killed Rordan Rath and you were supposed to kill the gargoyles that escaped my lands."

I close my eyes as I digest this new knowledge. Baelen's father died a year ago. I didn't have a chance to speak to Baelen about it and the details of his father's death were always kept from me. All I was told was that he'd died carrying out his duties.

Elwyn becomes defensive. "His son returned and got in our way."

"Well, as you can see, his son is no longer a problem."

Elwyn smiles. "Then you'll be happy to know that we recommenced our eradication efforts."

The gargoyles on the border? Dead?

"There aren't any gargoyles left on our side of the border, so you have nothing to worry about."

Howl's fist hits the table. "There are! There is a woman, little, with golden hair. She has a mark on her hip depicting the sun rising over the mountains. I want her back."

He's talking about the High Priestess Talia—the new High Priestess who is hidden in the mountains with Llion's children.

"Our intelligence tells us—"

"I don't care what your intelligence tells you. She's there. I want her brought to me." The heartstones begin to glow again. "Or we will have a problem."

Elwyn isn't as worried as I thought he would be. The air crackles around him, his form shimmering at the edges, a force bleeding into the air where he sits. It's sorcery. It has to be.

The Elven Commander I killed, Gideon Glory, was infected by sorcery, the same evil magic that the last Elven King dabbled in. When I left Erawind, only Gideon Glory appeared to be infected but now both Elwyn and Pedr openly stink of it. It makes my skin crawl even more than Howl's power. Howl's power comes from heartstones, but sorcery derives its power from death.

Howl exhales and relaxes, bringing the tension in the room down a few notches. "You will continue to look for her."

"Of course."

"Then let's talk about the future. What do you want?"

Elwyn flicks his head at me. "Her. Dead." Then at Baelen. "Him too."

Howl taps his fingers together. "That's a big ask. I've grown rather fond of her." He tangles his fingers into my hair, gripping the back of my neck. "What if I offer you an alternative?"

"I guess we will consider it."

"Baelen Rath buried deep in the heart of Mount Lightsworn. My miners have retrieved the heartstone from that mountain and there is now a deep tunnel that will be collapsed in a week. I can bury him under a mountain of rock."

"Very well. What about her?"

"I will marry her."

What?

The Elven Commanders scoff. "That doesn't address our problem. What about her power?"

"It's gone."

Their raised eyebrows say they don't believe him. "Prove it."

"Show them, Little Doll. Show them what you can't do."

I'm still stuck on his announcement that he's going to marry me. His demand only filters through when he repeats it. Show them I don't have my power? How can I show them something I don't have?

Howl launches upward but instead of grabbing me, he strides to the door. Music and voices wash into the room as the door opens and closes again. He drags one of the female slaves back with him. Five strides into the room, his hands close around her throat. She chokes and tries to scream.

"One twist and I'll break her neck. Show them, Little Doll."

I leap from my seat. "I can't show them something I don't have!"

Tears stream down the woman's face. Howl's grip closes so tight that the sound strangles in her throat and stops. She can't even whimper.

"Show them!"

I run at him, grabbing his arms, beating at his torso, trying to free her. The elves don't move, don't care.

I scream. "Let her go! I don't have any power!"

His heartstones flicker. A force knocks me backward and I tumble across the floor. I slide to a stop, scrabble against the ground, and jump to my feet, running back at him.

He roars, "*Show them!*"

The woman's eyes are closing. She has no time.

"Wait!" I cry, sudden clarity piercing my panic. "Give me a knife." I run to the table, snatching up the leftover cutlery, whirling to the Elven Commanders. "I've been sitting here eating with knives and forks and spoons, without gloves, all afternoon and you didn't notice!"

They actually focus on me for the first time since I entered the room. Until now, their eyes have glanced over me like I am a piece of furniture. For years they wouldn't let me touch metal because it triggered my power. It took the touch of a dagger for me to discover that I could harness lightning as a powerful force, lighting it up at a single touch.

"No electricity," Elwyn says, chin drawn back in surprise. "She's telling the truth."

"It's gone." I grip the knife in my fist. "King Howl, they believe you. Please let her go."

The woman slides to the floor, choking and spluttering, but alive. I run to help her, but Howl's fist connects with my stomach as I pass by. I double over, gagging, and collapse to my knees, before he drags the woman from the room. Sounds stop in the room beyond as he drops her in the doorway. "Get her out of here."

My hands form fists on the floor. Where is that shred of hope that filled my heart this morning? My whole body swells with anger, drowning my hope, even my sanity. Howl doesn't bother to wait for someone to help the woman. He spins back to us, but as his back turns, I catch a glimpse of massive wings and Cassian's blazing eyes. He scoops up the injured woman, supporting her head, and disappears with her as the door closes.

My tears drop onto the floor.

"If she has no power, why marry her?" Elwyn leans forward on the table, licking his lips. "What's in it for you?"

Howl scoops one arm under my stomach, carrying me back to my seat like a rag doll. He runs his fingers down my face and neck. "What isn't?"

"Fine. What do you want in return?"

"I want the Rath and Mercy Heartstones."

Elwyn and Pedr look at each other. "Why? They're worthless."

"Then you won't mind giving them to me."

They exchange another quizzical glance, clearly believing they are getting the better end of the deal. "We have an agreement."

"Good. Now. Let's go enjoy ourselves."

He drags me out and deposits me next to the door, waiting for the elves to move along. But instead of going with them, he grabs me again, almost wrenching my arm out of its socket. He hisses into my ear. "If you want your freedom, you will find me Prime's heart. He was the King's best friend, and with his heart, I will have the three most powerful Heartstones. I won't have to make deals with your weak Elven Commanders. Then you can go free."

He shoves me against the wall so hard that the impact rattles through my spine. "Stay there until I come back for you."

Lightsworn's blue light mingles with Virtuous's moss-colored glow as Howl strides away, the two heartstones a powerful reminder that Howl is invincible.

The crowd of dancing elves and gargoyles parts for him. Several of the women follow him to the dais at the other side of the room where plush couches await, along with drinks and food. I catch sight of Gilda and Carmen. I'm relieved that they're okay, but every moment they spend near Howl is a dangerous one. Like the other women, they maintain blank faces. They are a commodity. I want to snatch all of them and fight our way free of this place. I would feel better if Cassian was nearby but I'm glad he's helping the hurt woman.

As instructed, I remain glued to the wall, unmoving. There are too many women in this room that Howl can hurt if I disobey him. But his time will come. His end will come.

"Princess?" Eli's quiet question is almost smothered by the increasingly loud, alcohol-fueled laughter around me.

"Princess?"

I finally turn to him. "Eli."

"You're hurt." He doesn't touch me. The old rule: never touch the Storm Princess. He always respected it.

I ignore the growing bruise on my forearm. My stomach hurts too. The corset bones dug hard into my ribs when Howl punched me.

"I'll heal." I chew my lip, knowing I may not get another chance like this to ask about the people I left behind in Erawind. "Eli, can you tell me… how is my family?"

"I have news, but it isn't good."

"I can handle it."

"I believe you. But I want you to be prepared. Your Storm Command has been captured. So has Elise, your advisor. There are two new Elven Commanders. They are both powerful sorcerers, and one of them is… very dangerous. The five Elven Commanders are now completely consumed by sorcery's evil power."

My voice wobbles. Definitely not good news. "Jordan too? What about Sebastian and his mother?"

"They were the only ones who escaped. They're somewhere in the mountains. They haven't been found." He keeps his expression blank, giving nothing away. An observer might think we're discussing the weather. Nobody can know what we're really talking about. "The Elven Command has sold it to the people as a hunt for you. They have proclaimed that anyone aiding and abetting you is a traitor to the elven race."

"Because I killed Gideon Glory. They called it murder instead of self-defense."

"Yes." He gives me a short nod. "I've been doing my best to make sure the prisoners are treated fairly but they're being kept in very poor conditions."

"I have to get out of here," I murmur. "I have to end Howl and get back to Erawind."

"No." He breaks the rule. He touches my arm. It's a reflexive gesture, a worried one. He immediately lets go, regret washing across his face. "I'm sorry, Princess, but you must regain your power first. Otherwise, you will never be able to fight their sorcery. They are powerful and infect anyone they want." He glances across the room. His grandfather Elwyn is looking around––probably for him. "I have to go now. Please stay alive and come back strong."

"I will," I whisper to his retreating back even though right now, I have no idea how.

35

MARBELLA

I'm collapsing against the wall by the time Howl orders dinner to be brought in. It's impossible to stand up straight for hours on end. But my discomfort only increases when he sits me on his lap throughout the meal, feeding me things I really don't want to eat—rich, saucy meats and sweet, syrupy desserts. Each mouthful makes me gag. Who knew I'd crave gruel?

I put up with it for the sake of the women in the room. Howl is like a fire stick that could light up at any moment, and I won't jeopardize their safety. He loses all pretense of treating me civilly by the end of the evening. Ordering the staff to show the guests to their rooms, he grabs me by my hair and drags me down the opposite hallway, my eyes streaming tears of pain as he tugs on a combination of pins and curls. Whatever design my hair was in earlier today, it's a fallen mess now.

We finally reach our destination, a secluded part of the palace far away from everyone else. Quiet. Scarily alone. The only positive is that there's nobody here who he can threaten, but as we round the final corner and enter a short hall with a wide window on one side, Cassian straightens at the entrance to the room opposite.

"General," Howl slurs, waving the door open with his power. "What are you doing here?"

"I'm here to make sure you don't do something you'll regret."

"Why would I regret taking this sweet piece of—"

"My King? Think about it."

Howl grumbles. His lip curls in disgust. "Little half-caste heirs running around." He waves it away. "I don't care. Fuck my own rules."

Cassian doesn't budge. His wings twitch outward, obstructing the door. I eye the window opposite. There's no way I'm going into that room with Howl. If Cassian doesn't succeed in blocking him, the window is going to start looking pretty good. My observation of the palace walls when we arrived told me there are ledges everywhere so I shouldn't have far to jump.

"It's not about rules," Cassian continues smoothly. "It's about your life. Any heir is dangerous. Especially if it's born with the heartstone's power running through its veins."

So that's what Howl's really afraid of: passing the power onto an heir. That would explain why he only imprisons wives in his harem, women who have already had children since gargoyle women can have no more than two children in their life.

Howl sways on the spot, dragging me to and fro with him. I'm ready to punch his lights out and hang the consequences. If he swings me around one more time…

He shoves me at Cassian. "Get her back to the mines tomorrow. Stay here on this door tonight. Nobody enters this room. And you…" He topples forward to grab my shoulders one last time, almost shoving me over. "You will bring me Prime's heart."

He swerves down the corridor, wobbling side to side, too inebriated to walk straight. I don't stop watching until he's gone. Even then, I stare at the dark space he left behind, waiting for his footsteps to completely retreat.

When I'm certain Howl's gone, I round on Cassian, pushing away from him. "How can you serve him?"

He glares me down. "Do you think I have a choice?"

"Everyone has a choice! Who does he have imprisoned? Your wife? Sister? Children? Parents?"

He flinches at each word. "Nobody! I have nobody." He reins

himself in. Takes a deep breath. Stares past my shoulder. He fixates on the other side of the hallway as he says. "Until a month ago, I had nobody, but—"

I'm too angry to care that he had nobody to love. I've been mauled and abused all day and it spills out of me in an angry rush. "Oh, so a month ago you found somebody to care about? To maybe start thinking about whether Howl is any sort of leader you should be following?"

"Yes."

I glare at him, expecting more but that's all he says. His gaze returns to me, slides from my eyes to my arm. His brow furrows at the dark bruise circling it, and I sense a growing anger in him, but he reins that in too.

"You should get inside," he says. "Rest while you can."

"You mean freeze while I can."

"Not if I can help it."

I close the door in his face. If I freeze like last night, then I'm going to need his help, but right now I'm too angry to accept it. Right now, I'm furious at my own powerlessness to help my family and friends. To help Baelen or the Storm. To help the miners or the women stuck in Harem Hell. Right now…

Right now…

My eyes shoot wide.

The room is lit with soft lamps and contains a large bed, a bathroom through another door, a massive mirror on one side and…

Baelen!

His cage rests against the far wall, taking up most of the space between the floor and the ceiling and right next to him…

"Storm!"

She's a puddle of silver next to his cage, her head resting on her bent knees, her dress spilling around her, and her silver wings curved around her shoulders.

I race to her, dropping to my knees. "Storm."

She doesn't lift her head, doesn't look at me, keeps rocking back and forth. My happiness at seeing her turns to fear. "Storm?

Look at me." When she doesn't respond, I try her name instead. "Elyria?"

She lifts her eyes, peering above her knees, unfocused, glazed. She blinks at me. "Marbella?"

"It's me."

"Marbella," she breathes my name, shaking her head, blinking, focusing. "Is it really you? There were other elves. I saw them and I stayed away from them. I stayed as far away as I could."

That would explain why she hadn't come out with Baelen when Howl paraded him before the Elven Commanders earlier today.

"Every week there are elves. Here. They shouldn't be here. Not here." She grabs my hands, squeezing them tightly, tears leaking down her cheeks. "Where's Jasper? I need him."

"He's back at the mine. But he's safe."

"At least he's safe." Her voice trails off. "Please, I can't be here anymore. I know it's not my home, not the home I grew up in, but it looks like my home, and I can't stand it. I can't stand being here. I need to get out. Please, Marbella. Please."

"What happened here, Elyria? What happened to make you the Storm?"

She shuts down, dropping her head to her knees again. "Jasper," she murmurs. "I need Jasper."

She won't talk to me. She won't tell me. I sit with her for a long time, careful not to squeeze her broken wing too tight, stroking her hair as she continues to cry softly.

"It will be okay," I murmur. "You'll be okay."

Baelen's cage is exactly the same. He is exactly the same. My greatest fear is that he won't remain suspended in time and his wounds will progress and I won't be here to help him. I want to talk to him, but I can't risk drawing him out like before. Just seeing him has to be enough, even if it's here in this… Bedroom…

I glance from the bed to Baelen. The sheer perversion of Howl's mind sends a shudder down my spine. The only one who can move Baelen is Howl, which means he deliberately moved Baelen here, in front of this bed, where Howl intended to break me. I've never actually feared rape. In Erawind, nobody touched me because I could kill them instantly. But here… And if Cassian hadn't got in the way… Maybe I would have made it out the window but maybe I wouldn't have…

I hug the Storm tighter. "You were Supreme Incorruptible," I whisper. "You were the heir to the throne."

She draws a shaky breath, head down, her voice muffled against her knees. "I was. But then I died."

Her voice trails off. Her breathing deepens. She told me she doesn't sleep much, but I'm certain she's fallen asleep by the time I uncurl myself and seek the bathroom nearby. Once I've washed off the sensation of Howl's hands all over me, I debate whether to put the dress back on or wear the simple pajamas that have been provided. In the end, I opt for the pajamas.

I emerge from the bathroom to the sound of voices out in the hall: Cassian's and a female voice. I patter across to listen at the door, but the sound is too muted to make out what they're saying. The door opens and I jump back as a soft female voice floats inside. "Very well, if she's asleep, I won't wake her. But if she's awake…"

I recognize the old Priestess as she pokes her head around the door and pronounces, "She's awake."

She shuts herself in with me, leaving Cassian in the corridor. She's small and bony, but the air tingles around her. Howl may well be right when he says that deep magic recognizes itself. Just like the first time I saw her, the Priestess's presence makes my skin warm like stepping into a shaft of sunlight.

Her eyes are bright and assess me quickly. "Howl has passed out on his bed. Clutching his heartstones of course." She gives me a quick grin, and I'm surprised at the way her cheeks turn into dimples. "Paranoia is the illness of kings."

She tucks her long, straight hair behind her ear. "General Cassian has brought me here because he believes that there's something in this palace you need to see. It requires you to leave this room, however, which in turn means danger for everyone involved. Are you willing to accept that danger?" She leans forward, peering into my eyes. "For everyone involved?"

"You mean… including for Cassian?"

"Yes."

"I… have no idea."

She cocks her head to the side. "That's good enough for me. Put this on and come with me please." She hands me a coat and as soon as I pull it over my arms, she darts from the room before I have a chance to blink. I glance back at Elyria but she's fast asleep.

I follow the old Priestess out, my forehead creasing as I pass Cassian.

"Don't be long," he says. "If Howl comes back, I'll only be able to stall him for a short time."

The Priestess hurries down the hall. A minute later, she says, "It looks like General Cassian has found something to care about."

"Other than himself you mean."

Her voice is laced with warning. "Do not let your anger blind you to the truth, Marbella Mercy. Or you will lose more than you ever knew you had."

Okay, why am I following this old lady anyway?

"How have you been sleeping, dear?" she asks before I can rethink my current course of action and head straight back to my room.

"Well, but not well."

"How about tonight?"

I'm not cold. It only now dawns on me that I'm perfectly warm. Which means it must have something to do with the underground mine. I only freeze at night when I'm there. But… why?

The Priestess suddenly says, "Before you judge Cassian too harshly, you should know that he was barely sixteen years old when Howl killed King Roman. Howl killed Cassian's family too, but gave Cassian a choice. Cassian chose life. My point is… nothing in this place is straightforward."

Before I can respond, she places her finger to her lips. We've travelled from one secluded part of the palace to another, up a flight of stairs to a landing and another door.

"Nobody is supposed to enter this room," she says, leading me inside. "It's not locked because Howl expects his word to be obeyed, but I'm in a rebellious mood."

I'm still reeling from what she told me about Cassian. I'm not sure how to process it. As the Priestess draws me into the room, I see that there are only two objects inside it. One I recognize and the other I don't.

"My armor," I whisper, racing to where it hangs. I'd left it in a satchel on the phoenix's back when Howl surrounded us on Mount Erador. I hadn't seen it since then.

The other object rests on a simple wooden pedestal. "A book?"

"A very special book. It's the only object that Howl saved from the old palace before he destroyed it." She positions herself beside the door. "I will keep watch. Go on, open it."

I peer at it. The inscription on the front says:

Incorruptible.

That was the Gargoyle Queen's name. The pages inside the book progress through a rainbow of different-colored sections: starting with white first, followed by shades of purple, blue, orange, green, and finally, red.

As I turn to the first page, it's clear that it's a journal: Queen Incorruptible's journal, written hundreds of years ago. I flip through the entries until I get to one that stops me.

It wasn't Hideaway's fault. It was mine. I was the one who wanted to see the humans—the ones with the strange metal sticks that cause animals to fall down dead. I tried to tell the King that I put myself in danger, but he didn't want to believe me. Hideaway is such a loyal friend that he took the blame.

I guess now I know why Cassian's family was born into servitude. As I read on, the entries become more and more despairing. The humans hunt the gargoyles like animals—the women especially are hunted for their beautiful wings and the men are hunted for their wing daggers. Some of the descriptions of what they face are so horrifying that I have to skim over them.

The gargoyles flee across continents, trying to find a safe place to live, joining up with the elves to travel through a vast continent called Europe all the way to a place she calls the "New World." Along the way, the Queen begs her husband to allow her to fight back, to kill the humans, but they argue about the morality of a pre-emptive strike versus self-defense. She is close friends with Prime, Lightsworn, and Virtuous, and they all want to fight back, but in the end, the King says he won't become the monster that the humans think he is.

Finally, I reach the passage where the gargoyles and elves reach an accord: a desperate plan to leave the Earth's surface and descend together into the earth.

I reach the very last passage before the white-colored section ends.

I am Incorruptible and this is my last written vow.

My husband, the Gargoyle King, has already given his life to part the Earth. The Elven King has given his life to create a new sky. Today I will ascend with the Elven Queen. I will become the moon, and she will become the sun. I give my life willingly, but it is with one regret.

I am true and loyal to my husband, King Supreme. I am true and loyal to my people. I have never betrayed them. But my truest heart, my deepest love, belongs forever and always with Prime.

When I ascend with the phoenix today, my final thoughts will be of him.

My heart lurches. I understand her pain. The Queen was in love with Prime, but she never acted on it. She couldn't be with him the same way I couldn't be with Baelen. But I'm determined that our story will end differently. We will be together.

I suddenly feel like I'm eavesdropping on someone else's life. I mean, I guess I am. As I flip through the other sections, I realize that each one belongs to a different Queen: each successor who came after Incorruptible. I flip to the final section of the book, its pages crimson.

The first entry is marked with a date four hundred years ago.

The name written at the top of the page is:

Bethesda.

My mother gave me this book today. As the daughter of the Queen, I am heir to the throne. When I marry in a week, she will step down and I will be Queen.

She told me that when I write my name, the pages will turn the color of my life. I'm not sure what it means that they have turned the color of blood.

Two days later, she wrote:

I met the Elven King today. He is here for my wedding. My mother told me not to trust him, that he is treacherous, but I don't know why she would say that. He has been nothing but polite and attentive. I'm not afraid of him.

The two entries after that contain only dates, but no writing, which is odd that the pages were dated but left blank. The third entry says only:

Now I am Queen.

I flip through the pages and details of her life and her husband; sometimes, she talks about her brother, who seems fiercely protective of her. In fact, it reads as if that's his job. He doesn't seem to have a wife or children. I guess that if the throne passes from daughter to daughter, and the brother never has children, that means there's no fighting about the rightful heir.

I reach the end of the book, the last passage.

My children were born today. My son came first, which is not how it should have been. He should have been born second, to be his sister's protector. He struggles to breathe, and his wings are not strong.

It's my fault. I know it is.

But... my daughter is perfect. There are no signs that she is not what she is supposed to be. She will be Queen one day. The fact that she was born second doesn't change that. In fact, it is as if she is her brother's protector, and not the other way around. I have named her Elyria, because she will need to be unbreakable.

If she ever learned the truth—

"How did you get in here?"

I jump, spin, and drop the book. It hits the floor with a *thud*.

"Were you reading that?" Howl pounds into the room, wings spread, both heartstones shedding an angry glow, lighting up the rage oozing from every angle of his body.

"No," I squeak. Luckily the book landed closed. "Just looking at the cover."

Where is the Priestess? I can't see her anywhere. I didn't hear her leave, but I tuned out everything, so she could have left at any stage.

Howl veers toward me, and it's abundantly clear that he's no longer intoxicated but sharp and angry. I backpedal fast, angling for the door, but I don't quite make it out of there before he grabs me by my shoulders and presses me hard up against the wall. "Nobody reads that book!"

"Okay."

"Do you understand?"

"I understand."

He releases me and I jump away from him. Luckily, I memorized the way here, because I was going straight back to my room before he grabs me again. I race to the door and stumble down the stairs, glancing back to check whether he's following me.

He isn't. He's bending to the floor instead. I pause for a dangerous moment, watching as he picks up the book, but he doesn't place it back on the pedestal. Instead, he curls both hands around the outside covers and pulls.

It doesn't open.

He tries again, straining, the heartstones glowing brightly with the effort, but it remains closed.

He slams it onto the pedestal. "Humph. Nobody reads that book."

I race away as fast as I can. Halfway back to my room, the old Priestess jumps out at me. I swallow a scream that turns to anger. "You left me there."

She takes my elbow and steers me down the corridor toward my room, whispering. "You needed to see that."

"See what?"

"That the book can't be opened."

"But I opened it."

"Yes." She grins. "You did."

Cassian paces outside my room. He pulls up as soon as he sees us. "Did she?"

"She did."

He blows out a breath, staring at me. He suddenly launches into action. "I'm not waiting for the morning. I'm taking her back to the mine right now. She's not safe here. If Howl scents her, she's dead."

"Agreed. Especially because Howl is on his way here." The Priestess's whisper is a quiet hiss as she hurries back down the corridor, darting away into the darkness.

"Wait… what… but… I can't just leave." Baelen is here. The Storm is here. I have to talk to the Storm about what I just read. I'm certain that the last journal entry was written by her mother. She wrote about her daughter Elyria and something about learning the truth. I need to face the Storm once and for all and find out what happened.

I don't realize I've backed away from Cassian until he says, "I'm not going to hurt you. The mine is the safest place for you. You have friends there who will protect you. And the further you're away from Howl, the better."

"It's not that I don't want to go back—I actually really want to get out of here—but I don't understand what all of that book stuff was about."

"I… can't tell you."

Footsteps sound down the hall. Heavy ones. Howl ones.

I won't be able to say goodbye to the Storm. I try to gather my thoughts. Howl told me to find a heartstone. Once I'm free, I can find out everything I need to know about the Storm. There will be time for that. Right now, Cassian believes my life is in danger. I hate leaving Elyria, but I can't help her until I help Baelen, and I can't do that until I find a heartstone… which I don't want to do because that will only make Howl more powerful.

I seriously want to scream right now.

Cassian holds out his hand. "We have no time for a crate. I will carry you. Through the window." His eyes meet mine. "Please."

I step onto his feet, wrap my arms around his waist, and hold on. Howl turns the corner as Cassian lifts off the ground. There's only just enough room for his wings to stay aloft.

Howl seems more perturbed than angry. "What are you doing?"

Cassian says, "What you asked: making sure she stays alive."

"Very well. Take her back to the mines. But Princess," he addresses me. "You will bring me Prime's heart by the end of the week. Otherwise, I will bury Baelen Rath under a mountain of rock."

And the Storm with him.

I shudder so hard that my knees knock against Cassian's legs. He zooms up and out of the wide window, taking me with him.

36

MARBELLA

We fly in silence. The moon is a large white circle above us. I wonder if Incorruptible still thinks and feels like the Storm still thinks and feels. I suspect it's a bit different because Incorruptible became a stable part of nature and the Storm, well, she is a deliberately unstable one.

"Hideaway helped the Queen," I say into the silence between Cassian and me. My loose hair cascades between us. Cassian is wearing armor, but it's made of thick leather straps, so it's not too uncomfortable against my cheek. After we first ascended, once he was sure we were far enough away from the palace, he stopped mid-flight to tie parts of his armor around me, making sure I wouldn't fall.

"The Queen wanted to find out more about human weapons—guns I think they're called. The King thought Hideaway put the Queen in danger and wouldn't forgive him. Not even when the Queen said it was her idea. Anyway…" I shrug. "I thought you might want to know."

"I do. Thank you."

I clear my throat. My voice is small. "When you… said that you found something to care about a month ago…" I was too angry when he told me, but I've had time to think since then. A month ago was when I arrived at Mount Erador. I guess I find it difficult to believe that he means me.

He starts to speak but stops. Starts again. His voice is scratchy in the night air. "I felt something when you leaped from the cliff's edge with that dagger in your hand and smashed through Howl's shield. It was the night you first got here. Do you remember it?"

"Of course."

"You sliced through Howl's deep magic like nobody ever had before. Even the Priestesses. They tried getting through his defenses. Died trying, actually. They weren't strong enough. I watched them die and I… gave up. I followed him out of self-preservation."

He swallows. "But you broke through. Without even realizing what you'd done. You were terrifying and ferocious and… I had no reason to fight Howl before you did that. You changed everything. With one strike."

He stops talking and doesn't start again. When I came to Erador, I had a singular purpose: save Baelen. But now I need to do so much more than that. Howl has taken his people prisoner and enslaved them in his thirst for power. And worse, he is in league with the Elven Command, who have succumbed to sorcery.

For weeks, I've been mining side by side with gargoyles who have shown me friendship and loyalty, courage and bravery. For weeks, I've been falling asleep cold and pushing away a hum in my ears that tells me which of the Kings' bones to pick, ignoring a whisper telling me to choose the fifth tunnel, the fiery tunnel, the one that the gargoyles fear the most. But it calls to me. It called to me the moment I first stood at its entrance.

As we fly toward Mount Prime, I stare up into the light of the moon. I remember Badenoch telling me that he can sense Prime's Heartstone, that it pushes him away. But it doesn't push me away. It calls to me.

The closer we fly to Mount Prime, the colder I become. At first, it's only my toes and fingers, but as we enter the mountain, my skin frosts over.

"It's happening again," Cassian says, shivering next to me. "We need to get you to a hammock and get you warm."

"No," I say. "Cassian, I think I understand now why this is happening. I think I understand why I'm so cold."

We soar down the first opening, the Cavity moments away.

His brow furrows. "I don't think I'm going to like what you're about to say."

"You aren't."

"Then don't say it."

But I do anyway. "I need to go to the fifth tunnel."

We touch down inside the quiet Cavity. The gargoyles are all asleep in their hammocks above us. Three sleepy guards jump to attention as soon as they see Cassian, but he dismisses them. "It's fine, I'll take watch."

The only thing that needs watching is me.

I step off Cassian's feet. As soon as my bare feet touch the rocky ground, ice crystals spread out from them. I must have been hurting him again, but he didn't say anything. I rub my hands together and puffs of ice waft up around me.

I'm a walking snowstorm. "I have to go to the fifth."

"Not alone."

"You can come with me."

"I mean that you should take your team."

He's right. "Will you wake them for me? Jasper and the other team leaders as well. I need them to be a part of this. It's not about me finding a heartstone to take for myself. They need to know that."

His brow furrows. "What is it about then?"

"Finding a heartstone for all of them."

He doesn't understand. I don't exactly yet either, except that a plan is forming in my mind, a plan that might free us all.

I wait at the entrance to the mine shaft. I don't expect the gargoyles to trust Cassian, so I stay in plain sight even though the cold is killing me. Perhaps literally.

Cassian keeps his distance as the others make their way to me, wiping the sleep from their eyes. It's the middle of the night. The coldest time.

Jasper is the first to reach me. "I'm glad to see you're okay."

I resist the urge to hug him. I want to tell him that Elyria needs help, but it will only worry him, and I need this plan to work first.

"I need you all to come with me to the fifth," I say, not mincing words.

Llion is the quickest to get on board, his golden eyes flashing in the dim light. "I don't understand why you're asking us to do this, but if we're going to the fifth, we need to prepare water, protective clothing—"

"You won't need it." I point at my feet, my hands, the ground I'm standing on, and the rock wall directly behind me, all covered in ice. "I need to go quickly, I'm afraid. I don't have much time." Already, I sense my heartbeat slowing, the ice eating away at my insides. "Cassian?"

He flies forward, snatches me up, and plummets down the mineshaft with me. I don't have time to wait for the others to make their decision. "You're freezing up," he says, swooping across the entrance to the first tunnel and down the next mineshaft.

I catch my breath after the sudden motion forces the air out of my lungs. "I hope I'm right about this or I'm going to need your help. Big time."

By the time we reach the fifth tunnel, my teeth have progressed from chattering to jaw-locked. A blast of warm air up the mineshaft is the only thing keeping me alive. We touch down and Cassian soars toward the nearest flame. It sizzles and dies as soon as we reach it, the fiery surface freezing over as I approach.

I force sound out of my throat. "Let… me… warm… my… feet…"

Cassian allows me to slide to the ground but doesn't touch it himself. When my feet connect, it's like heaven. Heat, glorious heat, shoots up into my legs. I run for the nearest tower of flame, disappointed when it sputters and diminishes as soon as I get near it. I hurry to the next one. Each time the flame dies, my body absorbs the heat. Every time a fire warms me too much, my body reacts, freezing the fire down.

When I'm warm enough to function properly again, I look back the way I came to see that the tunnel where I walked is free of flames. Its hot surface has turned black, coated with a glossy-looking substance.

Cassian touches down on the ground, and I gather from his expression that the floor isn't scorching anymore. The other gargoyles join us, crowding into the tunnel, looking around, touching the cool walls.

This time, I can stop to speak to them. "I freeze every night, but only here on Mount Prime. Here… Prime's heart calls to me. I tried to stop listening, but it didn't work. Prime's heart wants to be found."

"No, Lady Storm. Please." Badenoch is the first to step forward. The pale scars across his chest are highlighted in the glow around us. "If we find the heart, we have to give it to Howl."

"Do we?" I look around me. "Tell me why."

"We can't control it and we can't use it against him. Rhain tried…"

"Because he tried to control it alone. Howl is one gargoyle. We can beat him if we work together. I know we can."

"Lady Storm…"

"It calls to me, Badenoch. I have to believe that's for a reason."

He's worried. I would be, too, if I were him, but he eventually nods, taking a massive leap of faith with me.

I can't ignore the hum in my ears anymore. Cassian hangs back, but the other gargoyles follow as I head further down the tunnel, finally reaching a fork. One side of the tunnel veers left into a wall of flame. It's almost impossible to see what's behind it or how far back the flames extend. The other side veers right and is potted with random fires but extends much farther into the distance.

At my elbow, Roar says, "The teams before us have been mining down the right side. Nobody can get through the wall of flame down that way." He points left and gives me a wry smile. "I'm guessing that's the way you're going."

I place my hand out in front of me. I'm about to walk through a wall of flames, and honestly, I'm not sure if I'm cold enough. I glance back, searching the faces of the watching gargoyles. Shadows flicker over them now that the fires have died down. I look past Roar, Welsian, Iago, and even Llion, whose trust in me was the greatest from the beginning. Past Jasper, whose loyalty has been unbending, to Erit and the other team leaders, all the way back to the gargoyle who took the most convincing that freedom is worth fighting for.

Cassian hovers in the shadows. I wait for him to make a move. I wait a long time. Finally, he steps into the light, tucks his massive wings into his side, and says, "Go on, Princess."

More certain now, I step into the flames.

Brilliant golden fire leaps away from me as if I'm the one burning it. The further I extend my hands, the further it retreats, conforming to the shape of my body for seconds before it begins to die. The rock wall hiding behind it glistens with threads of a rust-colored substance. It looks like copper, but I can't be sure.

"I need to get through this wall. I need a pickaxe… something… anything…"

The gargoyles mumble and shift. Nobody brought anything. I didn't exactly give them time to gather tools. I scrape my hand across the surface and place my ear against it. The touch of my skin cools any remaining heat. I can't be sure how thick the wall is, but the hum is almost unbearable, calling me from beyond.

"Excuse me, Lady Storm," Iago says. "May I assess the situation?"

I step back. "Of course. Thank you, Iago."

He studies the copper seam, tracking his finger across it from left to right, further up, and then down. He closes his fist and taps it at two points, one on the left and the other on the right, that consist of clear patches of rock without as much copper. "Here," he says. "And over here. Beneath the main seam."

He gives way to Roar and Llion who focus on those parts of the rock. "How thick is it, Iago?" Roar asks, to which Iago replies, "About six inches."

Roar grunts an acknowledgement. I'm not sure how they're going to break through. I don't see any pickaxes.

"Excuse me, Lady Storm," Llion says, picking me up and putting me safely out of the way.

There's a pause as he and Roar angle their wings forward and brace. I press back against the tunnel wall, waiting with everyone else…

They ram their wing daggers into the rock wall. Rock cracks and dust wafts into the air. They focus on the parts Iago showed them and follow the seam around in an oval shape. The pierce points they make with their daggers become dark dots, waiting holes. The wall cracks in multiple places but doesn't break, fracturing beyond each impact point.

Finally, they step back, chests heaving. Roar says, "Welsian?"

"My pleasure," Welsian answers, flexing his enormous arms and cracking his knuckles.

He chooses two spots on opposite sides and fits his fingers into the holes, bracing his giant feet against the bottom portion of the wall. The others step back.

Welsian's muscles flex and strain. With a roar, he rips the wall right out from itself. Tiny shards scatter across the tunnel, but he's left holding the main piece. I'm impressed. In fact, I'm impressed by all of it, from Iago, to Llion and Roar, to Welsian. I place my hand over my heart as Welsian leans the stone portion against the tunnel wall and gestures me inside. "Lady Storm. When you're ready."

"Thank you."

A soft glow spills through the opening they made, alternating between golden and white light. It glints in my eyes as I step through.

The cave beyond is several paces wide and deep, not big enough for everyone to fit inside. In the center, two pillars of stone rise up from the ground like two waves of molten rock that each froze at their crest. A stone sits at the highest tip of each.

I freeze to the spot.

Two heartstones. Not one.

I can't find my voice. All air has left my lungs. I'm not sure how much the others can see from outside, but I need Badenoch to come in here and identify which one is Prime's heart.

I whisper, "Badenoch!"

The older gargoyle squeezes through the opening to the cave, needing to bend to make it through. His eyes shoot wide when he sees what I see. "Two!"

I can't raise my voice above a whisper. I'm in too much shock. "Which one is Prime's heart? You're his descendant. You can tell me, right?"

He points to the golden one. As the light through the opening catches it, it reflects warmth, a sense of calm purpose. "It's that one. But, Lady Storm, it doesn't want me to be here." He shifts slightly, his intelligent eyes studying the other heart before he takes a step back. "That other one… *really* doesn't want me to be here."

The stone on the other pedestal is pure white, glittering, a diamond the size of my fist.

At odds with what Badenoch feels, the white stone calls to me. Not like a compulsion that I can't control, but like a kinship. A recognition of all the emotions I've ever felt and of who I am deep in my core. I step closer to it, studying its surface, the most dazzling stone I've ever seen, shining with an inner light.

Oomph. Badenoch catches me, wrapping both his arms around my waist and pulling me backward. "Don't touch it!"

I allow him to carry me backward, placing me back on my feet at the entrance. He steps away from me as fast as he puts me down. "Forgive me for grabbing you, but you can't touch that stone. Nobody can."

"I know, Badenoch. It will kill me."

It's not a stone.

It's a piece of the moon.

It's Queen Incorruptible's heart.

37

———

MARBELLA

er heart must have fallen after she became the moon, embedding itself in Mount Prime beside the heart of the one she truly loved: Prime.

"We need to tell the others."

Outside the cave, the fires that still burn deeper inside the fifth tunnel cast an eerie light across the waiting gargoyles. Cassian remains in the shadows at the back, and I have to wonder, some sixth sense asks me, did he know what I was going to find? I now know that it wasn't Prime's heart that was calling to me all this time—it was Incorruptible's. Together with reading her journal tonight, it doesn't feel like a coincidence.

Badenoch remains in front of the opening, but defers to me, indicating that I should give everyone the news.

I say, "There are two heartstones."

The news travels through the group like the flames that used to burn in the cave. The gargoyles' responses vary from exhilarated to fearful, turning to each other, asking questions, but by far the most common is: "What does this mean?"

"Badenoch has confirmed that one of the hearts belongs to Prime." If that news is enough to cause a stir, the next will be worse. "The other heart belongs to Queen Incorruptible."

Shock ripples through the gargoyles, stunning them into silence. It's thick and heavy around me until Jasper breaks it.

"That makes it the deadliest heartstone, correct?" he asks.

"But useless to Howl," Llion says. "Only the King could have touched it."

Cassian speaks for the first time, lifting himself off the wall at the back. "Or someone with royal blood."

The other gargoyles step away from him. With everything that's going on, I suspect they forgot he was there or who he is—Howl's right hand. A dangerous threat in our midst. He seems content to ignore them as he strides toward me, forcing them to part as quickly as he walks.

Cassian reaches me, his eyes blazing, towering over me, forcing me to tilt my head back. "Someone with the royal blood of a gargoyle queen can use that heartstone."

I stare up at him, confused. "I don't know what you're trying to say."

But my eyes widen as the shocking realization shoots through me: the Storm!

Cassian told me she was royal, that she was the heir to the throne before she became a force of nature. He'd arranged for me to see Incorruptible's journal, so I'd read it for myself.

What if… Cassian somehow knows that the Storm has taken the form of a woman with a mind, heart, thoughts, arms, legs, and everything which means she can pick up a heartstone and use it. And what if… Baelen wasn't brought to my room as some sick perversion of Howl's but because Cassian arranged it. Maybe he knows that the Storm stays with Baelen.

I don't know how any of that is possible, but I do know that Cassian told me she was royal, and then he brought her to see me.

My heart leaps. Elyria can use the royal heartstone. She can use the stone against Howl, strike him down, fight him, and he won't be able to stop her—

Except… she can't.

My hope fades, plummeting so hard, so fast, that tears fill my eyes. The Storm swore to never harm a gargoyle. She already tried to stop Howl once. She told me so herself. She may be able to pick up the heartstone, but she can't use it to help us.

Everyone is waiting for me to speak. Cassian hasn't taken his eyes off me, and I'm sure I'm a display of intense emotions right now: all the way from wonder to hope to… smashed and crushed.

"It can't be done." My final emotion isn't lost on the other gargoyles. I didn't mean for it to have this result, but they respond to my grief with protective anger, knowing only that Cassian has caused it.

Erit pushes forward, nearly barreling into Cassian. "Why are you here? You're not one of us." Erit's wing daggers angle forward, an aggressive gesture, and I'm reminded that he's from the Grievous Clan, who settle their disputes with violence.

I push between them before Erit does something dangerous. "Erit, listen to me, General Cassian is subject to Howl's whims just like the rest of us."

Erit doesn't back off, turning on me in confusion but not anger. His expression softens as he digests my earnest speech. "Why are you defending him?"

"Because he saved my life." The space between them is so small that I press back against Cassian, my arms pushed against either side of him. "He saved my life when he didn't have to."

Cassian's voice rumbles in his chest, a quiet statement murmured in my ear. "You don't have to protect me, Princess. He's correct. I don't have any right to be here."

"But…"

He places me to the side, putting me away from him, and faces the others, his wings tucked tight, wing daggers held carefully back, palms out, non-threatening. It occurs to me that he hasn't worn his bone lash for the last three days.

"When the sun comes up, everything changes," he says. "You have to decide whether you're going to fight or give up. Either way…" His blazing eyes meet mine before he turns away. "The Princess must not die."

They part for him as he strides away, his steps turning into a run before he spreads his wings and soars away into the dark mine beyond.

"What happens now?" Roar asks, always the leader, focusing everyone back on task.

"First, I need you to tell me what happened with Rhain. Howl can carry a heartstone around without any harm to himself, so why couldn't Rhain? Howl used to be a gargoyle just like you, didn't he?"

Roar says, "He was, Lady Storm. But a violent one. He killed the King years before he got hold of a heartstone and terrorized our people even without it."

"By brute force," Llion adds. "And a Grievous Army backing him." He clears his throat. "I mean no offense to our clan, Erit. We are the proof that not all Grievous follow Howl."

It was easy to forget that both Erit and Llion were born into the Grievous Clan. They are both such dedicated, loyal, and surprisingly kind gargoyles.

"No offence taken," Erit replies. He folds his arms across his chest. "I can tell you what happened to Rhain, Lady Storm because he was my friend."

He tucks his wings tight into his sides. I recognize the gesture as self-protective. The gargoyles might not know they're doing it, but they pull their wings close when they're facing something difficult.

Erit says, "The short version is that he found the heartstone and was ordered to place it in a wooden box without touching it, which he obeyed. When he heard that Howl was coming to Mount Virtuous to get it, Rhain became very agitated. He knew that if Howl got the stone, he'd be unstoppable. So Rhain killed the guards and flew off with the box. But he also knew that Howl would kill Carmen in retaliation, so he went to free her, to escape together."

Erit exhales, sighing into the quiet around us. The way he clenches and unclenches his fists at his sides tells me he's fighting to remain impassive and unemotional, as he recounts what happened to his friend. "Howl caught them and Rhain opened the box. As soon as he touched the stone, he collapsed. That was the end of it." He clears his throat. "That's the short version."

I know what the long version involves: the aftermath, the

consequences, Rhain losing his wings, his wife forced to remain in Harem Hell. I wipe away my tears. "Thank you, Erit. You've helped a lot, because now I know why the heartstone didn't hurt Howl."

"Lady Storm?"

"Howl told me that a heartstone awakens at first touch. The first surge of deep magic is like lightning: powerful, angry, and ferocious. I know because I went through it when I became the Storm Princess."

I shake my head, trying to dislodge the memories that flood back into me: memories of light pouring around me and unimaginable pain, but nothing so bad as my heart being torn apart because I believed that Baelen was dying in front of me while I couldn't help him.

My voice catches as I continue. "Rhain awoke the Virtuous Heartstone. He took the brunt of its first force. If Howl had touched it first, he would have collapsed too."

I wait for this information to sink in before continuing. "When Howl awoke Lightsworn's heart the other day, it hurt him, but it didn't knock him unconscious because he already had a heartstone to protect him."

Llion, Roar, Erit, Badenoch, all of the gargoyles catch on at the same time. "After the first touch, any gargoyle can use the heartstone."

Jasper finishes for them, "Including the heartstones that Howl already has."

"Yes," I say, a small smile breaking across my previous sadness. "Now… I'd suggest that one of you takes the brunt of the awakening right now so we can use Prime's heart against Howl immediately, but the problem is… Howl will feel it. The same way I felt Lightsworn's heart awaken the other night. As soon as he feels it, he will descend on us with his entire army in tow. For now, he doesn't know we've found a heartstone." I pause again, hoping they will follow me. "Right now, we control the outcome."

"What is your plan?"

I answer Roar's question with a question. "Do you all trust Llion?"

Llion himself shoots surprise my way. He won't understand yet why I'm asking, but I intend to make it clear very soon.

Roar looks around, checking every single gargoyle here. Jasper nods too, and I know his support is not lost on Llion since they haven't exactly been best buddies from the start. Llion still calls Jasper "Twisted Metal," but I sense that Jasper no longer minds.

Roar says, "We trust Llion without question."

"Then here's what we need to do."

Hours later, Llion flies me back up into the Cavity. Each team leader has quietly woken their team in turns, explained the plan, and got all of them on board. Meanwhile, Iago and a team of gargoyles have been hard at work fashioning the things we need from wood and metal, working deep inside the mine where the sound won't carry to the sleeping guards in the Cavity. To Llion, I gave the task of creating weapons for us—weapons that don't look like weapons.

"That is a difficult task," he'd said to me.

I'd raised my eyebrows in a mock challenge. "I was told you could make a weapon out of anything."

He'd grinned. "I can."

Now, despite the adrenaline still shooting through me, I'm exhausted. I haven't slept all night, and I won't make it to the next one without collapsing if I don't rest. All of the gargoyles need to use the last hours of the night to sleep as long as they can.

Llion carries me in the direction of my hammock. Our group has crept back in stages so we don't wake the guards. I tug on Llion's arm before we pass the Cavity's center, whispering, "I need to see Cassian." I'm a little embarrassed to ask because I don't know the answer to my next question. "Where does he sleep?"

Llion halts mid-wing sweep, coasting the air for a moment. "Are you sure, Lady Storm? Can you trust him?"

"I'm sure, Llion."

In response, he changes direction, soaring across to a concealed nook on the far side of the Cavity closest to Cassian's bathing room. Llion places me down and indicates the darkened cave beyond. "Over there. But please be careful."

"I will, I promise."

"Should I wait for you?"

"No, thank you, Llion. I will ask Cassian to fly me up to my hammock." The worry on his face makes me pause. "I trust him, Llion."

"Okay," he says, but he doesn't look convinced, shooting a suspicious glare in the direction of the shadowed cave before he takes flight again.

I pause at the entrance. Webs light the way inside, but only to a point. I can't see much beyond the first few paces. I wait for my eyes to adjust, finally making out vague outlines: a chair, a small table, and a hammock against the wall at the back with a figure lying in it. I can't fly up to it so I pick up the chair, careful not to make too much noise while I carry it across, hoping there are no unseen obstacles along the way that might trip me.

I hop onto the chair and take hold of the side of the hammock, listening to figure out if Cassian is sleeping.

"You're here because you need my help," he says.

He sweeps his wings aside and out of the way, holding them tight to his sides so he can face me.

"Yes," I say, gripping the hammock and struggling up into it. It swings wildly back and forth before I manage to clamber over the edge and inside. I would ask him for help to get in, but two of us moving around will only make it worse. Hammocks are made for lying in, not sitting, so I stretch myself against the outer side of it while he remains on the inner.

I say, "I need you to carry the box to Howl."

"Because he won't suspect me."

"Yes, but also because it means none of the miners will be singled out as making a claim to it. This only works if we all go together."

He knows I'm not finished. "What else?"

"I need you to send a message to Howl convincing him that this should be a grand event. Like that day at Crimson Court. I need all the old clan leaders there: Lightsworn, Prime, Virtuous, Sunflight, Denrock, all of them. I need the old High Priestess there too, but not Baelen Rath. I can't take the chance that he'll wake up if I'm in danger. Can you do that?"

"Can I encourage Howl to show off his power?" Cassian scoffs. My eyes have adjusted enough now that I can see his expression, the wry glint in his eyes, and the solemn press of his lips together before he speaks. "That won't be difficult."

"Then you'll help us?"

"Yes."

I didn't realize I was so tense until relief floods me. I really wasn't sure if Cassian would agree to help. It means he'll put himself in as much danger as the rest of us. Possibly more since his actions will be a betrayal of Howl.

The hammock isn't made for remaining on one side. I've slowly slipped further toward the middle as we've been speaking, and now my right side presses against his chest and legs. There's still one more question I have for him. "Howl let you fly away with me tonight. I honestly didn't think he would."

Cassian's expression is dark. "He would beat and torture you, but he won't risk your death."

"Why not?"

"He believes that if you die, Baelen Rath will wake up. Even if that means Baelen will die soon after, Howl fears what he will do if he wakes to find you dead."

"Kill Howl?"

"Possibly." He shifts his wings, rustling them. "Baelen Rath's fearsome reputation precedes him. Combine that with the Storm's power and Howl has something to fear for the first time."

"Thank you for telling me." Knowing that Howl is capable of fear is a source of hope. "Can you fly me back to my hammock?"

"No."

His response is so abrupt that I search his face and body

language for some explanation. The faint light from the distant webs reflects depths of emotion in his eyes. The web's similar blue color highlights every shade of his irises, accentuating each shadow that falls across his cheekbones and lips. Is he refusing to fly me back or… is he refusing to let me go back?

He returns my questioning look with a ferocious one. He moves so fast, I have no time to react. His upper wing shoots over us, an instant cocoon, and at the same time, he rolls with it, placing one hand on either side of my head, holding himself up off me, one knee between my legs and the other outside my right knee. His body balances directly above me.

His demand is short and swift. "Why are you in my bed?"

I struggle to catch my breath at the sudden change of tone. "I came to ask for help."

"You could have stayed on that chair and asked for my help."

He's right. I could have, but it seemed wrong to ask him to put his life in danger without looking him in the eyes.

He shakes his head at me. "I'll forgive you for not knowing our customs, Princess, but before Howl took power, before he changed everything, there was one custom of true respect that applied in every clan."

Tension rushes through me as he catches his own breath, his lungs expanding, causing his chest to brush against mine.

"The woman chooses her mate," he says. "Not the other way around. Do you know how she does that?"

My heart has stopped beating. "How?"

"She comes to his bed."

I was wrong: my heart hasn't stopped beating, it's hammering so hard in my chest that I can't tell the beats apart anymore. My breathing is short and rapid. I don't know their customs. I certainly never knew anything about choosing a mate. In elven culture, marriage is arranged, public, nothing so intimate as what he's described. How was I to know? I have no idea how many times I've stomped on something culturally important to them. But this…?

"But… I'm not a gargoyle."

"You are to me!" His earnest declaration cuts my heart. He

doesn't see me as an elf anymore. He doesn't see me as an outsider. He sees me as one of them. A gargoyle. A woman.

"Now here you are… in my bed," he says. "And yet I know that your heart belongs to Baelen Rath. What am I to make of this?"

I whisper, "You said you'd forgive me."

A perplexed crease sweeps across his forehead. "What?"

"You said you'd forgive me for not knowing your customs."

His expression softens. "I did." He sighs. "Which is why… I'll take what you want to give."

He lowers himself against me but angles to the side, sweeping his arms under me and pulling me with him so I'm lying on my side, pressed against his chest. Hooking his upper leg over mine, he sweeps his hand into my hair, smoothing it down my back in a soothing gesture. He plants a kiss on my forehead, a brief and confusingly gentle touch.

"You will sleep here," he says. "After tonight, you will never come back to my bed again."

I nod against his chest, just once. I can't speak. My heart is a whirlwind of emotions. Cassian is like another storm to me—unpredictable, protective, surprisingly loyal, and compassionate in astonishing ways. The emotions I feel for him are equally unsettling. I feel for him the same care I feel for Jasper and Llion, two men I count as true friends. But I can't deny that if Baelen wasn't in my life, I might see Cassian in a different light. I might see a possibility that… can't exist because Baelen is everything to me. My heart is already spoken for.

Cassian said that he would only take what I want to give. Right now, I want to fall asleep feeling safe, because I know that when the sun rises, I won't be.

None of us will.

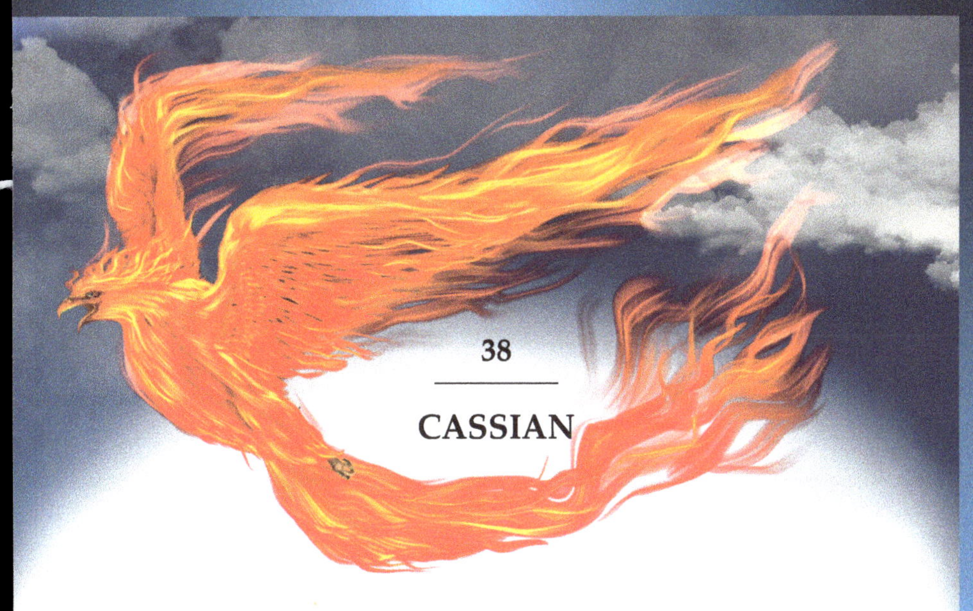

38

———

CASSIAN

Remember not to be so polite.

Marbella asks me if I will fly her back to her hammock and my response is the truth. "No."

Her eyes widen slowly as she searches my face. I've never been so abrupt with her, even when I've given her orders. But I'm finally ready to fight for what I want. I have no guarantees that I'll be alive at the end of tomorrow. I can't go to my grave not knowing what could have been.

I release my upper wing. It shoots in a curve over her, cocooning us inside the hammock. I roll with the movement, positioning my hands on either side of her head, balancing my body above hers, one knee between her legs. She lies beneath me, and it takes all my willpower not to lower myself, gather her body up to mine, and reposition her legs around my hips.

I demand an answer from her. "Why are you in my bed?"

She catches her breath, startled by the suddenness of my movement. "I came to ask for help."

"You could have stayed on that chair and asked for my help."

Her lips part, her gaze passing across my face, following the shape of my cheekbones, eyes, and finally my lips. There was a time when she looked at me with fear and distrust, but not anymore.

Now she has come to my bed, clambered right in. She's the first who wasn't sent by Howl. The first woman to choose me.

I growl. "I'll forgive you for not knowing our customs, Princess, but before Howl took power, there was one custom of true respect that applied in every clan." I inhale, trying to breathe, my chest expanding and brushing hers in tantalizing ways, making the distance between us agonizing. "The woman chooses her mate. Do you know how she does that?"

Marbella is frozen, her voice a whisper. "How?"

"She comes to his bed."

Her lips part in shock. I can see her thinking about what she did, rapidly going through the choices that led her here. She doesn't know the true weight of what she's done. By coming to my bed, she has given me the permission I crave to touch her, the permission to love her like I want to. Not only that, but she has made a declaration of commitment. Gargoyles don't have weddings like elves do. If she knew our customs, she would know that by coming to my bed...

She has become my wife.

Elaina was supposed to be my wife. She stole my heart a long time ago and until I met Marbella, I didn't think I would ever get it back.

But I won't touch Marbella—not until she makes a conscious choice.

She's stunned. "But I'm not a gargoyle."

I stare into her eyes, my heart suddenly bleeding. "You are to me!"

I don't know how to make her understand that I stopped seeing her as an elf from the moment I flew her up to her hammock, from the moment I inhaled her dangerous scent, from the moment she dragged her fingertip across her lips in front of the mirror I gave her.

I fight the bitter ache growing in my chest. "Now here you are in my bed. But I know that your heart belongs to Baelen Rath. What am I to make of this?"

I want her to tell me that she doesn't love him. I want her to tell me that she will forsake the past and be mine. I want her to look at me the way she looks at him.

But instead, she whispers, "You said you'd forgive me."

I'm confused by her response. "What?"

"You said you'd forgive me for not knowing your customs."

I search her eyes for a long moment, not wanting to shift from above her, not wanting to acknowledge that I'll never hear what I want her to say.

I do forgive her. With my whole heart.

I sigh, releasing my hope, letting it go. "I did. So tonight I'll take what you want to give."

Friendship. Loyalty. Trust. Gifts I haven't been given for a long time. Gifts that I'm willing to accept.

I lower myself to her side, sweeping her into my arms, stroking her hair and upper back the same way I did when she was cold. I leave a kiss on her soft forehead, the briefest touch.

"You will sleep here tonight," I say. "Then you will never come back to my bed."

She nods just once, burying her face against my chest, finally relaxing in my arms.

I stare at the ceiling for a long time until she falls asleep. Elaina gave me her unconditional trust and then she died because of me. This time, there's more at stake than my heart. Marbella holds the key to the future of my people.

I slowly, carefully, fold up my feelings for her, putting them away before I extricate myself from her arms.

Like the shadow panther I killed all those years ago, I steal into the darkness of the tunnels, returning to the fifth, where the Queen's heart is hidden under loose rubble at the back of the cave. After tomorrow, this tunnel will be collapsed and the Queen's heartstone will be buried forever. Howl will never know it was here.

Elaina told me that one day I would understand why she gave her life for me.

I finally do.

39

———

MARBELLA

I wake to hushed voices inside the entrance of the cave. I stay very still, listening, making out Llion's silhouette opposite Cassian's.

Cassian says, "She's sleeping. I don't want to wake her before we need to."

Llion's accusation is laced with threat. "You didn't bring her back to her hammock."

"She climbed into my bed."

There's a pause. "Oh."

Cassian sighs. "She didn't know what she was doing. Don't worry, I didn't take advantage."

There's another pause. When Llion finally speaks, it's a growl. "She trusts you, Cassian. Don't betray her." He spins on his heel, but Cassian follows him out.

"Llion… We used to be brothers."

"That was before you chose to side with Howl."

Cassian's wings curve forward, another self-protective gesture that I've come to recognize, but this one is connected with remorse. "My actions are unforgivable. I'm trying to make up for it now."

"I hope you can."

Llion strides away and Cassian leans against the cave's entrance,

304

staring at the other side, basically at nothing, for a long time. It gives me a chance to wake up properly and gather my thoughts. A shot of adrenaline forces me upright when I remember what today means. I try to wriggle out of the hammock on my own, but Cassian swoops over and helps me down.

"I sent the message to Howl," he says. "Now I'm waiting for a response. In the meantime, I've ordered the guards to stay away from the heartstone or I will kill them." He's wearing his bone lash again. He's already dressed in armor. "You can use my bathing room this morning. I've put something in there that I think you should wear today."

So far, he's done all the talking, which is good, because I don't know what to say. There are no words for what we'll face today. I'm not sure if I'll be alive at the end of it. I enter the bathing room, curious to see what clothing he was talking about.

My armor.

I run to it, checking it over. It's in perfect condition and it's definitely the strongest, safest thing I could wear today. "How did you…?"

"I brought it back from the palace. The old Priestess, uh, borrowed it. You were so engrossed in the book that you didn't notice her take it. I guess you didn't notice the satchel on my back either."

"I was busy focusing on a safe getaway from Howl." I chew my lip, trying to find a way to tell him that this armor could mean the difference between life and death for me today. That it is a priceless gift. What I end up saying is far from what I feel. "Thank you. I will wear this today."

He accepts that, but before he leaves, I ask, "Did you let Llion go?"

He blinks at me. "What?"

"Llion told me that after he thought his wife died, you were supposed to kill him."

Cassian shifts, uncomfortable, as I continue. "But you threw him into prison instead and I'm guessing… it wasn't the most well-guarded prison. So, I want to know: did you let him go?"

His expression is answer enough. He stares at the floor for a moment before he turns and leaves me in privacy. I suddenly realize that that might be the last private conversation I have with him. Everything is in place and ready. He's agreed to his part in it. I lurch after him, not sure what else I want to say, but he's already disappeared.

The next two hours are the longest of my life. Finally, at lunchtime, a messenger arrives, and Cassian resumes his authoritative persona as he strides into the food hall, the messenger in tow. "Listen up! Howl expects to receive the Prime Heartstone at Crimson Court this afternoon. I expect you all to be ready to fly in an hour."

He glares around the room, tapping his bone lash. "If any of you attempt to touch the heartstone before we leave, you will lose your head."

A deathly silence follows him out. I lean across to Llion, "Get ready." My voice wobbles. I want to say more but words fail me.

"Don't worry, Lady Storm." He places his hand over mine, strong and comforting. My team nods around me: Roar, Iago, and Welsian. Across the way, Jasper and Badenoch are waiting for my signal. "We know what to do."

"It's time," I say, meaning so much more than it's time to get ready. It's time for Howl to end.

As a swarm, the gargoyles stand up, quiet and resolute, and scatter in the directions they need to go. Jasper catches my arm before I leave, waiting for the food hall to empty around us.

"You're very quiet," he says. It's been a long time since we spoke alone. I haven't told him about Elyria yet—there hasn't been a chance, but I know I have to take the opportunity now.

"I saw Elyria at the palace."

His expression softens. He's the only other person who can see Elyria and speak with her and the first person she opened up to before we were separated. "How is she?"

"Not good, Jasper. Howl is violent and cruel. I can only imagine the things she's seen."

"She can't fight back." He grips my hands, sudden and

determined. "We'll do the fighting for her."

I try to swallow past the lump in my throat. "I came here to save Baelen. Now I need to save an entire race of gargoyles." I hang my head, the weight of responsibility heavy across my back and shoulders. "What if I fail?"

He pulls me into a hug. A month ago, I would have frozen up in complete shock at the contact. Now I melt into it, needing the assurance that I'm on the right path and that he's willing to walk it with me.

"Marbella," he murmurs. "You've already won." He pulls back with a steely glint in his eyes. "Now get ready."

I head straight for the bathing room and pull on my armor, brushing my hair back and braiding it tightly to keep it out of my face. Once my boots and gloves are on, I stride from the room feeling different, feeling like I still have my storm power.

Outside, I find the gargoyles all lined up and ready.

They have no armor, but they do have sturdy boots and they're all wearing shirts for the first time, some tucked into their long pants with belts made of rope. If they're surprised to see me in armor, they hide it well.

"Princess," Cassian orders. "You will come with me to retrieve the heartstone."

The messenger seems surprised when I slide down the ladder at the side of the mineshaft. I'm pretty quick about it now, the thick gloves protecting my hands and the slides on the inner sides of my boots making fast work of the downward descent.

Reaching the fifth tunnel, Cassian wastes no time taking the messenger into the cave we discovered. A single, wooden box rests on one of the crests.

Last night we removed the Queen's heart with a very long pair of pliers wrapped in leather—just in case the touch of metal set off the heartstone—and placed it in a second wooden box, locking and burying it under rubble at the back of the cave. Even if Howl wins today, every miner has vowed that if they survive, they will return to this cave to collapse it, burying the Queen's heart forever, and never tell anyone what we found.

Cassian slides the wooden box containing Prime's heart into a leather satchel that he carries attached to the straps crisscrossing his armor. He slides it onto his back, and we return to the Cavity where the miners and guards are all waiting.

"Fly out!" Cassian orders.

As a single, coordinated unit, the miners take to the air, and the guards follow, leaving me to scramble into yet another crate. Cassian locks the hatch. Within moments we're airborne, and all I can see are the light changes—soft blue changing to bright yellow as we fly into the sun.

When we reach our destination, all my emotions are tucked away, honed into a pinpoint focus: Howl.

I roll out of the basket as soon as Cassian opens the hatch, moving smoothly to my feet, and lift my head high. The gargoyles are lined up in five rows of five on the cliff's edge. Llion, Roar, and Jasper are in the first row, while Welsian, Iago, and Badenoch join the last row. I need them in those positions to guide the others if things go bad.

I stride to the head of the group, giving them a single nod before turning in the direction of Crimson Court and the beating drums. Shadow panther flags flap in the wind, the breeze cooling us as the sun begins its descent. Sunset is still two hours away, so we have plenty of light.

Cassian removes the wooden box from his satchel and places it on the wide, wooden tray that he asked one of the guards to bring. He balances it in his arms like an offering, walking ahead of us. In the distance, brilliant flashes of sapphire and emerald light from Howl's heartstones tell me that he has chosen to wait inside the Court. He wants us to bring Prime's heart to him.

I judge the number of guards lining the Court at about one hundred. There are more guards outside Harem Hall, another legion outside the palace itself, and even more within each mine. The number of guards I see here are just the beginning of what we'll have to fight.

Another forty or so free gargoyles stand in rough rows on the right-hand side inside the Court—each of the former Clan elders, plus some advisors. I recognize many of the faces from the last time we were here, including Lightsworn Liliana who waits next to the old High Priestess. Liliana is dressed in simple black pants and a shirt, but it's overlaid with leather armor. I'm guessing that Howl's announcement about marrying me has had a positive impact on her life. At the very least, it looks like he no longer controls what she wears.

She doesn't take her eyes off Llion as he approaches and it's easy to see why she chose him. Like Llion, she's focused and intent. She doesn't carry any visible weapons—none of us do—but I sense her quiet rage.

The other gargoyles are equally unyielding and silent, but their Clan cultures are visible in their dress and manners. While the Lightsworn and Virtuous clans are regal, the leaders of the Denrock and Sunflight clans are dressed in functional, earthy-colored clothing.

Sitting on the throne of the dais, Howl wears a grin that fades only slightly when he narrows his eyes at my armor. He won't call me out on it because that would mean admitting that someone succeeded in stealing it from him, but the tick at the side of his jaw tells me he's not happy. The two heartstones glow against his bare chest, but he wears a new molded metal harness with a third, empty circle ready to place the new stone into. He's alone on the dais this time—no trophies in the form of Baelen or the phoenix—but I guess the Prime Heartstone will be trophy enough.

"My King," Cassian says, stopping at the foot of the dais as the drums stop beating. "I bring you Prime's heart."

Howl doesn't make a move to take it yet. "Which gargoyle found it?"

"They all did, my King."

Howl scoffs, his thick fingers thrumming against his armrests.

"All of them?"

"Yes. The Princess found a way through the flames in the fifth tunnel. That gargoyle there—Iago—determined where to puncture the rock wall behind it. Those two—Roar and Llion—weakened the wall, and that one—Welsian—finally broke the wall apart. Then this one here—Badenoch—identified the heart as Prime's. That one over there devised a way to pick up the heart without triggering it and—"

Howl cuts him off. "I get your point, General Cassian." His narrowed eyes slide over to me. "We'll deal with who can claim the prize soon enough. Bring me the stone."

Cassian turns to Roar and orders him to take the tray, remove the wooden box from it, and ascend the steps.

I thrum with tension as he places the box on a waiting pedestal. He draws himself off to the side, wings partially spread, tips forward. It's a defensive pose, but Howl is too pleased about his new prize to notice. He lifts himself from his throne and gleams at the box, running his hands over the top of it in a caress. "Finally. The trio of heartstones."

Howl lifts the lid with a wide grin. I hold my breath. My heart begins to pound but I accept it, the force of adrenaline, the need to fight.

Howl blinks down at the box. Anger follows confusion and it's all the reaction I need.

"Positions!" I scream.

The front line of gargoyles, including Roar and Llion drops to their knees. Roar uses the same movement to knock the tray onto the floor. It splits into twenty straight pieces that had been held together with the same gum that Roar plastered over my eye after my fight with Arlo. At the same time, the other lines of gargoyles drop to their boots, retrieving the pickaxe heads hidden in them in one hand, and deftly catch the handles that Roar and the front line throw back with their other. Suddenly they're all armed with the weapon of their trade. In the next breath, they form a semi-circle around Llion and me, pushing outward as the guards push in, reacting to my scream.

Roar takes the lead and shouts at the Clan leaders to get to the back of the Court. They don't waste time, hurrying out of the way of the guards. The old Priestess runs with them, but Liliana jumps into line with the miners, taking position beside Welsian. We're left with two rings: guards on the outside, miners on the inside, Llion and me in the center.

Howl is still fixated on the empty box. His angry fist closes around it so tightly that the wooden structure cracks and splinters, strewing shards across the dais.

He roars at Cassian, "Where is the heartstone?"

Cassian points. "There."

Llion spreads his wings. He rips off his shirt to reveal his own molded metal straps crossing his chest. The Prime Heartstone rests inside them.

Howl screams, "That's not possible!"

"Believe it," Llion says as he takes flight, his strong wings lifting him up into the space over our heads. "You want it? Come and get it."

Howl's corded muscles bulge. Powerful green light pulses through the veins in his wings as he speeds into the air, flying faster than normal with the power of the heartstones behind him.

The two gargoyles collide mid-air. The collision is all it takes to send the guards into action, but we're ready for them.

"Lady Storm!" Roar throws me a pickaxe as several guards target me. It doesn't take me long to get the hang of using it as a weapon. After all, I've used one of these every day for the last month. When I don't use it for its sharp end, I use its handle in the way my Storm Command taught me to fight with a wooden rod. I duck under the sword swing of the nearest guard and drive the blunt end of the pickaxe once into his chest and again under his chin, knocking him backward.

Nearby, Welsian disarms a guard, and Liliana snaps up his sword. When Welsian loses his own weapon in the chest of another guard, his fists become his weapons until he pulls out the rope belt he's wearing, which happens to have a small chisel attached to the end of it. It's not quite a bone lash, but it does enough damage when swung around and let loose on his opponents.

The fight continues around me, and so far, we haven't lost any miners. But up above us, Llion appears to be tiring—and getting sloppy because of it.

"You can't control Prime's heart," Howl jeers at him. "You don't know how."

Knocking both of Llion's arms outward, he exposes Llion's chest and snatches at the heartstone. "Now it's mine."

Watching from the ground, I grin. Iago designed the harness well.

Llion says, "I was waiting for you to do that."

As Howl's bare hand closes over the front of the heartstone, his muscles bulge, and his eyes widen. There's a pause as he realizes his mistake. "You didn't wake it yet…"

The blast knocks Howl backward, all the way across the Court into the side of the mountain against which it's built. Every creature in the room that ever controlled deep magic, including the Priestess, flies backward in the blast. It hits me too, but I'm ready for it this time. I allow the wave to carry me up and over the stunned guards, preparing to drop and roll on the way back down. The awakening hurts—I can't deny that it hurts—but I welcome it because now Llion can use the stone. He can fight Howl for real. Now the fight will be fair.

"Princess!" Cassian flies through the air and catches me before I fall, carrying me safely back to the ground.

Howl tumbles to the dais, stunned. His concussion won't last long, but Llion uses the seconds wisely, taking hold of the heartstone for real this time, ripping off the protective covering at the back of the harness that stopped the stone from making contact with his skin. It was the same method I'd used in Erawind so I could handle metal without causing a lightning storm.

The change is instant. Golden light streams through his veins, visible in his wings, lighting up his eyes even more golden than they were before. Nearby, Liliana has frozen in shock. As a guard cuts the air beside her with his sword, Llion reacts in her defense, his palm shooting outward. The guard is flung backward from the force. She barely notices, racing to her husband. "Llion!"

He scoops her up, kisses her fiercely, and then puts her down again. "Be safe, my love."

He flies up again and swoops toward Howl. The King rises from the ground, clawing at the side of the mountain to regain his feet before leaping toward the front of the dais, his wings spread.

Beside me, Cassian suddenly stiffens. "Princess! Watch out!"

It takes me a split second to realize that Howl isn't coming for Llion. He's coming for us, or more particularly, his pinpoint focus is Cassian.

"Traitor!" Howl feints around Llion's right wing, barely evading his wing dagger. In the time it takes for Llion to spin, reach out, snatch hold of Howl's wing, and wrench him backward…

"*Death.*" Howl's palm shoots out. A bolt of green light the size of my arm spears toward Cassian. I sense its power the moment it leaves Howl's hand. The memory of deep magic inside me screams at me in warning. He's injected his cruelest thoughts into the heartstone and forced it to give life to savage pain and slow death. Nothing will be able to stop it once it reaches its target.

I don't think. I react.

Both my arms shoot out, palms flat. I take one step forward for the strength I'll need for my smaller body to have the impact I want. I shove Cassian hard in the side, pushing him out of the way, registering the shock sparking from every angle of his falling body, his eyes shooting to mine.

The step I took positions me directly in the bolt's path, and even with my quickest reflex, it's too late to move out of it. The bolt's explosive light fills my view and I brace for the pain that will come first and the death that will follow.

Beyond it, obscured and barely visible, Howl's expression morphs from rage to fear; the deepest fear he's ever shown. It stretches his skin and drains his face pale.

If there's such a thing as a moment within a moment, I use it for my last thought.

Baelen will kill you when I'm dead.

40

MARBELLA

A gray curtain shoots up in front of me, thick webbing lighting up green as the bolt strikes it from the other side. Another protective curtain shoots up behind me. Wings… *Wings!*

Cassian must have let them unfold as he fell, using the strength of my push to trigger his reflex to extend his wings at the exact moment that I pushed him away.

No! Cassian!

The death bolt strikes Cassian's wing and shrieks through his wing bones, lighting them up green, sizzling through them to his shoulders, chest, arms, legs, and up into his head. He hits the floor with a crack, his back arched over his satchel, the smash of breaking wood filling my ears.

The light vanishes. The bolt met its mark.

"Cassian!" *Damn his massive wings.* No other gargoyle could have done what he did, using his wings to shield me and take the bolt himself.

I drop to his side, grasping at his torso, sliding my hands behind his back, trying to pull him up. He's heavy, all bulky muscle. He shudders against me. He's hurting. Badly. His eyes are shut, but he's still breathing. Gasping for breath.

"Cassian… No…." I have to get him out of here. Tears of fright replace my shock. I don't know what I can do to stop the death that's coming, but I need to try. "Somebody help me!"

Jasper is closest to me, but as soon as he tries to get to me, three big guards step into his path, jeering at him and me. They heard my cry. They know what they're doing, blocking Jasper from helping me. I memorize their faces, because I'll be coming for them soon.

For now, I'm on my own. With a scream of effort, I pull Cassian's bulky torso into my arms, his wings flopping to the ground behind him, a dead weight pulling him backward. It takes me too long to snatch and grab them forward, using their weight to keep him leaning against me, and in the meantime, he's trying to speak.

"Satch…el."

"Cassian?"

His eyelashes flicker against my cheek. "Satchel."

Finally managing to slide his wings to either side of me, I lean his head against my shoulder and pat the floor. I'm unable to really see the satchel and finally feel its strap so I can pull it up from the floor. Shards of wood poke out from it and I don't want to drag it into the space between us.

Cassian seems to understand my dilemma. His hands rattle against mine, weak, but he takes the satchel, splinters and all, and reaches into it.

He pulls a smaller leather bag out of it and lets the rest of the satchel and shards drop back to the floor. He breathes heavily with the effort but drags the little bag into my lap. "I brought this… for you."

"Cassian, I need to get you out of here. Llion can hold Howl for now. You're hurt. You're…" *Dying.* My voice chokes up as blood drips onto my hands, falling onto the little bag resting in them. It's coming from his mouth, telling me he has internal injuries. "You're badly hurt."

"I'm not going to make it. We both know that." He tilts his head up a little, his forehead against my cheek, his shoulder against mine. "Please… open it."

What could be so important that he would rather give it to me than get help? As he slumps against my shoulder, I pull apart the cords holding the leather bag closed.

"Now, tip it… into my hands." He pushes his shaking palms together, cupping them above my lap, ready to receive whatever is in the bag.

I don't question him. I stopped questioning him a long time ago. He saved my life, my dignity, and didn't take anything from me. I trust him. But as I tip the bag… I realize that I shouldn't.

He lied to me.

He lied to me because he thinks he can help me because he thinks that he can help his people and make up for what he did in the past. He lied to me because he believes something that can't be true. He lied to me, and he's about to accept death into his hands, and I don't want that.

I don't want him to die.

My muscles fire. My hand flexes upward, intent on reversing what I've done—to stop the object from falling into his waiting palms, but he anticipates my move. One of his hands flies upward, grasping mine in an iron, determined grip, and by then, it's too late.

The brilliant, white diamond—the Queen's heart—drops into his other palm.

There's a moment of silence, a heartbeat in which he pulls the Queen's Heartstone to his chest, covers it with his fist, and says, "Hold on to me."

I throw my arms and legs around him, he wraps his wings around me, and the cocoon he creates fills with a blast so pure that it rips through every part of me, lifting us both upward, suspending us in the quiet eye of a different storm.

He told me that his wings were just like his ancestor's. That they can form a barrier against deep magic. Now he's sealing the stone's awakening inside his wings with us so nobody else will feel it.

"Cassian…"

His blue eyes blaze at me. His free arm wraps around me, stroking my back and tangling in my hair as we remain suspended.

I don't know how long it lasts. It could be seconds or a lifetime as he says, "I need to tell you what you smell like."

He presses his cheek against mine, inhaling deeply before he draws back to cup the cheek he just pressed against. "You smell like the Queen whose home I grew up in. You smell like her daughter who died when we were young. I don't know how but you carry the blood of the Supreme Incorruptible."

The fist he holds between us, containing the Queen's heart, pushes at me. "Take it. Her heart is awake now, and it belongs to you."

A sob builds in my chest. "I'm not what you think I am, Cassian. I'm not a gargoyle."

"You are to me…" His eyes begin to close. "Take it, Princess. Take it and strike."

Gravity returns and we fall together. I hit the ground with Cassian beneath me, my knees knocking the ground, the heartstone rattling between us. He cushions my fall, holding me safe in his wings so I don't hit my head, even though his back cracks against the hard floor and his body finally goes limp.

His free hand slides away from my hair, stroking down my neck, falling. A final breath sighs out of him. "Maybe in another life… Marbella…"

It's the way he says my name that breaks me.

Sobs tear out of me as his fist opens, and the stone remains very still on his chest. Tears pour out of me, blurring my vision. He wanted me to take the stone. He wanted me to believe him. And now he's gone.

The Queen's heart is deadly to everyone. Only a gargoyle of royal blood can touch it. It killed Cassian, ended his suffering, and he was one of the strongest gargoyles I know.

I reach over to close his eyes, my palms brushing across his cheekbones. Sobbing, I take hold of his left wing and pull it over his body, covering the stone at the same time.

I'm reaching for his other wing when something hits my back. I'm thrown forward against Cassian's chest, the force pushing all the air out of my lungs. Pain rips across my back as if a hook raked over the top of me.

Screaming out the fire in my spine, I look up just in time to see Llion tumble through the air over me, his left wing damaged and dangling.

It was his wing that clipped me. If it wasn't for my armor, it would have ripped my back open. But he never would have done that deliberately. He's hurt.

Ducking, I slide off Cassian, crouching beside him as the fight rages around me. With a savage roar, Howl takes flight after Llion, spearing through the air, doing everything he can to kill him. Llion reaches the side of the Court and angles left but another bolt hits him. *Death bolts.* Just like the one that hurt Cassian. Only the Prime Heartstone is keeping Llion alive.

On my left, Jasper fights three guards at once. Two of the guards who kept him from reaching me before are dead at his feet. As one of the guards dislodges Jasper's weapon, he ducks, rolls, and grabs a sword from a dead guard, spinning right back into the fight. Welsian and Liliana fight side by side nearby, bodies building up around them, but more guards keep coming. Roar and Badenoch hold position on the far side, and Erit and Arlo fight further away from the mountain side. All of them are cut and bleeding. There are many bodies on the floor, and not all of them are guards. The miners are fighting as hard as they can, but the next wave of guards will soon arrive.

The only way to end this is to defeat Howl.

Another blast hits Llion right where his hurt wing meets his shoulder. He's close enough to me that I hear the bone snap. Unable to fly, he loses elevation and drops to the ground several paces away from me, shouting in agony.

"Llion!"

His tortured eyes meet mine. He's trying to heal, but he's still learning how to control the heartstone's power. Howl has had much longer to master the deep magic.

I jolt backward as Howl flies over my head and hovers over me with a sneer, his wings beating the air around me, sending tornados swirling around my body.

"You will watch all of your friends die today, Little Doll." He soars over my head and grabs hold of Llion's shoulder with one clawed foot and his broken wing with the other. Llion thumps at him, trying to get up, pushing at Howl with all the force he can muster, but Howl doesn't let go.

His feet shift, one pulling and the other pushing.

He's going to rip Llion's wing right off.

Howl's focus is on me. His threat is for me. "When the Prime Heartstone is mine, you will be too. Watch, Little Doll. Watch and understand that there's nothing you can do."

I can't let it happen. I can't let him hurt anyone else. He hasn't seen the Queen's heart hidden under Cassian's wing. He didn't feel the blast when it awoke because Cassian's wings sealed it in. It was another gift Cassian gave me—concealing the heart's awakening from Howl.

Cassian held the Queen's heart for more than a few seconds before it killed him. If I pick it up, I'll have that long to use it against Howl before it kills me. All I have to do is make sure he holds it too.

My gift to Howl.

I tell myself it's simple. I push all thoughts of Baelen and freedom out of my mind as I dive under Cassian's wing, feeling his weight around me for the last time. One last cocoon to keep me safe before I throw myself into the path of danger. Before I challenge death to claim me.

If I had time to find the bag Cassian carried the stone in, I would. If I had time to pick it up safely, I would. But Llion's scream of agony tells me he won't be alive long enough for me to find a way.

I can do this. It's only four steps, one after the other, simple: pick up the stone, run, jump, shove it into Howl's harness. It will lock into the place he saved for Prime's heart. And then he'll die.

Don't think.

My hand closes over the Queen's heart. Its surface is smooth beneath my fingers, tingling. I'm ready for the pain, channeling it into speed. My body's already moving, rising up, muscles firing. Howl is only five paces away. The hardest part will be rising to his height, but Llion can help me there. He's crouched, one knee bent. It's the same technique I used to tangle with Arlo: knee, shoulder, *up*. It's going to hurt him because of the way Howl's gripping him but I have no other option.

"Llion! Up!" I don't have time to scream anything else. My right foot hits his knee, then my left hits the shoulder Howl isn't clutching. Llion rises at the same time. He can't move much, but it's enough to give me a lift.

I launch myself at Howl. Even if I don't place the stone exactly in the harness, as long as I can wedge it against his skin, it will work.

He must think I'm trying to fight him, to push him away from Llion. As I crash into his chest, he catches me in his thick arms, the momentum tipping him backward. Mentally, I beg Llion to tip with us because Howl's feet are still attached to his wing and shoulder and a sudden wrench backward will rip him apart. At the last moment, Howl lets go, releasing Llion from his claws and flying up into the high ceiling with me in his arms.

I swing my legs around his hips and wrap them tight because the last time he held me in the air—the first time I met him—he drained the air right out of me by squeezing my lungs.

As my legs wind around him, a chuckle rumbles out of his throat. "Little Doll, you surprise me."

Yes, I've wrapped my legs around you, asshole. But I won't have to stomach your nearness for long.

My chest heaves, my heart hurts, and my hand burns like I plunged it into fire. I'm shaking, rattling so hard I won't be able to function soon. I only have a moment before everything ends. I have nothing I want to say to him and no time even if I did.

The Queen's heart clicks neatly into the harness around Howl's neck. The sound echoes around and around inside my head.

Click.

The effect is instantaneous. Not like with Cassian at all. White light shoots through Howl's chest, through the corded muscles in his arms and shoulders, through his wing bones, and all the way to his wing daggers. It spreads, grows, ripples, and then… it starts shredding.

Terror fills his eyes and a scream of pain blasts from his mouth. His hands close around my waist, squeezing my rib cage painfully tight. His fingers claw at me while his skin visibly boils.

"What did you do?!"

I don't answer. I'll never have to answer him again.

The stone's impact is rapid and ruthless. It's over in seconds. Like acid, the light burns through his wings and cuts them to pieces before my eyes. His bones pop, crack, and implode from the inside. We lose altitude as his wings disintegrate and he can't stay airborne. It wouldn't matter if he tried.

A final streak of light shoots up his thick neck, reaches his eyes, and lights them up. For a moment, everything he did, everything he is, every cruel act he committed presses in on me. Then there's a crack…

… and his neck breaks.

His head sinks forward, and we plummet toward the ground, tipping the wrong way so that I'll hit the floor beneath him.

It doesn't matter.

I did what I needed to do. Howl is dead. He can't hurt the gargoyles anymore. He can't threaten, torture, or imprison them. Cassian's death wasn't for nothing. I did what he asked me to do.

Now I can let myself feel what I need to feel. Sadness that I won't see Baelen's eyes open, that I won't be there when he wakes. Faith that Jasper will find a way to open the deep springs and heal him. Fear for my family and Storm Command—for the elves who are loyal to me—because I can't help them now. But Baelen will. He'll discover the power he now holds, and he'll use it to free them. I trust him to.

Baelen, I love you. I always will.

Howl's dead hands open, releasing me into the air like a butterfly into a hurricane. I unwrap my legs from around him. The Queen's heart floats up and away from his shoulders as his body plummets down on top of me. At the last moment, my floating fingers rise up to tap the stone.

A glow ripples out from me like dying sunlight, and a hiss fills my ears: *Choose.*

Choose what, I wonder?

Choose life or death.

It's too late to choose life. My world is already darkness.

EPILOGUE
CASSIAN

The light shifts. I lift my hand to shield my eyes, squinting into the brightness before I lower my hand to study my fingers. I don't know much for certain, but I know I'm standing upright. My fist is what I remember it to be. Real and tangible. My wings are partially spread. I'm dressed in my battle armor, but I'm not in Crimson Court.

I don't know how I got here. Or why. I don't know where 'here' is.

As the light clears, I make sense of the trees soaring skyward on every side of me. The path I stand on begins on the very spot where I stand, forged into the earth by a scorch mark before it becomes spotless farther ahead, clean pebbles pointing the way through the forest. The only way is forward.

The memory of battle, of death, makes me shudder as I tuck my wings to my sides and take a step.

Sunlight glints through the leaves as I head toward the sound of water. I peel off my armor as I go, ridding myself of the heavy reminder of all things in the past.

I died. Willingly. I know that much.

By the time I reach the path's end, I'm bare-chested, wearing only leather pants. I would get rid of those too if it wouldn't leave me naked. My instincts are basic: wash, breathe, figure out where the hell I am.

A still lake opens out in front of me. The path leads right up to it, the trees extending to the edge of the quiet water, obscuring my surroundings on either side. I make my way toward it, determined to wash off the memories of the things I can't change.

"Cassian?"

A woman rises to her feet at the edge of the lake only a few paces away. I startle. I didn't see her there, but she must have been hidden by the trees. Another path extends along the edge of the lake, leading away on that side.

My forehead creases. Her voice triggers long-distant memories. She's about my age—mid-twenties. Her sunset hair is tied back into a loose braid that extends past her waist. Her eyes are a deep cornflower blue. She carries a basket of flowers. Cherry blossoms.

She drops it to the ground, her lips parted in surprise. Then caution. She ignores the scattered flowers as she approaches me, her white dress diaphanous in the sunlight, barely concealing her curves, her wings so translucent that they fragment the sunlight as she walks.

Daring to lift her hands to my chest, she travels a path to my neck, my cheeks, one fingertip finally settling on the edge of my lips.

Her touch is seeking, searching, her eyes studying mine.

My startled breath washes across her fingertip.

Her expression clears. "It *is* you." She bites her lip, a gesture of uncertainty. "Do you remember me?"

I breathe her name. "Elaina."

A smile lights up her eyes. "Yes."

Pain strikes through me. I can't take any more cruel acts of fate. My voice is a demand. "What is this? How are you here?"

If she disappears, I'll turn to darkness. If she's an illusion, I'll rage like the Storm. If she's here to taunt me with things I can't have, I'll—

Alarm crosses her features, her hands becoming firm against my

cheeks, forcing me to meet her eyes. "Don't, please, Cassian. Don't wish to become darkness."

She has grown so tall that her head could rest comfortably in the crook of my neck. She rises up on her tiptoes to plant a kiss on my lips that steals the breath from my lungs and clears the anger from my mind.

It's only when the sunlight glints off her wings again that I realize the sun disappeared behind clouds as soon as I let rage consume my thoughts. I'm not sure how, but my emotions changed our surroundings. Or maybe they changed me.

My forehead creases with confusion as she speaks quickly. "This is a place of deep magic. It is the place of choice for those who triggered the deep magic when they died." Her expression becomes deeply sad. "You're here because you gave your life for something greater than yourself."

My lips burn where she kissed me, not a painful burn. A burn I want again. "I don't understand."

She gestures to the sun. "The Elven Queen gave her life to become the sun. The Gargoyle Queen gave her life to become the moon." Elaina lowers her hand to my heart. "I gave my life for you. And now you gave your life for your people. We triggered the deep magic, Cassian."

"But what does that mean?"

She attempts another smile. "It means we get to choose what we become." Her hand rises to the sun again, gesturing to the path, then the flowers. "Sunlight, pebbles, a tree. Or… we can choose to stay here and remain who we are."

I inhale a sharp breath, but she hurries on, "Please don't become darkness, Cassian. There's already a storm. There's already night and shadows. I don't need more of those. I… need… *you*."

She lets me go, sliding her arms away from me, lowering them to her sides as if she's leaving me free to make a choice.

The full meaning of what she said is slowly sinking in. *Stay here and remain who we are.*

I don't reach for her. Not yet. "How are you still here after all these years?"

The breeze presses her dress against her body, the outline of her breasts and hips becoming clear before the material puffs in the other direction. It scatters my thoughts, not only because she's gorgeous but because she's completely vulnerable, her heart open to me as she waits for me to make my choice.

"Because I waited for you," she says.

If I could go back to the first time we kissed and change the course of the future, I would run with her as far as we could. I would never become Howl's General, never fight my own people, never descend into darkness. But I can't change any of that. All I can do is choose my future.

I cross the distance and pull her to me, encircling her waist to plaster her against me. "You're older."

She tilts her head back, a surprisingly sultry smile on her lips. "I decided to age at the same rate you did so that when you arrived, I wouldn't be as young anymore." The corner of her mouth twitches into a smile. "Even if you arrived here as an old man, I wanted to be the same age as you. Although… I'm not sure you would recognize me with gray hair."

"I would know you, Elaina," I say. I mean it as a promise that I would know her no matter what she looked like, but the way her lips part, an intensity growing in her eyes tells me she heard something much more provocative.

Her gaze falls to my lips. "Are you still as polite as you used to—"

"No."

I crush my lips against hers, exploring the curve of her mouth. My hands seek to know the shape of her back and shoulders, her waist, her hips, all the way back up to her slender neck. I thought I'd lost her forever. I never thought I'd see her again.

Now she's here, but the past—my life—weighs heavily on me. I've lived a life without her, fallen in love with another, made choices that horrify me, done things I'm ashamed of, and tried to find redemption. How can I put all of that behind me?

She moans against my lips, but I force myself to pull back, not pushing her away but breaking our kiss. I stroke the soft curls at the side of her face. "I'm not the same gargoyle you knew."

She presses her hand to my heart again, easing the pain in my chest. "You're hurting and I won't ask for anything you can't give. I don't expect you to forget everything you felt. All of it makes you who you are. But I want you to know that I accept that. All of you. Good and bad. All I ask is that you let me in."

She looks up at me with a question in her eyes.

My voice breaks. "How can you still love me?"

She lowers her head to my chest, turning her ear as if she is listening to my heart. "You think you've changed, but you haven't. Your heart is still true, Cassian."

"How can you know that?"

She tips her head back. Her smile becomes gentle, serious. "Because you found me."

I pull her close, kiss her, and inhale the scent of freedom.

Find out how the story ends in
Storm Princess: Book 3
the final book with no cliffhanger.

STORM PRINCESS: BOOK THREE

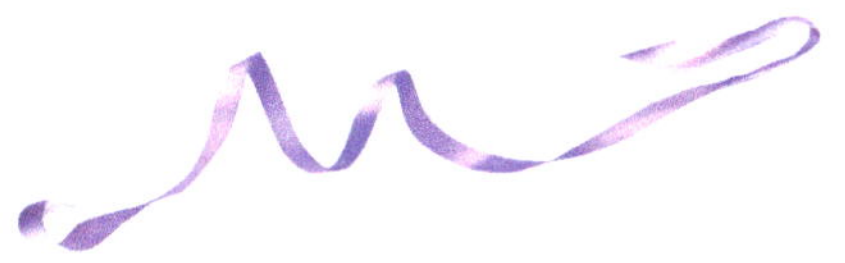

**"You are everything to me.
I would wait a thousand years to hear your voice, kiss your lips,
walk beside you."**

Complete Baelen and Marbella's story in Storm Princess: Book 3.

Content information: Storm Princess: Book 3 is high fantasy romance, the third and final book in the complete Storm Princess series.

Recommended reading age is 17+ for sex scenes, mature themes, violence, and language. Ends on a cliffhanger.

ALSO BY JAYMIN EVE

STORM PRINCESS - COMPLETE

(Fantasy Romance)

1. Storm Princess: Book One

2. Storm Princess: Book Two

3. Storm Princess: Book Three

Shadow Beast Shifters

Book One: Rejected

Book Two: Reclaimed

Book Three: Reborn

Book Four: Deserted

Book Five: Compelled

Fallen Fae Gods

(Romantasy Duet)

1. Gilded Wings

2. Crimson Skies

Demon Pack

(Dark Paranormal Romance)

1. Demon Pack

2. Demon Pack: Elimination

3. Demon Pack: Eternal

Supernatural Academy

Year One

Year Two

Year Three

Supernatural Prison Trilogy (Urban Fantasy)

Book One: Dragon Marked

Book Two: Dragon Mystics

Book Three: Dragon Mated

Supernatural Prison Stories

Broken Compass

Magical Compass

Louis

Royals of Arbon Academy Series (Dark College Romance)

Book One: Princess Ballot

Book Two: Playboy Princes

Book Three: Poison Throne

Dark Legacy Series (Dark High School Romance)

Book One: Broken Wings

Book Two: Broken Trust

Book Three: Broken Legacy

Secret Keepers Series (Paranormal Romance)

Book One: House of Darken

Book Two: House of Imperial

Book Three: House of Leights

Book Four: House of Royale

Titans Saga

Book One: Releasing the Gods

Book Two: Wrath of the Gods

Book Three: Revenge of the Gods

Curse of the Gods Series (RH Fantasy Romance)

Book One: Trickery

Book Two: Persuasion

Book Three: Seduction

Book Four: Strength

Book 4.5: Neutral (Novella)

Book Five: Pain

NYC Mecca Series (YA Urban Fantasy)

Book One: Queen Heir

Book Two: Queen Alpha

Book Three: Queen Fae

Book Four: Queen Mecca

A Walker Saga (YA Fantasy Series)

Book One: First World

Book Two: Spurn

Book Three: Crais

Book Four: Regali

Book Five: Nephilius

Book Six: Dronish

Book Seven: Earth

Hive Trilogy (YA/NA Urban Fantasy)

Book One: Ash

Book Two: Anarchy

Book Three: Annihilate

Sinclair Stories (Contemporary Sports Romance)

Songbird

ALSO BY EVERLY FROST

STORM PRINCESS - COMPLETE

(Fantasy Romance)

1. Storm Princess: Book One

2. Storm Princess: Book Two

3. Storm Princess: Book Three

KINGDOM OF BETRAYAL

(Fantasy Romance)

1. A Sky Like Blood

2. A Sin Like Fire

3. A Soul Like Glass

DARK MAGIC SHIFTERS

(Dark Urban Fantasy Romance)

1. Wolf of Ashes

2. Bond of Flames

3. Crown of Fate

SUPERNATURAL LEGACY - COMPLETE

(Angels and Dragon Shifters)

1. Hunt the Night

2. Chase the Shadows

3. Slay the Dawn

4. Claim the Light

BRIGHT WICKED - COMPLETE

(Fantasy Romance)

1. Bright Wicked

2. Radiant Fierce

3. Infernal Dark

SOUL BITTEN SHIFTER - COMPLETE

(Dark Urban Fantasy Romance)

1. This Dark Wolf

2. This Broken Wolf

3. This Caged Wolf

4. This Cruel Blood

DEMON PACK - COMPLETE

(Dark Paranormal Romance)

1. Demon Pack

2. Demon Pack: Elimination

3. Demon Pack: Eternal

ASSASSIN'S MAGIC - COMPLETE

(Urban Fantasy Romance)

1. Assassin's Magic

2. Assassin's Mask

3. Assassin's Menace

4. Assassin's Maze

5. Assassin's Match

ASSASSIN'S ACADEMY - COMPLETE

(Dark Academy Romance)

1. Rebels

2. Revenge

3. Rogue

MORTALITY - COMPLETE

(Science-Fantasy Romance)

Mortality Complete Set: Books 1 to 4

1. Beyond the Ever Reach

2. Beneath the Guarding Stars

3. By the Icy Wild

4. Before the Raging Lion

<u>Stand-alone fiction - dark romance</u>

Corrupt Me: Immortal Vices and Virtues

ABOUT THE AUTHORS

Jaymin Eve is the Wall Street Journal and USA Today Bestselling author of paranormal romance, urban fantasy, and sci-fi novels filled with epic love stories, great adventure, and plenty of laughs. She lives in Australia with her husband, two beautiful daughters, and a couple of crazy pets. To date, she has sold close to two million ebooks, and still can't believe that she gets to create fantasy worlds as a job.

Everly Frost is the USA Today Bestselling author of fantasy romance, urban fantasy and paranormal romance novels. She spent her childhood dreaming of other worlds and scribbling stories on the leftover blank pages at the back of school notebooks. She lives in Brisbane, Australia with her husband and two children.